Praise for Jenny Hale

"Jenny Hale writes touching, beautiful stories about people and places I love visiting."

—RaeAnne Thayne, *New York Times* bestselling author

Summer at Firefly Beach

"A great summer beach read." —*PopSugar*

"A perfect beach read about rediscovering oneself, second chances, and the power of healing." —*Harlequin Junkie*

It Started with Christmas

"This sweet small-town romance will leave readers feeling warm all the way through." —*Publishers Weekly*

The Summer House

"Hale's rich and slow-building romance is enhanced by the allure of the North Carolina coast... North Carolina's beautiful Outer Banks are the perfect setting for this sweet, poignant romance, and authentic characters and a riveting story make it a keeper worth savoring."

—*Publishers Weekly* (Starred Review)

"Like a paper and ink version of a chick-flick... gives you the butterflies and leaves you happy and hopeful." —*Due South*

Christmas Wishes and Mistletoe Kisses

"[A] tender treat that can be savored in any season."

—*Publishers Weekly* (Starred Review)

"[Jenny] Hale's impeccably executed contemporary romance is the perfect gift for readers who love sweetly romantic love stories imbued with all the warmth and joy of the holiday season." —*Booklist*

the house on firefly beach

ALSO BY JENNY HALE

Christmas Wishes and Mistletoe Kisses

The Summer House

It Started with Christmas

Summer at Firefly Beach

A Christmas to Remember

Summer by the Sea

Christmas at Silver Falls

the house on firefly beach

JENNY HALE

FOREVER
NEW YORK BOSTON

Forever
Hachette Book Group
1290 Avenue of the Americas, New York, NY 10104
read-forever.com
twitter.com/readforeverpub

Originally published in 2020 by Bookouture, an imprint of StoryFire Ltd.
First Forever Edition: May 2022

Forever is an imprint of Grand Central Publishing. The Forever name and logo are trademarks of Hachette Book Group, Inc.

The publisher is not responsible for websites (or their content) that are not owned by the publisher.

The Hachette Speakers Bureau provides a wide range of authors for speaking events. To find out more, go to www.hachettespeakersbureau.com or call (866) 376-6591.

LCCN: 2021952441

ISBN: 9781538708422 (trade paperback)

Printed in the United States of America

LSC-C

Printing 1, 2022

the house on firefly beach

Prologue

Sydney Flynn skipped along the beach road toward Nate's house, her auburn curls pulled into a ponytail to combat the swell of afternoon pre-summer heat. It was their senior year in college, and they were both graduating in a week, the clear, humid days of summer quickly approaching. Having spent four glorious years together, much of their winters separated by a lengthy drive between their two universities, Sydney couldn't help but feel the excitement of their uninterrupted future together bubbling up.

She fiddled with the purple stone of the toy ring Nate had given her as a placeholder for the real diamond he promised once they graduated—she wore the ring every day. Nate had called her this morning before she'd awakened and left a message to come see him right away. He'd sounded oddly breathless and nervous, and she wondered what the surprise could be. He wasn't usually this mysterious.

The sun was already beaming in a gloriously blue sky, birds flying overhead, the waters of the gulf that rippled by her side shushing relentlessly onto the Florida shore as she walked the familiar path toward the one person in this world that she adored the most—it was the perfect day to start the rest of their lives. She didn't want to jinx it, but she did wonder: Would he propose today? Could that be it?

Of course, she wanted it to happen in his time, but she was so in love with him that she was ready to start their lives together right now. Last night they'd celebrated her incredible news that she'd been invited to travel around the U.S. for three months, as a writer, documenting the work of a famous humanitarian. She didn't even want to go if she could start planning her wedding right now, but Nate had convinced her to follow her passion to be a professional journalist, so she'd decided to take the trip. If they had a year before the wedding, she could still get all the planning done if she started after she returned. Her excitement made her laugh because she knew she was getting ahead of herself.

Sydney came up the drive, bounding with the thrill of seeing Nate and hearing what he had to tell her, but she paused, the sight in front of her baffling. "What's going on?" she asked, as Nate hurried out, locked the door behind him, and stopped cold, his arms fumbling with a pile of boxes as he picked them up off the drive. He lumped them into the back of his truck, which was completely full of his things.

Were they going somewhere?

"I'm leaving," he said, his gaze fluttering up to her, but only briefly.

"Where are you going?" Her heart was beating uncontrollably, as if her body had caught up to the situation before her mind could process it.

"I don't know," he nearly snapped. "New York? LA? Somewhere I can write my songs and make something of myself." He shifted a box in the back and secured it with a bungee cord, his movement swift and focused. "I'm getting out of here. There's more to life than Firefly Beach," he said. "I just wanted to say goodbye."

A cloud drifted in front of the sun, casting a gray shade on everything, but she barely noticed through the tears that were forming in her eyes.

"I'm not coming with you?" She already knew the answer, but she was pleading with the heavens above to help her by casting some kind of reconsideration onto his heart before he broke hers into pieces.

"No."

"Why not?" she asked, her body beginning to shake all over, her world crumbling in front of her.

He swallowed, not answering or meeting her eyes. "I wanted to say goodbye, but… There's no good way to do this."

"Nate, what are you doing?" Why was he hurting her like this? "Explain to me what is going on," she cried, unable to keep her emotions from coming through.

He pushed another box into his truck and lifted the tailgate, shutting his belongings into the back.

"Talk to me!" When he didn't respond, she tried to push herself in front of him, but he darted out of her way. "I deserve an explanation! You can't just leave like this after four years. What happened between last night and now?"

He didn't answer, leaving her to wonder if he, too, had given thought to forever with her, and suddenly realized that it wasn't at all what he wanted.

"Sorry," he said quickly without even a look in her direction.

He paused in front of her and stared into her eyes, the hint of something in them, as if he wanted one last chance to make sure this was the right decision. Then before she could say anything, he got in his truck, starting the engine and shutting the door. She stepped back instinctively when he put the truck into gear, his face like stone. He pulled away, leaving her standing there, struggling to clear the tears from her vision enough to see him look back at her in his rearview mirror, but he never did. Sydney stood in the driveway of his dark, locked house, and watched his truck pull further away from her until it disappeared. Nate was gone, taking her happiness with him.

Chapter One

In her conch-shell-pink chiffon bridesmaid's dress, Sydney stood with the rest of the wedding party, at the end of their beloved family's pier, and locked eyes with Nate Henderson. She barely noticed the unseasonably perfect weather or the lapping of the sparkling Gulf of Mexico behind them, all of it fading away at the sight of Nate. Nate was the man whom Sydney had always considered to be the true love of her life. And now, with his Valentino suit and over-priced haircut, he was someone she barely recognized.

His cell went off. He quickly left his seat and bowed his way down the aisle, stepping off to the side to answer a call right in the middle of the service. *Mr. Hollywood can't even shut it off for a wedding?* she thought, irritated already. He had seemed slightly mortified, but it hadn't stopped him from answering. He slid back into his seat.

Knowing every rocky detail of their break-up and the scar it had left on Sydney's heart, Sydney's sister Hallie and Hallie's fiancé Ben Murray had warned her that Nate would be invited to their wedding. Ben had tried to convince Sydney that she'd misunderstood Nate all these years and that she should give him a chance to explain himself, that it would help her get through the wedding at the very least. Sydney had assured the couple she'd be just fine with him there whether she spoke to him or not. She was completely over it. Not until this very moment, under strands of summer twinkle lights and festive bouquets of hydrangea, had she felt like her knees were going to buckle.

Nate smiled at her guardedly from his aisle seat, while tucked in to the row next to him were the two women in his life: the plus one that had been written on his wedding RSVP card—an international supermodel and reported girlfriend named Juliana Vargas—and his sister Malory. If Nate was expressing his happiness to celebrate Hallie and Ben's wedding, that was one thing, but if that smile had been his feeble attempt to bury the hatchet with Sydney, given their history, he was completely delusional. She pushed herself to focus on someone else, her gaze landing on her friend Mary Alice, who gave her a tiny wave. Sydney smiled back at her before breaking eye contact. But her thoughts remained with Nate, her stomach in knots.

It had been years since she'd gotten her heart broken by Nate, and both of them had moved on with their lives. But two things had lingered, spiking her emotions when it came to him: the first was the fact that all those years ago, his leaving had made her feel like she wasn't good enough; the second was the overwhelming loss of the person he'd been and the gaping hole it had caused in her life. The four years she'd dated him, he'd been amazing, perfect for her, actually—he'd been her best friend.

Now, no longer Nate Henderson, he was known to the world as Nathan Carr, most eligible bachelor and songwriting superstar, not even his name recognizable to Sydney anymore. And he'd had the audacity to smile at her like everything had been mended between them. Wouldn't "I'm sorry" come first, at the very least?

"Benjamin," the preacher said, pulling Sydney back into the present where she should be: her sister's wedding at their gorgeous family beachside retreat, Starlight Cottage.

Sydney gripped her bouquet to steady herself and tore her eyes from Nate to focus on her sister and her soon-to-be brother-in-law. This was their moment, and it couldn't be more perfect. Hallie gazed up at the love of her life while Sydney looked on, under the cedar-shingled roof of the enormous gazebo, the southernmost point of the dwelling. The gazebo sat at the end of a pier that reached up to the shoreline where it met the boardwalk leading to the house Sydney and Hallie had spent the entire season renovating.

Growing up, Sydney had spent every summer at Firefly Beach, and when her divorce was finalized, she'd moved back for a few months to recharge, but returned to where she'd grown up in Nashville, since Hallie and her mother lived there. Then last summer, when Uncle Hank had been struggling with Aunt Clara's death, and Sydney had been given Aunt Clara's dying wishes to follow her heart, she'd moved back to Firefly Beach full time. Her mother divided her time between Starlight Cottage and her home in Nashville, but this summer she'd been there full time to help with renovations.

The gazebo where Sydney stood had been remodeled especially for the evening, widened to accommodate the throng of wedding guests in their rows of white chairs. The wedding had given them a timeframe, but their love of this place had been their motivation for restoring it.

Starlight Cottage was the home that had seen them through all their ups and downs. It had been revived originally with love and magazine-worthy décor by their great aunt Clara, designer extraordinaire, and when she'd passed it had fallen into disrepair. Now Sydney, Hallie, and their mother, Jacqueline Flynn took care of it. With the grief that had been filling the hallways, her sister's wedding was like a warm coastal breeze flushing through the whole property, breathing life back into it again. The family's energy buzzed through the entire place, laughter filled the empty rooms, footsteps and banter tickled the hardwoods, and it was becoming the retreat that it had always been for them.

The ever-present salty air blew Hallie's veil despite the fact that they were all sheltered from the wind and the setting sun in an orange and pink sky. Ben's Labrador-spaniel mix, Beau, sat at his master's side, sporting a coral-colored bow tie. The dog tilted his head, his ears perking with interest as the preacher spoke.

"Will you take this woman to be your lawfully wedded wife? And whatever the future may hold, will you love her and stand by her, as long as you both shall live?"

"I will," Ben said, Hallie's hands in his as he peered down at her adoringly. Ben leaned toward her, clearly lost in the moment and ready to press his lips to his soon-to-be wife's.

"Wait," the preacher said, gently placing his hand on Ben's shoulder to stop him. "I have to get the rest of my lines out before you kiss her… That's my job."

The crowd chuckled and Ben looked back at the preacher, playfully impatient.

"Hey, I didn't write the rules for the wedding," the preacher added. "You two did."

Everyone laughed again, and in her amusement, Sydney let her eyes roam the front row of the guests, searching for her mother, to share in the moment of humor, but her attention was pulled toward Nate once more. This time, he was whispering something to the supermodel, the woman's eyes hidden behind her enormous designer sunglasses. She nodded at whatever he'd said and then fanned her perfectly smooth and professionally made-up face with one of the programs that Sydney had picked up from the printers herself yesterday to allow Hallie time to attend a final meeting with the wedding design team before the big night.

As if he could feel her gaze upon him, Nate looked back at Sydney, and his interpretation of her mood was obvious. This time, there were silent words in his stare. He had something to say, and the minute the ceremony was finished, she knew, by that look, that he'd find her to tell her whatever it was. Her mind wandered to places she could go to avoid him. She wasn't going to let Nate derail this evening. Sydney turned back toward her sister, basking in the happiness on Hallie's face as she and Ben continued their vows.

Sydney's eight-year-old son Robby, dressed adorably in his little tuxedo, his light brown hair combed perfectly to one side, held up the lace ring-pillow made from a swatch of Aunt Clara's vintage honeymoon gown that had been meticulously preserved over the years, in the back of her great aunt's closet. Their Uncle Hank had offered the dress to Hallie as a wedding gift, telling her that Aunt Clara would've wanted her to have it, and that he knew she could do something amazing with it. The soft blue satin had floated like the waves of the gulf over Hallie's arm when she held it out that night, deciding right then and there that it would be her "something blue" at the wedding.

Robby held the pillow above his head, just like he and Sydney had practiced all week, as the preacher untied the rings.

While Ben's friend from college sang the couple's song, "Marry Me" by Train, about knowing beyond a shadow of doubt that The One is right there in front of him, Sydney tried to sort out the best way to avoid Nate at the reception while still being able to enjoy her family. She had planned to spend the entire night celebrating with her loved ones, rather than reliving old wounds. But what alarmed her was the pattering of her heart, just knowing Nate was out there. It was an involuntary response that she used to have every time he met her on the front porch of his parents' small beach cottage, bare feet, sun-kissed hair, those stormy blue eyes that used to swallow her like he couldn't get enough of her…

She looked back at the bride in an attempt to refocus, but her racing mind wouldn't allow her to. Life seemed to move along neatly for her sister Hallie. Sure, she'd had her moments of uncertainty, but she was a successful designer, and she'd found the love of her life. Sydney's path wasn't quite so obvious. She had wanted to be in a better place before she'd come face-to-face with Nate again, but as fate would have it, she was still at her aunt and uncle's estate, Starlight Cottage, in Firefly Beach where he'd left her, the dreams of writing that they used to share now a distant memory for her, just like those long-ago days with Nate.

Memories floated into her consciousness, one in particular lingering: she and Nate were on a blanket in the sand one night. She was tired from too much sun and the rum-and-pineapple cocktails they'd been drinking. With their writing notebooks strewn out around them, he sat cross-legged on the blanket and she lay down and propped her head up on his knee, the fireflies swirling around them like restless stars. Laughter floated over the dune from Starlight Cottage behind them, both of them twisting around to see Uncle Hank and Aunt Clara in rocking chairs together on the porch.

"That will be us someday," Nate said, pushing a rogue piece of hair behind her ear adoringly.

Sydney rolled onto her belly and propped her chin on her hands. "You sure you want to spend every single day of your life with me?" she asked.

His smile fell into a serious affection, his eyes devouring her. "Yes," he said with a quiet determination. "When you find the right person, it feels like you've found the rest of yourself. And that's how I feel about you. Without you, I'm not really me—just some half-empty version of myself."

He leaned down and kissed her, and even now, Sydney could still drum up the mix of fruity cocktails and the unique scent of him as his lips touched hers.

"I now pronounce you man and wife," the preacher announced.

Sydney blinked away the distraction, frustrated that Nate could still have that effect on her. She breathed in the briny air to steady her nerves.

"You may *now* kiss your bride."

Ben dipped Hallie, her arm dropping by her side, the bouquet dangling in her hand against the satin fabric of her vintage French couture wedding dress as the train fanned out along the boards of the gazebo. Their silhouettes were a picture of perfection in front of the glorious sunset that had materialized as if on cue over the water behind them. The crowd cheered. Beau barked. When Ben righted Hallie, the couple turned toward the onlookers, and Hallie was positively glowing.

The preacher stepped behind them, calling over the couple, "I now present to you Mr. and Mrs. Benjamin Murray."

Ben, a top Nashville music producer, had organized one of his new bands to play their jazzed-up version of a wedding march. He took Hallie's hand and gave her a spin, Hallie's train fluttering out around her ballet-slipper-style shoes. Then he dipped her one more time and kissed her again, the whole crowd whooping and clapping. While the music filled the air around them, mixing with the rustle of the palm trees in the ocean breeze and gentle lapping of the gulf, the wedding party made their way out of the gazebo and down the pier toward the reception.

Sydney took Robby's hand, grabbed Beau's leash, and walked in the procession, behind her sister and Ben. She kept her eyes straight ahead and tried to avoid the loaded look from Nate as she passed him. But walking across the lawn, her flats treading lightly down the path of rose petals, she knew just by his stare, that no matter how hard she tried, there would be no avoiding whatever it was that Nate had to say.

Chapter Two

"I just saw the food table," Hallie said to Sydney, swishing over to her in the incredible chiffon vintage gown with an open back and lace-edged empire waist that she'd picked out only a week after her engagement, when the two of them had gone out shopping.

Sydney smirked deviously.

Chewing on a grin, Hallie teasingly shook her sister by the shoulders. "Why do I have bowls of Doritos snack chips on the table between the dishes of lamb and rosemary appetizers and the prosciutto wrapped persimmons? Is this a football game?" Hallie broke her mock-seriousness and bent over laughing.

"That's what you said you wanted," Sydney said, unable to hide her own laughter. "There are also crystal dishes of pink bubble gum—did you see them? Dubble Bubble," she added as if that upped the status of the gum.

"Wait till your next wedding," Hallie said. "You're getting a Jell-O mold, a big, wiggly bride and groom in wild cherry."

Sydney burst into laughter.

When Sydney and Hallie were in elementary school, they'd planned out their weddings. Sydney had wanted Jell-O for her reception, while Hallie had drawn a map of the table she'd wanted to see at her nuptials, which included Doritos and Dubble Bubble, both of which Sydney had managed to hide from her sister until this moment.

"You deserved the wedding of your dreams," Sydney said, still giggling. "Think of me as the magic maker."

Hallie rolled her eyes, still smiling from ear to ear before being pulled away to accept congratulations from a group of Ben's relatives.

Sydney waved at Robby from across the makeshift dance floor that had been built with old wood from original planks in the cottage. Aunt Clara had ripped them out in her previous renovation and saved pieces of them that were stored in the guesthouse basement. Hallie had decided they would be perfect at the reception. Together, Ben had sanded the edges, and Sydney and Hallie had oiled the boards, encasing the whole thing in an oak frame. It now sat in the center of the lush green grass, dotted by lanterns and hanging lights.

While couples filtered onto the dance floor, the band kicking up to a slightly more festive beat, Robby was at the dessert table, helping himself to the wedding-bell cookies and sneaking some to Beau. His light brown hair was disheveled, the sleeves of his tuxedo shirt were rolled to the elbow, and his jacket, shoes, and socks were long gone.

Robby was Sydney's whole world, the last remnant of the life she'd worked so hard for, which had come crashing down around her a few years ago when Robby's father Christian had left her for another woman. Sydney had known Christian since his family had moved down the road when he was fifteen but growing up, they'd never been anything more than friends. In her late twenties, he and Sydney reunited, falling in love quickly. They'd started dating seriously and soon after Sydney found herself swept up in a romantic whirlwind, everything moving in a flash. Not long after they started dating, they both admitted they had fallen head-over-heels. Christian rushed over one night, breathless, telling her he couldn't live without her, and before she knew it, she was planning her wedding. He'd ended up finding someone else, their relationship falling apart after only five years. She should've known it wouldn't last by the lackluster romance they had once they'd settled into their daily routine. It seemed he was more interested in the chase than the actual happily ever after.

As her sister began the wedding planning, Sydney feared he'd be invited, but Hallie had told her that even though they'd all known him forever, and he was Robby's father, she'd never put her sister in that position.

However Nate was a different story entirely. He most certainly got an invite.

A darling of the music industry, Nate Henderson had left Firefly Beach after college to pursue a career as a songwriter, and Sydney wasn't sure even *he* had been prepared back then for the future that lay ahead of him. In his career so far, he'd already achieved thirty-seven number one hits, and eleven movie soundtrack titles. His success, which earned him the title "King of the Ballad," and his unprecedented gorgeous good looks propelled him into the public eye and won him a spot on quite a few magazine covers. One of them had even titled his rise to fame as "extraordinary" and named him "Man of the Year." He and Ben, having grown up together, were easy collaborators in their line of work, and they'd teamed up on many major albums. A prominent Nashville news show had labeled them country music's dream team. So when Ben and Hallie began to make the guest list, Sydney knew that having Nate there would be inescapable.

Sydney allowed a little glance in Nate's direction, and it looked as though he was passing his business card to one of Ben's producer friends. *Ugh, figures,* she thought. She wondered if this was nothing but an opportunity to network for him.

She pushed her thoughts of Nate aside and swayed on the edge of the dance floor. The yard was full of candles and strings of lights in the trees, their branches hanging over masses of white tables adorned with magnolias and more hydrangea blooms bursting from centerpieces. It couldn't be a more perfect night. The weather was unusually cool for June, the evening temperature topping out at seventy-five degrees, without a cloud in the sky. With the sun now sinking low on the horizon, the fireflies had come out and were mingling with the crowd. Against the swells of champagne as the bottles were uncorked, and the live music, it was like a summer dream.

"Mom!" Robby said, running over to her with a handful of cookies. Beau chased him across the yard, both of them coming to a stop in front of Sydney. "Ben said later, when all the guests leave, if I'm still awake, he'll play football with me!"

With the wedding planning, Hallie and Ben had spent a ton of time around the cottage, playing with Robby to free up Sydney so she could plan with her sister. They were inseparable.

"It might be very late before everyone leaves, but perhaps you'll get a chance to play," she said, taking his free hand and swinging it back and forth to the music while he nibbled on the cookies in his other hand. Beau got tired of begging and trotted off. "Thank you for helping me hang the lanterns today," she said.

"You're welcome," Robby replied before popping the last cookie into his mouth. "It was fun!"

"You just liked sitting on my shoulders." Sydney reached over and tickled his sides, making him giggle. She wouldn't admit to him that he was getting so big that she'd had a pinched nerve from him being on her shoulders all day hanging the lanterns. She'd had to take ibuprofen to make the ache stop. But she would do it every day if he'd let her.

"Robby!" Hallie called from the dance floor. She twirled her train out of the way and beckoned for him to join her. "Come dance with me!"

Robby gave Sydney a bashful look. "She wants me to dance," he said. "Yuck."

Sydney stifled her laughter. "Aunt Hallie is only going to get married one time. This will be the only night you'll probably ever have to dance with her. . . . Unless you want to dance with her at your own wedding."

"I'm not getting married! Girls are double yuck!"

Hallie waved him over again.

"Go on. Ben dances with her." Sydney knew that Robby would do anything his new uncle did.

"Okaaay," Robby said, running over to the dance floor.

Hallie grabbed his hands and gave him a spin, introducing him to a few people around them.

Taking in the sight of him, Sydney thought about how wonderful he'd been while they'd restored the cottage and planned the wedding. He'd helped any chance he could get, sometimes sticking labels on the favors or folding the invitations, and when he couldn't help, like with the floral arrangements, he spent time drawing or playing outside. When she allowed the thought to filter in, she wished he had siblings and a better father. Robby only saw his father on the random holiday. Christian would call up out of nowhere, as if he'd remembered suddenly that he had a son. He'd offer to take Robby to a movie or some other location that didn't require a lot of parental supervision. Then he'd buy him something and bring him home.

If she were honest with herself, her life—and Robby's—wasn't what she'd hoped for the both of them. Growing up, she'd always envisioned that perfect little family, playing games together, reading stories at bedtime, taking summer vacations. That hadn't happened for the two of them…

Breaking through her reflections, Nate's voice sailed over Sydney's shoulder tentatively, and he was suddenly by her side, his hand outstretched to her. "May I have this dance?"

He had to be kidding.

"Shouldn't you be asking your date?" she asked, keeping her eyes on the crowd that had filled the floor around Hallie and Robby.

"Juliana didn't feel well..." he said, sounding shaky. "She went back to Malory's cottage... "

Sydney had been hoping to spend some time with Malory tonight. Malory and Sydney had spent their summers in Firefly Beach with one another, and the Hendersons and the Flynns were always together in those days. In fact, that was one of the things that had brought Sydney and Nate closer. He'd been that annoying big brother type, splashing her and Malory while they sunned themselves on the dock or chasing them around with the water hose when he was washing his truck. As they got older, he took on a more protective role and began to watch over them, walking with Sydney whenever she went home after dark to be sure she was okay.

Malory had been a driving force in getting Sydney and Nate together. She'd urged Sydney to spend time with Nate, telling her more than once that they were perfect for each other. She invited Nate to every activity the two of them did together. He was there for Sydney's softball games, he magically showed up at the ice cream shop when she and Malory got mint chocolate chip ice cream cones. He found his way to the beach on the nights they made bonfires and roasted marshmallows... When they'd finally started dating, Malory teased them, telling them that if they ever got married, Hallie would have competition for maid of honor. "You're like a sister to me," she'd told Sydney.

When Nate left them all for LA, it was clear that Malory held on to a lot of guilt over Sydney's heartbreak. One night, as they'd sat together in near silence at the top of the lighthouse, the gulf, as big as Sydney's emotions, stretching out before them, Malory had apologized to Sydney for hurting her so badly by encouraging her brother's advances. And even though Sydney assured her that she'd done nothing wrong, the two of them drifted apart, the absence of the laughter that they used to have in Nate's presence settling heavily between them. About two months after he left, when Nate finally began making contact with his sister, calling her to catch her up on what he'd been doing out in Los Angeles, and Sydney had moved back to Nashville for the winter, Malory stopped calling Sydney altogether under the strain of the whole situation.

"I want to dance with *you*," Nate said.

Sydney forced herself to focus on the ruggedness that was still present on his face despite the years spent in the land of beauty and excess, and shook her head. His date had gone back to the house alone, and he'd wasted no time at all moving in on someone else. He was unbelievable.

"Sydney..." he said quietly. "Will you let me talk to you?"

He placed his hand on her arm, but she flinched, jerking it away instinctively. The reaction surprised even her. It had been a long time, and the wound was still very much there. She scanned the crowd, making sure they weren't drawing attention to themselves before she finally looked him in the eye, but she was at a loss for words. There was nothing more to say. She didn't like the man he'd become, and he'd made it pretty clear when he'd left that this was the lifestyle he'd wanted. Well, he'd gotten it.

"Look," he said under his breath, his voice tender, "we don't need to do this here. The last thing I want is to upset you—you deserve to be happy." There was a long pause, deliberation on his face. Finally, he said, "I won't bother you anymore tonight."

The disappointment and sadness in his eyes as he walked away made her second-guess her response to him, but she didn't trust it. All she had to do was remember how he'd left. The night before, they'd celebrated her huge accomplishment. Sydney had received a letter inviting her to travel around the U.S. for three months, documenting the work of Eugene Storer, a famous humanitarian who was collaborating with students from various universities.

One of her professors had asked her to apply, and she'd gotten accepted as a staff writer. Nate had brought over a bottle of champagne to commemorate the occasion.

"You're amazing!" he'd said that day, picking her up and giving her a squeeze, the champagne bottle in his grip, swinging with her as he turned her around.

"Do you think I should go?" she'd asked once he'd put her down, and she could still remember the complete bewilderment on his face.

"Why wouldn't you?" He leaned over and nibbled at her neck playfully, his arms finding her again.

"It means we'll be apart for a while," she said, earnestly. The thought bothered her more than she wanted to say.

When she said that, something registered on his face. "It's okay to be apart. We can make things work."

"I'd rather stay here with you, even if it means making different choices in life. All these things pulling me away… I feel like it would ruin us."

He stared at her, clearly working something out. "Is that why you didn't transfer to Emerson College like you'd wanted to? Because you were worried about being away from me?"

"It's in Boston, Nate. We'd never see each other."

"It's *the* top journalism college in America, and you were accepted," he countered. "You'd told me that living in the north would be too cold and busy…"

"It all means nothing if I can't be with you. Relationships are about compromise, right? Being with you is more important than some fancy college. And the same holds true for this trip."

"Syd, I *overwhelmingly* support you going on this trip. I've never met anyone as talented as you are. You can't let your feelings about us hold you back from what you were born to do."

"I don't know…" she replied, unable to articulate how much it would bother her to be away from him. She knew this was a fantastic opportunity, but was now the right time? "Let's celebrate that I got it," she said with a smile. "We can decide if it's the right thing for me to do later."

As the evening went on, he'd seemed slightly withdrawn, but it was late, and she figured he was tired. She remembered how much love she felt for him that he was working so hard to mark the occasion given how worn-out he clearly was, and she hadn't thought a thing about it when he'd decided to go home alone instead of staying over like he usually did.

She had no idea what awaited her the next morning, so full of joy and anticipation.

She just couldn't understand it, the grief of losing him stinging her like a pack of bees, swarming her for the longest time. They'd dated exclusively throughout college—madly in love with one another—and they'd talked about "forever" as if it wasn't just a possibility but a reality. They'd been so in love that she just knew after graduation, he'd pop the question and they'd live happily ever after. But instead, out of nowhere, he'd broken her heart, moved to LA, and begun to build a larger-than-life persona that included dating actresses and supermodels and jet-setting across the world, leaving his old life—and her—behind.

She'd gone on that trip with Dr. Storer after Nate left, but she'd spent the entire time missing him, and she never really felt much like writing after that.

When the two of them had sprawled under the oak trees together with their pencils and notebooks, their aspirations floating around them like untouchable butterflies, she'd never considered that their lives would turn out so differently.

Now, he was a famous songwriter, and she'd ended up leaving Nashville unemployed and moving back to Firefly Beach for good, having quit her job as a paralegal on the advice of her Aunt Clara, who had told Sydney in the inheritance letter that the one regret she never wanted Sydney to have was to look back on her life and know that she hadn't used her talents.

Sydney took in a deep breath and tried to get her emotions under control, the music from the dance floor filtering into her mind again as she returned to the present.

"I heard Justin Timberlake is here somewhere," Uncle Hank said, walking up to Sydney.

Uncle Hank had really come a long way this past year. They hadn't been able to get him to see a counselor for his grief over the loss of Aunt Clara, but he'd made strides, and restoring the house back to its original condition had seemed to help.

"And did you see that woman Nate was with? She's famous too, you know." His bushy gray eyebrows danced animatedly. "She's a swimsuit model in that magazine." He waggled his finger in the air, clearly trying to remember the name of it.

"Yes," Sydney replied, his excitement making her feel a little better.

"And there are so many country music stars here that I can't keep track of them all," he carried on. "I've had my eye on the guestbook to make sure no one runs off with it. With all the signatures in it, someone could retire if they sold it on eBay."

Sydney laughed. "Uncle Hank, I'm so happy you came up just now. I needed that." She wrapped him in a warm hug, the tight squeeze of his arms around her taking her back to her childhood. He was in good spirits, and it was so wonderful to see.

For the last year, Sydney and her son Robby had lived at Starlight Cottage along with her mother and Hallie when they came for long stints as their work schedule allowed. They'd thrown themselves into restoring the cottage and helping Uncle Hank get back on his feet after the death of her beloved Aunt Clara. But now she was at one of those turning points in life where she knew change was about to take place; she just hadn't actually figured out how to make it happen.

Uncle Hank was doing incredibly well, and he'd even asked his brother Lewis who lived alone in his own cottage down the road to stay with him some of the time so her uncle needed her less and less. Sydney had been looking at jobs over the last year and none of them had hit the mark yet, but she had found a few new ones to look into. On a bet with Hallie, she'd sent her résumé and a significant writing sample to a major New York magazine called *NY Pulse* that was offering a remote content editor position in the world and humanities section, but with no formal writing experience, she knew nothing would come of it. The one thing she was certain about, however, was that Firefly Beach was where she wanted to be, and the right opportunity would come along.

Uncle Hank's expression sobered. "I saw Nate walking away," he said, his disappointment in Nate's choices made evident by his frown.

Nate hadn't just left *her*; he'd left them all. Uncle Hank had checked the oil in Nate's truck and topped it off whenever it was low; he and Nate had gone fishing all the time together; and any evening that Nate was at Starlight Cottage after five o'clock, he was certain to get an invite to dinner, many nights staying over on the sofa. "I never liked that boy anyway," Uncle Hank said, but his smirk and the fondness in his eyes gave away his lie. "And he was a *terrible* football player."

Sydney burst into laughter then. Uncle Hank had managed to get away with the first fib, but that whopper was too difficult to let go. Nate's team had won the championship his senior year, and he'd been offered college football scholarships to a few small universities, but he'd turned them down to pursue songwriting and attend Belmont University in Nashville. She'd loved visiting him there. In the winters, he'd been right down the road from her mother's home in Nashville, and then, when the universities would let out for the summer, they'd travel to Firefly Beach together. She would stay at Starlight Cottage with Uncle Hank and Aunt Clara, and he'd stay with his parents down the road.

"You plan to talk to him?" Uncle Hank asked.

A server came by with a tray of champagne and Sydney grabbed one, tipping it up against her lips and swallowing a sip before answering, "Probably not."

"You gonna spend the night with that champagne instead? I know Nate's a headache for you, but I can guarantee the champagne packs a stronger punch."

She offered a half grin.

"You know he's moved back, right?"

"What?" She nearly spilled her champagne, her hand going limp and the glass tilting precariously to the side.

"He couldn't wait to get out of Firefly Beach all those years ago. Why would he want to come back here?" she said, nearly spitting the words at her uncle.

"You could ask him." Uncle Hank nodded toward a group of tables where Nate now sat, fiddling with the stem of a wine glass while he talked to a family member from Ben's side. The woman was getting up as they finished whatever it was they were chatting about, leaving him alone at the table.

"I'd rather not," she said, finishing her champagne and switching out the empty glass for a new one when the server came back by. But then, her fears subsided just a little when she remembered an article she'd read on him, highlighting all the homes he owned and noting how he'd barely lived in any of them. Every time, he spent a few months in a new place, immersed himself in renovations, and then he'd get bored, leaving it to sit vacant while he moved on to the next place.

Robby skipped across the grass, coming to a stop beside them. "They're almost ready to cut the cake, Mama! Ben told me!" he said, swiveling toward Uncle Hank at the same time. "Hi, Uncle Hank." He beamed up at him. "Are you gonna have cake?"

"Absolutely!" Uncle Hank nodded with vigor.

"I know *I* am," Sydney's mother said, joining in on the conversation. She straightened her white rose and baby's breath wrist corsage, the smile she'd had all day still plastered across her face.

"Hallie just has to throw her flowers at people first—that's what she said." Robby added, "What's that all about?"

Sydney laughed. "Not throw them *at* people; she probably said she was going to throw them *to* people. It's the bouquet toss—an old tradition."

"All the single guys are gathering for the garter now," Jacqueline said, pointing to the group of men huddling around Ben as he pulled out a chair for his bride. Hallie sat down, to the whoops of the crowd, her wedding dress puffing out around her. Sydney noticed Nate's seat at the table where he'd been sitting was now empty. She tried to locate him in the crowd but was unsuccessful. Maybe he'd gone. She could only hope.

Ben walked around the chair and kneeled down in front of Hallie, a playfully suggestive look on his face as his hands disappeared beneath her gown to a drum roll, not emerging again until he'd pulled the garter over her foot. He twirled the little slip of lacy elastic on his finger and the single men roared again. Ben turned his back to the group, waving it in the air. Then he tossed it behind him, the garter sailing over the heads of some of the men as they jumped to get it. An arm shot up from the center of them all, and Sydney recognized the suit sleeve immediately, her disappointment surfacing. It was definitely Nate's. The garter disappeared in his fist and the crowd parted.

Sydney's attention went straight to her sister. Hallie was already looking back at her, and Sydney subtly shook her head. Her sister nodded, telling her with that silent gesture that she wouldn't throw the bouquet in Sydney's direction. The last thing Sydney wanted was to allow Nate to push that garter up her leg. She wasn't superstitious, but she couldn't be too careful. She didn't need anything pointing toward her marrying Nate. No way.

"Are you going to try to catch the bouquet, Mama?" Robby asked.

She squatted down to eye level with her son. "Do you want me to?"

She knew, after her explanation to him that, as legend had it, the person who caught the bouquet would be the next to marry, Robby would be worried. Sydney would love Robby to have a solid father figure in his life, and to witness a happy marriage, but, over the years that his new uncle Ben had been with their family, Robby had bonded with him so strongly that he wouldn't give anyone else a chance. Sydney had introduced him once to someone she'd met at the coffee shop in town and he'd refused to even say hello. Later, Robby fretted that she was going to get married to the guy, and he didn't want her to. They'd spent so many years, just the two of them, that anyone moving in on that dynamic would be a major disruption.

"You don't need to catch it, do you?" he asked.

Sydney glanced over at Nate. "Definitely not."

Robby grinned.

"I'll tell you what: I'll go out there so I can be a part of Hallie's big night. There are lots of single girls who would love to catch it." Then she leaned toward him and whispered, "And I've already told her not to throw it to me." No sense in worrying Robby over a silly wedding tradition. "But I'd better hurry so we can get to the cake-cutting, right?"

"Yes, Mama!" Robby pushed her forward lightheartedly.

Sydney hustled out to the group of girls, waving her arms early to give Hallie her coordinates before her sister turned around. Hallie gave her a silent okay and, with her back to Sydney, she raised the flowers into the air. Nate was at the edge of the group, his eyes on Sydney, the garter dangling by his side from his pointer finger. She stared back at him and offered her best don't-even-think-about-it look while the girls counted down, "Three! Two! One!"

Hallie threw the bouquet, the heaviness of it creating an unforeseen arc. It sailed straight for Sydney. She quickly stepped to the side, the bundle of flowers landing with a thud onto the grass. One of Ben's cousins scooped it up, waving it in the air.

Sydney offered one more look at Nate before walking back toward Mama and Uncle Hank. On her way to them, a striking man about her age, with wavy blond hair and a friendly smile, whom she hadn't met before stepped into her path.

"Hello," he said with a kind smile and gentle eyes. He was strikingly handsome—probably one of Ben's new singer-songwriters. "Bride or groom?" he asked.

"Uh, bride—technically—but both, really. You?"

"Groom."

She knew it.

"I'm Logan." He held out his hand in greeting. "Logan Hayes. And you are?"

"Sydney Flynn." She returned his handshake. "It's nice to meet you, Logan."

"Likewise," he said, with a smile. "Having a good time?"

Sydney thought about her evening so far, wishing Nate would disappear. "Yes," she lied.

But there was a flicker in his eye and he tightened his focus on her.

She felt her cheeks flush at his observation. "What?" she said, caught off guard, her pulse rising.

"Your face just went all red."

"Oh, it's just my blush. Blame my sister. She did my make-up for the wedding. I had to stop her before she gave me eyelids that rivaled a Jackson Pollock."

"Mmm," he said with a chuckle. He looked out at the crowd. "It's a beautiful wedding. Probably one of the most perfect weddings I've ever been to."

"Yes," she said, looking over at Hallie who was positively glowing as she nearly floated across the grass from guest to guest in her exquisite gown, Ben on her arm. "I agree."

"It would be a pity not to enjoy it." He eyed the dance floor. "Want to go out there?"

Sydney considered Logan's request as she looked around for Robby. He was at the edge of the yard, playing games with a group of kids, so he wouldn't notice her. Then she caught sight of Nate. He was standing in a group of people, but his gaze was fixed on her. "I'd love to," she said, grabbing Logan's arm and hurrying to the dance floor.

As soon as they hit the dance floor, Logan took her by the hands and moved her arms to the music, spinning her around and pulling her into him. His grip on her was commanding but careful in a way that made her feel completely comfortable. Her satin dress slid up and down against her with the movement of his hands, and she allowed herself to enjoy the night, to relish the attention, and to shut off from everything except for this moment under the rising moon and twinkling string lights.

They danced until she'd forgotten all about her worries. Logan was an enjoyable partner, slipping in little funny comments as they moved to the music of the band. When they finally stepped off the dance floor, he turned to her. "We should get a cup of coffee sometime."

"That would be nice," she said, the reality of Robby's issues regarding men sliding into her consciousness now, making the idea of going on a date more difficult than giving a simple yes.

Logan leaned over to a nearby table and swiped a cocktail napkin. With a pen from the inside of his jacket, he scribbled on it and handed it to her. "This is my cell. If you ever want that cup of coffee, give me a call."

"Thank you," she said, folding it and securing it in her fist.

"It was wonderful meeting you," Logan told her.

"Same." Sydney felt a lift in her spirit as he walked away.

*

The wedding guests had dwindled and Jacqueline had taken Robby up to bed. Ben was spinning a now barefoot Hallie on the dance floor while Sydney sat amidst a table full of empty glassware and leaned on her hand, her eyelids drooping from such a big day. She'd hit the ground running at about five thirty this morning, helping Hallie finalize the last few details. She'd organized the wedding party breakfast at Starlight Cottage, gotten five women through hair and make-up, and picked up Beau from the groomer's in town—all while trying to keep her own appearance wedding-ready, wearing one of Uncle Hank's button-down shirts and flowers in her up-do. The wedding couldn't have been better—she was so happy for Hallie. Her sister deserved this night.

Sydney contemplated heading in to the cottage, all the champagne and festivities making her feel like she hadn't slept in weeks.

"You could've caught the bouquet," a familiar voice settled over her, making her fatigued shoulders tense up.

Nate dropped down into the chair beside her. His jacket and tie were gone, the top button of his shirt undone, and his sleeves rolled. He looked as tired as she felt, but she sort of liked it, because when he relaxed, he seemed less like Nathan Carr and more like Nate Henderson. It gave her a rush of nostalgia, and for the first time in quite a while, she considered how much she missed him.

"Is your date still sitting alone at your sister's cottage?" she asked, ignoring his first statement.

"Malory's with her."

She'd have liked to have been a fly on the wall when Nate had faced his sister. It was no secret that Malory wasn't happy at all with the fact that Nate hadn't been back to see anyone since he'd left. While he'd called his sister fairly often, he hadn't bothered to come back for any length of time, until now.

When his parents passed away, they'd left him their cottage in Firefly Beach, and it held so many memories for Sydney. There were six mailboxes between Starlight Cottage and the tiny little house where Nate Henderson used to live. She'd counted them every day that she'd made the walk between the two homes. On those lazy summertime days when she'd traveled that route with Nate, their faces warmed from a day in the sun, both of them barefoot, her sandals swinging from her fingertips, she'd never have imagined this. Nate had returned once a few years ago, and everyone wondered if he'd finally come back to spruce up the cottage his parents had left to him and his sister, but instead, he'd leveled it and created two separate lots: one with Malory's new cottage and another that sat abandoned while the weeds got cut twice a month; nothing had been done with it. He'd left in less than twenty-four hours.

Sydney twisted toward Nate to figure out exactly what he wanted when he'd said himself that he wouldn't bother her any more tonight.

"Can we talk?" he asked, surrender in his eyes. In that light, he looked just like he had all those years ago. She could almost swear she saw that same love in his eyes now that she'd taken for granted when they were younger. She'd have never imagined that she'd have to go so long without it.

Sydney was completely drained. Her head ached, the pinch in her shoulder was back in full force, and she'd had too much alcohol to have any kind of major conversation. All she wanted to do was crawl under the crisp covers of her bed, up at the cottage, and sink into glorious sleep.

"It's a little too late for that," she whispered and to her complete surprise and panic, tears welled up in her eyes. She was clearly exhausted, and had definitely had too much to drink. She blinked away her emotion. It had been easy to be strong when his face was on a glossy magazine cover, but with him right there in front of her, it felt too much like old times, and her resolve was slipping. She cleared her throat to keep the lump from forming.

"I feel like we never really got any closure, and that was my fault," he said, the softness of his voice as warming for her as the morning sun under the crisp coastal breeze. He looked out over the yard, littered with party debris. The gulf shone like diamonds under a full moon as fireflies danced along the edge of its lapping waves. "I haven't been able to get any of this right," he admitted. He looked back at her.

"And I just want you to know I'm sorry, Syd. I'm so sorry."

It was surprising how much her heart ached still when she let him get close enough. She'd thought she was over it. And now he'd just apologized, which was the one thing she'd wanted in all this.

But there was a part of her that was cautious about his motives. Right before her wedding to Christian, Nate had called her out of the blue—it had been the first time they'd spoken since he'd left that day for California. Things had started with her being angry, just like they had today, but he had sweet-talked his way into an easy conversation, and she'd found herself wondering about what could've been. It had terrified her, since she was on her way to the altar with someone else whom she thought she loved, and she'd cut the call short.

Later, she'd heard from someone in town that he'd tried to buy his sister's cottage out from under her, asking her to move, and Sydney couldn't help but wonder if he'd wanted something that day, which only made her feel more terrible for allowing her feelings for him to bubble to the surface. He'd upped his game tonight with an apology. Did he want something now?

Nate stood up and held out his hand. "Take a walk with me?"

She stared at the slight pout that his lips made when he was asking a question; it was an expression that she knew so well. There wasn't a shred of arrogance in his eyes, and she wanted so badly to believe the honesty she saw.

But life was about forward movement, not getting stuck in something from the past that obviously wasn't going anywhere, judging by his wedding date who was still sitting back at Malory's. She knew what she had to do. Sydney picked up the shoes that she'd kicked off earlier and stood in front of him in her bare feet.

"I don't think so," she told him. Then she walked off toward Starlight Cottage, feeling a swell of pride but knowing that the minute she got to her room, she'd let the tears come.

Chapter Three

The old farm table in Uncle Hank's kitchen at Starlight Cottage was abuzz with family this morning. The coffee pot gurgled, filling the room with the heady, chocolaty aroma of ground coffee, while the small television on the kitchen counter chattered in the background, offering up a day of glorious weather ahead.

Hallie and Ben had wanted to stay for breakfast before leaving for their honeymoon—their suitcases were already packed and ready against the wall. Sydney tried unsuccessfully to ignore the reading material for the plane that Hallie had stacked with their bags. The magazine on top had a giant photo of Juliana with a thumbnail of Nate in the corner. The headline read, "The It Couple's Decision to Leave the Spotlight: Is It a Publicity Stunt?" Had they fled to Firefly Beach to drum up interest in some new project? She took in a gulp of air to clear her mind and turned back toward her family.

Uncle Hank and his brother Lewis were chatting about the local news while Robbie wriggled up next to Ben to find out when he'd be back from the honeymoon so they could play football in the yard. Beau sighed from his dog bed in the corner. The regularity of the scene was comforting to Sydney, given the events that were invading their normalcy.

Sydney and Jacqueline had been up cooking since the early hours like they did sometimes. Sydney had come downstairs to find all the kitchen windows open, allowing a picturesque view of the turquoise Gulf and a warm breeze to blow in intermittently. Sydney hadn't slept well last night, and she wondered if the alcohol from the wedding had made her restless. She certainly wasn't going to admit to herself that it had anything to do with Nate being right down the street. Her mother hadn't asked about Nate, which only made Sydney more uptight about him. When Jacqueline was quiet, she was thinking. Well, her mother shouldn't have *anything* to think about when it came to him.

Sydney took the serving bowl of potato casserole over to the table and sat down with the rest of the family, her mother following with a platter of eggs.

"So what's everyone else doing today?" Ben asked, grabbing a few pieces of bacon from one of the dishes with the serving tongs and placing them on his plate before passing the dish to Hallie.

"I'm starting my new job today," Sydney said, buttering a biscuit. Sydney had been hired to write a small column for a section in a national magazine called *You* where she answered letters that were sent in. "I've chosen my first week's letters," she said. "I'm hoping the writing might get my creative juices flowing again." It wasn't the job of her dreams or anything, but it was a step toward her goal of getting into the business of content writing. "And I'm seeing Mary Alice for lunch. She says she has a favor to ask."

"Oh, that's wonderful!" Jacqueline said. "I haven't seen Mary Alice in so long. Remember when you two used to do that lemonade stand together?"

"I do," Sydney said, remembering her friend.

Uncle Hank beamed at her. "You're going to be writing again?"

"Well, writing letters, yes, but it's a start."

"It certainly is," Uncle Hank said, clearly delighted.

Growing up, Sydney had wanted to write about world events, interviewing people and bringing light to humanitarian issues, dreaming of traveling to faraway lands and documenting all the splendor of the human race. Once she got in to college, her interests widened to more social topics, but her love of writing never left her. She'd consumed entire days climbing shelves in the local library and gathering all her information to help her understand culture and history, and then she'd meet Nate, spending evenings after he'd gotten off at the beachside bar and grill where he worked on his summer break from college, both of them scribbling in their notebooks for hours—Sydney writing her articles and Nate writing songs.

Nate had written her more love songs than she could count over the four years they were together; she'd cherished every one of them. Her favorite moments were the ones when he'd drop his pencil, roll onto his back and play with melodies, humming the words to different tunes. Then he'd turn back over and scratch down a few more notes. During creative lulls, he always wanted to read her pieces. He said it recharged him. He'd been so supportive of her writing, telling her that she was going to do great things one day, and to remember him when she shot up so high that she'd have to look down to see everyone. Funny how ironic life could be sometimes.

She'd heard some of those songs on the radio, but every time one came on, she turned it off as fast as she could. She didn't want Nathan Carr's version of them to taint those precious moments they'd had together.

"Local Firefly Beach residents are going to face the largest summer crowd on record for this small village…" the television said, pulling everyone's attention over to it. "The current public beach area downtown," the reporter continued, "is the busiest location in all of Firefly Beach. From May until September..." The video footage showed the steady stream of people as they filtered through the access point to the shoreline, leaving bottles of sun lotion, trash, and swim gear in their wake to litter the coast. "And it's getting worse," the reporter said. "Local contractor Colin Ferguson, builder of the new beachfront hotel Luxury in the neighboring village of White Sands, is hoping for the opportunity to build on Firefly Beach's unspoiled shores, which will send even more people to the village as they look for uncrowded beaches."

Jacqueline clicked off the TV.

Uncle Hank picked up his cup of coffee but didn't drink it. "Lewis and I will be attending the town meeting today to show our support for maintaining our coastline," he said, filling the quiet that had settled over the table.

With the wedding and everything on her mind, Sydney had totally forgotten about the potential problem facing Starlight Cottage. Some people on the town's board of supervisors wanted to lessen the foot traffic downtown, so they had proposed a public beach access down the road from Starlight Cottage. "What's the latest?"

"They're still pushing the public beach access that would run along the lots right next to Starlight Cottage, and the most recent development is the additional plan for expansive parking and retail. That's where Colin Ferguson is getting involved."

"From what I've heard, the shops are supposed to stretch the length of road between the old Henderson lot and us," Jacqueline said. "I'll be very interested in hearing the specifics after you attend the meeting today," she said to Uncle Hank.

With the growth of tourism in the surrounding villages, the number of visitors finding their way to Firefly Beach had increased, and it was only a matter of time before the town would be facing the same summer gridlock that its neighbors were already dealing with.

It had taken two crews to maintain the cleanliness and quality of the public beach last summer, so to alleviate the growing congestion, the local government was planning to open a second access point, bulldozing all the trees and small cottages that separated Starlight Cottage from the town.

Starlight Cottage had been in the family for generations, but her great Aunt Clara and Uncle Hank Eubanks were the first to give the home a name. They'd called the cottage Starlight because of the lighthouse that sat on its own private peninsula, jutting out into the sea, behind the main building on the Eubanks' sprawling property. For years, the lighthouse had illuminated the water over a distance of nearly twenty miles, assisting the usually dazzling stars when cloud-cover hid them. With the increased use of electronic navigational systems, it wasn't a working lighthouse anymore, but Aunt Clara had always maintained it, and on Christmas, she lit it. She said that, on that night in particular, she wanted just one more opportunity to get sailors home to their families where they belonged.

Earlier this year, Sydney and Hallie had organized the revitalization of the lighthouse along with the surrounding structures—everything had been painted a bright white, the gazebo widened, landscaping along the seashell paths leading to the shore, boat docks, spacious patios out back... It was completely restored to the way it had been when Aunt Clara was alive—a little oasis, secluded just enough to make Sydney feel like she could escape the stress of real life for a while. But if the planning commission had anything to do with it, things wouldn't stay that way for long. As a girl, Sydney used to take in the sweeping coastal views from the top of the lighthouse, but now there was a possibility that she could be looking down at a mass of out-of-town cars instead of the palm trees and little southern cottages that she loved so much.

"There's no way that plan will ever get off the ground," she said. "The city would have to knock down all the houses between us and the corner lot. I can't imagine that the neighbors would give up their land," she added, holding out hope.

"Well," Lewis piped up. "Yesterday, I ran into Tom McCoy from down the road, and he told me he *would* sell if they made him an offer he couldn't refuse. The growth in the area recently is what made him finally decide he'd let it go. He wants to move down the coast. The sale of his land could give him enough to retire."

A wave of uncertainty washed over Sydney. "Then he wouldn't be running the fruit stand anymore…" she considered aloud.

The McCoy fruit stand was anything but a simple stand. It was an enormous expanse that stretched the side of the McCoy home and across part of the front lawn. Tom hosted hayrides and face painting for the kids; he offered free dog biscuits for pets of anyone stopping by, and he always managed to have the sweetest peaches in Firefly Beach. On walks between their houses, Sydney and Nate would always stop there. Since they were kids back then, Tom would give them each a peach free of charge every time.

"When are you gonna let us pay?" Nate would tease him.

"When you bring your kids here," Tom told him.

If only they'd all known how things would turn out…

"Will you tell me anything new you find out today?" Sydney asked Uncle Hank and Lewis, not bothering to hide her concern.

"You know I will," Uncle Hank replied.

She wished she could go with them to offer her own opinions on the matter, but she knew that Uncle Hank wasn't shy about sharing what he thought. The future of Starlight Cottage was in good hands.

"Text me to let me know what happens," Hallie said, apprehension written on her face.

Sydney laughed. "I'm not texting you in Barbados! You and Ben deserve this time together."

Unable to have children, Hallie and Ben had decided to adopt, and they'd completed and passed the home study. They'd gotten everything filed at the agency they'd chosen, and they were currently awaiting selection as adoptive parents. Hallie and Ben were so excited, but Sydney knew, from raising Robby, how important their time as a couple was.

There were eight chairs at the table and seven family members at Starlight Cottage. They'd said, after Aunt Clara passed, that the empty one was for Aunt Clara, but Sydney was more than willing to bet that Aunt Clara wouldn't mind sharing her chair with the newest member of the family when he or she arrived. It was as if the spot were just waiting to be filled, and now the empty chair felt less like an old memory and more like Aunt Clara, with her arms open wide, poised like she used to be, ready to grab on to her loved ones as they rushed toward her.

After breakfast, Uncle Hank took his coffee and went out to his spot on the back porch overlooking the sea, where he'd been going every morning recently. Sydney joined him, lowering herself into one of the rocking chairs. Uncle Hank rocked back and forth, his eyes on the turquoise water as it caressed the white sand, ebbing and flowing in a hypnotic way, while the breeze turned the paddle fans that lined the porch ceiling above them.

"When your Aunt Clara died," he said, still gazing out to sea, "what struck me most at first was the silence. It was just me in this big house and the quiet was so loud that I couldn't stand it." He took a drink from his mug and tipped back in his chair, rocking. "I didn't have Clara's chatting about nothing." He grinned at the memory.

Uncle Hank had struggled with Aunt Clara's death for a long time, but having his family around, and Sydney and Robby living there with him, had helped him. He was back to himself again. And he enjoyed talking about Aunt Clara, often telling Sydney stories she'd never known about her great aunt.

"She was always buzzing around," he continued, "asking me questions about something she'd noticed in town, or deciding out loud whether she should make us new cushions for the outdoor porch swing, or she'd point out the change in color of the palm trees that I never could see… My whole life with her, I'd never prepared myself for what it would be like to be without that. But every morning since the whole family has been here for the wedding, I feel that buzzing again, as if Clara's spirit is in all of us."

"I thought about her this morning," Sydney said. "Her chair at the table… I miss her, but I feel like she's here."

"Me too."

"What do you think she'd say about the public beach access coming our way?" Sydney asked.

Uncle Hank laughed. "I think she'd have already been in their offices, driving them crazy. She'd have produced an entire alternative plan, and it would almost certainly be something they'd never thought of, *and* it would work better than one anyone else could've devised. 'Firefly Beach is in our soul,' she used to say. She wouldn't let them come near it."

"She was so creative and talented."

He nodded, content.

They both looked out at the tranquil gulf, its crystal waters rushing in and out all the way to the lighthouse and beyond. Something told Sydney to take it in. She couldn't help but feel like this was the calm before the storm.

Mary Alice Chambers looked exactly the same as she had as a girl. Her white-blond hair was swept up in a bun, accentuating her sky-blue eyes.

"Thank you for meeting me," she said to Sydney as she sat down at the little bistro table on the deck at her favorite restaurant. The red and blue bungalow known as Wes and Maggie's was surrounded by palm trees and sat right on the water in a strip of sand. Matching red and blue flags, fighting madly against the coastal wind, lined the outdoor seating, which was usually full of vacationers, but it was early afternoon and, as she looked out to the shoreline, the beaches were still crowded with visitors. She could remember when that beach was only dotted with a few residents, and now it was towel-to-towel, on the strip of sand.

Next to Wes and Maggie's was Cup of Sunshine, the coffee shop, where Sydney had spent many mornings reading and job-hunting since their WiFi was stronger than the connection out at Starlight Cottage. Locals and visitors alike couldn't get enough of their signature butter pecan latte or their homemade pumpkin pie breakfast bread, and the owner Melissa was a master at preparing delicious French toast served with a drizzle of cream cheese syrup. Every patron, no matter how small the purchase, went home with a complimentary dark chocolate truffle that had an icing-piped chocolate sunshine on the top. As Sydney had walked past this morning, on her way to Wes and Maggie's, Melissa caught her eye through the window of the shop and waved like she always did.

"Hey, pretty ladies," Wes said as he came over to Sydney and Mary Alice. He was an old family friend and owner of the restaurant. "What kind of day is it for the two of you—an iced tea day or try-my-new-Passion-Punch day?"

"Passion Punch?" Mary Alice replied, as she shifted her bag to get comfortable in her chair.

"It's got two kinds of rum, strawberry daiquiri puree, and a splash of pineapple and coconut. I've been selling 'em like hot cakes to the tourists. I even have new painted paper umbrellas with coconuts on them." Wes, an artist, was known for the hand-painted little umbrellas he placed in every drink he made at the bar.

"I'm up for one if you are," Mary Alice said, consulting Sydney.

"Two Passion Punches then," Sydney said to Wes.

"Comin' up! Anything else?"

"I'm fine for now," Sydney replied. "Mary Alice?"

"We'll start with drinks, but I'm not going to definitively say I won't be ordering your seafood sampler."

Wes laughed. "If we make one for someone, I'll have them throw a few extra bites onto a small plate for you, on the house." He gave her a wink and headed toward the bar.

Once Wes had left them alone, Mary Alice placed her forearms on the table, leaning closer. "Your mother told me at the wedding that you got a new writing job."

"Yeah, it's nothing too grand, but I'm hoping it will get me warmed up in case something bigger comes along. I'm writing a daily column called 'Dear Ms. Flynn' for the *Panhandle Gazette.*"

"That sounds interesting."

"People write in with things that are weighing on them and I answer." She shrugged to convey that it wasn't the most glamorous of writing jobs but it was a start. "But enough about me! Tell me what you've got going on—it sounds huge."

Mary Alice beamed, pulling a glossy brochure from her bag. "I had these made this week," she said, her eyes shining with excitement as she pushed it across the table. "It's for my new wellness center."

"Oh wow," Sydney said, opening the brochure to view the services offered by the center. "This is great."

"Thank you." Mary Alice beamed. "It's a big leap, but I've decided to start my own center here in Firefly Beach so I can give back to the community that I love."

"That's amazing," Sydney told her, setting the brochure down. "I'm excited for you!"

"Thanks!" Mary Alice offered her a big smile. "I was wondering if I could ask a huge favor."

"Of course," Sydney said. "What is it?"

"I'm offering a free magazine for my patients... and I was wondering if I could ask for you to use your content editing skills? It needs a front cover, would you be able to help with the layout and photo shoot for that, and maybe offer me some quick ideas for the organization of the magazine? I can't afford a full staff and I know how good your attention to detail is."

It would be nice to be a part of something with such passion behind it, Sydney thought. She still had her inheritance and the money from the sale of her house back in Nashville, so she didn't mind taking this time to do a little something for herself. It had been a long time since she'd allowed herself to be solely in the creative field, and she still wasn't sure she could do it, but she'd never know until she tried—it was where she was always the happiest.

Mary Alice ran her hand over the brochure that had a photo of a family gathered on a picnic blanket with the title in block font:

SEASIDE FAMILY CALM AND WELLNESS CENTER
A complete approach to a healthier you.

"Absolutely." Sydney felt a thrill just looking at the pamphlet in front of her. This type of work was right up her alley. "I can see the title *A Better You* on the cover of the magazine. Just thinking out loud, you could have a range of sections that might go something like... 'Find Yourself,' covering organic and cruelty-free products, vitamins, local spots to get outdoor exercise... Maybe a section on the latest in psychology, for example, a spot on meditation or mindfulness... You could call it 'Mind over Matter'?" She kept going, the ideas flooding her. "You could even do another piece with celebrity spotlights—people in the public eye who are making a difference in their environment and themselves, and then ways to help and get involved..."

When she looked up, Mary Alice had her hand over her mouth, covering a giddy smile, her eyes wide. "I *knew* you were the one to ask," she said. "I already love it all. Would you be free to come in to the office when we open tomorrow at nine? I have counseling clients already lined up first thing, but I'll show you some of the ideas I've got to get you started."

"Of course I would!"

"That's amazing. I'll set up a table for us in one of the spare rooms at the center so you and I can have a quiet place to talk."

"That sounds marvelous."

Wes brought their drinks to the table—tall narrow glasses filled to the brim with dark pink liquid, a slice of pineapple on the rim, and his signature umbrella, speared through mixed fruit, floating on top.

"I suppose these drinks are celebratory," Mary Alice said, her eyes dancing with enthusiasm for the project.

Sydney, nearly overflowing with hope, raised her glass. "Cheers to that."

Chapter Four

Sydney clicked on the lamp as she sat at the desk in the small office she'd converted from Aunt Clara's sewing room, leaning back in the chair she'd chosen during the renovation of the cottage because of the oatmeal color that matched so nicely with the linen drapes. She opened her computer to begin her first response for her column, under the banner of "Dear Ms. Flynn." She opened the first letter:

Dear Ms. Flynn,

I'm writing you with a heavy heart. I've taken a new job and had to move away from my entire family. Now I'm all alone in a new city…

Best wishes,

Rebecca

Sydney copied and pasted the letter into a new document and began her response, addressing the sender:

Dear Rebecca,

It must be terribly difficult to be without your family.

Her fingers stilled and she stared at her screen, thinking, but nothing was coming to her. What should she say to this woman that could make her feel better? Should she take the approach that this kind of thing happened sometimes and this too shall pass? Sydney tipped her head up and focused on the crystal light fixture in the ceiling, trying to think of just the right thing to say. What would it feel like if she moved away from everyone? Well, she wouldn't. But if she did… Sydney placed her fingers on the keys but they just hovered there. None of her ideas seemed heartfelt enough.

A wave of fear washed over her. She hadn't written in years. What if she didn't have the ability to do what she used to do? What if she was too jaded to be that open? Sydney closed her eyes, trying to force the creative energy, but she was coming up empty. How had Aunt Clara done it? She'd been a successful designer and no matter what was going on in her life, she could just create. Almost on command. "Tell me what to do," she said silently to her aunt, praying she'd hear her in the heavens and send some sort of magical answer down to her.

She leaned back, her eyes falling on the new drapes she'd hung and a memory of Aunt Clara came to mind, making Sydney smile. When Sydney was about fifteen, she'd gone in to the living room once when Aunt Clara was hanging a new pair of curtains. Her aunt was up on a ladder with a pencil in her mouth and a measuring tape stretched out between her fingers. "Why do you keep changing the curtains?" Sydney had asked her.

The measuring tape zipped back into its spool, and Aunt Clara took the pencil from her lips and tucked it behind her ear. "Well, darling, the first set of drapes were an idea I'd had years ago. But if you keep relying on the old ideas about what works, you may never actually let enough light in. There's always room for change." That had never made sense until right now.

A knock at the door pulled her attention away from the screen. She shut her computer. "Come in."

Uncle Hank peeked into the room. "What are you doing?" he asked, curious.

"Trying to let the light in," she said.

Uncle Hank frowned. "Isn't it already coming in?" he asked, peering over at the window.

"The creative light," she clarified.

"Ah," he said, sitting on a nearby chair.

Sydney scooted over to give him more legroom.

"The elusive creativity."

"It's just not flowing right now," she said, wondering again about Aunt Clara's advice.

"Not being the artistic type, it's difficult to know how to help you. What did you used to do to get into an imaginative mindset?"

Sydney chewed her lip. She didn't want to say that she used to talk to Nate. He could always help her. But just as Aunt Clara had said, if you rely on the old ideas about what works, you may never let enough light in. Nate definitely didn't let her see any light now. His star was so large that it overpowered everything in his path. No one else could even twinkle. "I can't remember what helped me," she lied. "Did you need me?" She set her laptop on the floor.

Uncle Hank looked around the room. "This house has grown with us," he said. "I just assumed it would continue to do so…" He took in a deep breath and let it out slowly. "They only sent one of the board members to the meeting today," he said. "And he was there simply to jot down our questions."

"Do you think they're listening at all?"

He shook his head. "No. Tom's the only one who's agreed to sell his property, although he hasn't signed a contract yet. The others are all against the project, but I could see their interest when they heard what was being offered for their land. I don't know how the county is getting the kind of money they're proposing."

"It's not right," she said. The image of their quiet street crowded with cars and people filing onto the beach along their side yard flashed in her mind, causing a lurch of panic. Starlight Cottage had always been Sydney's safe place, away from the noise that life could bring. It was the place where she'd stayed in the years following Nate's leaving, the house she'd retreated to when her marriage dissolved, where she'd spent every childhood summer, and now it was her home. The calm of this estate had been her quiet getaway from life's stresses. She'd never have imagined that one day she might have to survive without it.

"We've asked for another meeting, and we want the full board there." He pursed his lips in disapproval. "But it's not looking good for our case. The impact on residents is small—the public beach would only affect five of us on this street, since the area isn't built up. I'm worried the other Firefly Beach residents will be in favor of the project, or at the very least not be opposed."

Jacqueline came in with a plate of leftover wedding cookies, setting it down on the side table next to the chair. "I thought you could use a pick-me-up," she said. "How's the writing going?"

"I haven't really gotten started," Sydney replied, the seed of fear sprouting in her gut. "I was just reading the first letter when Uncle Hank came in."

"Are you talking about the meeting?" she asked.

"Yes," Sydney said, the weight of the impending decision sitting heavily on her.

"There's nothing we can do about it right now. We've offered up our questions and concerns, and asked for another meeting." She grabbed a cookie. "Try not to dwell on this," she told Sydney. "Focus on your new working adventure."

Despite her worries about the cottage, with the support of her family, Sydney felt something moving within her, and she wondered if this would be the change she needed. It would certainly take her a while to get acclimated to a creative mindset again. But she couldn't wait to get started.

"It's strange without Ben and Hallie here," Jacqueline said as she fiddled with the petals of one of the geraniums in a pot on the back porch. She'd come out to enjoy the salty evening air before starting supper, and Sydney and Robby had joined her.

Sydney settled on the porch swing they'd installed just before Hallie and Ben's wedding. The couple had had their engagement portraits taken on it—Ben sitting with Hallie lying beside him, knees up, her head resting on his knee. They'd looked incredible. Even Sydney noticed the absence of the calm they both brought with them anywhere they went together.

"I miss Ben," Robby said.

Sydney's chest tightened. Ben had been with their family for years—Robby's entire life—and he was the only man who'd ever really connected with him. With Ben starting his own family, Sydney couldn't help but worry for Robby. When the adoption came through, Ben would be with Hallie, and where would that leave her son? Robby was too young to understand the demands of adulthood, and he was bound to feel left behind by both Christian and Ben.

Robby's father was barely around. He'd moved on with his life, leaving them behind. He showed up at major holidays but only ever stayed a few hours. And now his new wife was expecting a baby, so he'd be wrapped up in his new family.

"I miss Ben and Hallie too," she said, keeping her thoughts to herself.

"Can we call Ben?" Robby asked, climbing up onto the swing with her.

"Sorry, honey. When two people are on their honeymoon, they're usually pretty busy sightseeing and spending time together," she said with a discreet wink to her mother. "We need to give Ben and Hallie their privacy."

Robby's face dropped, and Sydney already felt the disappointment that would unquestionably settle upon him as time went on. She wanted to give him more healthy role models, but she just didn't know what to do. She'd tried to take him to see Gavin Wilson, who owned the art gallery in town, thinking they could connect on a creative level this summer, but Robby refused to talk to him. Then he'd worried incessantly that Sydney was going to date Gavin, which couldn't be further from the truth. He was only an acquaintance, a friend of Hallie's. It wasn't healthy, but she didn't know what to do. She figured she might run it by Mary Alice at some point to see if she had any suggestions from a counseling perspective.

The crunch of gravel on the walk leading around to the porch where they sat pulled her from her introspection. A lone, overlooked paper napkin, the last remnant from yesterday's wedding, blew like a tumbleweed across the lawn until a masculine hand stopped it, balling it up in his fist, and shoved it into the pockets of his jeans. Sydney followed the arm up to the face, her mouth drying out. She stood up.

"May I help you?" she asked Nate.

"Hi," he said, his hand raised in greeting. When she didn't say anything, he lowered it slowly, his eyes full of silent messages to her that she couldn't decipher, and really didn't want to.

"Robby," Jacqueline said. "I need your help snapping the ends off the green beans for supper tonight. You're so good at it. Think you could help me inside?" She eyed Sydney. Her mother knew all about Nate, and she also knew exactly what Sydney thought of him.

"Okay," Robby replied, regarding Nate cautiously. He followed Mama inside.

Nate stepped onto the porch. "I thought I'd stop by," he said, moving toward her tentatively.

Sydney backed away, her heart racing.

"I didn't push you at the wedding because it wasn't the time nor place, but I was wondering if you'd hear me out." He took another step forward, and this time she allowed the proximity, her curiosity getting the better of her. "Let me get this off my chest and then you can tell me to leave. Because if I don't say anything, I'll regret it, and when it comes to us, I have enough regret already."

At least he wasn't entirely heartless. Although, judging by how quickly he'd moved on to better things in LA after leaving Firefly Beach, she doubted he'd spent long nights, his heart breaking until the tears were literally flooding him, the emptiness so raw that he didn't know how he'd pick up the pieces. Seeing him brought it all back for her, and she scolded herself for letting him affect her.

"Can we just be us for a little bit?" he asked. "Just you and me, Syd?"

She felt the swell in her chest at the thought of him and her, like old times. But the problem was that they'd been irrevocably changed by everything that had happened. "We've both moved on with our lives," she said. "You're not who you were anymore and neither am I. Dragging each other through our muddy past isn't healthy for either of us."

His gaze dropped to the floor, but it was clear that his thoughts were somewhere else. "I hadn't meant to change..." His voice trailed off.

Sydney wondered if he regretted leaving, and despite her anger about how he'd handled things, she felt an odd sort of guilt for making him question something that had led to his success. "Your life now is your destiny," she said. "I know that because you are an incredible songwriter. You deserve to be right where you are. You don't belong under the oaks at Firefly Beach anymore, Nate. *We* are a casualty of that success, no matter how rocky the journey was to get you there."

Sadness seemed to wash over him, and before she could act on it, his arms were around her, his familiar scent of fresh cotton and spice overwhelming her senses and making her lightheaded. The feel of his chest against her face took her right back to those years they'd spent curled up together all night after they'd stayed up writing and talking about their future, neither of them wanting to move as the sun broke on the horizon, the day inching between them and making them finally get up. She fought back the prick of tears.

"My heart will always be under those oaks with you," he whispered into her ear. Sydney worked to swallow the lump forming in her throat, the ache that had been long forgotten surging through her with a vengeance. In that moment, how he'd left wasn't what surfaced, but instead a deluge of memories from all the wonderful times they'd shared together, and she realized that even though she kept telling herself that she shouldn't, she loved him, and if she allowed herself to admit it, she was *still* in love with him.

Nate pulled away and looked down at her. "Even after all this time, it feels like yesterday," he said.

Sydney knew that telling him she felt the same way would do more harm than good. Keeping him at Firefly Beach because of her would be like caging a wild bird—his wings were too big for this town, and it was only a matter of time before he'd leave again.

She was still swimming around in her feelings when the reality of the whole situation set in: it wasn't fair to Juliana to have her boyfriend running around after an old flame. So why was he? That single question pulled Sydney back into the certainty that Nate Henderson was no longer the person standing in front of her. The very best Sydney could hope for was to have the strength to keep her emotions in check until Nate had his fill of Firefly Beach and pulled away from town and away from *her* for good.

"Mr. Carr," she said quietly, purposely using his pen name to drive home the point, "it isn't yesterday." Sydney had to literally push the words from her lips when all she wanted to do was to fall back into his arms as if the time that they'd lost had been just a bad dream. "If you're here to say you're sorry, then apology accepted. But I'd appreciate it if you would, *please*, let me move on with my life." Her heart slammed around in her chest, and she feared that he could see through her.

Nate stared at her questioningly. It seemed like she was hurting him, but what did he expect? He might be used to girls falling at his feet these days, but Sydney wouldn't be one of them.

"Mama?" Robby's voice tore through the moment.

Sydney whipped around to address him. "Hi, honey."

"I'm all done helping with dinner." His little eyes fluttered over to Nate.

"This is… an old friend," Sydney said. "His name is Nathan Carr." The name rolled heavily off her tongue.

Robby moved slightly behind her when Nate bent down to say hello.

"You can call me Nate," he said gently. When Robby refused to acknowledge him, Nate stood back up.

"Will you say hello to Nate?" Sydney asked him.

"Hello," Robby said bashfully. Then he turned to Sydney. "Will you come inside soon?"

"I'll be inside in just a minute," she told her son as he ran back into the cottage.

"Your son looks like you," Nate said. After that, he was quiet, unspoken words on his lips.

Sydney remembered the article she'd read where he'd said he couldn't see himself with children, so his comment seemed laden with the screaming reality that what they wanted in life was very different.

They both stood together—so many obstacles stacked between them—and then he spoke again. "I wish things could've been different. I thought I was doing the right thing at the time…"

That call he'd made to her right before her wedding came to mind. Despite the way things were between them, he'd made her laugh, bringing up an old memory. And now, here he was, trying to tell her how he felt, when his girlfriend was down the road. In both instances, his timing was unbelievable, and absolutely selfish of him.

He shook his head as if he were jostling the emotions free, an exhale bursting from his lips. Sydney wondered if he, too, was thinking that he shouldn't be there. She felt guilty for the tiny bit of pleasure she got in his presence. It seemed as though there was unfinished business between them, as if something was still left unsaid and they had this minute to say it.

"I should probably get inside," she said, wishing all their problems could be like helium balloons and they could both just let go, watching them float away until they were so small they didn't matter anymore.

"Well, look who the cat dragged in," Uncle Hank said, stepping outside. His expression was playful but also a little cautious. "I've missed ya."

Nate smiled. "Caught any redfish in the slot?" he asked Uncle Hank.

That was always their first conversation when they hadn't seen each other in a while. Nate would come home for the summer, sneak up behind Uncle Hank on the shore, throw his arm around him, and ask him that question. Sydney had grown up fishing at Firefly Beach with Uncle Hank so she knew that "in the slot" meant that he'd caught a fish that measured between seventeen and twenty-seven inches in length. Law only allowed fishermen to keep one redfish per day that was in the slot.

"Caught a bull in the Choctawhatchee Bay. Thing weighed twenty-nine pounds."

Nate raised his eyebrows in interest. "Did you keep it?"

"Nah. I threw him back."

Nate chuckled. Uncle Hank was never one to keep the fish. Nate had said once that he thought Uncle Hank actually enjoyed setting them free more than hooking them. He'd never harm a soul.

"I didn't get to talk to you at the wedding," Uncle Hank carried on, rotating toward the sun and closing his eyes briefly while the orange light washed over his face. "But I've got time now." He turned to Nate. "Wanna come inside and have dinner with us?"

"What about Juliana?" Sydney heard herself ask. Just saying her name out loud caused a torrent of remorse to pelt her insides. Sydney was letting old feelings for Nate seep back in, and now Uncle Hank was asking him to dinner—*not* a good idea.

"She's having a spa day with Malory. They aren't getting back until tonight," he said. "They're going to a new beachfront restaurant down the road, in Rosemary Beach."

Juliana was getting to know Nate's sister, spending time with her… People didn't do that unless things were serious. But then Sydney's feelings turned to frustration. Why was Nate even standing on her porch? Had he left for Starlight Cottage the minute Juliana was out of his sight? Sydney had seen the magazine headline: things were looking up for them. Well, maybe Juliana would like to know that her boyfriend had run off to his ex-girlfriend's house… It all gave her a bitter taste in her mouth.

"I don't think he's hungry," she offered, sending an icy glance in Nate's direction. The ease with which he could pull her in unnerved her, and all she wanted was for him to leave.

"I'm starving, actually," Nate said.

Uncle Hank threw his arm around Nate. "Well, come in then. We've got an extra seat at the table."

Was this really happening? How would she hold a normal conversation with him there? What were they all going to talk about anyway? She wouldn't be able to eat a single bite; her stomach would be in knots. Suddenly, Sydney wished she would have crawled into Hallie's suitcase and shipped herself right off to Barbados because right now, as he looked back at her with those unspoken words of his, she wanted to be as far away from Nate Henderson—or should she say Nathan Carr?—as she could be.

Chapter Five

Over the years, Sydney had allowed moments of affection for Nate, but the more she thought about it, the more she convinced herself it was simply a longing to have the old Nate back. Seeing him in Firefly Beach, those blue eyes on her in the same way they had looked at her so long ago—it was toying with her rational side. She'd gotten very good at building up the walls that could keep her safe from heartbreak, and until Nate went back to LA, she'd have to put that skill to the test. Because he *was* going back to LA, and back to his life and back to his girlfriend.

Judging by the sparkle in Uncle Hank's eyes when he talked to Nate, she wondered if he'd missed Nate as much as she had. Uncle Hank had asked him all about Malory and the cottage, how he was doing, and whether he was happy to be back in Firefly Beach again… Sydney had focused on bringing the food to the table and tried to have a regular conversation with her mother to drown him out. She barely even looked Nate's way.

Nate's phone went off at the table, the irritation scratching down her spine as he picked it up. "I'm so sorry," he said, "may I take this call?" Nate put the phone to his ear and stepped over toward the door. "Nathan Carr," he said into his phone in a business-like tone that she'd never heard before. "Hey… Yes… I was going to touch base when we're all in the same room for the Grammys…" He stepped outside for a second, an awkward lull hanging in the air as everyone tried to ease the disruption. Soon he was back inside, setting his phone on the table, and dropping into his chair.

It frustrated her to see him sitting in Aunt Clara's chair. In her mind, that place was reserved for family, and he didn't feel like family at all anymore.

"So Nate," Jacqueline said with an uneasy smile, "how's the songwriting business?" She passed him a plate and a handful of silverware.

"Busy," he said. "But in my business, busy is good." He took a roll from the platter and passed the plate to Lewis. "I thought coming home would give me a break from the madness, and it has, but I can't stop writing songs here. I've written three new ones in the last two days." He glanced over at Sydney.

Sydney remembered how he'd get stuck sometimes when writing. He was always in motion, telling her how movement helped him think, so she'd tacked little stories about their lives—memories—to the trees around the property to inspire him. As they walked together, talking and reminiscing, he'd stop and jot down a few lines. Before she knew it, he had notebooks full of them. "You're my muse," he said once, before pulling her in for a kiss and wrapping his arms around her. He'd always insisted she was a more talented writer than he was—now, judging by his success, it was clear he'd been so wrong.

"That's wonderful," Jacqueline said, dragging her from her thoughts. "Sometimes we just need to have a new perspective for the ideas to come. Would you share one of your songs with us?"

Nate buttered his roll, his mind clearly heavy with something. "Okay," he said, and his gaze landed on Sydney. "I've got one in particular that I'm writing and I haven't gotten the beginning yet, but I have the chorus. Here it goes…" He started to sing.

"*If only I had that moment back*

That day, that hour, that minute

Would life have carved out something more—

A life with you in it?"

Sydney dropped her fork, the utensil clanging to the ground, stopping Nate. The lyrics were too close to her own heart to bear, but that was what he was great at, right? He used to take her feelings and turn them into songs, but this was too much. He was a master at storytelling. He could spin fiction until it was difficult to know what was real and what wasn't. Sydney stood up to get the fork, bumping the table and jostling everyone's glasses. Nate's juice sloshed over the rim of his glass, spilling onto the table. "Sorry," she said, picking up her fork. She sat down and handed Nate her napkin.

"It's okay," he replied with a look of questioning interest.

"That sounds like the start of another hit," Uncle Hank said, once everyone had settled again.

"I truly think my creativity has spiked because I'm getting back to my roots. It feels good to be home."

"Too bad Ben's not here," Uncle Hank said. "We could all go fishing like old times. Have you been since you've been back in Firefly Beach?"

"I haven't." Nate took a drink of his iced tea and swallowed. "I don't have a fishing pole anymore."

"Good grief, son! What kind of life are you livin' out there in that big city?" Uncle Hank teased, making Nate laugh.

"I'd love to go fishing," Nate replied.

"Just say the word." Uncle Hank leaned over to Robby and whispered, "You could come too," he said. "We can show him how it's done."

Robby grinned up at Uncle Hank, but all Sydney could think about was the fact that she didn't want Nate at dinner or fishing with Robby… She just wanted him to leave.

"I'm free all evening," Nate said, his expression serious and intentional.

Uncle Hank's face lit up. "I've got bait and rods out back if you're looking to shore fish tonight."

Nooooo. Sydney did not need Nate hanging around Starlight Cottage any longer than he was already. Why was Uncle Hank being so accommodating when he knew how she felt? Her uncle had been there the day Nate had left her. He'd seen her moping around for weeks, for months, unable to get her head around the fact that the future she'd been building in her head for years had come shattering down around her. Uncle Hank knew how much Nate had hurt her. What was he doing?

"I'd love to."

Robby sat up on his knees. "May I fish with you, Uncle Hank?"

"Of course you can!"

Was Sydney on some kind of hidden camera show? Didn't anyone realize that Nate hadn't bothered to contact a single one of them in years, but now they couldn't seem to get rid of him—wasn't that a little too weird?

"Uncle Hank, after dinner, can I speak with you?" Sydney asked to the hush of the table.

"Of course you can." Uncle Hank seemed unfazed by her request. "But you'll have to make it fast, unless you'd like to fish with us…"

"I think we need to show him how great life is here at Firefly Beach," Uncle Hank explained when Sydney had pulled him aside to find out why in the world he'd asked Nate to dinner and then to stay this evening.

"Why, when he's moved on from us and from here?"

"When you're young, it's only natural to move beyond where you came from, to see the world and push yourself to find your own limits. I watched your Aunt Clara do that with her design business—it took her all over the world. But once a person has that perspective, if they're lucky enough to get the chance to look back, they'll see what's most important: the people they love. That's why your Aunt Clara always came back to this home and to her friends here. These people are more important than any *place* in the world. Nate has experienced success; he's been away. We've been blessed to have him return. Let's show him what he's missing in that big city of his."

Uncle Hank had good intentions. He wanted to fill that silence he'd spoken about earlier, and he truly enjoyed having all his loved ones around him. But Sydney wasn't so sure he'd want *this* Nate back. She worried that Nathan Carr would disappoint him. After the year she'd spent helping Uncle Hank deal with his grief and get back onto his feet, she felt extremely protective of him.

"I'm fishing too," she said, the tension in her chest rising at just the thought.

Uncle Hank, obviously misinterpreting her decision, beamed. "Excellent. I'll need help with the supplies."

When they all got down to the shore, Nate cast his line into the gulf as the salty tide rippled around their ankles. Sydney reeled hers in just a bit and waited, the way Uncle Hank had always taught her to do. Robby and Uncle Hank were down the beach from her—Robby wouldn't speak to Nate, so they'd fallen into an odd pairing because Robby still needed quite a bit of instruction and Uncle Hank was the one who did that best.

"I know Ben was happy you came to the wedding," she said, trying her best to make small talk.

Nate nodded, reeling in when he got a tug on the line, but then evidently deciding it was a false alarm, so he let it be.

"What does Juliana think of Firefly Beach?" she ventured.

Sydney had read that Juliana Vargas, a swimsuit model, had traveled the globe and lived in luxury at various sought-after beach locations like Fiji and Belize. She was the third highest paid model in the industry and her Instagram feed looked like an advertisement for the diversions of the rich and famous. The quaint little village of Firefly Beach was probably quite a different experience for her.

"She likes the quiet," he said, not taking his focus off his line. The breeze coming off the gulf rustled his hair like it used to do when they were young. "And the seclusion."

His answer was surprising. "I just assumed, by what I'd read about her, that she preferred things that were more—I don't know—fast-paced."

Nate finally looked her way. "She grew up in a little village in Argentina. Her grandfather owned a small winery. She said that her only companionship there was the breadth of the grape vines on their fencings and the mountainous rock that jutted into the sky. She showed me a photo of it once."

Sydney gave him her full attention.

"The red-rock hills around the town have these incredible stripes on them; they're beautiful." He reeled in, checked his bait, and then recast his line. "All that to say that she's not used to the craziness she's been immersed in lately. It doesn't come naturally for her, and while it's exciting, she feels like she can breathe when she's here."

Hearing such personal information about Juliana made the situation more real, which only caused Sydney to feel more uncomfortable about being with Nate. While they weren't doing anything wrong, she felt the pull of their past whenever she was with him, and there was the fact that he'd come over today at all. The whole situation was unsettling.

Sydney got a tug on her line, jerking her attention to the rod in her hand. The line began to pull harder, her rod bending with the force of whatever was on the other end. She started to reel, gripping the handle with all her might.

"You got something?" Nate reeled his line in quickly and set his rod onto the powdery sand behind them, ready to help her like he used to do so long ago.

The line was taut between the end of her rod and the lapping water as she reeled, barely able to get the spool to rotate an entire turn fast enough. Her breath caught when Nate was behind her, his arms around her and his breath at her cheek. His hand was on top of hers, reeling faster now. Panic shot through her and she felt woozy from the sheer proximity. She ducked out of his grasp, leaving him to reel the fish in on his own.

"You don't want to claim the catch?" he asked with a sideways grin.

"Nope," she said. "You can have it."

Nate reeled it in, grabbing the line just above the fish's mouth. "It's a redfish," he said proudly. "Hey, Hank! Syd caught a redfish!" His use of the nickname he used to call her crawled under her skin like a swarm of fire ants.

Uncle Hank and Robby both looked over from their spots down the beach. "In the slot?" Uncle Hank asked.

"Looks like it could be a keeper!" Nate called to them. "Got a measuring tape in your fishing gear?" With the rod in one hand and the line in the other, the fish dangling from his fist, he jogged over to Uncle Hank and Robby. Sydney followed.

"You can throw him back," Uncle Hank said, predictably.

Nate held the fish lower. "Robby, want to see what your mom caught?"

Robby set his rod in the sand but didn't step toward Nate.

Nate held the fish a careful distance. "Has your Uncle Hank told you about the spot here on his tail?"

"No," he said, looking away.

"It's said," Nate nearly whispered, his voice dramatic, despite Robby's quiet protest, "that they grow spots on their tails so other fish will think it's their eye." Carefully, he moved closer to Robby.

Robby took a step backwards, but his interest was undeniable. "Why?"

Nate continued, "They can heal a lot more easily if the other fish takes a bite out of their tail instead of their head."

Robby leaned in just a tiny bit and peered closer at the tail of the fish, fascinated. "That's cool," he said.

"Syd, can you grab those pliers for me?" Nate asked.

"I've got 'em," Robby said, running over to the plastic box of supplies, most likely to get away from Nate. He grabbed the tool and carried it over to his mother, handing it to her.

Sydney walked the tool to Nate.

"I'm going to cut him loose. Want to watch him swim away?" he said to Robby.

Robby kept quite a distance but followed Nate into the water until it was up to his knees. With swift, fluid actions, Nate used the pliers to release the fish. It dropped from the hook and shot through the surf, disappearing. Robby smiled, a genuine sparkle in his eye as he looked up at Nate, taking Sydney's breath away. There, in the setting sun, Nate and Robby were side-by-side grinning at each other like some sort of family postcard. But then Robby quickly moved away from Nate, running back up onto the shore.

"Robby, it's probably time to go inside and get your bath," Sydney suggested, the look they'd shared a little too close for comfort.

"Ah, let him stay up," Uncle Hank called over, holding his fishing rod, his line still sunk in the waves.

There was no way Sydney was allowing Robby to warm up to Nate. Yes, she wanted him to have a male role model in his life, but Nate was *not* the one to serve that purpose. And there was no way this would end well, because Nate would undoubtedly leave and Sydney knew she couldn't count on him to keep in touch. Nor did she really want him to anyway.

Nate took the pliers over to the box and stopped by the bag of fishing line and lures. "Oh, look what's in here," he said, pulling out the football that they'd used for family games in the yard. He backed away from them. "Hey, Robby! Can you catch?" He held up the ball. "Go long!"

Robby seemed torn between the game he loved so much and the fear of allowing Nate to interact with him. But he started to run, hands in the air, his eye on the ball as Nate let it go. The ball fell perfectly into Robby's arms and he cradled it as he ran through the yard toward the house. Sydney couldn't deny the similarities in interests between Robby and Nate. Her mind moved to Robby and his newly found love of drawing, the image of him on his belly in the grass with his notebook open, scribbling away, and a pang of trepidation shot through her.

"Nate's a heck of a football player," Uncle Hank called up to Robby as the little boy headed to the house.

Robby stopped and turned around to listen to Uncle Hank.

"He was a famous receiver in his time." Uncle Hank reeled something in on his line. When he realized he'd pulled up a clump of seaweed, he dislodged it and threw it back into the water.

"Can you catch this then?" Robby called to him. He threw a pass to Nate, who caught it, the ball coming to a silent stop in his hand.

"Good throw!" he said, looking over at Sydney in surprise.

"I think Nate should come over and play a football game with us tomorrow," Uncle Hank offered.

"Okay!" Sydney butted in, putting a hasty stop to the conversation. "Bath time. Ask Nana if she'll get your water to a good temperature. I'll be up in just a bit."

"Okay…" Robby replied.

"I'll go up and make sure he gets his bath," Uncle Hank said, setting his rod down next to his tackle box, "if you two would bring these things up to the house for me when you're done."

"Thanks," Sydney said.

"I'd love to play tomorrow, Robby!" Nate called up to the house.

Sydney's pulse was throbbing in her ears. Nate had been awfully chatty with Robby despite what she knew about him never planning to have children. If he was using Robby to get Sydney to change her mind… He wouldn't dare do that… She began to question even his hug earlier. As soon as her son was out of earshot, she stomped over to Nate. "What do you think you're doing?" she snapped through gritted teeth.

"What do you mean?"

Nate's look of innocence was infuriating. "Listen, you can come waltzing back here, throwing out lines about how sorry you are, trying to make amends for leaving everyone who loved you with barely a goodbye, and we're all adults; we can handle it. But don't you dare pull my son's fragile emotions into this."

"I…" Nate shook his head, stunned and obviously at a loss for words, but Sydney was so terrified at the possibility of her son getting hurt that she didn't bother to decipher Nate's feelings on the matter. "I just got caught up in the nostalgia and excitement of fishing here at Starlight Cottage again. I found that football and I wasn't even thinking… I was just playing around. I miss this…"

"Well, Robby isn't someone to play around with. And neither am I." She grabbed the rods, collecting them all into her arms, her hands shaking as she shut the tackle box and secured the latch, picking it up. Then she snatched the football and shoved it into one of the bags, her arms full.

"Here, let me help you—"

"I've got it!" she barked, jerking away from him, all the fishing gear in her small arms. To her frustration, tears were surfacing again in her eyes, and she didn't want him to see them. He'd crossed the line tonight.

"Syd…" He came up beside her, trying to take something off her hands.

She pulled away again, his efforts only making the tears worse. "Go home," she said, her voice breaking as she attempted to swallow her emotion.

"Talk to me." His hand brushed her arm softly, sending a shiver down her spine.

"I'm done talking," she said, refusing to make eye contact with him for fear that her resolve would crumble into a million pieces when she looked into his eyes. This was the last straw. She lugged the fishing gear through the yard, dumping it at the edge of the back porch, and she went inside without looking back. She had to be strong. For herself and for Robby.

Chapter Six

Sydney held her mug of coffee in both hands, the caffeine a welcome sight this morning when she'd come downstairs to a full pot still warming. Her mother had made it for her, with a note that said, "Have a great day!" Sydney was heading in to the wellness center to chat with Mary Alice about the magazine.

The house was still quiet as she sat in the crisp morning air—that slip of time before the sun brought the intense heat of the day—the French doors ajar, the porch open to allow the breeze to come inside. She walked over to the open living area that was adjacent to the kitchen and ran her fingers along the whitewashed chest Aunt Clara had bought because she thought it resembled the color of a sand dollar. Everything in this room was hers, down to the creamy textured walls and the carved driftwood moldings along the doorframes and windows. Sydney could still remember Aunt Clara's excitement as she'd shown them all once they were installed. "Feast your eyes on this!" she'd said, delighting in customizing this cottage to make it feel uniquely theirs.

Beau got off his cushion and greeted her. She reached down and patted his head and his tail wagged weakly. It was clear that he missed Ben.

"I know, boy," she said to him. "Ben won't be gone too long."

Beau's ears perked up at the mention of his master's name.

Sydney took a long drink from her mug, savoring the nutty, smooth flavor of it and stared out of the bay window at the gulf. It was another perfectly clear early summer day, the palms dancing in the breeze, the bleached sand nearly glowing like a winding strip of white paint out at the shoreline. One of the groundskeepers was up early, cleaning the glass of the lighthouse. She'd had to hire a brand new staff to take care of the Starlight Cottage estate after Aunt Clara had passed away. Uncle Hank wasn't great at managing the property himself, and in his grief of losing Aunt Clara, he'd let the place fall into disrepair, but now Starlight Cottage was just as it had been growing up, and Sydney couldn't imagine being anywhere else.

She was glad for the comfort of the cottage this morning. She'd been up a lot of the night, thinking about what had happened yesterday, wondering if she'd overreacted. Nate had no right to offer to spend time with Robby without discussing it with her first. But she kept thinking that if it had been anyone else, she would have been overjoyed to have an opportunity for Robby to warm up to someone.

"You look nice," Jacqueline said, coming into the kitchen. She walked over to the window and put her arm around her daughter.

"Thanks," Sydney replied, giving her mama a side-squeeze.

Sydney had curled her hair and put on make-up. She'd even decided to wear the pink summer dress she'd found on sale at the beginning of the season that matched her flats almost perfectly. After helping Mary Alice, she was heading to the coffee shop to make some headway on her first Ms. Flynn response. Today was the start of something great—she could feel it—and she wanted to step into this day believing change was coming. Mary Alice had texted yesterday to confirm with Sydney that she had a therapy session at nine o'clock, but she'd be ready to meet with Sydney a few minutes before, and she would have some ideas laid out. Just the idea of working on something new filled her with a buzzing excitement.

"I heard you tossing and turning in your room last night," her mother said. "You were restless. Was something on your mind?"

"Nate being back has been hard." She hadn't wanted to bring it up before she left for work for fear that it would own her thoughts all day.

"I know," her mother said, consoling her with another little squeeze. "Do you think he regrets leaving?"

Sydney shrugged, still unable to process her own feelings on the matter. There was a side of her that reverted to the twenty-two-year-old who still struggled to cope with the grief of losing her best friend. But the woman she'd become knew better and wanted to put up the protective shield that she'd worked so hard to erect over the years.

"I think he misses you," her mother ventured.

"He made his choice," Sydney said.

"You're right," her mom replied, clearly being agreeable so as not to upset her before her day got started. "I'll go make some more coffee. Uncle Hank and Lewis will want some when they get up and you'll have enough to fill a travel mug for the road."

Sydney sat down at the kitchen table and let her eyes fall on Aunt Clara's seat that always remained empty. She wished her great aunt could be there to help her. Aunt Clara would lean over her steaming mug with an intense stare and tell Sydney exactly how to handle the situation. That was how she was. And now that they'd all come through the initial blur of grief from her death, the whole family was scrambling to find their own direction. Sydney's mother didn't have the answers for her any more than she had them herself because they were all trying to get their footing without Aunt Clara's wisdom to fall back on.

Sydney wasn't really sure how Aunt Clara had done it. She'd been a world-renowned designer, running her company Morgan and Flynn while simultaneously being there for every single one of them. She'd been a wife, mother, nurturer, friend, neighbor—everything to everyone. She'd made it look so easy that none of them had considered how to navigate their own hardships by themselves.

Sydney was a thinker. She didn't often share her feelings with people. Instead, she kept them inside, protecting them from judgment. But Aunt Clara could always tell when something was bothering her. She never had to say anything. She could hear Aunt Clara's sensible voice in the back of her mind, saying, "The minute you stop thinking so hard about it is the minute the answer will come to you." That was exactly what she would do: Sydney decided right then and there to put all her focus on what made her happy. If she did that, she couldn't go wrong.

Sydney walked up to the white clapboard storefront that Mary Alice had converted into her practice. The old display window had been renovated into a window-seat with coordinating patterned pillows in calming shades of green and cream. An oval sign that read "Seaside Calm and Family Wellness Center" hung by the door. Sydney straightened her dress and squared her shoulders, the anticipation of the day humming within her. But when she opened the door and stepped into the main room, she had to keep her mouth from dropping open.

Nate and Juliana were sitting together on the sofa in the waiting area. They both looked at Sydney just as Mary Alice walked in from the back.

"Oh, hi!" she said to Sydney. "I'll just show you to the back room." Then she turned to Nate. "I'll be with you two in just a second."

Nate's gaze was on Sydney but she ignored it completely, her mind whirring.

"Nate is your first client?" Sydney said in a whisper as they reached the spare room where they'd be meeting. The room was a crisp white with a small desk in the center and a window view of the strip of grass that ran along the back of the building outside.

Sydney wondered if Nate and Juliana were there for couple's therapy but she didn't need to confirm it. She'd read that Nate and Juliana had had a rocky relationship—on-again-off-again—but they were working things out. And now, here was Juliana, with him, in Firefly Beach. Surely it would be easier to get therapy here, without the glare of the media spotlight.

Then the thought occurred to Sydney that there was a slight possibility that Nate might actually not tire of Firefly Beach and leave the way she'd hoped. He'd said himself that Juliana liked it here, that it was remote like her childhood home. And now he was moving back, getting therapy. They were clearly settling in. Sydney's breakfast sat like a cinder block in her stomach.

"Hey there, Miss Sydney," Melissa said with a giant grin. The owner of the local coffee shop Cup of Sunshine greeted everyone with Mr. or Miss and then their first name. Her chocolate-colored hair was piled on top of her head in a messy bun, and her reading glasses were perched on the end of her nose.

"Hi, Melissa." Sydney slid her laptop onto the counter so she could fiddle around in her handbag for her wallet. She pulled out a crumpled napkin and two receipts, and set them aside.

"No Robby today?" Melissa asked.

"No, I'm going to try to get a little work done."

"Ah," she said, grabbing a square of parchment and taking a small button cookie out of the glass display case, handing it to Sydney. Whenever Robby went in with her, Melissa always gave him a button cookie. "You'll have to eat this for him then," she said with a wink. "What'll it be?"

"Definitely the Butter Pecan Latte. What else is there in this world?"

Melissa's large bosom heaved with her light laughter. "Absolutely nothing," she said, ringing up the drink.

Sydney handed over her credit card.

"I'll bring it out to you," Melissa said, swiping the card and handing it back. "Want me to throw this stuff away?" She took the receipts and napkin and held them up.

Sydney thanked her for taking care of her trash.

Then something caught Melissa's eye. "Hang on," she said, holding out her hand. "Do you want to keep this one?" She held out the napkin. "It's got something on it."

"Definitely not. Why would I want to use a napkin that's got something on it?" she teased, looking down at the writing that was scratched onto the napkin.

Melissa laughed, handing it over.

"The rest is trash, thanks." Sydney peered down at Logan's name and number. She remembered at the end of the wedding, taking the napkin inside and stuffing it into her handbag. Logan had been so nice. He'd made her laugh on the dance floor… She headed to an open table while nibbling on her cookie, thinking. She'd made some good headway on the magazine cover with Mary Alice, and she was feeling excited about starting her response for Ms. Flynn. Perhaps it was her good mood, but after she set her things down, she picked up her phone and texted Logan:

This is Sydney Flynn from the wedding. Just wanted to say hello. Thanks for a fun evening at the wedding.

Then she put her phone away and opened her laptop.

What should she say to Rebecca who'd moved away from her family? She considered her own life…

Sydney began to type.

Hi Rebecca,

It must be difficult to be alone. But perhaps you were meant to be on your own so that you could think through your circumstances properly. Consider the people around you—those are the people who have been put in your path. If you could pick one person you'd like to impact—a coworker? A neighbor?—who would it be? And now, if one person could impact you, who do you think has the best chance of being that person? Seek the person out, and find ways to spend time with him or her. At the end of the day, life is about the connections we make, and starting over with a fresh slate for making those connections could be an exciting adventure. Good luck with the new job!

Best wishes,

Ms. Flynn

Sydney sat back, happy with her first response. She'd done it. The words had rolled off her fingers effortlessly as she typed.

"Your coffee," Melissa said, gingerly setting down her mug.

Sydney admired the heart that Melissa had drawn in the foam. "Thank you," she said, feeling accomplished. The answer to Rebecca's dilemma had come easily to her today, and she remembered Aunt Clara's advice: "The minute you stop thinking so hard about it is the minute the answer will come to you." There was something to be said about that.

Her phone lit up on the table with a text.

I'm delighted to hear from you. Let's get coffee soon. Logan

Maybe she could apply Aunt Clara's idea to the harder things in life…

Sydney arrived back home at Starlight Cottage with a notepad full of ideas. She'd spent the rest of the day jotting down ideas for the magazine cover and choosing the next few Ms. Flynn letters. The creative outlet had been good to get her emotions into a calmer state and to push away thoughts of Nate. But when she saw who was out in the yard, she felt like the wind had been knocked out of her. She got out of her car and shut the door.

Robby ran around one end of the grassy area with a football tucked under his arm while Nate jogged over to him.

"That was a good move you made," Nate said, laughing, slightly out of breath before he caught sight of Sydney and offered that eerily familiar smile that made her feel like she was twenty again. Nate and Robby together was an unnerving collision of past and present that made her want to shrink in on herself, unable to face her emotions. But she forced herself to be strong, marching across the yard.

"Hi, honey!" she said, giving Robby a bear hug, lifting him up. She offered a half smile at Nate before turning her attention back to her son. "How was your day with Nana?"

"Good." He twirled the football in the palm of his hand, the oblong shape of it causing it to wobble. He tossed it into the air.

Nate reached out and caught it above Robby's head. "Ha! Got it," he said.

Robby smiled uneasily at Nate, not attempting to get the football back. Clearly reading him, Nate offered him the ball.

Sydney's blood was beginning to boil. "Robby, do you mind if Nate and I go for a little walk?" she asked.

"May I come?" he asked.

"Not this time. But I'll come inside in a minute, and we can talk all about your day, okay? Why don't you see if Beau needs to be let out?"

"Okay," he said.

"Thanks, buddy."

Shyly, Robby turned to Nate. "Can we play again?"

Nate kneeled down to get on Robby's level. "That's up to your mom. But I'll try to convince her on our walk."

After Robby had run off, Sydney whirled around to Nate. "How dare you put me in that position? If I don't allow you to see him anymore, it will make *me* look like the bad guy," she snapped.

"Why wouldn't you want me to see him?" he asked.

"You don't even like kids, do you?"

"What?" His face crumpled in confusion. "What ever gave you that idea?"

"It doesn't matter," she said, frustrated that she was spending time with him instead of being inside with Robby.

"Syd, why wouldn't you want me to see Robby?" he repeated.

She gritted her teeth, trying to keep her emotions in check, but it was a losing battle. "Because he doesn't warm up to just anyone. And he doesn't need someone who will walk out of his life without notice."

Nate stared at her. "I won't do that to you again," he said, his face full of remorse.

"What do you want, Nate?" she asked, her tone now resigned.

He walked over to the pier and sat on the edge of it, his forearms on his knees, his hands clasped, and his head lowered as if he needed a moment to decide what he wanted to say. "That's not an easy question," he finally said.

So he *did* want something. She knew it. "Well, just come out with it."

"I knew coming back would be hard..." He looked up at her. "I've ruined everything, and I don't know how to make things right." He stood up to face her. "I'm trying, Syd. But you won't let me in. I miss you so much it hurts."

"Why did you come back?" she asked, not replying to his admission—she didn't know how to respond. She just wanted him to leave her in peace so she could get on with her life.

It seemed as though the answer were on the tip of his tongue, yet something was holding him back. Finally, he spoke. "Because this is home for me."

Sydney knew exactly what he meant; she felt the same about Firefly Beach. But she wished he didn't feel that way. Why couldn't he have just stayed in LA or Nashville and left her and her family alone?

"Where will you live?" she asked, the idea that she'd have to face Nate and Juliana for the rest of her days settling hard in her gut. She remembered how, all those years ago, they'd talked about finding an old farmhouse right on the water and restoring it. How naïve they'd been...

"Right now I'm staying with Malory but I bought a lot on the other side of town and I'm building there."

"And what's wrong with the lot you already have?"

He didn't answer.

Without even knowing it, he'd just betrayed her again. It made sense, though, that he wouldn't want to wake up with Juliana down the road from his ex. The ex he'd run away from, the one he'd planned on marrying at one time.

He'd put a quarter in the bubblegum machine in town and gotten Sydney a ring with a plastic purple stone. He'd said she could wear it until he could afford to get her the best ring money could buy. One day, Robby had found it in her jewelry box and asked to play with it. She couldn't bring herself to let him. She wasn't sure why she kept it, but to this day it was still in the same spot in her jewelry box. She'd taken it off the day he'd left and initially, she hadn't had the strength to take it out of the little velvet cushion where she'd placed it that day. Then the days turned to weeks and weeks turned to months and… that was it.

He caught her looking down at her empty ring finger. "Whatever happened to…" he began before evidently deciding not to bring it up.

"I don't have it anymore," she lied, and their eyes met. She looked away for fear that he'd be able to see through her answer.

When she turned back to him, Nate nodded, but the disappointment was clear.

"Look," she said. "This is difficult for both of us. There's too much between us to keep going on like this. I don't think we can see each other without bringing our history back up, and it's not something I want to keep reliving. If there's something you want from me, then ask me now. But then I'd appreciate it if you would give me my space."

"Something I want from you?" he asked, his brows furrowing.

"Is there?"

He took a step toward her, reaching for her arm, his finger trailing down it. She let him, although she could feel the tears welling up. She blinked them away. "Somehow… I just want to make you happy," he said.

"You can't do that anymore," Sydney told him honestly.

His hand found hers and he caressed her empty ring finger the same way he used to do when she was wearing the ring. The hollow feeling that she'd thought she'd gotten over came rushing back. She pulled her hand away gently, wishing things could be different. "I have to go inside," she said, unable to keep her emotions at bay. She needed to get a handle on herself so she could spend time with Robby.

"Wait," he said, stopping her.

"Wait for what, Nate? Why aren't you putting this much effort into making Juliana happy right now?"

"Because I'm not in love with Juliana," he said, matter-of-factly. Then it was as if he'd wanted to suck the words back in, and she realized what he was implying: that he was spending his effort on the person he *was* in love with. That didn't make any sense, given the way he'd left without a care in the world. Then she wondered if his reaction was simply due to the guilt he felt by betraying his girlfriend with his words just now.

"That's a pretty big admission," Sydney said. "You'd better let Juliana in on that bit of information." The whole situation made her feel uneasy. This was definitely not how she'd wanted a reconciliation to happen with Nate if he ever came back. Early on after their break-up, she'd fantasized about what it would be like to have him run into her arms and tell her how it had all been such a terrible mistake. Lost and confused, she'd prayed for it, but now she wished he'd have never returned to Firefly Beach; not like this.

"Juliana knows," he said. "She's known for a while."

Juliana knew that Nate felt something for Sydney? And she was still with him? Sydney wasn't even going to get into their off-again status. Who knows what they'd talked about in therapy today, and it was none of her business anyway.

"If you had some kind of change of heart, why didn't you come find me years ago?" she asked.

He took in a deep breath and blew it out loudly, tipping his head back. "I tried, but we were never in the same place emotionally at the same time. You were getting married..."

She didn't dare tell him that had he actually been honest about why he'd called that day, it would've shaken her so badly that she probably would've called off her wedding. And she'd have never had the love of her life—her son. That was proof that all of this happened for a reason and they were trying to hold on to something that was never meant to be theirs. Sydney shook the thought free from her mind. She was letting Nate get to her. He was simply on the rebound from whatever falling-out he'd had with Juliana. If Sydney allowed him to continue to make these little appearances, she would undoubtedly let him in, only to have him break her heart when he realized that he was better suited for someone like Juliana. They'd run back to LA together, leaving Sydney shattered, and she didn't think her fragile heart could take Nate leaving a second time.

"I don't know any other way to tell you that I'm not interested, Nate. How can I make you understand?" She didn't bother to clarify that it was Nathan Carr that didn't interest her. Nate Henderson would always have her heart.

Nate pursed his lips, clearly unable to find the words to convince her. She'd made it pretty clear. "I'll just give you this," he said, pulling a card from his pocket and handing it to her. She opened the envelope. "It's Malory's birthday tomorrow. I'm inviting a few friends over to her house after work tomorrow night. She'd love to see you—she told me herself. Bring Robby. I'm sure he'd like to get a piece of cake."

"I don't know, Nate. I love Malory, but it's too difficult..."

"I won't make it weird, I promise." He held up his hands in surrender. "Just friends. No pressure." When she didn't answer him, he gave her that crooked grin she loved so much. "Come on," he urged. "It won't be much fun with no one to say, 'Happy birthday.' I need you." His smile widened. "And I've already invited your mom and Uncle Hank, and they're coming."

Sydney really would like to see Malory… "Fine," she said.

"Ah!" He picked her up and twirled her around, making her laugh despite herself. "I *knew* you'd cave! It'll be fun." He set her back down.

Sydney shook her head.

"It's a party! What's the worst that could happen?"

Chapter Seven

"Is Nate coming again tomorrow?" Robby asked as he climbed under his covers, his eyes sleepy from a busy day.

"I'm not sure," Sydney said.

Sydney wasn't lying to him. She had a feeling that Nate was going to do what he wanted to do regardless of her wishes. Protectiveness over Robby surged through her. Nate's commitment to them and to Firefly Beach was just too uncertain for her to allow anything to develop between him and Robby. Ben would be back from his honeymoon in a few weeks, which would buy her some time to figure out what she could do, if anything, for Robby. But allowing him to see Nate certainly wasn't the answer.

Out of nowhere, he asked, "Do you like him, Mama?"

Unexpectedly—perhaps out of worry for her son or wistfulness over what was lost with Nate, she felt tears surface. She must have been just as tired as Robby. To keep her mind from wandering any further, she busied herself with tucking the covers around his little body while clearing her throat to keep the lump from forming. Despite her best efforts, she couldn't avoid one sniffle.

Robby was paying close attention to her, which made her anxious. She smoothed out his covers and tugged on the end of them to make sure he was snuggled in.

"You love him?" Robby asked.

An icy sensation spread over her. "What?"

"You're crying."

"I'm fine," she lied.

But Robby shook his head. "No. You're crying. You used to cry about Daddy when he left too, and when I asked you why once, you said, 'Sometimes we cry over people we love—that's how you know you really love them.'"

Her little boy was so perceptive.

This was different. When she and Christian divorced, Robby was only four years old—too young to understand what was happening, but too old to be oblivious to it. "Why isn't daddy coming home tonight?" he'd ask, literally tearing her heart out. One day she'd found him in the closet, staring up at the empty hangers on Christian's side, and she could see the confusion on his face. While she was managing her own loss of love, she also had the burden of what Christian's leaving had caused for her son.

And now, how would she explain to him that she missed the person Nate used to be, terribly, and her tears were because she could never have him back? "Nate used to be my best friend," she said, stumbling over the words because "friend" just didn't even begin to cover what they'd been. "And he had to go away. I missed him so much that it still makes me sad."

Robby seemed to understand. "I miss Ben like that," he said. "But when I play football with Nate, I don't feel as sad." He sat up. "Will he come over again?"

"We'll see," she said, unable to provide the answer he wanted. "I'm glad you had fun with Nate." Sydney kissed her son's forehead. "Now, let's get a good night's sleep, okay?"

"Okay, Mama. I love you."

"Love you too."

Sydney settled onto the porch swing outside, next to Uncle Hank. They sat in silence together, watching the fireflies dancing through the trees at the edge of the property. The sun had already disappeared below the horizon, and the night sky had just begun to emerge, the first few stars making an appearance.

"You look tired," Uncle Hank said, pushing them back and then lifting his feet so the swing could rock them. "Something on your mind?"

She let the air out that she only just realized she'd been holding in. "Nate has me in a tizzy," she said.

"What's new?" Uncle Hank smiled knowingly at her, lightening her mood.

"I think Robby might *like* him," she confessed, still totally baffled that Robby was warming to Nate at all.

"He's a likeable guy."

"If I let him come around, I'm afraid Robby will get hurt when he decides to leave again. He'll get his heart broken."

"Is it only Robby's heart you're worried about?"

She dared not say, so she turned her head toward the wind, a warm gust blowing across her face.

"Have you ever talked with him about the day he left?" Uncle Hank asked.

She shook her head.

"I wonder what went through his mind." Uncle Hank pushed them again on the swing, the movement having a lulling affect on Sydney, and she could feel the heaviness in her eyes. "He's a good man. We all make mistakes, Sydney."

"But he isn't the same person anymore," she challenged. "Even if he regrets that day, he's not the same boy who pulled out of our driveway in his old truck. Time just keeps moving us all forward and we can't go back."

"That it does," Uncle Hank agreed. He turned his head to look down the beach, the lapping waves nearly invisible against the night's sky. "You two used to walk all the way to his house at the end of the shore," he said, pointing to the strip of sand that ran along the coast past the lighthouse. He fell silent just long enough to get Sydney's full attention, something washing over him. Then, his mournful eyes met hers.

"What's on your mind?" she asked.

"There are so many memories here… Are we going to have to sell Starlight Cottage?"

"What?" The question seemed to come out of nowhere.

"Clara and I bought this house because of the serenity of this view. But soon it will be gone, the trees leveled, and the coastline full of out-of-towners…"

"So you're thinking about selling?" Just the idea sent an ache through her temples.

"It's a lot of house for just me."

"Robby and I are here too."

"Eventually, you'll want your own space, I can imagine."

"Not necessarily. I love living here with you."

"At some point, Sydney, you're going to move forward with your life, settle down with someone wonderful, and you'll want somewhere that you can be a family."

She let that comment register. "Are you saying that I'm not moving forward with my life right now?"

"I am incredibly grateful to you for helping me get back on my feet, but you can't spend the rest of your life taking care of an old man. You've made a good start by taking a job that's using your gift of writing. Keep going! Get out there. Take risks. Let Robby play a few football games if he wants to… Stop worrying so much about getting hurt. You have to live like there's no such thing as heartbreak. If you tiptoe around, trying to keep yourself safe from it, you'll miss all the moments that will make you who you are."

They rocked together, Sydney contemplating Uncle Hank's advice. Sydney always took the predictable route, the path with the least amount of resistance. She considered herself to be the levelheaded one of the family—stable, reliable. But had she missed out by not taking chances? Had Nate felt like she was holding him back—was that why he'd left her behind? She tried to conjure up what her perfect future would be, but she came up empty, not knowing what she really wanted for herself and Robby. She'd had such a clear picture when she and Nate were dating, but when he left, he took all her dreams with him.

"I don't know what I want my future to look like," she worried aloud.

"You don't have to have all the answers right now, Sydney. You just have to want to find them. The minute you let that desire take over, your future will show up right in front of your eyes."

Sydney had spent the last decade focusing on being a wife and a mother. At the time, she felt that that was what she was meant to do. But now, it was time to concentrate on what would make her the happiest and also the best role model for Robby. He deserved the world, and she decided right then and there that she was the one who could give it to him.

Chapter Eight

Not a cloud in the sky, the gulf sparkled like diamonds. A lone sunbeam made its way past the thickly painted white windowsill and onto the rustic plank wood of the kitchen floor.

Sydney sat at the kitchen table, opened her work email the next morning, and found a new Ms. Flynn letter, the subject line catching her eye: Heartbreak. She could definitely relate to that… Mama must have opened the window to let the morning breeze in, and it brought with it a swirling scent of briny air mixed with the coconut aroma from the candle that was burning on the table next to a note that said she and Robby had taken Beau for a walk. Sydney made herself a cup of coffee, opened the message on her computer, and read.

Dear Ms. Flynn,

I have a problem. I'm in love with someone who isn't in love with me. I can't live without her and I feel like my heart is breaking every time I see her. What do I do?

Best,

Mel

She stared at the letter, trying to find the right words. This wasn't a simple issue. She copied and pasted the email into a new document and sipped her coffee, savoring the nutty, bitter flavor, as she began to try to construct her response.

Dear Mel,

There's no easy answer for this. It's something that only time can fix…

But then Sydney deleted the line she'd typed. Because it wasn't true. Time hadn't repaired her heart after Nate had left her, so it was insensitive of her to believe time could fix Mel's life. She imagined what she'd say to herself, and started again.

There are things in this life that aren't meant to be fixed. They will always hurt. But the human heart is resilient in that it can beat again after even the toughest blow. I'd like to say we're stronger because of it. We can't know true joy until we've experienced absolute heartbreak. My hope for you is that one day you'll be able to see that person and be happy for her because you loved her enough to let her go and find whatever it was that made her complete. That is love.

This would be her next submission. She signed the letter, checked the piece for errors, and emailed it to her editor. Once she got the okay from the *Gazette*, she'd email mel4221 and let him know his letter would be published.

Then she headed over to the wellness center to get to work on Mary Alice's magazine. It was going to get her full attention today, and she was planning to knock everyone's socks off with her ideas.

*

Mary Alice had a concept that people could relate to: finding balance for the whole self. It had been done before, but how could Sydney spin the idea to make it something everyone was dying to find out more about? She started brainstorming: What about people who had never been to a wellness center? What could they begin to do at home that would start them on the path to better health? She started typing slogans, her mind buzzing: *Reinvent Your Life*, *Discover the Real You*, *Reclaim Your Destiny*...

Sydney grabbed her pad of paper and scratched down a note to talk to Hallie when she got back. With Hallie now running Morgan and Flynn, Aunt Clara's worldwide design company, her sister had media contacts across the globe that would gladly do her favors, like giving a quote for a little Firefly Beach magazine, for an exclusive peek at Hallie's upcoming designs. Perhaps Hallie would be interested in collaborating on a new holistic décor line, and Sydney could write the press release copy, including Mary Alice's philosophies. It could be their first feature in the magazine.

But today was about the cover. She needed photography—a big, glossy image to draw in the consumer. She'd call local photographer Gavin Wilson, who owned the gallery in town, to see if he'd be interested in doing a photo shoot for her. Gavin had only moved to Firefly Beach last year, but he'd done some painting for Uncle Hank, and he'd taken her uncle fishing when he was at his lowest over Aunt Clara's death. Sydney had had coffee with him a few times, and he was always willing to lend a helping hand.

If Gavin agreed to let her hire him, she'd need a design concept as soon as possible. She imagined a couple on a cover with all the calming colors: blue, violet, light pink, green, grey... Easy. She needed a couple on the beach at sunset. The woman in a white dress. Holding hands with someone. Hair blowing in the wind as they faced away from her… Sydney sketched the image onto her pad of paper.

The bells at the front door jingled, pulling Sydney out of her creative cloud. She leaned over and peered through the open door to find Juliana taking a seat on the sofa. She had on the same big sunglasses from the wedding, her rounded lips set seriously. It seemed to be just her for this visit, and Sydney couldn't help but wonder if Nate had said anything to her about the talk he and Sydney had had at Starlight Cottage yesterday. Juliana took off her glasses and Sydney swore the rims of her eyes were red. Regardless of Nate and Juliana's relationship issues, Sydney wasn't in the business of breaking up couples, and the guilt from her own thoughts about Nate was enough to make her get up to shut the office door before Juliana saw the flush of crimson that had certainly taken hold on Sydney's cheeks.

She walked over to the door to close it but stopped cold when, to her surprise, Juliana's perfect lips turned upward, her face lifting cordially from under the flowing waves of hair she'd been hiding behind, and she offered a dainty wave in Sydney's direction. So obviously Nate hadn't said a thing. Typical. No matter how sorry he told Sydney he was, she couldn't change that truth about him: he was a selfish person. Judging by Juliana's expression and the defeat in her eyes, she was in a fragile state, which only made Sydney feel worse. She smiled weakly and waved back, then shut the door.

Despite forcing herself to turn her attention back to her work, Sydney was unsuccessful at shutting out the image of Juliana's meek smile. The photos of her in the magazines and on television made her seem so self-confident, so sure of herself. But even in her delicate state now her beauty was undeniable. Sydney tried to refocus, sending Gavin an email through his website and telling him she'd call him later.

Photography locations were key to grabbing the readers' interest; she needed buy-in. Serene, casual, happy… There was only one place that came to mind: Starlight Cottage, down by the lighthouse, the couple standing together on the sand, the gazebo out of focus in the background. That would be perfect.

There was a knock at the door and Mary Alice poked her head in. "I was just checking in before I begin with my first client. Everything going okay?"

"Yes," Sydney said with a smile. "I'm organizing my thoughts at the moment." She turned her pad of paper around to show Mary Alice a quick look at her sketch. "I emailed Gavin to see if he'd do a photo shoot. I want to put a couple on the beach at Starlight Cottage. I can tell you more about it when you have time."

"I'm excited! It sounds fantastic."

When Sydney and Mary Alice left the wellness center together, headed for their cars, Sydney told her she'd gotten confirmation from Gavin to do the photo shoot, and he'd said he had everything for the lighting and staging at Starlight Cottage. Mary Alice had been thrilled with the idea as well as the articles Sydney had come up with so far.

"We just need to find a couple for the shoot," Sydney said as they reached the parking lot.

"I thought about that when I saw your sketch," Mary Alice told her.

"Any ideas?"

"Well—confidentially—even though I promised to keep it a secret," she leaned in and whispered, "Nathan and Juliana didn't want a paper trail of any kind that the press could get a hold of, so they aren't technically on my books, and, because of that, I wouldn't let them pay me, so Nathan said he owes me one. I'm sort of counseling them as a favor and I'm only seeing them here at the center because it's easier than making Malory leave the house to keep things confidential if I made a house-call. If I asked for a favor in return, they'd most likely do it for me. They'd be a gorgeous couple for the magazine and the photo would be from the back, right? So no one would recognize them anyway."

Of all people.

"Juliana told me earlier that you're going to Malory's birthday party tonight," Mary Alice continued. "I hate to suggest this…" she said, making a face. "Maybe you could find a quiet moment to ask Nathan then?"

Why had Juliana mentioned Sydney at all? While Sydney hated the idea of putting herself in Nate's path again, she knew that they'd be the perfect couple for the cover. Perhaps she could avoid asking Nate altogether and approach his girlfriend—as a business venture. After all, this was what Juliana did for a living, so she would probably welcome it. And she felt like she needed to be friendly with Juliana to assure her that there was absolutely nothing going on between her and Nate.

Maybe the project would be helpful for all of them. They could see each other in a different light and move on from whatever moment it was that Nate was having. Perhaps he'd realize he was trying to relive the past and he'd finally leave Firefly Beach for good.

The thought crept in that Sydney should face this, put Juliana right in the line of her vision to drive home the point to herself that the old Nate wasn't coming back, no matter what she wished for.

Sydney's phone pinged with an email, but she ignored it. She stood in the yard after work, her hand on her forehead as if in salute, to shield her eyes from the glare of the sun, just enough to make out the enormous boat that was sitting on the shore out back of Starlight Cottage. The massive shiny white vessel looked out of place next to the rustic pier. Its front was pressed against the shoreline, its back end bobbing in the lapping water.

"Mama!" Robby said, running through the front door of Starlight Cottage and bounding down the porch steps toward her. "Can I take a boat ride?" he called to her, excited and out of breath, pointing to the yacht.

"Whose—?" She was about to finish her thought when Nate appeared in the doorway with his hands raised in surrender, his cell phone pressed against his ear with his shoulder.

"Go ahead and pitch it to the label," he said into his phone, his eyes on Sydney. "I'll call you back with the idea for Timberlake." He ended the call and gave Sydney all his attention. "Don't yell at me," he teased. "It isn't my fault I'm here this time. I was minding my own business working, but Uncle Hank invited me over."

"And you came in that?" she asked, jutting a finger toward the boat.

"It's my first purchase since moving back," he said. "I can't be by the water and not have a boat."

Sydney didn't want to consider the fact that buying that boat would make it more difficult for him to just pick up and leave. She'd hoped he'd get tired of his old small-town life sooner rather than later.

"Take a ride with me," he said, walking toward her. "Just friends, I promise; no pressure. I brought Juliana," he offered when he reached her, as if that would make the situation any better. "She's on the boat."

"Can we go, Mama?" Robby pleaded.

"I just got off of work..." she said, knowing her excuse was flimsy at best.

Robby clasped his hands together, begging her with his eyes to say yes. The boat ride was so enticing that it was overpowering his reluctance to be with Nate.

"Why did Uncle Hank ask you over?" Sydney asked, still trying to make up her mind.

"He said he wanted to talk about Starlight Cottage, but then Lewis asked him if he'd take a walk, and he said he'd catch up with me later."

Sydney wondered what in the world Uncle Hank would want to discuss with Nate regarding Starlight Cottage. She was definitely going to ask when he and Lewis got home. But right now, Robby was tugging on her arm, giving her puppy-dog eyes.

"I've got food on the boat," Nate said. "Why don't you put your swimsuit on and come with us? Robby wants to jump off the back so I'm going to take him out in the gulf."

She opened her mouth to protest but he cut her off.

"I've got a life vest for him. And an inner tube. And goggles."

Sydney tried to come up with some reason to say no.

"…And peanut butter sandwiches," he added. "Syd, come on. Have a little fun."

Was he implying that she didn't have fun? She might be having a blast right now and not need his fancy boat to give her a good time.

"I'll go get my towel!" Robby said, running off toward the cottage, clearly trying a different persuasion tactic.

Nate took a step closer to Sydney. "I remember when you were a fearless dreamer who could outthink me in a second. You wowed me at every turn. You'd have been the first one on the boat, probably even driving it yourself. You're so cautious now."

She didn't dare tell him that he'd broken her when he'd left. His leaving had caused her to grow up quickly, to get her head out of the clouds. All those dreams and possibilities that she'd pondered—he'd taken them with him when he'd left.

"Things change," she said, her tone less harsh than it had been before. They couldn't change how he left, so all they could do was move on from this.

"They definitely do," he replied, his mind clearly heavy with thoughts. He cleared his throat. "Juliana wants to meet you," he said, changing the subject.

Sydney's heart pounded. Talking with Juliana would give Sydney closure on the whole thing; meeting her would solidify the idea that Nate Henderson was in her past and Nathan Carr was the person standing opposite her now. And Sydney had wanted to talk to her about the photo shoot anyway…

"Come on," he urged. "I need you to guide me back into the water."

That made her smile. Years ago, whenever he'd bring the boat down from his house, Nate had always gotten it stuck on the sand, and the two of them had to push and pull until it floated free.

"I won't be able to move that monstrosity," she teased.

"I just bought it. You don't like it?" There was a twinkle in his eye when he asked, which made Sydney take another look at the boat.

"Is that a bridge boat?" she asked.

He nodded. "A Sea Ray."

A distant memory floated into her consciousness. "When we're both old, I still want to sit together just like this," he'd said as they rocked in two chairs on the porch at Starlight Cottage, both of them looking out at the glistening water that seemed to stretch forever, just like the years ahead of them.

"Nah," Sydney told him. "We'll be too famous. No one will ever leave us alone if we sit out here on these chairs. We'll have to float way out to sea on our yacht if we want to be alone."

Nate had laughed. "Yes, we'll definitely need a yacht. How about a Sea Ray?" he said, naming one of the boats he'd pointed out to her once in his fishing magazine.

"Yes!" she replied happily. "A Sea Ray will do. A nice big yacht."

"Which one of us is going to buy that big yacht first?"

"You will," she'd told him without hesitation, and it was at that moment that she'd noticed something shift in his expression, almost as if he didn't trust her suggestion. Or maybe he'd already considered leaving her by then… She remembered thinking that she'd only been kidding with the whole idea anyway, so why had he become so serious? His look and the fact that she couldn't decipher it had scared her, and she'd let the conversation die on the wind. Well, he might have doubted it at the time, but her guess had been dead-on. She hoped he hadn't purchased the boat just to prove a point—that would be a very expensive way to tell her she was right.

"What are you thinking about?" Nate asked, pulling her from her memory.

"I've got my towel!" Robby came running toward them, ripping through the moment. When he got to Sydney, he asked, "You coming?"

There was nothing left to do but grab her swimsuit and climb aboard.

Chapter Nine

When Sydney stepped aboard the yacht, Juliana was in a string bikini and sunglasses, lying on a towel at the back of the vessel. As she neared her, Sydney took in her perfect red pedicure that matched her swimsuit, the rounded softness of her knee on her flawless leg that was bent, her foot flat on the towel, her long dark hair fanned out around her, puddling at the nape of her neck in picture-perfect waves. She looked so different than she had at the wellness center and even at the wedding. Her body was made for this, and her star power was undeniable, making Sydney suddenly nervous as she realized for the first time that she was in the presence of a superstar. Juliana's stillness and relaxed appearance were hypnotizing.

She turned her head slowly and then popped up, pulling small wireless headphones out of her ears. "Sorry," she said, a slight accent still present even after so many years living in California. "I didn't hear you walk up."

She swung her legs around and scooted to the edge of the platform, hopping off of it, every part of her body in impeccable form as she moved about the boat. She placed a large hat over her hair—the brim of it covered her face down to her sunglasses—and sat on the bench to pick up a cocktail that had been resting in one of the cup holders.

She stirred around the melted ice before evidently reconsidering and placing the drink back into its spot.

"I'm Sydney." She tried to keep her nerves down as she held out her hand to Juliana, willing it to remain steady.

"Yes," Juliana said, her dainty fingers gripping Sydney's hand briefly but warmly. "It's so nice to finally meet you. Nathan speaks very highly of you."

"Oh?" Sydney sat down beside Juliana. "That's… interesting." What had he told Juliana?

"He was so happy to get back to Firefly Beach to see you."

"Is that so?"

"He adores you," Juliana said with a smile that showed off her bright white teeth.

Clearly, he hadn't divulged his true feelings. He couldn't have, given Juliana's reaction.

"Are you all right?" Juliana asked.

This was ridiculous. She couldn't just sit there next to Juliana, knowing all the things Nate had told her, and act like everything was just peachy. "Sort of," she said, unsure of how to answer the question.

"Are you sure you're okay?" Juliana tilted her head, her eyes curious.

Besides not understanding this odd relationship you have with my ex? Her heart pattered fiercely in her chest—a mix of nerves and awkwardness.

Juliana seemed as befuddled as Sydney was with this conversation.

It was time to get some answers once and for all. "This is a weird question, but are you and Nate… dating?" she asked.

Juliana broke eye contact, her gaze moving to the floor of the boat nervously. "Uh…" She looked over at Nate through her lashes. "No."

The answer came out quickly and quietly as if she didn't want anyone to hear.

Juliana's response surprised Sydney. What was going on?

"Mama!" Robby said, running down the boat. "Nate has his fishing rod and he said that we could fish once we anchor out in the water!" Despite his excitement, she noticed his slight trepidation when his eyes moved to Nate, and she guessed that their shared interests were driving her son to accept the fact that Nate could fill something for him that hadn't been there since Ben left. It made Sydney queasier than a day at sea.

"That's exciting!" she said, ignoring her own baggage, genuinely happy to see her son so enthusiastic.

"I'll let you drive the boat, if you want, Robby," Nate said to him, as he took a seat at the wheel. "Your mom just has to help me out of the sand."

Sydney looked over at Nate and they shared a moment of reminiscence, making her smile despite everything. His face lit up at the sight of her, and for an instant, the fondness in his eyes, the heat of the sun, and the salty air, made her feel like she was in her twenties again. Robby climbed up onto Nate's lap, breaking the spell, but she couldn't pull her gaze from the two of them together. The rush of emotions made her need a minute.

"You're going to just hold the wheel like this," Nate told Robby. Robby gripped the silver wheel of the yacht. "Yep, just like that. I'm going down onto the sand to help your mom. I'll be right back up."

"Okay," Robby said, his face serious.

"Think you can drive it, Captain?" Nate said, tussling Robby's hair.

"Yes, sir!" Robby said.

"Hold it with the same strength as you hold the football when someone's about to come in for a tackle."

Nate turned to Sydney and gestured toward the ladder on the side of the boat. "After you."

Sydney climbed down onto the sand and went straight to the front of the boat to push it. The whole time, she was taking in slow, steady, deep breaths and trying to erase the image of Nate and Robby from her mind. She had to, or her heart would break all over again. When she and Nate were together, she'd imagined a family with him—they'd talked about it. He'd wanted lots of land so they could play outside, fish by the water, build sand castles… All the things Robby liked to do. The "if only" of it all was already eating away at her, and they hadn't even left the shore. She pressed her hands against the warm fiberglass of the boat and channeled her emotions into her strength, pushing with all her might.

Nate's phone began to ring on the boat.

"Nate!" Robby called. "Want me to bring you your phone?"

"That's okay, buddy. You just hold the wheel," he replied, ignoring the call.

"Whoa," Nate said, placing his hands beside hers. "You don't give yourself enough credit. You can probably move this boat all by yourself."

"Are you jealous of my biceps?" she said.

He smiled, and positioned his hands next to hers, his scent intoxicating. "On the count of three, ready? One, two, three."

They both heaved, the boat grinding against the powder white sand as it shifted.

"One more time and I think we've got it," she said, glad for the diversion. "Then you jump in the boat and I'll guide you around the pier."

"All right," he said, his arm brushing against hers.

He seemed to notice their proximity, giving her a little glance out of the corner of his eye. Given what Juliana had said, all of the attention he'd been offering Sydney was some sort of rebound for sure. And why was Juliana still in Firefly Beach if they weren't together? They'd been getting therapy… It didn't add up. Well, Sydney wasn't going to play his games. He and Juliana could do their little back-and-forth romance, but Sydney didn't want to have any part in it. Her heart wouldn't be able to survive when he decided that Juliana was the better fit for him, because she knew it was true. Nathan Carr would take nothing less.

Nate started counting again, "One, two, three."

The boat suddenly became light against Sydney's hands, its body bobbing in the gulf waves that splashed around them. Nate jumped onto the ladder, climbing it quickly, and moving over to Robby. He lifted Robby, and placed him back into his lap. Sydney looked away, focusing on the pier.

"Give it a hard right!" she called up to them.

The nose of the boat gently glided around in an arc.

"Straighten it up slowly and I'll jump on." She guided the boat, pushing against it, until it was completely clear of the pier and grabbed the ladder, pulling herself out of the water. Once she was on deck, Nate cranked the engine and began moving the boat out to sea, causing the wind to pick up and blow her hair behind her shoulders. It was the best feeling in the world. Only then did she grasp how long it had been since she'd been on a boat, her feet wet like they used to stay all summer.

Sydney took a seat next to Juliana just before the boat picked up speed, slicing through the cobalt blue water, the spray dancing on her skin. The wind rushed through her ears, nearly drowning the constant buzzing of the engine. Nate and Robby were in her peripheral vision as the coastline zipped past them in a blur. The total assault on her senses made her feel alive for the first time in a very long time. Being out on the gulf gave her so much joy. She needed to do more of this, stir up that old creativity that used to come so easily for her. Now she knew why her ideas had come so effortlessly when she was younger: she had to feed her imagination with sunshine and happiness.

When the boat began to slow, Nate lifted Robby off his lap and stood up. "You know how to do it now, Captain," he told Robby. Nate cut the engine. "Just keep her straight ahead for me while I drop the anchor."

"Yes sir," Robby said with authority.

With Robby and Nate both busy anchoring the boat in place, Sydney turned to Juliana. "So," she said, "are you enjoying Firefly Beach?"

Juliana spread her slender arm along the back of the bench seat where they were both sitting and nodded. "It's very beautiful and quiet here," she said. "It is the kind of place where I could live."

"Are you planning to stay?"

"For right now, yes."

By staying, was Juliana hoping for some sort of reconciliation with Nate? Probably. According to the tabloids, they didn't dare move their things out of each other's apartments because they'd be back together before they could get it all unloaded. "Will you be staying with Nate?"

"If he says it's okay. We haven't really discussed all that just yet."

With the boat anchored down, Nate grabbed a fishing pole and walked over to Robby. "Want to see what we can catch out here?" he asked.

Robby's head bounced up and down, his face beaming with delight.

"Perfect. Okay, here's how you work this rod. Put your thumb against the line here…" He showed him where to place his thumb on the spool to keep it from unwinding too quickly—a trick Nate had learned from Uncle Hank on one of the countless fishing trips when Sydney had tagged along.

Sydney turned her attention back to Juliana. "So will you be doing any work while you're here?"

"No, I'm taking some time off from modeling," Juliana said. "The schedule is hectic… Things became so crazy. My soul was suffering."

"Your soul?"

"I was so busy trying to… manage things… I lost who I was."

Juliana showed an intense sadness just then, the emotion surfacing even through those big sunglasses of hers. Her honesty seemed brave, given the fact that she looked like she wanted to close in on herself. And now she was dealing with relationship issues with Nate. Poor girl. Looking at her, it was clear that the Juliana in all those glossy magazines wasn't necessarily representative of who Juliana was. She was hurting and uncertain—a far cry from the self-assured bikini model who seemed to have the world at her fingertips.

"What will you do now?" Sydney asked.

Juliana grabbed her sarong and draped it over her lap, smoothing it out on her legs. "I'm not totally sure. I have been modeling since I was fifteen. I have no experience doing anything else." She dragged her manicured finger under her glasses and sniffled before she turned toward the wind, her dark tresses cascading down her back.

Nate let Robby hold the rod by himself and came to join them. "That's why you're here," he said, his voice gentle and calming. "Take your time; don't rush it. You are one of the most resilient and passionate people I know. Breathe in this air and let it soak down to your bones. I find inspiration everywhere here. I'm hoping it'll do the same for you."

Nate's fondness for Juliana was clear, which only left Sydney feeling more confused, and hurt.

"I got one, Nate!" Robby called, reeling as fast as his little fingers would allow him to, the rod bending at the tip, giving him quite a struggle.

Nate rushed over to him to help pull in the fish.

"I wish I had your talent," Juliana said with a sigh, still clearly immersed in their prior conversation. "Nathan said you are an amazing writer."

Her comment surprised Sydney. "I don't know about that."

"One thing I can say about Nathan is that he tells the truth. If he tells me you're a great writer, I believe him." She took off her dark glasses, revealing her tired but beautiful almond-colored eyes. "He says you're a better writer than he is."

Completely baffled, she turned to look at Nate, only to find his eyes already on her, those unsaid words crashing upon her like the roll of a stormy tide. He quickly moved his attention back to Robby and the fish that was dangling from his line.

"Do *you* like to write?" she asked Juliana.

"I don't think so. I would like to design things. I really love choosing the layout for my photos. Sometimes I was able to collaborate with the photographers on the photo shoots, and tell them my ideas. The ones who would listen usually liked them."

"So perhaps you'd like to be a layout editor for a magazine?"

Juliana smiled. "That is exactly what Nathan suggested. But we searched online and for most of the jobs, I need a graphic design degree. I do not have a degree or any formal experience."

If someone had told her even a day ago that she would be suggesting this to Nate's on-and-off girlfriend, Sydney might have died laughing at the absurdity of the idea, but Juliana seemed genuinely kind, and it only made sense, given what she'd shared. "I'll tell you what. If you enjoy that sort of thing, maybe you can show me some of your ideas for the magazine I'm working on as a favor for Mary Alice for the wellness center. I'm designing the cover."

Juliana sat up straighter, her interest clear.

"I wanted to talk to you about the cover anyway. I was going to ask you… Would you and Nate pose for the cover image?"

"Oh, I am sorry," she said, "I am no longer modeling." Tears swelled suddenly in her eyes. She slipped her glasses back on.

Sydney thought she said she was taking a break from it, but Juliana's reaction just now told her something totally different. Then, as though Juliana could read her mind, it was as if she realized her blunder and wanted to take her words back. Sydney's question had put her on the spot and caused her just enough anxiety that she clearly couldn't hide her feelings anymore. Had Juliana Vargas, one of the world's top supermodels, literally at the height of fame, left modeling for good? And was Sydney the first to know of this decision?

Nate quickly got Robby's line baited and talked him through casting it before rushing over to Juliana. "You okay?" he asked quietly in her ear but Sydney heard. Juliana nodded, wiping a tear from her cheek. The exchange made Sydney feel like she was eavesdropping, so she got up and walked over to Robby.

"What did you catch?" she asked him, turning all her attention to the rocking sea surrounding them to give her calm.

"Nate said it was a snapper," he told her, reeling in, checking his line, and casting back out. He was becoming quite skillful, and she had to wonder if Nate had taught him a thing or two in their short time together.

"Hey, what do you say we pull up the anchor and do a little tubing?" Nate said to Robby, appearing next to him. "I can pull you and your mom behind the boat."

Juliana had taken her spot again, sunning herself on the towel at the back of the boat, her headphones in her ears. Sydney considered the fact that it might be an effort to shut everything out. A tear escaped from under Juliana's sunglasses, and she wiped it away. What had happened to her? Nate was right about one thing: if there was anywhere on earth that could make her feel better about whatever it was she was going through, Firefly Beach was the place.

Chapter Ten

Sydney clicked on the radio in the kitchen, the sun from the day still on her skin, and pulled out Aunt Clara's lemon bar recipe. She was going to make some for Malory's party tonight. Aunt Clara had said, "You never know when life will give you lemons, so it's best to have all the ingredients for lemon bars on hand. That way you can make something sweet out of the whole thing." With a nod in the direction of Aunt Clara's chair at the table, Sydney lumped an armful of lemons onto the counter. They all began rolling in different directions as she scrambled to get control of them.

Out of nowhere, Nate caught one before it tumbled to the ground and set it on the table. "Hi," he said, helping her roll them into a pile. He'd showered, his hair still wet, and his cheeks pink from all afternoon on the boat. He surveyed the kitchen, the counter filled with sugar, flour, a bowl of eggs, and the utensils she'd need for baking. "You're trying to drum up good luck for something," he said, the idea causing a sparkle in his eye.

Sydney took one of the lemons and ran it under the water at the sink, drying it off. "What gives you that idea?"

A tiny smirk formed on his lips. "When you want something to go well, you bake and, by the look of that pile of lemons, you're making Aunt Clara's lemon bars. Something big must be on your mind."

"The lemons were already here," she said. "Mama had them in the center of the table to look nice."

"Whatcha making, Mom?" Robby said, coming in to the room and crawling up on the barstool to see better. "Hi, Nate," he said a little more bashfully than he had on the boat earlier.

"Lemon bars," Nate told him, clearly not needing confirmation.

"Oh, I love those!" Robby wriggled on the barstool. "She always makes them before I have big tests in school."

Nate eyed her and raised an eyebrow, and Sydney's cheeks burned with the memory that she knew had been conjured up with Robby's comment.

Sydney ignored his look and started shaving the zest off of the lemons. "I wanted to bring something summery for Malory's birthday," she said. "That's why I'm baking them." She tried to hide the fact that she was hoping things went well with Malory tonight. She missed her.

"Do you remember when we made these together?" Nate asked. But before she could answer, he turned to Robby. "Your mom and I both grew up here in Firefly Beach, and we used to make these before our big tests in college like she does for you." He grabbed two lemons, cradling them in one hand, and then took a third. "Your mom and I can juggle these lemons, each of us only using one hand."

Robby lit up. "You can?" He looked over at Sydney for confirmation.

She smiled, unable to deny the fondness she had at the memory. It had started as a bet.

"You should ask him out," Nate told Malory, all those years ago, when the subject of his sister's crush had come up, as they all stood together in the Hendersons' kitchen baking. "Put the moves on…" His eyebrows bounced up and down. "I can give you some pointers if you need them."

"Absolutely not," Malory said, rolling her eyes playfully.

"Oh, come on," Nate teased his sister. "You know I've got all the moves," he said, grabbing Sydney and tickling her, making her squirm and wriggle away with laughter. He grabbed two lemons from the counter and juggled them high in the air.

"Gross," Malory said with playful disgust. "I do *not* want to know about my brother's moves."

"I'll tell you what," he said, grabbing a third lemon and adding it to the two already circling in the air. "If I can juggle these for one minute straight, you have to ask him out."

Malory laughed. "Too easy," she said. "You have to juggle them with one hand."

"Of course!" he said, the lemons coming to a stop one by one in his hand. Start your timer." But before he began, he walked around the kitchen island and stood next to Sydney. "I can't juggle with one hand," he whispered to her and then nuzzled her ear, making her giggle. "Remember how I taught you to juggle?" he asked.

Nate had taught Sydney how to juggle using Aunt Clara's scarves. When she'd gotten good enough at it, he had her try tennis balls, and she'd gotten to be a pretty smooth juggler. She nodded, wondering what he had up his sleeve.

"I'm going to be your right hand, and you be my left. Think we can juggle together?"

Malory piped up, "That's totally cheating, but I can't wait to see if you can pull this off, so I'll let it go." She leaned on the counter with her elbows and put her chin in her hands.

"Can we have a practice round?" he asked.

"Nope." Malory's chin remained in her hands, amusement on her face.

"Fine," he said. "But if we can do this for one minute, you have to ask Brian out."

"Okay," Malory said, getting up and setting the kitchen timer. "On your mark, get set, go!"

Quickly, Nate faced Sydney, putting his arm out and tossing a lemon in the air. To Sydney's surprise, she was able to manage, keeping the lemon in the air.

"Here comes number two," he said, tossing it into the mix with his free hand.

The lemon sailed up in the air and came down in her hand as if she'd tossed it up herself. She kept it going. He threw the third one up, and there they were: both of them working together like they'd done it all their lives. She kept her concentration, not wanting to break for a second, but wondering how long they'd been going.

When the timer finally went off, Malory moaned a loud, annoyed groan. "I cannot *believe* you two pulled that off!"

Aunt Clara had burst into the room and asked, "What in the world is going on in here? You all sound like you're having too much fun." She winked at them.

"*They* certainly are," Malory said.

She'd asked her crush Brian out, and they'd ended up dating for about six months before they finally decided they were better off as friends.

"Show me!" Robby said.

Sydney swam out of her memory.

"We might be a little rusty," Nate said, positioning himself up next to her, making her pulse rise. He handed her a lemon. "We had gotten pretty good at it—we used to do it at parties."

"Why did you come over again?" she asked, recognizing the incredible distraction he'd caused. She was running out of time to make the lemon bars.

"Stop trying to change the subject. Let's show Robby," he said, already tossing a lemon in the air.

Just like they'd never stopped practicing, she caught it, sending it back into the air. The lemon went around a few times before Nate sent the second one up. Pretty soon, they were juggling all three to Robby's cheers.

Nate caught them one at a time, stopping and setting them back on the pile where Sydney had originally put them. "We make a good team," he said, but when he said it, there was more to his observation than what was on the surface. "And by the way," he added, "I just came by to say hi. Malory and Juliana have the whole cottage full of hairspray fumes while they get ready for the party, and I had to escape." He gave Robby a wink, making Robby giggle. "Looks like we'd better get a move on with making these lemon bars. Wanna help, little guy?"

"Sure," Robby said. Sydney couldn't deny the curiosity in her son's eyes when he looked at Nate right then, giving her two juxtaposed reactions: the first was the flutter in her chest at this little moment they were having together and the second was the utter fear that Robby could fall for Nate's charm as easily as she could.

The last of the lemon bars had come out of the oven, filling the air with the sugary sweet nectar of lemon and butter, and Nate had gone home to help get things ready for the party tonight. While Jacqueline ironed the shirt Uncle Hank was wearing to the party, Sydney grabbed her phone to check the time, and only then did she remember the push notification of the email she'd gotten. It had been from someone she didn't recognize, but seeing the subject line now, it made her pause: *NY Pulse Magazine Content Editor Position*. Quickly, she set down the strappy sandals she was holding, opened up the email, and scanned the message.

Thank you for reaching out… The team has reviewed your submission and we'd like to set up a call… Could you send us available times and days…

Sydney clasped her hand over her mouth in complete shock. "Oh, my gosh," she said from behind her fingers.

Jacqueline stopped and set the iron upright, turning down the radio that was playing beach tunes and fixing her eyes on Sydney. "What is it?"

"Uh… It could be nothing," she said, the insecurity about her ability to compete with the applicants for that level of a writing position surfacing. "Hallie and I were messing around a few weeks ago and we sent my résumé to this big magazine in New York… They want me to call them."

"Oh, Sydney, that's amazing!"

"Well, let's not get too excited," she warned. It was more directed to herself than her mother.

Robby wandered into the room, wearing the new shorts Sydney had gotten a few weeks ago for church and a two-button Polo shirt. "How do I look?" he said, holding out his arms and tapping his feet in the loafers she'd asked him to wear tonight.

"If I was eight, I'd date ya," Sydney teased.

Robby squeezed his eyes shut with embarrassment. "Mo-om."

"What?" She dropped her phone onto the bed and took his hands, dancing with him. "You're a chick-magnet," she teased again.

"Mom!" he said, shaking his head. "That's gross."

Sydney laughed. "One day, you won't think so."

"I will always think so." He made a face.

"One day, when you grow up, you might get married," she said.

"No way. I want to live with you forever." He wrapped his arms around her and squeezed her tightly, making her glow with adoration for him.

"You're welcome to," she said, kissing the top of his head.

"I'll live with you..." He pulled back. "As long as you don't make me wear these shoes very much. Yuck."

"It's good to dress up every now and again," Sydney told him.

"Your mother's right," Sydney's mom said. "How else will you appreciate the comfort of your sneakers?"

"I already had to wear fancy clothes at the wedding," Robby said, tugging on the collar of his shirt.

"You'll be a pro at dressing up then," Sydney said. "Your *girlfriend* will be impressed!"

"I don't have a girlfriend," he said, giving her the side-eye.

"What about Susie Jones at school?"

"She's not my girlfriend! She just talks real weird around me. *Like this.*" He said the last two words in a sultry voice, making Sydney and Jacqueline laugh out loud.

"Watch out," Jacqueline said. "With that kind of talk, she'll be your girlfriend before you know it."

Robby rolled his eyes. "What time are we going to the party?"

"We'll leave in about twenty minutes," Sydney replied.

"Okay! I'll go get my football!"

"Try to stay clean!" she called after him as he ran down the hallway.

Sydney walked along the road toward Malory's house with the rest of the family, the birthday-themed bag containing an expensive bottle of wine and the gift card they'd all pitched in to buy swinging by her side, while Jacqueline carried the tin of lemon bars.

Robby strolled along next to her, tossing his football into the air and catching it. "Think Nate will play a game or two with me tonight?" he asked.

"It's his sister's birthday, so I'm not sure, but probably," Sydney said. She'd started to get her mind around the idea of Nate and Robby spending time together, although she still wasn't certain if it was the right thing to do or not. Robby just seemed so relaxed around him. Even after all his fame, Nate had that effect on people.

"I heard that Nate managed to get his hands on one of Sally Ann's peach cobblers for tonight," Uncle Hank said, pacing up beside them. "Between that and the cake, you'll need to play some football to burn off all that sugar."

"How did he get one of Sally Ann's cobblers?" Sydney's mother asked. "The bakery's been sold out of them for a week now, since the tourists have started arriving."

Sally Ann, the town baker, was famous for her homemade peach cobbler. The whole village knew how good they were, and in the summer months they had to be ordered specially, because they sold out faster than one could say "pie."

"I asked her when I saw her in town this morning," Uncle Hank said. "She was so star-struck by Nathan Carr entering the bakery that she gave him one from her personal stash in the back that she reserves for special occasions. She took a photo of him holding it, and then ran straight to her phone and posted the picture on all the bakery's social media outlets."

"Why does Nate have two last names?" Robby asked.

Unaware that he even knew that fact, Sydney tried to hide her discomfort while she tried to figure out the most concise way to explain a pen name. "When he's writing, he uses the last name Carr."

"Why doesn't he just use his regular name?" Robby asked.

"I think it's easier to remember a short name like Carr than a long one like Henderson, and it isn't as common, so people will remember it." She didn't want to mention her own opinion about it: that she'd felt Nate wanted to get as far away from who he was as possible—as far away from *her*—and that he wanted to reinvent himself as a superstar with no connections to his past.

"Oh, that makes sense," Robby said. "When he's with us, his last name is Henderson, right? That's what I heard Hallie say at the wedding. But someone else called him Mr. Carr. *I* think it's because he's like Superman." Robby grinned. "Superman has two names."

"I doubt Nate would consider himself a hero..." she replied. She certainly didn't.

"You certainly have taken a liking to Nate," Uncle Hank said, moving over and walking beside Robby. "You like him?"

"Yeah." Robby tossed his ball into the air and caught it with both hands. "He's as much fun as Ben."

"It's good to have those kinds of people in our lives, isn't it?" Uncle Hank said. He winked at Sydney, but she didn't find the humor in this conversation. It terrified her. Nate clearly had too much going on in that head of his to be what Robby needed.

Sydney's mother waved at Nate, who was headed toward them. Speak of the devil.

"Robby! Go long!" he called down the road, his hands in the air.

Robby's face lit up like the sunrise on a clear day and he cocked back and then let the ball go. It landed right into Nate's hands.

"You've got a good arm on you," Nate said to Robby when they reached each other. He tossed Robby the ball. "I've got a big spot in the back yard cleared out for us to play."

As they reached Malory's cottage, Robby ran ahead, "Show me, Nate!" he called, not stopping as he got to the grass.

"Guess I'd better follow him around back," Nate said, running off before Sydney had even had a chance to redirect her son.

"Here, let me take that." Sydney's mother hooked her fingers through the handles of the gift bag. "You need to go inside and relax. It's been ages since you've spent an evening with Malory. I'm sure she'll be delighted that you've come tonight."

"I should probably go find Robby," Sydney said, but her mother caught her arm.

"He'll be okay," she replied, unspoken words in her eyes. "He's just playing football. Let's go in, say hello to the birthday girl, and get a drink."

When they got inside, Malory rushed over to them happily. "Hi!" she said, giving Sydney and her mother a big squeeze of a hug. She seemed genuinely delighted to see them, despite the undercurrent of unease that had slithered between Malory and Sydney because of Nate. "Uncle Hank! I'm so glad you could come too."

"Glad to see you," Uncle Hank said. Everyone in town who was Sydney's age had referred to Hank and Clara as if they were family, and Malory was no different.

"I was hoping to get to talk to you at the wedding. I had to take Juliana home," Malory said, linking her arm with Sydney's like they used to do. Her actions contrasted with the lingering questions in her gaze.

Sydney missed the days when they'd skipped along the side of the road between their houses without a care in the world.

"I know; Nate told me," she said, wishing Malory could've spent more time at the wedding, too. Sydney longed for the lighthearted atmosphere that used to follow them wherever they went.

Clearly sensing the dynamic, Uncle Hank said, "Malory, I'm so happy to see you invited the Fergusons. Jacqueline and I should say hello." Sydney's mother lit up at the sight of their long-time friends and followed Uncle Hank over to the owners of the bait and tackle shop in town.

"Can I show you something?" Malory asked the moment they were alone, noticeably taking advantage of the short lull in conversation with her guests. She took Sydney to a bedroom in the back.

The room was tidy, the bed made; the only evidence that anyone was even staying in the room was the lump of Nate's clothes that were draped on a side chair beside a pair of stilettos. Sydney sat down on the bed, trying not to imagine the two people who had slept in it last night.

Malory opened a drawer, and Sydney immediately recognized the old notebook she pulled from it. "That's mine," Sydney said, the surprise over seeing it again after all these years making her breathless. "I wondered where it went."

Malory sat down beside her and handed Sydney the tattered leather-bound book. Gingerly, Sydney opened the cover and ran her fingers down the words. "I couldn't think of anything to say…" She looked up, swallowing to alleviate the lump that was forming. "Nate got me this notebook because mine was full, and it was so clean and perfect that I remember I had trouble knowing what to write first because I didn't want to ruin the beauty of it." She looked back down at that first entry. "Nate told me to harness that emotion and write the first thing that came to my mind. All I could think about was how, one day, I wanted my writing to be worthy of such a gorgeous gift as this book and a sort of manifest destiny rushed through me. I wrote this." She turned the notebook around and showed Malory what she'd written:

I am destined for great things.

What had happened to that drive? Sydney knew exactly what had happened to it. Nate had been that voice in her head, cheering her on, telling her how talented she was, and when he left her behind, it had made her feel like all his words had meant nothing. She'd suddenly felt like she'd been weighing him down. Looking back on her adult life so far, she hadn't lived up to such a colossal statement as the one glaring back at her from the open page in her hand—in fact, just the sight of it made her feel like she'd been nothing but a silly child when she'd written that. Yet Nate had actually done so many great things. Perhaps he really had known back then how ridiculous that declaration was for her to write, he'd been wise enough to see that she wouldn't be able to achieve her dreams. Maybe leaving them all had actually been the best decision he could've made…

"Nate had this book in his suitcase," Malory said, tapping the notebook, grabbing hold of Sydney's attention once more.

Sydney looked up at her friend, losing her breath for a second.

"I don't know what's going on," Malory told her. "He's secretive, and he's never like that with me. He's overly protective of Juliana, but then I see him reading that journal of yours at night by the lamp in the living room, completely consumed by it, tears in his eyes… You and I both know that he wouldn't be unfaithful to his girlfriend—I don't care what kind of celebrity he's become; he wouldn't do that. But you're all he talks about whenever it's just the two of us. I think he's come back here for you, Syd."

"That's ridiculous," Sydney said with an incredulous laugh.

"Is it?" There wasn't a shred of amusement on Malory's face. "You two dated for four years—that's longer than he's ever dated anyone else. He told me back then that you were the only person he could ever imagine spending his life with."

"People change," she countered. "And it doesn't make any sense." Sydney shook her head, completely baffled. Where had all this come from after so many years?

"I know he's my big brother, so I probably give him the benefit of the doubt above and beyond what I should, but something tells me that there's more in that head of his than what we're seeing on the outside." She leaned forward into Sydney's view. "Think about it: nothing has brought him home for any length of time in all these years. He told me he called you before your wedding, but he wouldn't elaborate as to why. All he said was that you shot him down and made him realize that you'd moved on with your life and he needed to do the same. Then you move back to Starlight Cottage—single—and within the year, he's staying at my house, buying property, getting involved with local events—he's even been working on his old truck."

"He still has that thing?"

"It's what he pulled up in. I've never seen Juliana Vargas so out of place in my life!" Malory said, giggling. "That's why I jumped at the chance to take Juliana back to the house during the wedding. I was hoping he'd open up and tell you what all of this is about."

Suddenly, those thoughts Sydney had seen in his stare at the wedding began to match up with this revelation of Malory's. She considered how he kept coming back to the cottage to see her, pouring out his heart. Was there more to his gesture than just making things right between them?

"He might have tried to tell me… But the whole situation rubs me the wrong way. I don't want him coming back here for me. Not like this."

"It's been a long time, and after he hurt you the way he did, I thought long and hard about whether I should tell you my opinions on the matter, but it would eat me up to not say anything. Talk to him, Sydney. Ask him your questions. Let him get whatever this is off his chest completely and then make a decision. You owe it to the both of you. Maybe, now that you two have grown up, this will be your chance for happiness."

"He lost his chance the day he decided I wasn't good enough for him." Sydney closed the journal and handed it back to Malory. There was a part of her that still held on to that magic of the past, that wanted to run into his arms, but the other side of her wouldn't allow it. She just couldn't, given the way things had ended between them. She had her pride and self-worth to think about, not to mention Robby.

A knock sent them both jumping, the notebook slamming down onto the floor.

Nate was in the doorway, his eyes on the notebook, looking as white as a ghost. "I was just checking on Juliana, but then I wondered why the birthday girl was tucked away in a back room," he said, coming in and picking up the book. He handled it gently as if it were fragile and then held it out to Sydney. "This belongs to you."

"You can keep it," she told him, her tone laced with the pain of what was written on the pages: all her dreams that had never happened.

"Is everything all right?" Juliana said from behind Nate in her Argentinean accent that sounded as comforting as home cooking.

Nate tossed the book gently onto the chair with his clothes, and turned to Juliana, a new sense of purpose overtaking him. "Don't go outside." There was warning in his words.

"Why not?" Juliana stepped up in front of him, concern written on her face.

"There's a photographer out there taking pictures of the yard from the tree line."

Juliana's eyes glistened. "Do you think he got any photos of me when I went out to bring you a drink earlier?"

"I don't know. I was playing football with Robby. I only just noticed him. I have no idea how long he's been there."

"How did they find us?" Juliana asked, her voice shaking.

Nate shook his head and ran his fingers through his hair. "I let Sally Ann post photos of me online." His jaw clenched, and he was noticeably remorseful about his error. "I should've been more careful." He balled his hands into fists by his side. "Damn it."

"It's okay," Juliana said, rubbing his arm. "It was only a matter of time anyway. I can't hide from them forever."

That familiar unease Sydney felt when Juliana and Nate shared intimate moments like this came rushing back.

"I know. But I feel like it's my fault. I wanted to give you more of an opportunity to work through things before you had to deal with all that."

"Would someone like to fill us in?" Malory asked, standing up from the bed and walking over to Nate.

"It's just our daily struggle with the press. They connect their own dots about our lives, and they couldn't be further from the truth. And right now, we don't need any speculation about Juliana's life or what she's doing here." Just as the words came out of his mouth, the intensity melted as he looked at his sister. "I'm sorry. It's your birthday. Let's not let that one guy ruin your party. Juliana and I will stay inside for the night, and we'll close the blinds on the east side of the house so they won't get even a glimpse of what's going on."

"That's no way to live," Malory said.

"We're used to it." Juliana blew a frustrated breath through her red lips. "My aunt owned a restaurant in New York and my mother thought it would expand my horizons if I went abroad, so she let me visit. I was only sixteen when my first modeling agent saw me through the window of the restaurant and contracted me right there on the spot. All of the glitter in her talk and the promise of so many things—how could I say no? But she never told me about this." Juliana waved her hand at the window. "She never taught me how to live as a prisoner. And Nathan has it worse than I do—they hound him like crazy. I only hope that now that I have stopped modeling, after a while, people will tire of me and leave me alone."

"So that's why you're leaving modeling…" Sydney said.

"Part of the reason, yes."

"What's the other part?" Sydney asked.

Juliana paused. "I'd rather not say." There was a definite shift in her demeanor, and it was evident that whatever it was had certainly affected her. That was when Sydney noticed Juliana's hands shaking like a leaf.

Nate must have seen it at the same time, because he rushed over to her and put his arms around her. Feeling awkward and suddenly stifled in that tiny room while Nate consoled Juliana, Sydney took Malory's arm, and they slipped past the couple.

As they entered the living room, Malory got pulled into a conversation with some friends of hers and Robby ran up to Sydney.

"Where's Nate?" he asked.

"He's helping Juliana with something. He'll be back in just a minute," she said, her mind in such a muddle. She needed to refocus. "I see a table full of snacks. We better get over there before Uncle Hank finishes all the cheese." She pointed past a bunch of balloons to a table against the wall where her uncle was helping himself to a cracker with cheese. "Should we go over and see what's on it?"

"Yes!" Robby moved through the now crowded cottage to where Uncle Hank was still standing and Sydney followed.

"Hey, bud!" Uncle Hank said, ruffling his hair.

Robby wrapped his arms around his uncle. "This is a fun party, isn't it?" Robby said, pulling away and snagging a brownie from a platter of confections.

But before they'd been able to start any sort of conversation, Robby left them, running off toward Nate as he came into the room. Juliana settled in a chair and started making small talk with a couple that was nearby, still noticeably shaken but doing well at hiding it. The woman speaking to her clearly hadn't noticed. Nate squatted down, saying something to Robby, and with the noise in the room, Sydney couldn't make out what it was.

"Those two get along famously," Uncle Hank noted, something clearly on his mind as he pointed it out. "...You know, I called Nate today."

Sydney nodded, her head still clouded with everything she'd just taken in, remembering what Nate had said when she'd gotten home from work. "Why did you call him?" Sydney asked Uncle Hank.

"I wanted to find out which realtor he used to buy his land."

"You mean the lot he bought?" Sydney asked.

Uncle Hank laughed. "I suppose you could call it a 'lot.' That is, if you think fifty-seven acres of beachfront property is a 'lot.'"

"Fifty-seven acres?" She looked over at Nate, processing this. "That's *millions* of dollars."

"He has it, Sydney."

With that kind of investment, Nate was most certainly planting roots here. A future with him in it was solidified in her mind now, and she scrambled for what to do. Could she handle that? Should she move back to Nashville? She didn't want to leave—she loved it in Firefly Beach. But all his back and forth was too difficult to handle, and she just wanted to escape it. Was it so wrong to want to run away? After all, that was what he'd done.

Suddenly, the question occurred to her: "Why did you need to know his realtor?" she asked Uncle Hank.

"I have to have the best, and I knew that he'd have chosen a top agent to help him find his property." Uncle Hank looked down at the balled napkin in his hands from his cookie. "I'm seriously considering selling Starlight Cottage."

Aunt Clara's smile as she waved to Sydney at the front door of the cottage flashed in Sydney's mind, all the memories flooding her like some sort of movie reel gone haywire. Starlight Cottage was part of the Flynn family. It had seen them through thick and thin. It had seen Flynn weddings over the years, the birth of babies, and it had seen Aunt Clara through her last days; it had been her great aunt's solace and sense of peace her entire adult life…

"I didn't think you were serious about selling," she said, her temples beginning to ache. She wished she could get Aunt Clara's opinion, at the very least, see her face—her expression would speak volumes about whether or not selling was a good idea. "There's no dilemma too great to conquer," Aunt Clara explained to Sydney once. "The hard part is knowing what it means exactly to 'conquer' it. The answer isn't always what you want or even think should happen, but it's what was in the cards all along. The 'conquering' occurs within sometimes, but everything can be conquered."

"It won't be the same once the public beach access is built," Uncle Hank said, drawing Sydney out of her memory. "The Starlight Cottage that we love will be forever changed the moment the clearing begins." He straightened his shoulders and grabbed another cookie. "Let's talk about it later. We need to enjoy the birthday party."

"You know what? You're absolutely right," she said, needing a break from everything.

On her way into the kitchen, she spotted Nate. She grabbed a cracker for herself and decided to head to the kitchen in search of a glass of wine. She couldn't conquer the issues facing Starlight Cottage tonight or the problems surrounding her and Nate, but she could completely conquer the rift that had formed between her and Malory. It was Malory's birthday, and she was going to celebrate with her friend.

Chapter Eleven

Sydney tipped her glass toward Malory as her friend topped it off with the last of the wine. They'd finally opened up about their feelings surrounding the break-up.

"I felt like it was all my fault for getting you two together," Malory told her, shaking her head. "It seemed like you two were perfect for each other. You were so perfect that it never even occurred to me that you'd ever break up. After, I felt naïve, like I had my head in the clouds, when maybe I could've focused more on your lives and at least warned you."

"Malory, it was my choice to date Nate. You couldn't have foreseen this, nor was it in any way your fault," Sydney told her. "I'm just glad I came over tonight. I should've come to find you sooner."

Malory smiled. "I missed you."

"Same." Sydney held up her glass to toast her friend. "To us," she said, clinking Malory's glass.

It had been just the two of them for a while. She had no idea where Nate was and everyone else had gone home. The two women sat together on the sofa, their feet kicked up on the coffee table that was littered with streamers and scraps of wrapping paper. Uncle Hank and her mother had refused to let her leave, telling her she needed to unwind, taking Robby home and putting him in bed for her. After everyone else had gone, she and Malory had stayed up talking, neither of them worried about the fact that they both had to work the next day.

"I'm calling in sick," Malory declared, giggling.

"I might sleep in late." Sydney forced the words to come out evenly through the buzz of the alcohol. "I need to get home soon though, or I'm going to end up falling asleep right here."

They both laughed. Malory snorted, only making them giggle harder.

"I've missed you," Malory said. She put her arm around Sydney and offered a slow smile under her drooping eyelids. "I'm getting sappy from all the wine." She took another drink from her glass.

"I've had so much wine," Sydney said, "that I caught myself considering whether Tommy Simpson from down the road might have actually been attractive and we just hadn't noticed it…"

Malory fell over laughing in fits of loud inhalations and cackling. Tommy Simpson had had a crush on them when they were younger. He was just a regular guy, nothing flashy, kind of quiet, bad haircut…

"But seriously," Sydney said, sobering, "I've missed you too." She sat up. "Happy birthday."

"Thank you. It was the best birthday ever with you here."

"Let's get a coffee tomorrow. I think we'll both need one…"

They both laughed again, but their merriment was interrupted when Nate came into the room. "Did I hear you say you need to go home?" he asked Sydney in a whisper that she could only assume was to avoid waking his girlfriend. "I'll walk you."

Sydney looked past him down the hall. "You should really stay with Juliana," she said, the wine giving an edge to her usual sadness. She cut her eyes at him.

Nate followed the track of her earlier gaze to his bedroom. "Juliana is sleeping across the hall," he said. "The one you were in earlier is *my* room."

"But you both had your things in there…" She was struggling to make sense of what was going on, given the buzz in her head from the drinks and a long day.

"Her room is too small for her bags, so she keeps them in my room." With a playfully annoyed look, he walked over to her and grabbed her hands, pulling her up from the sofa. "Stop being stubborn. I'm walking you home. You've had too much wine to go alone."

Sydney stood, the alcohol giving her courage. She wasn't drunk. She was just relaxed enough to give him a piece of her mind. She got onto her tiptoes and looked him in the eye. "I'm a big girl. I've done it alone for many, many years now, thank you very much," she said, glaring at him.

The corner of his mouth twitched upward and he gently pushed a strand of hair out of her face with his forefinger. With that one touch, her knees felt like soft butter and she wobbled. Nate caught her.

"I've got the key. Lock up after we leave," he said to Malory, his arm still around Sydney.

The street was dark and quiet, as the two of them walked toward Starlight Cottage. Neither of them said a word. The only sound between them was the soft caress of the gulf against the shore. She'd walked beside him so many times, but this time was different. She was aware of every breath he took, every stride he made, the way his shoulders tensed just a little when he slipped his hands into his pockets. A tiny subconscious part of her wanted the moment to stretch into the night, and with every mailbox they passed, she found herself willing him to keep walking with her past her house so he wouldn't have to say goodnight.

When the long drive to Starlight Cottage came into view, Nate took her arm to stop her. He looked around at the black of night and then leaned in to her ear.

"I don't know if we're being photographed," he said quietly, "so I'm going to whisper this to you." He put his lips right by her ear, his breath on her skin sending a chill down her spine. "Juliana isn't my girlfriend. But the press doesn't know that. There's a lot going on, and I hadn't really prepared for it all." He pulled back and looked her in the eye. "Can we talk tomorrow?"

Sydney wanted to be relieved by his admission, but the truth of the matter was that it didn't change the way he'd made her feel about herself. And even if she could get over that, there was that tiny voice in the back of her mind that whispered, "What if he left again?" This time, it wasn't just her he'd be abandoning; she had Robby too.

"Please meet me tomorrow," he said, interrupting her inner battle.

"I have to work tomorrow," she replied, knowing how feeble the excuse seemed. Sydney's head was starting to pound. She needed to get inside where she could clear her mind.

Nate reached out and caressed her arm. Just when she was about to take a step, a white-hot flash, like a lightning strike, burned her eyes. She blinked to try to clear it, but all she could see was a gray haze, her vision affected by the intensity of the light. Unexpectedly, Nate's hand was at her back, moving her forward, startling her and burning through the alcohol in her system. She stumbled alongside him blindly as the images in front of her slowly came back into focus.

"If I try to run from them, it will give them more ammo to make up stories about you and me," he said in her ear as another flash went off. "We have to look like we have nothing to hide." Then, he spoke urgently, "And I still don't know if they've realized Juliana is here in Firefly Beach. She doesn't sleep well, and she gets up in the night. I'm not even sure if the press is aware that I'm *staying* at Malory's; they could just think I was at the party there tonight. If I go back there, they might camp out until the morning to get a good shot. Once they know where I'm living, they'll be back every day. I'm coming inside."

"They got my picture?" Sydney didn't know how to feel about the possibility of being in Nathan Carr's circus of a world.

"It's dark. The photo's probably too grainy to use," he said as they neared the cottage. "I'm just being proactive."

There was something very unsettling about learning she'd been watched. Had the photographer been with them the entire walk home? She and Nate climbed the few stairs leading to the front porch together, and she noticed how calm he was in all this. His movements were deliberate and well practiced. This was his reality all the time. When she used to fantasize as a girl about being famous, this idea of it had never entered her mind. She suddenly felt glad that she hadn't become the famous one. This was not something she wanted to deal with every day.

"So you mean they might camp out at Starlight Cottage now?" she asked, slipping her key into the front door lock as she sent darting glances over her shoulder.

Nate ushered her inside and shut the door quickly behind them.

"It's possible," he said, regret filling his face. "I'm so sorry. I really didn't think that letting Sally Ann post a photo would cause this. They hound me at public events, but at home, they usually leave me alone." He stopped cold. "Unless…" He pulled out his phone and fired off a text. After staring at the screen for a long pause, he dialed a number and put the phone to his ear.

"Malory, I'm at Sydney's. Is Juliana awake, by chance? … Go check." He began to pace in front of the doorway. Sydney stepped aside, trying to make sense of the call. "Hey," he said, his whole body straightening up. "Juliana, don't go outside until I'm back. The photographer followed me here. But I started thinking… What if he isn't with the press? You have three months left in your modeling deal, right?" Nate walked over and shut the window blinds. "Are you in breach of contract being here right now?" He went over to one of the two matching dark blue bergère-style chairs that Aunt Clara had delighted in when she'd redesigned the living room and sat down. "What if it isn't a reporter? What if the camera man is an investigator?"

Investigator? Sydney took a seat on the floor next to Nate's chair.

"I'll be back the minute I think this guy's left, all right?" Then he listened quietly for quite a while before telling Juliana it would be okay.

"What's going on, Nate?" Sydney asked when he'd gotten off the phone.

He blew out a frustrated puff of air and rubbed his eyes. "I'm not sure. At first I thought it was just a rogue photographer, trying to make a buck on a quick story—and it could be. But then it hit me that Juliana's four-year contract will expire in three months, and her lawyer will be presenting her thirty-day notice to the agency to terminate the contract. She has about two working months left before the lawyer gives notice. I wondered if the agency has sent someone to find her because contractually she's under obligation to work, no matter what her mental health is like."

"Would they do something like that?"

"They would do a whole lot of things to get what they want…" He gritted his teeth and stood up.

"So why would the photographer follow *us*?" she asked, pressing her fingers against her temples that felt as if they would throb right out of her head.

"Hopefully, if they didn't see her earlier at Malory's, it was to document the fact that Juliana isn't here. That's our best hope. Maybe the photographer will assume she's somewhere else, and he'll go back to wherever he came from."

"And if it's the press? Would that be any better?"

"Not really." He leaned on his knees and put his head in his hands. "I wasn't even thinking about the agency when I posed with Sally Ann for that photo—if that's even what it was that caused this." He looked up at her with tired eyes. "I just… I feel more like myself here, instead of this celebrity figure that people have built me up to be. I guess I forgot who I'd become for a second." There was a tremble in his voice that made him seem more vulnerable than Sydney had ever seen him before.

"It's okay," she said in an attempt to console him. "It was just one tiny sidestep, but it will pass."

He shook his head. "I feel like I can't ever get anything right."

"What?" Sydney asked, nearly breathless by his confession. When it came to getting what he'd wanted, he'd achieved an incredible amount.

"I'm not happy," he admitted. "I've made a complete mess of my life, trying to do the right thing."

She looked into his eyes, and it was as if time stood still. She missed him so much. He stared at her, so many unsaid words between them, and she could've sworn by his look that he was trying to tell her how much he missed her too. Her forearm prickled, every nerve ending on high alert as he trailed his finger along it lightly, and she knew right then that she was still completely in love with him. In an instant, she wanted to put her arms around him and kiss his lips. They shared that space together, just the two of them, locked in that moment with one another. With the flutters going on in her belly the way they were, she considered whether she'd forgiven him for leaving her the way he had. Before she could contemplate her answer, however, he hastily broke his gaze and paced across the room.

"I feel like I'm having some kind of breakdown," he said. "I don't know what I'm doing."

The insecurity she'd felt all those years ago came slithering back in. Why had he pulled away just now? Had he realized that he was staring into the same future he'd left so many years ago?

"I… uh… I'm going to go up to bed," she said, trying not to let her hurt show. "Lock up when you leave."

He grabbed onto her with his stare, urgency in his eyes, but she turned away.

Then something came over her: she felt sorry for him. He was only a shadow now of the boy she'd known. That life he'd chased, gambling everything he loved and rolling the dice, was eating him alive. She went over to him and kissed his cheek. "Good night, Nate," she said, her tone telling him that they were done here.

"Good night," he said, barely audible under the confusion and defeat in his voice. And as she left his sight and walked up the stairs, she stopped, sharpening her hearing. But all she heard was silence. Her mind must have been playing tricks on her because she could've sworn she heard him whisper, "I love you, Syd." But perhaps that was simply wishful thinking.

Chapter Twelve

The first sound that entered Sydney's consciousness was the tinkling of the wind chime on the porch outside, signaling a gentle breeze, but she couldn't quite swim out of her sleep enough to move. The morning sun streaming in through her window didn't even help. But then Nate's laugh sailed into her room from downstairs and her eyes flew open. Robby's giggle followed. It was seven a.m. What was he still doing here? Sydney grabbed her bathrobe and threw it on.

When she got downstairs, Nate and Robby were side-by-side on the floor in the living room, notebooks open, drawing together. A folded blanket sat on the sofa with a toothbrush on top from the packs that her mother had gathered for guests when they'd redone the bathroom. Nate was still in his clothes from yesterday, a shadow of stubble on his face. Ben's dog Beau greeted Sydney before retreating back to the sunspot on his dog bed in the corner of the room.

"Nate showed me how to draw a dinosaur," Robby said to her when she neared them.

Nate looked up at her, a fond grin spreading across his face. "Sleep well?" he asked.

It was only then that she realized she hadn't even looked in the mirror yet. Her hair was still disheveled from sleep, and she had no recollection of taking off her mascara last night, which made for an amusing appearance, she was certain. She ignored his question.

"I'm just going to get a cup of coffee. And a glass of water."

Judging by the sandpaper feel of her tongue, she started to wonder if maybe she'd had more wine than she should've last night.

Nate twisted his notebook toward Robby. "Here's how to do the tail. Give it a try while I get a cup of coffee with your mom." Nate stood up and walked over to her. Once they were facing each other, she thought she saw a tiny bit of hesitation, as if he didn't know what to do around her anymore.

"What's wrong?" she asked.

He nodded toward the kitchen, so she led them down the hallway.

She could see her mother and Uncle Hank through the window. They were out on the porch like they often were before the heat of the day settled in. A full pot of coffee was waiting for Sydney, a familiar gesture by her mother. She slid the milk and sugar over before pouring two steaming coffees, but then abandoned the mugs and faced Nate, waiting for any kind of explanation as to his tentativeness a minute ago.

He swallowed, a gentle smile surfacing. "I miss seeing you like this," he said. "Remember when we'd get so tired writing that we'd fall asleep at one another's houses and we'd wake up the next morning and look at each other like that night's sleep together had been some sort of secret prize we'd both won? You'd always raise your eyebrows at me, your face looking like Christmas morning. Remember that feeling?"

"Like it was yesterday," she replied, allowing her emotion to show. His obvious adoration for her this morning was confusing her, and she could barely keep her mind straight, answering truthfully.

He stared at her, his face full of thoughts. Out of nowhere, it looked as though he were going to kiss her, a move she wasn't sure how to navigate, the two sides of her brain in stark conflict over it, causing her pulse to rise. He'd hit a nerve with that memory—waking up beside him had been her most favorite thing…

Nate leaned in, the warmth of his breath at her ear as he said, "I miss you."

Every nerve was on high alert, her mind totally clouded and unable to create a single thought other than the fact that she missed him too. In fact, if she wanted to be totally honest with herself, she'd never stopped missing him. She'd just pushed it down where it would stop hurting so much.

Just then, Uncle Hank came in and the two of them flew apart. "Ah, Robby let you have a break from the drawing lessons?" he asked, seemingly not noticing their proximity.

"Yes," Nate said, still clearly recovering from the moment. He cleared his throat. "I don't mind, though. I enjoy being with Robby. He's very creative."

"That, he is. Just like his mama," Uncle Hank replied, getting himself a coffee. He threaded his large fingers through the handles of all three mugs and brought them to the table. "Have a seat with me. I want to pick your brain."

Nate pulled out the chair.

Last night's conversation with Uncle Hank came rushing back to Sydney, and she knew that she wanted to be a voice of reason in this little chat. She sat next to Nate and stirred her coffee.

"I need a good real estate agent, and I was hoping you could give me a reference," Uncle Hank said over his mug. "I'm considering the possibility of selling Starlight Cottage."

"Really?" Nate asked, his expression oddly unreadable.

"Yeah." Uncle Hank shook his head.

"Are you downsizing or something?" Nate's gaze flickered over to Sydney and then back to Uncle Hank. He was clearly trying to get a read on the conversation. It seemed to be making him uncomfortable, but he also didn't appear to be against the idea of selling.

"Everything is changing in Firefly Beach, and if the new shopping area they're proposing creates an environment anything like the massive influx of tourists that downtown has been facing every year, I'm not so sure I want to be this close to all the development." Uncle Hank looked down into his coffee.

Nate tapped his fingers against the table, clearly buying time before he responded. "If it's seclusion you want, you could build something by me. I've been talking it over with Malory. She's planning to sell as well, and I'm giving her ten acres of the parcel of land that I bought. I could definitely make room for you and the family."

Uncle Hank pressed his fingers to his lips in thought, clearly wrestling with the kindness of Nate's gesture and the anguish of losing the last tangible piece of Aunt Clara's legacy.

Sydney's opinion wasn't as diplomatic. Was Nate serious? He'd spent quite enough time here to know how much Starlight Cottage meant to Aunt Clara and to the family. And Uncle Hank was actually giving this ridiculous idea thought?

"You two can't be considering this," Sydney said, her heart rate quickening. None of it had seemed real until this moment.

"I'll bet we can even have the lighthouse moved," Nate carried on.

"Starlight Cottage is a lot to take care of..." Uncle Hank said, but she could see the sadness under his casual expression. He was stuck and deciding to settle.

"That has never bothered you before," she said. "That stupid public beach access—it's ruining everything. We need to fight it!"

"I will," Uncle Hank said. "In fact, they've scheduled an emergency meeting on Friday, and Lewis and I will definitely be there. I think we should all go to show our disagreement."

"Absolutely. I'm with you," Sydney said.

"I'll call around and see if I can drum up some more support. We need numbers at this point."

"Yes," she agreed, determined.

"But sometimes, Sydney, despite everything we do, things just change, and, while I'll do what I can, I'm too old to fight unnecessary battles." He leaned across the table and took her hand. "Would it be so bad to call another four walls home?" The uncertainty in his voice gave away the fact that he needed her to convince him. And that, she could never do.

Sydney looked over at the chair that had been empty since Aunt Clara had passed, wondering what her aunt would say. She tried to tell herself that Starlight Cottage was Aunt Clara's vision, and that maybe now it was time for them to all move forward, but just the thought of it brought her to tears. It had been hard enough to face being here without her favorite aunt. But losing Starlight Cottage would be losing the last shred of Aunt Clara, and something inside her screamed out how wrong it was to let it go.

"Do you know what Aunt Clara told me once?" she asked, trying to keep the wobble out of her voice. She had the attention of both Nate and Uncle Hank. "She told me that the name Starlight reminded her that even in the darkness that life could sometimes bring, this place shined—just like a star in the black of night. It brought her into the present, and she swore that she was her truest self when she simply existed in that single moment. She said that the past had already been and the future had yet to be dreamt. The present—this—" Sydney waved her hand around. "This is what matters most. This place was what made her whole again when the world made her feel less than that."

"She was a wise woman," Nate said, his knowing eyes on Sydney. "I like the idea of existing in the present moment. It makes everything else fade away."

"What if we're all still trying to live in *her* reality," Uncle Hank said. "What if I might miss her less when I didn't have so many reminders?"

The pain Sydney had dealt with over the last year as she tried to help Uncle Hank manage his grief while she coped with her own sadness came rushing back to her, so much so that she almost didn't register the ringing of Nate's cell phone.

"Sorry," he said, waving his phone at them. "Juliana's calling." He hit the speaker and held it in front of him. "Hey, Juliana. You're on speaker with Sydney and Hank."

"Okay…" Her voice sounded small through the phone. "They are outside the house and I can't leave."

"The photographers?" he asked.

"Yes. I don't know what to do. I'm supposed to go to my counseling appointment right now."

Sydney jumped up and looked at the clock. It was seven forty-five. She needed to get ready; she'd told Mary Alice she'd meet her at the wellness center to look over some ideas she had for the magazine. The thought was jarring, since she had so much on her mind already this morning, but she tried to focus on the issues she could solve right now. "I can pick her up and she can ride with me," Sydney offered. "She could wear one of Mama's big sun hats to hide her face."

"Hang on," Nate said. "Juliana, call your agent and explain what's going on. We need to know if it's just paparazzi or if you need to be in LA for a few more months to finish your contract."

"I cannot go back to LA," Juliana said, her voice breaking on the last word, panic in her voice.

"We can make sure you won't even have to see Seth. We'll file a restraining order." Nate spoke as if he were the only person in the room.

"No," Juliana said quickly. "That will make him unhappy and I don't know what he will do."

Nate took in a long breath. "Okay. Call your agent and feel out the situation. Once we know who's out there, we can figure out how to handle it. I'll make sure Mary Alice knows you can't get to her, and I'll reschedule. I'll work from here today."

Juliana said her goodbyes and Nate ended the call. He turned to Sydney. "If they're outside Malory's still, they're probably outside here too. Is it all right if I ask Mary Alice if she can come to you today? Otherwise, the photographers might follow you, and I don't want them to connect anything to the wellness center. If it *is* the press, then even the tiniest inkling that Juliana or I might be getting therapy could be terrible. They'll blow it out of proportion. The next thing we know, they'll say we're unstable."

Uncle Hank stood up before Sydney could respond, and retrieved a pair of keys from the cupboard. He walked back over to them and set them down in front of Nate. "Take my boat," he said. "No one will see you if you leave from the back of the cottage. Pack what you need for the day and the two of you can work out on the water."

Nate took the keys and his phone and gave Uncle Hank a squeeze around the shoulders with one arm. "You are the best, Uncle Hank," he said. "I'll call Mary Alice now so she knows what's going on."

"We won't have any Wi-Fi… Give me a second so I can pull up a few emails for my column." Sydney was trying to get her head around the fact that she was going to spend the day secluded on a boat with Nate.

"Of course," Nate said. In the midst of the drama, a small smile formed at the corners of his mouth. "You're writing again," he said. It hadn't been a question but more of an observation.

She nodded.

"I'm so happy to hear that." He turned to Uncle Hank. "Great idea," he said. "We'll take the boat."

"Excellent," Uncle Hank said as he opened the large bag of dog food and scooped up a cup of it, dumping it in Beau's bowl. The dog ran over and sniffed his new meal. "Then when you get home, perhaps you can fill me in on what in the world is going on."

Sydney patted his shoulder.

Nate, who'd stepped outside to make the call, came back in and dangled the keys in front of Sydney. "Mary Alice is completely fine with it. Get your swimsuit. It might get hot out there."

Jacqueline came in from outside. "I heard you two are taking a little boat ride today," she said with a cautious smile. "I'll make y'all some lunch and put it in the cooler."

Sydney's day was suddenly turning out a whole lot differently. And she wasn't quite sure about it at all.

Chapter Thirteen

Sydney stretched her bare legs out on the bench seat of Uncle Hank's center-console fishing boat, scooting back so that her laptop was under the shade of the overhang above the captain's chair and opened the few emails she'd quickly copied and pasted, praying she'd gotten something with substance. She'd been in such a rush that she hadn't read a single one before now, and she noticed that one of the emails was a response from Mel4221. She read that one first.

Dear Ms. Flynn,

I definitely hear you that there are things in this life that aren't meant to be fixed, and I question whether this is one of those things all the time. She isn't coming back to me, and I can hardly manage, knowing that she was the one person in this life who completed me. I haven't found anyone who can fill her shoes since. What if I've ruined everything by letting her go?

Lost,
Mel

Sydney's mouth dried out, her heart pattering. Mel's experience was exactly how she felt about Nate, but she couldn't help but let him go.

He hadn't given her any other choice. What could she say to this man other than the simple fact that she totally understood. Her heart ached for him because there was no easy answer to heartbreak. She didn't dare tell him that a decade later, his pain might still linger in his chest and that the dreams he'd had of their life together would hang in front of him as lost opportunities for the rest of his life.

"What are you working on?" Nate asked, making her jump. He walked over with his notebook under his arm, drying his hands on a towel after dropping anchor.

They'd made it out of the house and down to the dock without incident, and now they were secluded out in the middle of the gulf, rocking in the endless expanse of the turquoise waters, nothing around them but the bobbing markers telling local fishermen where they'd placed their crab pots. Nate picked her legs up, plopped down, and put her legs in his lap, resting his notebook on them as if they were twenty again. Juliana floated into her mind like a strong wind. What would she think of Nate's actions just now? Was she okay with this, or would it break her heart to see it? She tried to suppress the butterflies that swarmed her stomach, telling herself it was only old feelings surfacing.

When she realized he was waiting for an answer, she wriggled upright a bit and said, "I'm writing a response to an email for my column."

Nate's hand rested on her knee. "I can't wait to read it."

"How do you know I'll let you," she said before she'd thought it through. That was what she'd always used to tell him when he'd said he was going to read the pieces she'd written. But this had been a knee-jerk reaction to hide her feelings for him. She didn't want to get into a conversation with Nate, and possibly compare their opinions regarding Mel's experience.

He didn't answer her, but his thumb moved affectionately on her knee, his gaze on her, making her jittery.

She pulled her legs free and twisted around to a sitting position. "We need to work," she said.

Nate sighed dramatically and opened his notebook.

Sydney stared at her screen, rereading the same sentence a couple of times before it finally sank in. This was going to be more difficult than she thought. She needed to focus. With her fingers poised on the keyboard, she forced herself to recall the memory of the taillights of Nate's truck as he left Firefly Beach that day. He'd made her feel so insignificant… That was all she needed to regain concentration on her work. She pulled up another email and started to read about a woman considering a full-time nanny for her only child, the ideas beginning to flow as seamlessly as the lapping waves under the boat.

The heat of the sun bore down on her skin, the salt settling on her lips as her fingers moved on the keys, and she started to get into the groove of writing. The energy of her thoughts as they moved down her arms and through her fingers was like finding a long-lost friend after years apart.

But as she worked, she was increasingly aware of the fact that Nate was staring at her. "What?" she asked, pulling herself from her screen to address him.

He was leaned back, his notebook open with quite a few lines scratched down, the pen in his hand hovering over the paper, his total attention on her.

"Will you please work?" she asked.

"I am," he said, looking into her eyes. "You inspire me." He smiled, giving her a flutter against her will. "It's been a long time since I've had this much to say at once. The ideas have flooded me since the moment I came back. Check this out. I can just hear the island beat in the background and the steel guitars…" He turned his notebook around, showing her the lyrics he'd written:

Sunny days
How I'd like to be castaways
Sailing out on the ocean blue
Spending all my time with you

"Why did you come back?" She could hear the defensiveness in her tone; it came out as irritated and short, when she was only trying to protect herself from getting hurt. It was time to answer the question once and for all.

Nate opened his mouth to say something but his pause gave away the fact that he'd reconsidered whatever it was he'd wanted to tell her. "Juliana needed to get away from someone awful in her life, and she called me to help her."

Disappointment swelled in her stomach as she realized that she'd been hoping for a different answer. But what did she expect?

"The most secluded, restful, comforting place I know is right here in Firefly Beach." He looked out over the gulf, squinting in the sunlight, those familiar creases forming at the corners of his eyes. He took in a deep breath as if the briny air were giving him life, and it made her wonder why he hadn't come back before.

"If it's so inspiring," she said, "then why didn't you come back sooner?"

"I didn't want to… disrupt everyone's lives. I'd made a mess of things and I felt like it might be better to stay away and let everyone enjoy their own happiness."

What did he mean by that?

"When Ben sent me the invite," he continued, "I knew it was the perfect time to bring Juliana here. What a wonderful way to spend a day in a new place: a wedding, where everyone is celebrating love."

How ironic, she thought. She and Nate certainly weren't celebrating...

"Did you bring her here because of that Seth person you mentioned on the phone?" she asked, pushing herself back into the conversation.

"Yeah. His name is Seth Fortini. He's the CEO of the modeling agency where Juliana works, and he's her ex-boyfriend, if you want to call it that." Nate closed his notebook and set it on the bench beside him. "He hurt her..."

Sydney's eyes grew round. "Physically?"

"Yes."

"Oh, my goodness." She put her hand over her mouth to stifle the complete shock of this revelation. Juliana's images in magazines and on social media feeds were alight with glamor and good times. The press had reported that Nate and Juliana were a couple, only having the odd on-again-off-again moments. They were pictured together: grainy street shots of Nate with his arm around her while she nestled into his chest, with dark sunglasses, a cup of coffee.

"Was it during one your break-ups?" Sydney closed her laptop, placing it in the little spot of shade on the bench beside her.

"We only had a two-week relationship," he said. "We realized pretty early on that we were better as friends and we've been strictly platonic for years... It was a little like kissing my sister." He smirked. "Every time she took a trip or had a date, the press played into the rumors that we'd had some sort of huge fight. And when she started seeing Seth, Juliana didn't want the press to know she was dating him because it wouldn't reflect well on her, since he was her boss. Seth suggested that they keep it quiet, so we didn't let on that we weren't a couple."

"It seemed so believable that you two were an item…"

"We're great friends. After her break-ups, sometimes we'd go out for coffee together. I'm like her big brother, so I was the one she'd call, and I'd run right out to console her."

Sydney knew all too well about Nate's big-brother instinct; she'd felt protected by him her entire life.

"One shot of us walking together and the press can make up whatever they want, to sell magazines. I'm worried that's what's going on right now. Juliana hasn't told Seth where she is, so we don't want anyone taking photos, although I think it's probably too late for that."

"What will happen if Seth finds her?"

"I think he's pretty angry that she disappeared without warning. He left his marriage for her, falling in love with her while they were working. Although Juliana had nothing to do with the marriage breaking up. By the time she knew he was interested, the divorce was only weeks from being finalized."

"Wouldn't he just get the picture, given that she's gone?"

"He doesn't like to lose. When he gets angry, he snaps on her. She's terrified."

"Can Juliana report him?"

"I tried to encourage her to file charges. She doesn't want to. If anyone got wind of their affair, her reputation would be ruined; she's worried she'd never work a day at a reputable agency. She says she doesn't want to model anymore, but she also believes that she has to keep her options open and maintain her clean-cut appeal. At the end of the day, that's how she makes her money, and she may have to go back to that if she needs to."

"She doesn't want to model because of Seth?"

"He was hard on her. He pushed perfection in every shoot, and if she didn't fit that image, he told her to lose weight or to work out. He'd often assign trainers to focus on a specific part of her body, when I could never see what the heck he was even talking about. He told her that by pointing out her flaws, he was only trying to better her career, but no one should have to deal with what she endured. He pushed her through insane workouts that would have her so sore she'd have to take painkillers to move the next day. He only allowed her to eat food prepared by his personal chef, but I counted the calories and, given the workouts she was doing, she was way under. She felt lightheaded all the time, passing out at the end of a long day's shooting. Seth told her she was just frail, and it was a hurdle she'd have to manage if she wanted to survive at the top. For a while, she believed him. She trusted him. He was the person who'd gotten her where she was today. But once things became romantic, she started to notice the cracks. When she began to question him, he'd lash out at her, telling her she was nothing without him."

"My God." Sydney shook her head, trying to process it all. "I wish I could do something to help her." Her shoulders were tense, just thinking about it. "I asked her to model for my magazine. I hope it didn't upset her too badly."

"It's what she does. She wouldn't think a thing of it. But Seth ruined the allure for her. He stole the joy she used to find in it—that's why she doesn't want to do it anymore. It just brings back all those feelings of insecurity and pain."

She looked Nate in the eye and reached for his hand. "You're so good. I'll bet she's incredibly thankful for you."

Sydney couldn't help but draw upon her memories of how Nate had protected her in her younger days. It made her feelings for him surface, and she worried about her resolve with just the two of them out on that boat. But she had to remind herself that he hadn't come back to Firefly Beach for any length of time for her, but that he'd dropped everything and moved his entire life there for someone else.

"I'm hungry," Nate said, causing Sydney to look up from her computer.

She'd written her next two weeks' worth of email responses for the column, the inspiration coming easily to her out on the water, next to Nate. After their heavy exchange regarding Juliana, they'd settled into their work, both of them quietly creating, absorbed by their own energy, but inspired by the depth of conversation and being next to one another. Sydney hadn't felt that in so long; it was like finally getting her breath after being under water.

"Want me to get our lunches?" he asked.

She closed the various screens full of research she'd pulled up using Nate's hotspot, and saved her document, only realizing then that her stomach was growling.

"I wonder what Mama packed us," she said.

"Sandwiches," Nate said with a grin, walking over to the cooler. "I know because I caught a peek when I threw a bottle of wine and two cups into the cooler before loading it onto the boat."

She wondered why he'd gone to so much trouble to pack wine when it was just the two of them on the boat. She wasn't ready for this to get anywhere near romantic…

"I did ask Uncle Hank if I could swipe it." He popped open the lid of the cooler and dipped his hand into the ice, retrieving the bottle of white. With the bottle in his hand, he fished around in one of the bags, grabbing a corkscrew.

"I'm glad you asked Uncle Hank this time," she said with a smile.

He became still as he absorbed her statement, and then the memory passed across his face. Nate threw his head back and laughed. "We took all three of his bottles on that hike through the mountains!" He chuckled again. "How were we to know that he'd ordered them especially for Aunt Clara's business meeting and they were two hundred dollars apiece?"

The cork made a hollow pop when Nate freed it from the bottle.

"I had to clean his boat for three weeks to pay for it—one week for every bottle." He poured the wine into two plastic cups and handed her one.

Sydney took a sip, the icy cold bite of alcohol sliding down easily in the humid air outside. She grasped the cup, cooling the skin on her fingers.

"You're getting red," Nate said. "I think you should probably reapply your sun lotion."

"I'm not used to spending my workday in a bikini," she teased, getting up and digging out the lotion from her bag. She took another big drink of her wine and set it on the bench before squirting a line down her arm and rubbing it in. She followed with her legs and stomach, rubbing the excess on her towel.

Nate handed her a plastic bag with a chicken sandwich. "Let me get your back," he said. "No wonder you're so red. Have you put any on your back at all?"

"I put some spray on this morning but I can't reach it."

Nate squirted lotion into his hands and rubbed them together as she turned away from him, pulling her hair to the side. She felt his cool touch against her lower back and she had to force herself to breathe. His fingers moved up her spine and found her shoulders, kneading them softly, causing her eyes to close. His thumbs went up her neck, and it was the most amazing thing she'd felt in a long time. Nate had always been great with his hands.

"You're tense," he said, rubbing her shoulders more.

The motion and pressure of it robbed her of coherent thought.

He pressed against the muscles of her shoulders, knowing her exact pressure points. Under his touch, it was as if he were releasing the stiffness that had been there all the years she'd been without him. She opened her eyes as she felt him take the sandwich from her and then the wine and set them down, before returning his hands to her shoulders. She tried to turn to protest, but he gently turned her back around and continued working his fingers, under the tie on her swimsuit and along the large muscles on her back. She let her head drop, her shoulders slumping under the complete relaxation of it.

As he moved back to her neck, she was aware of his body closing in behind her, his breath near her ear, and the lightening of his touch to a soft caress, making her breathing become shallow. He nuzzled against her neck, his hands dropping to her waist, his fingers moving around her until he was embracing her from behind.

"I miss you, Syd," he said into her ear in a whisper. "I miss you so much it hurts."

He turned her around to face him and he put his hands on her face. She hadn't even accessed her rational brain before his lips were on hers and everything else faded away except the fireworks going off inside her. In that kiss, she felt Nate Henderson again—the sweet, loving, protective Nate that had stolen her heart all those years ago. It was like coming home. His lips moved on hers urgently, the salty taste of them making her lightheaded. She put her arms around him as if she were holding on for dear life, praying that all the things she'd known about the person he'd become over the last decade had been some sort of bad dream. The boat, writing, kissing him—it was all more her than she'd ever been.

But slowly her brain started working again. She remembered that he hadn't come back to Firefly Beach for her, and that he was no longer the boy who'd driven out of town all those years ago. He was the man who'd come back to Firefly Beach, in essence, to hide; he was the man being chased by photographers; he was the man who'd only called her once in all those years. The truth of the matter was that he felt their old chemistry being back here, and she was an easy escape for his problems. She'd let her guard down, but if she kept going on like this, it would eventually rip her heart out. She needed to find herself, to decide what exactly she wanted in life, and then she had to go get it. And if she let him, he'd pull her right back down where she was when he'd walked out on her.

She gently pushed him away. "I don't want this," she said. It was the truth. She didn't want the heartbreak anymore, the ache that she felt whenever he wasn't with her, the tears that surfaced every time she recalled how wrong she'd gotten it when she thought they'd spend forever together.

He stared at her, pain in his eyes, and she'd never seen him so exposed. Then he tipped his head back and gazed up at the clouds as if some sort of answer were hidden in them. He swallowed, blinking rapidly, and cleared his throat. "Let's pack up our stuff," he said quietly. He went over to the side and started to pull up the anchor. "I'll get you home."

"What about the photographers?"

"It's my problem, not yours." He dropped the anchor onto the boat floor and sat down in the captain's chair, leaving her still catching her breath and trying not to still feel the lingering buzz on her lips from his kiss.

With a rev of the engine, the boat was moving, making its way back to Starlight Cottage.

Chapter Fourteen

"Guess what, Mom!" Robby said, running up to Sydney when she came in. The entryway was aglow with lamplight and the smell of peppers and onions from her mother's cooking filled the air.

Nate had been unusually quiet on the boat ride home, and she was still trying to shake the pain in her chest at the thought of not seeing him anymore. He certainly wouldn't be coming by the cottage now—she could tell by the finality she'd felt between them when he'd started the engine to head home. Their last exchange seemed to have been his final effort to make amends and she'd shot him down. Nate wasn't the type to continue on pursuing things if he knew she wasn't reciprocating his feelings, and she hadn't given him even the slightest hint that she still felt anything for him. It was for her own good, she told herself.

She dropped her bags inside the front door at Starlight Cottage and squatted down to address her son. "What?" she said, trying to allow his innocence to alter her mood.

"The informational night for football is tonight."

"Tonight?

"Remember you'd asked me to sign up Robby for little league football this fall—we'd talked about it before the wedding?" Jacqueline said from the other side of the room as she came in to join the conversation. But then she seemed to catch up with Sydney's disposition, despite her daughter's attempt to hide it. She looked around. "Where's Nate?"

"He went back to Malory's." Just the mention of his name gave her a rush of guilt and confusion.

"So the photographers are gone?"

Sydney shrugged. "I have no idea."

"We get to find out our coaches and team members tonight, Mama!"

Sydney had already missed the fact that Robby's football meeting was tonight because Nate had distracted her. She wouldn't allow herself to be distracted anymore. "I'm excited!" she said to Robby, dropping the conversation about Nate, but today's events lingering in her mind. "Maybe we can get ice cream after."

"Yeah!" Robby bounced up and down, clearly delighted.

Beau must have sensed the anticipation in the air because he barked and then gobbled up his tennis ball, loping over to Robby and dropping it at his feet. Robby picked up the ball and opened the front door. "Wanna chase the ball, boy?" he asked. "Let's go!" Robby and Beau sprinted out the door toward the yard.

"Your face looked like a storm cloud when you came in," Jacqueline said. "Want to tell me what's going on?"

"Not really," Sydney replied, offering a weak smile. She never did like talking about things. "But I got a few responses done for my column and I'm ready to relax. Know what I think you and I should do?" She draped her arm around her mother, ignoring the fact that all the little moments with Nate were still buzzing through her mind.

"What's that?" Jacqueline grinned at her daughter.

"I think we should dig out the margarita mix and make ourselves some frozen drinks in the blender."

"I like this plan," her mother said. "We've got tequila in the cabinet."

They went into the kitchen and Mama plugged in the blender. "It's weird making drinks without Hallie," she noted. "The three of us are usually together when we do this."

"I miss her," Sydney said. "I hope she and Ben are having a blast."

"Has she texted you at all?"

"It's only been three days since they left," Sydney laughed. "I give her one more day before we get the text."

"I think she'll last five days. She and Ben are surely too… busy." She winked.

"No. She won't be able to stand not telling us what they're doing." Sydney grabbed the bag of ice from the freezer, topped up the blender, and poured in the margarita mix.

"I hope she brings something back for us." Mama handed Sydney the bottle of tequila. "I need a new keychain—one of those gold ones with the word 'Barbados' in brightly colored letters would be nice."

"I'd like a coffee mug."

"That's boring." Jacqueline smirked at her while salting the rims of two glasses. "You already have an entire cupboard of mugs."

"But I don't have one that says, 'I know you think I'm hotter than this coffee.'" She laughed.

Jacqueline rolled her eyes playfully.

"Or how about, 'I never intended to be the best sister, but here I am crushing it.'"

Her mother burst out laughing. "Ooooh," she said, putting a hand on Sydney's arm to interrupt her. "How about one of those woven beach bags—maybe one with an island picture intertwined in the rattan on the front. I'd like one of those."

"She needs to text us now," Sydney said with wide eyes as she hit the button on the blender, drowning out their conversation for a few seconds. When it finished mixing, she shook it around in a circle to get the slushy concoction off the sides. While she poured the margaritas into their glasses, she said, "Should *we* text *her*?"

"We shouldn't…" Jacqueline said before taking a sip from her glass. She eyed her phone, second-guessing her statement.

"You're right. It's her honeymoon. Let's leave them alone." Sydney held up her glass. "To this opportunity to be two Flynns instead of our usual three. We never get time with just the two of us and I'm thankful to have it."

"Cheers." Jacqueline tapped the rim of her glass against Sydney's. "Why don't we take our drinks outside and watch Robby and Beau play?" she suggested. "That way we won't be tempted to pick up our phones!"

With a laugh, Sydney followed her mother out of the kitchen, hoping she could put her memories of Nate's kiss aside and enjoy the moment.

They headed out the front door and then settled in the old rockers on the porch that overlooked the large expanse of wiry beach grass that made up the yard. Robby was at one end of it, running around in circles while Beau honed in on the ball that was in Robby's hand. Robby chucked it into the air, sending Beau in a frenzy of hopping and sprinting to retrieve it.

"Robby's so excited about football tonight," Mama said.

"He loves the sport. I know he can't wait for fall to get here so they can begin practices."

"I hope he gets Sam Baldwin again. He's such a good coach. I've asked him to put in a word if he gets a chance so that Robby can be on his team."

Sam had coached Robby when they'd moved back to Firefly Beach briefly after the divorce. Football had been such a help in getting Robby through the traumatic changes and disruptions that hit them when Christian left. At the tender age of five, he'd signed up for football that first year after his father had gone, and fell in love with the sport. A skinny child, Robby wasn't built for football, and he'd gotten hurt the first time he'd tried to play in the recreational league, so Sydney had urged him toward baseball. But Robby wouldn't hear of it.

"I know." Sydney took a drink from her glass, the icy cold of it a shock against the warmth settling on her skin. "He loves Sam. They had such a good season that year."

"It should be fun tonight." Jacqueline rocked back in her chair. "The meeting is a cookout and a picnic. I knew you were really busy trying to work, so I've already gotten some potato salad and a few jugs of sweet tea to bring. I signed us up for the easy stuff."

"Thank you for doing that," Sydney said, considering the fact that she still had to respond to *NY Pulse*. "It is taking me a little while to get adjusted, but I want to make sure that I spend enough time with Robby. I won't get this time back, so I really want to make sure I don't miss a thing. He's getting so big." She looked out at her son.

"It flies, baby girl," her mother replied, her doting eyes on Sydney. "You were in that yard with your hula hoops and batons just yesterday, I swear. I blinked and you landed in this chair beside me." She tipped her margarita up against her lips and took a slow drink.

"Watch this, Mama!" Robby called over to Sydney. He tossed the ball high into the air, did a spin, and caught it on its way back down.

"Wow, good catch!" she said back to him.

"Wanna see me do it again?"

"Of course I do!" She was so happy just sitting on that porch with her mother. There was nowhere she'd rather be.

"I didn't want to bombard you with this right when you walked in," her mother said as they sat on the porch, their glasses long empty. "We should check on Uncle Hank. He's low today. I thought he was taking a nap earlier, but I found him in tears up in his bedroom."

"What's wrong?"

Her mother shook her head. "I'm not sure. Lewis tried to get him to tell him, but he wouldn't. He talks to you."

"Do you think he's worried about selling Starlight Cottage?"

"I don't know. Maybe you can get it out of him."

Robby poked his head out the door. "Mom, I can't find my football jersey for the picnic. Can you help me?"

"I'll go," her mother said, standing up and heading inside with her grandson.

Sydney went through the house and out to the back porch that overlooked the sparkling gulf and the towering lighthouse, its white brick reaching into the heavens, contrasting with the nautical colors of the gulf behind it. It was one of Uncle Hank's favorite spots at the cottage. He always sat out there when he was thinking things over.

"Hey," she said, sitting down beside him on the porch swing.

He didn't turn toward her, his gaze still on the white beach that snaked along the property, but he nodded, acknowledging her presence.

"Wanna tell me what you're thinking about?"

Uncle Hank let out a sigh, causing Beau, who had followed them out and was now sunning himself at the edge of the porch, to lift his head and assess the situation. Seeing no immediate threat, the dog put his chin down on his paws and closed his eyes once more.

"I've just been thinking about how things change," Uncle Hank said. He finally looked her way. "I understand that life continues to move forward, but it never bothered me until I was an old man." He rubbed his hands along his thighs, his fingers unsteady. "I keep trying to be normal in a world that doesn't work for me anymore. Clara's gone. The town I adore is about to plow through my favorite view. And I feel useless." His bottom lip began to wobble and he pursed his lips to keep it still, tears surfacing. "I'm being forced to sell this cottage—Clara's dream; the place we built together. I can't even have my home. What is my reason for being here?"

It was clear that Uncle Hank's mind had slipped back to the same sadness he'd felt when she'd first arrived in Firefly Beach after Aunt Clara's death. She understood how that could happen; she knew all too well how easily old emotions could bubble to the surface.

"This is just an idea, but do you think hearing someone else's perspective might help? Mary Alice could work through your feelings with you. She's really good."

He stood up with a huff, rocking the swing by the shift of his weight. "I don't need a counselor. I need my life back." He folded his arms, his weathered hands gripping his biceps so tightly that the ends of his fingers were white.

Sydney hadn't meant to hit a nerve. She'd only been trying to help. "She won't try to convince you that you don't need your life back. She'll just help you find a way to understand it that you hadn't thought of before, which can sometimes help you manage a little better."

His shoulders rounded. "I'm an old man, Sydney. I mean no disrespect, but I'm living in a world where kids are running my life, and sitting in a room with the little girl who used to sell lemonade with you on the corner isn't going to help me." He blew air through his lips. "I'll be fine," he said, but she didn't believe him.

Sydney stood up in front of him, wishing she could hear Aunt Clara's voice to soothe them both. "Uncle Hank, you're the wisest person I know. If I were battling with something big, what would you tell me?"

"I don't know." He shook his head.

"Yes you do. You've never just let us flounder when we have problems. You've gotten me through every single one."

He leaned on the railing, his arms stretched out, his fingers gripping the whitewashed wood. "I'd tell you to follow your heart, not your head. But that's just it: my heart is somewhere unreachable at the moment."

"So what does your heart say about Starlight Cottage?" she asked.

He dragged his finger affectionately along the railing. "It aches to keep it the same. For Clara. And for me."

"Then let's do everything we can to make that happen. I'll go with you to the meeting Friday." She took Uncle Hank's hand. "We can do this." A seed of resolution stirred inside her, and no matter what, she'd fight for Starlight Cottage until the end.

Chapter Fifteen

Sydney's phone lit up with a text as it sat on the table beside her computer while she tinkered around with the cover design for the wellness center. It was Malory.

Coffee?

With everything going on, Sydney had forgotten that she'd mentioned getting coffee with Malory at her party. She'd been busy working the rest of the day while Robby was at his friend's house, and she'd emailed *NY Pulse* magazine to give them days and times when she'd be available to discuss the content editor position.

With a couple hours before Robby's football meeting, Sydney decided it would be nice to spend some time with her friend. It was such a gorgeous evening that she decided it would be a perfect night to walk, so she texted Malory that she'd meet her at Cup of Sunshine in fifteen minutes if she was up to it.

Malory texted back:

Absolutely! Sliding on my flip-flops right now…

Sydney shut down her laptop and scribbled a quick note to her mom, letting her know where she was headed. Then she slipped on her sandals, grabbed her handbag and sunglasses, and headed out the door, deciding to take the shortcut past the lighthouse, down the beach, and along the coast.

The sea air wrapped around her like a warm hug, blowing her long hair behind her shoulders, and caressing her skin. Sydney walked through the yard toward the tree-laden area where she and Nate used to write in the shade of the palms. She ran her fingers down the spiny bark of a palm tree, remembering all the times she'd sat on a blanket under it, her notebooks spread out around her…

She walked further in, along the old path the people who lived on these lots had carved out to allow them to pass through until they reached the next clearing. She hadn't been down this path in years. The sun shined through the trees, casting long rays through their leaves, blinding her and then relenting as she walked along. Then suddenly, something caught her eye, making her gasp. A rusted thumbtack jutted out from one of the trees, a tiny torn piece of paper still speared into the bark. She touched it, remembering the notes she'd put up for Nate to give him inspiration. As she ran her hand over the remnant of it, barely even a visible piece of it left, she closed her eyes, hoping to hear Nate's voice calling her. Would he walk up behind her and pull her back to that time in her life when everything seemed to be perfect? She kept her eyes closed and waited, the shushing of the gulf mocking the silence.

She opened her eyes and started walking again. Every tree, every bend in the path ahead of her was like a graveyard for her memories, each one preserved in that space, lingering there and calling out to her to remember. She fought the swell of fear at the thought that all this would be a parking lot soon. Her memories bulldozed without a single thought. Suddenly, she wanted to run back to Starlight Cottage and plead with Uncle Hank not to sell.

When she finally emerged onto the main street in town, she surveyed the intersection. It was lined with tourists, the shop doors clogged with people, the stoplights congested and all the area picnic tables brimming, people spilling out of the outdoor dining areas onto the sidewalk, stopping foot traffic. She maneuvered around passers-by and made her way to Cup of Sunshine, plunging herself into the air-conditioned interior.

Malory waved from a table she'd saved for them.

"This is crazy," Sydney said, squeezing herself into a chair. "It's not even the weekend."

"It doesn't matter when it's late afternoon, in-season. All the vacationers are here for the whole week and they probably don't even know what day it is. On Sundays, I can hardly get in and out of the village with all the traffic leaving their rentals. It's a nightmare." She scooted a cup of iced coffee toward Sydney. "I got you an iced caramel latte."

"How did you guess my favorite?" she asked.

"Nate suggested it when I said we were getting coffee together." She offered a cautious smile. "He said, 'When in doubt, go sweet.'"

Sydney chuckled. "He always did know what I like." She took a sip, and settled in to the space between the two of them.

"How do you like being back?" Malory asked her.

"It's where I belong," she said. "The longer I stay here, the more I realize how much I need the sea air and the open spaces."

They both looked around at the coffee line that was nearly out the door, the trail of sand coming in on all their feet, the beach bags—full to the brim—bumping into people. "Open spaces," Malory said, and they both laughed.

Then a man in line caught her eye and raised his hand, his smile very familiar. She realized it was Logan, from the wedding. She smiled at him.

"Who's that?" Malory said, her tone playfully suggestive.

"His name is Logan Hayes. I met him at Hallie's wedding."

"He looks very happy to see you."

"He's really nice."

"You should go say hello… I would."

She noticed that Ariel Barnes was a few people behind him. Ariel worked at the candy shop in town and she'd made friends with Robby, offering him his favorite peppermint spinner whenever he came in—a candy that would actually spin on its stick. She'd talk to Ariel first. That would be a great way to break the ice.

"Okay. Be right back. And while I'm up there, I'll mention that you're single…" Sydney teased.

Malory's eyes got as big as saucers, and then she looked back at Logan, clearly considering, making Sydney laugh. "I wouldn't hold it against you if you did."

Sydney stood up and went over to Ariel. "Hi," she said, coming up behind her friend.

"Oh!" Ariel said, her two dark French braids swinging madly as she offered Sydney a warm hug. "It's so nice to see you!"

"Same. Robby is dying to get in for your peppermint spinner."

Ariel gave a warm smile, her freckled cheekbones pushing her black-rimmed glasses up. "Any time. You know, I've made a larger one now. And I found a way to get a rainbow-colored flash light on the end of the stick!"

"That's amazing! He'll love it."

"Bring him in soon. I need someone to taste-test my new chocolate line."

"I'd be happy to do that for you myself," Sydney said with a laugh.

The line moved, causing them all to step forward.

"Well, it was nice to see you," Sydney said.

"You too!"

She walked forward in line as if she were headed back to her table and when Logan made eye contact, she stepped back over to talk to him. "Hey," she said, joining him in the line.

"Hey there." He offered her a warm smile. "It's so nice to see you."

"Same. Would you like to join us?" she asked, nearly sure by Malory's response to him that she wouldn't object.

"I wish I could. I was running errands and I'm grabbing a coffee for my mom on the way back to the cottage. But I demand a rain check."

Sydney grinned. "Absolutely. Well, it was great to run into you."

"I'll text you once I get home and we can set up a time." He looked around at the crowds. "Maybe not *this* time of day."

"Definitely not." Sydney said her goodbyes and then headed back to Malory, glad to have seen Logan again.

"Okay, tell me the date and time," Malory said once she'd returned to the table.

"Date and time?"

"Of my date with Logan."

They both fell into their usual laughter. Sydney was so happy to be back with her friend again. If everything could be as easy as rekindling their friendship.

"Robby! Did you get your football?" Sydney called upstairs as she scrolled through the email on her phone that had all the details for tonight. The kids were all meeting at the park where they'd receive their coaches and team assignments.

She was about to put her phone in her back pocket when the screen lit up, drawing her attention back down to a text. Sydney swiped it open. It read:

Hey, it's Nate. I just wanted to warn you before you got here. I'm coaching for the Firefly Little League, and Robby's on my team. I just got the roster.

A barrage of conflicting emotions swarmed her: the thrill that he had her cell number and they were still somehow connected, the fear that she'd have to face him tonight after their talk on the boat today, the unsettling idea that Nate might be sticking around in Firefly Beach, and that he and Robby would be spending an entire football season together.

She texted back:

Thanks for letting me know. See you soon.

"Ready to go?" Robby asked, hopping down the last step from upstairs. He had his ball under his arm, his favorite jersey and shorts making him look more grown up than he usually did. He was visibly buzzing with anticipation.

"I sure am!" she said, sliding her phone into her pocket. "Let's go!"

Sydney opened the car door to let Beau out. She'd decided to leash him up and bring him with her since he'd been cooped up at Firefly Beach since Ben had left. She unhooked his lead and grabbed his tennis ball from the floorboard. "Ready?" she said to him.

Beau's feet were tapping unmercifully against the dirt, his tail swinging wildly in circles. Sydney chucked the ball across the field, and Beau went tearing after it. He retrieved it in seconds, and galloped back to Sydney, dropping it at her feet, his tongue hanging from the side of his mouth as he panted, his loyal eyes on her.

Sydney threw the ball again and Beau chased it once more.

"I know a little secret," she said once Robby had exited the car and walked around to her side.

"What is it?" he asked.

Beau dropped the ball and nuzzled Robby's hand until he picked it up and threw it again.

"I already know who your coach is and I think you're gonna be really excited."

At the end of the day, no matter what her problems were with Nate, one thing she knew without a doubt was that he'd be an amazing coach. He was so patient with Robby and he knew the game of football inside and out. Plus, the end of football season might provide her a nice, clean way to break the relationship with Nate and Robby. With Ben and Hallie staying primarily in Firefly Beach this year to be near family and prepare for their adoption, Ben would be right there to jump in and fill Nate's shoes. Then Sydney could finally cut him out of her life and move on. "Want to know?"

Robby's eyes grew round. "Who is it?"

Just then, she caught sight of Nate and turned Robby around, pointing toward him.

"Nate's my coach?" Robby broke into an enormous grin and went running toward him, Beau trotting after him. Sydney picked up Beau's ball and followed them.

"Hey, buddy!" Nate said. He reached down and petted Beau, the dog's tail spinning circles with pleasure. He met Sydney's eyes but then turned his focus back to her son. "Are you ready for some football this season?"

"Yes, sir!" Robby stepped back a few paces and lifted the ball into a pass position.

Nate put up his hands, catching the ball when Robby threw it. He tossed it back. "Let's go to the table and find out who else is on the team." He turned to Sydney. "May I take him?"

"Of course," she said, reaching down to take Beau's collar so she could hook up his leash. Beau sat dutifully and allowed her to get a hold of him.

As she let them go, Nate and Robby walked together, their backs to Sydney. Robby was looking up at his new coach, talking animatedly, the football under his arm, while Nate laughed at something he'd said. The sight of it pinched her chest.

All of a sudden, her phone went off, startling her. She peered down at the caller. "Ha!" she said to no one, wishing her mom was there to witness Hallie calling. She answered it immediately. "How is Barbados?" she asked without even a hello.

"Amazing! I got you a coffee mug."

Sydney smiled. "You know me so well."

"How's everything at home?"

"Apart from Robby running off with Nate, his new best friend and football coach, not much."

"What?!"

Sydney pulled the phone from her ear to save her eardrum. "Yes."

Hallie's voice came through muffled as she had evidently turned from the phone to relay this information to Ben.

"Sorry," she said, coming back to Sydney. "Ben and I are at the most incredible place right now having drinks. It's all pillars and white tablecloths with sparkling wine and the whole place hovers over the ocean. It's absolutely incredible."

"So why are you on the phone? You should be enjoying it!"

"I am! I just wanted to check in. Here, I'll put you on speaker. There's no one around at the moment and Ben wants to hear all about Nate and Robby."

"So have you two finally made up?" Ben's voice came through the phone.

Sydney started walking around the field with Beau in one hand and her phone in the other. "I wouldn't say we've made up. I think I've finally found some closure."

"I don't buy it," Ben said.

"Why not?"

"He's crazy for you. He's been in love with you since the day he rolled out of town."

She looked over at Nate in the distance. He was to the side of the team tent, kneeling down with a group of boys, smiling, making them laugh.

"He has a funny way of showing it," she said, Ben's comment making no sense at all. Why would he have left her and hurt her so terribly if he loved her? "I think you're mistaken. Nobody rolls out of town when they're crazy about someone."

"I'm not mistaken," Ben said. "But it isn't my place to get involved. I just thought he'd have told you, that's all."

Juliana waved from across the field and started making her way over to Sydney.

"Have you gotten Mama anything, Hallie?" she asked, changing the subject. She threw her hand up to Juliana.

"Not yet! I'm still looking…"

"You should get her a beach bag or a keychain," Sydney suggested, another grin surfacing at the thought of her earlier conversation with her mother.

"Oh, yes! I saw these cool woven bags at a corner market. I'll find her a really great one… I can't wait to see you."

"How's Beau doing?" Ben chimed in.

"He's missing you," she told him. "He loafs around most of the time. I've got him at the park with me right now while Robby's at his first football meeting. Here, talk to him. I'll put you on speaker." She tapped her phone screen.

"Hey, boy!" Ben called through the phone. "I'll be home soon, okay?"

Beau's ears perked up, and he lifted his head to sniff the phone, his tail wagging.

"He's rolling his eyes and telling me you'd better bring him back a new toy for the lack of ball-chasing he's had to endure in your absence," Sydney said with a laugh. Juliana had nearly reached her, so Sydney said, "I'm going to go, okay? But call me back later if you want to catch up some more."

They said their goodbyes as Juliana strolled up.

"May I walk with you?" Juliana asked from behind her sunglasses. She was wearing a form-fitting spandex workout suit with designer sneakers, her dark hair pulled tightly into a smooth ponytail at the back of her head, accentuating her high cheekbones.

"Of course." Sydney started to walk along the small track that circled the field while Beau jogged beside her. "No photographers today?"

"It seems like it was just the one. Not sure if they were after Nate or me. Sometimes they will do that when we are in remote places; someone will get word about where we are and they certainly aren't going to tell anyone so they can have the exclusive. When we didn't come out, he probably finally gave up."

"Dodging them all must be exhausting."

"Yes…"

"And you're sure it was someone from the press and not a hired photographer from your agency?"

"I am not sure," she said, her frown pulling down her features, showing her stress. "Nate said he told you about Seth." She pushed her dark glasses onto the top of her head and made eye contact with Sydney.

"Yes. I'm so sorry that happened to you."

Juliana peered over at Nate. "I am so thankful for that man," she stated, her whole body now turned toward him.

Sydney stopped walking to stand next to her, and Beau turned around to see what was going on. Then he sat, clearly waiting to keep going.

"He is easy to love," she said. "I fell head over heels for him, but he did not feel the same way for me, so we settled for friends."

Sydney was surprised by Juliana's admission. Here Juliana was, confessing that she'd loved Nate, and he hadn't loved her back. Sydney could definitely relate to that. How glamorous Juliana Vargas's life had seemed from the outside. Any bystander would assume she could get anyone she wanted. Sydney was learning that things definitely weren't always what they seemed. She and Juliana weren't all that different.

"I cannot see myself dating him now," Juliana said. "We have been friends for too long. But I always wonder who will have his heart in the end." She pivoted around to face Sydney. "Whoever it is, is a lucky woman." She let out a wistful sigh. "He is a good man."

"Do you think people change?" Sydney asked as she watched Nate running with the kids.

"I don't think people change entirely. They just learn more about what they are and are not capable of. And sometimes, you think you know someone, but you have not really *heard* them yet. My grandfather used to say, 'If you want to know someone, listen to their stories—every single one. Who they are is in their stories.'" Juliana slipped her glasses back down over her eyes and resumed walking.

"I definitely know Nate's stories," Sydney said, leaning more toward the idea that Nate was who he was and there was no changing him.

"Ah, but you have not heard them *all*."

"What hasn't he told me?" Sydney asked.

"I haven't heard them all either," Juliana said. "But when it comes to you, he definitely has stories to tell." She pressed her full lips together, seemingly thinking about something. Finally, she said, "He told me once that he loves you. I asked him how he could love someone he hasn't seen in ten years. He said, 'Because I know her soul.' That is pretty powerful."

First Ben and now Juliana. It didn't make any sense. "He left me," she said. "He just walked out on me, out of the blue, to pursue his music career. Not a call—nothing. Just gone."

"I'm afraid I have no answers for you," Juliana said. "He has never told me about this."

Perhaps Nate hadn't told Juliana that part of his little fairy-tale love story. Maybe Ben and Juliana were both wrong about him. After all, Sydney was the one who had known him best. She should stop allowing others to cloud her judgment.

"Will you ask him about this?" Juliana said.

"I don't have any questions about it," Sydney returned. It was pretty clear to her what had happened that day and for the years following. She deserved better.

Chapter Sixteen

When Sydney arrived at the wellness center to show Mary Alice a few ideas she'd come up with, her office door was closed. She checked her watch. Mary Alice had said to come by at nine o'clock. Sydney wasn't late. She was actually ten minutes early, so Mary Alice must have started her first session before the regular counseling time. On her way to the spare room they'd been using, Sydney had gotten both her and Mary Alice a coffee from Cup of Sunshine, but now she stood holding both cups, wondering how cold Mary Alice's would be in an hour when the door reopened. She walked into the small kitchenette area at the back of the office and set the paper cup on the counter. With nothing to do, she took her own coffee into the spare room and opened her email. Perhaps she could write a few responses while she waited, and get ahead.

Her skin prickled with anticipation as she saw an email from *NY Pulse* magazine. She opened the message. They wanted to talk today. She could hardly contain her excitement. Sydney looked up from her phone at the empty room, just dying to share the news with someone. This was the first big shot she'd ever taken with her writing. She typed back that today would be great and she was eager to hear what they had to say. Then she noticed she'd never responded to mel4221's last email. She reread the last bit of the message:

… She isn't coming back to me, and I can hardly manage, knowing that she was the one person in this life who completed me. I haven't found anyone who can fill her shoes since. What if I've ruined everything by letting her go?

This was definitely difficult to answer, given the fact that she replayed that last moment with Nate over and over in her head, wondering the same thing. If she'd run after him that day, would he have stopped the truck? Had he been waiting for her to stop him? But she knew that she was overanalyzing things. She'd given him a million opportunities to stay. It had been his decision to leave her, and he'd been pretty clear about it.

She hit respond and typed an email back.

Hi Mel,

Do you ever wonder why someone so perfect for you actually isn't The One? I had a similar situation and wonder that all the time. What leads people in the wrong directions?

Sydney stared at her response. It wasn't really a response at all, but more of a conversation she was starting with this person. But the problem was, there wasn't an answer to this. If there was, she certainly hadn't found it. She signed her name and hit send.

Then she pulled up the spreadsheet with Mary Alice's budget. Juliana wouldn't model for the cover, and she and Nate would've been perfect, not to mention she probably could've gotten them at a good price. She opened up a search screen on her computer and typed in a search for local models, but there wasn't a whole lot in the vicinity of Firefly Beach.

Before she could consider her options, her phone lit up, and to her complete surprise, mel4221 had responded again. She opened the email.

I think it comes down to bad timing and wrong choices. Do you ever wish you could rewind the clock and start again? Would things be different?
Mel

Sydney debated whether or not she should send another email to Mel, but as she considered this, she thought it might help the poor guy. He was really going through a rough patch, it seemed, and perhaps her personal experience could help him in some way. She typed back:

I agree. Definitely wrong choices. And if I were able to rewind the clock, sadly I don't think it would change a thing. Our paths are a muddle of ups and downs, but in the end, they are our paths—we can't unwind them and make them cleaner or straighter. They just are the way they are. I hope someday you can find some closure.

She sent the message and set her phone down on the table, the conversation with this stranger sitting heavily. But in a flash, she got a single-line response.

Have you been lucky enough to have closure? I haven't.

That was a tough one. She didn't dare tell him that she hadn't; that, years later, he may still be just as heartbroken. But cutting through her thoughts was another message from mel4221.

If you could write a letter to him, what would you say?

This was getting personal. Quickly, she fired off an answer.

I don't think my love letter to him would impact your dilemma.

Another email came back to her:

Love? Did you say love letter? You still love him?

Shoot. Did she say "love"? She reread her message and gritted her teeth. She hadn't meant to say that, but it must have just come out with her honesty. What could she say to his question, other than the obvious? She sent back an answer:

Yes. I will always love him.

She hated to dash Mel's hopes that he could move on, but she was just being honest. Sydney waited for his reaction to her answer, but her phone sat silent, the back-and-forth suddenly over. Then suddenly, a final response, and what it said surprised her.

I'm happy to know you still love him. I feel the same way about her. Thank you for chatting with me and for making my day.

Well, that went better than expected, she thought. But then a second email came through.

One day soon, I'm going to show her how much I love her.

While Sydney liked the romantic idea of this guy professing his love to the girl of his dreams, she did worry that things might not end the way he hoped. She opened another email to warn him. She considered telling him how her own situation hadn't worked so well, but then she reconsidered. It would be a long story, and she didn't want to bring Nate into this. And what if she deterred him, and it kept him from rekindling things with this woman? It would be best to let time take its course. With a sigh, she deleted the draft.

Mary Alice's door was still closed, so Sydney decided perhaps she should come back another time. She peeked into the lobby to see if anyone was waiting, and to her surprise, Juliana was on the sofa reading a magazine.

"Hello," Juliana said, raising a long, lean hand at Sydney. "I am early."

"I'm sure it's fine," Sydney said, moving over to her. "You okay?"

Juliana folded her hands, her shoulders tense. "The photographer must have been Seth's. He texted me and said if I did not go back and finish out my contract, he would have me in breach of the agreement."

"Oh no." Sydney sat down next to her, giving Juliana her full attention.

"I'm scared of him," Juliana whispered.

"Is there any way to work for him without actually being in the same place?"

Anger flashed in Juliana's eyes. "He does not want my work. He wants to make my life miserable. No one tells him no."

"How is he able to do this?" Sydney said, concerned for her new friend.

"Look at the life he gave me. Aspiring models die for that kind of life. They will put up with a lot and they will keep it quiet." She crossed her legs, her delicate sandal dangling from her painted toes. "I noticed how most of them kept their distance from him, but I was too naïve to read the signs and when he became friendly with me, I fell right into it. He loves the power of making people into superstars and he will not allow me to be successful if I am not working for him. I am worried he is going to hurt me…"

Sydney covered her gaping mouth. "Oh my God," she said, aghast.

Juliana's eyes glistened with fear but the noise of Mary Alice's door opening caused her to wipe her face clean of any worry she had.

Mary Alice came walking briskly toward them behind the couple that was leaving. "Oh my goodness!" she said when she saw Sydney. "I haven't had a minute to spare. I'm so sorry."

"No worries at all," Sydney told her. "We can catch up later."

"Thank you," she said with relief. "You're welcome to work here in the office today, if you need a quiet place."

"I actually have a call," Sydney said. "It might be good to take it here."

"Absolutely!" Mary Alice said. Then she turned to Juliana. "Hello. I'm so sorry you've had to wait." She peered down at her watch. "Oh good, I'm not too late." Mary Alice pushed a smile across her face. "Come on back."

It was time for her call from *NY Pulse*. She was oddly calm about the whole thing. It was so incredibly out of her league that she couldn't even feel nervous about it. The idea that she could beat out her competition with no real experience, on a single submission, was ridiculous, so she kept her excitement in check. She was more curious to hear what it was about her writing that had interested them.

"Hello, this is Sydney Flynn," she said, answering the call.

"Ah, hello, Sydney. My name is Amanda Rains. I am the editor-in-chief of *NY Pulse*. How are you?"

"I'm doing well, thank you," she said, her heartbeat rising at the thrill of speaking to Mrs. Rains herself. She'd read about her after submitting, and her experience in the field was unmatched.

"I'm glad to hear it," Amanda said with authority. "I have to say, I read your submission personally, and I was blown away. The intimacy you created in drawing connections between your family and the elements of renovation actually brought me to tears at one point. I loved the idea of the new layers of paint not covering over, but *protecting* the old, sealing it in, the way we internalize our family values. It was incredible. It's *exactly* what I'm looking for."

"Wow," Sydney said, unable to manage anything else.

"If you're still interested in the position, I'd want to give you a couple more writing tasks to see what you've got, with a pretty quick turn-around to get a feel for what you can produce under a time-limit. And if you can do it, the next step would be to fly you up to New York for a formal interview. What do you think?"

Sydney's hands were getting sweaty now. This was huge. Probably the biggest opportunity that she'd ever gotten in her life. And she hadn't even really been trying. It was just a whim, a sort of writing lottery she'd entered with Hallie. She'd never thought for a second she'd actually get a call…

"Would you like some time to think it over?" Amanda asked into the silence.

"Oh," Sydney said, realizing she hadn't answered. "I'd love to try to write the pieces for you," she said, thankful, now, that she was well ahead on her column articles for the *Gazette*.

"Perfect. Shall I send them to the same email from your original submission?"

"Yes, that would be great." Sydney's mind buzzed with the reality that this was actually happening.

"Lovely. I'll get them out to you today. It was so nice speaking to you."

"Great talking to you too," she said. "Thank you for this opportunity."

"You're welcome. I can't wait to see what you send me."

Sydney finished the call and sat in the middle of the empty room at the wellness center, stunned. Had that really just happened? She couldn't believe it. But once the excitement had worn off, a new fear set in. Was she ready for something like this? Chances were that she might not get this kind of opportunity again. Did she have what it takes?

Mary Alice knocked on the doorframe of Sydney's open office door and held up the coffee she'd left in the kitchen this morning. "Did you know you left a full coffee on the counter?" she asked, looking completely ragged. Her normally neatly tied-back hair was wispy, her cheeks red, her eyes tired.

"It was for you," Sydney said with a half smile.

"Oh, I'm so sorry," Mary Alice said, coming in and setting it on Sydney's desk before dropping into the chair across from Sydney. "I was so busy. I've got more patients than I have time to see." She ran her hands down her face and squeezed her eyes shut before looking back at Sydney. "It's a good problem to have, but I'm not sure what to do." She leaned forward and popped the lid off the coffee, obviously deciding if it was worth drinking the ice-cold, five-hours-old beverage. She must have decided against it, because she sat back in the chair with a huff. "My mom's coming to pick me up for dinner," she said with a smile. "I need a nice night out."

"I love your mom," Sydney said. The memories came to mind of Mrs. Chambers bringing them cupcakes with their names on them after field hockey games and dressing up for Halloween in the most extravagant costumes just to make them all laugh.

"She's going to be very excited to see you," Mary Alice replied. "She's asked about you a couple of times since you've been back."

"We should all get together soon." Sydney closed down her computer for the day. "I'll walk you out and tell her hello."

"You're welcome to grab Robby and meet us for dinner tonight," Mary Alice offered.

"Thank you, but I should probably get home and make sure Mama doesn't need any help with dinner.

Just then, Mary Alice's mother, Susan Chambers, walked through the door. She had the same friendly eyes and bobbed hairstyle she'd always had but her amber brown locks were graying now.

"Oh, Sydney," she said, her arms stretched wide to embrace her. "I have missed you, my sweet girl." She pulled Sydney into a bear hug, the floral scent of her perfume registering as one of the markers of Sydney's childhood. She pulled back. "Are you coming to dinner with us?"

"Probably not tonight," Sydney said, "but another time, I promise."

"I'm going to hold you to that." She fluttered her hands in the air, some sort of excitement hitting her. "We should have all of you kids together! Nate's back, you're here. We could get Malory to join us… It would be just like those days when I had you all in my kitchen after school, hanging out."

"Maybe we could," Sydney said. But she really wasn't ready to spend a night reminiscing about old times. It would only serve as a reminder of a life path she hadn't taken.

"Have you seen Nate since the wedding?" she asked. "Mary Alice told me he would be there."

"I have, actually," Sydney said, purposely not elaborating to keep the conversation light.

Susan fluffed one of the pillows on the sofa nearby, her mothering instincts still on high alert. "I'm so glad," she said as she reached for the stack of magazines, straightening them. She looked around the office waiting room where they were standing. "You know, he's the reason Mary Alice came back to Firefly Beach."

"Oh?" Susan's statement had completely stunned Sydney.

"Yep," Susan said with a doting look to Mary Alice. "He was the one who talked her into giving up her job, moving to Firefly Beach, and starting her own practice."

"Nate? Nate *Henderson*?"

"Yes," Mary Alice said with a nod. She gathered her bags and slid them up onto her shoulder.

Sydney walked with them to the door. "I'd love to hear that story."

Mary Alice cut off the lights. "I'll tell you one day, but I can't tell you *everything*. Patient confidentiality and all… But, as an old friend, not a counselor, I urge you to try to get him to open up."

As Sydney drove home, Uncle Hank's words went round and round in her head: *We all make mistakes, Sydney*. Could Nate have changed for the better? What had Mary Alice meant by "everything"? She couldn't tell her *everything*, she'd said. What didn't Sydney know? And after all, she wasn't so sure she wanted Nate to open up. If he *had* changed, he was going to have to convince her beyond a shadow of doubt that he had, because it would take a whole lot for her to let him into her heart again.

Chapter Seventeen

Frustration slithered through Sydney as she parked her car next to Nate's old truck. It had a shiny new paint job, but she could tell it was the same one he'd had all those years ago by the beach shop sticker in the back window.

She still remembered when he'd put that sticker on. They'd been on the beach all day. Sydney lay next to Nate on her towel in the sand, the warmth of the sun playing with her consciousness.

"Let's get ice cream," Nate said, rolling over onto his stomach, pulling her from her dreamlike haze that drowned out everything but the rushing surf and coastal wind. He leaned over her, his shadow allowing her to focus on the adoration in his eyes as he looked at her.

"I don't want to get up," she said, hoping he'd look at her like that forever.

He leaned down and kissed her. The salty taste of his lips was a sensation she'd never forget. It was the taste of every summer she'd spent with him.

He took her hands and pinned them playfully above her head. "You know you want some mint chocolate chip," he said.

"Stop." She giggled as she squirmed away from him. "You're all hot and sandy."

"Hot for *you*," he said, pulling her to him and nuzzling her neck.

"Get off," she squealed with laughter. "There are families on the beach."

"And they'll all know I adore you." He kissed her again.

She wriggled to a sitting position and he ran his fingers through her hair, pulling her to him for another kiss. "This is my ploy to get a cup of double chocolate swirl," he teased, kissing her over and over.

She laughed. "Let's go," she said, relenting and standing up.

They gathered their things and headed to the ice cream parlor, where they got ice cream cones—giant waffle cones with piles and piles of ice cream. Beside the ice cream parlor was the beach shop, and they walked the aisles of the store, licking their cones.

"I need to have these shades," Nate said, slipping on a ridiculous pair of blaze-orange sunglasses.

Sydney laughed and took them off him. "Don't hide that gorgeous face," she said.

He grabbed her with one arm, his ice cream coming precariously close to a rack of T-shirts. "I love you," he said, looking into her eyes. A grumpy shopkeeper glanced over at them from his spot at the register.

"Wonder what happened to *that* guy today? We should buy something so we can try to make him smile," he said, looking around.

"I'm not sure that's possible," she said quietly. "He looks like he's having the worst day ever."

Nate grabbed a sticker from a pile on one of the shelves and took it up to pay for it. "Hang on," he said to the guy and ran back to where he and Sydney had been standing to grab the orange sunglasses. "These too," he said, putting them on the counter. "The lady secretly loves them," he whispered, but the guy just rang up the items and handed him the bag.

When they got outside, Nate handed her the bag. "Wait right here," he told her. Then he strode off toward the ice cream shop and after a few minutes returned with a giant sundae.

Sydney eyed the dripping vanilla scoops with chocolate sauce and sprinkles. "Still hungry?" she kidded him.

He offered a mischievous grin and nodded toward the door of the shop for her to go back inside. Nate walked in and set the sundae on the counter. "Whatever kind of morning you've had is gone. All you have ahead of you now is sunshine and a sundae."

A tiny smirk broke through at one corner of the man's mouth. "I can't find my cat," the man admitted. "She's lost."

"What's her name?" Nate asked, sobering.

"I named her after the day I got her because I think she saved me." He looked down at the ice cream. "Her name is Sunday," he said, meeting Nate's eyes.

They both shared a moment, realizing that Nate had told the man that the only thing ahead of him was sunshine and a *sundae*.

Nate got a description of the cat and promised he'd look for it. And then when they got outside, he put the shop sticker on his truck. "I want to remember this," he said, "because when we first went in, I thought that guy was just having a bad day, but he was suffering." He smoothed out the sticker and looked at it for a while. "I want to remind myself not to take people's reactions at face value. Everyone needs someone to hear them."

Coming back to the present, Sydney could almost taste the ice cream on her lips, and she realized she'd been standing at Nate's truck for quite a while. She went inside and followed laughter, walking straight to the kitchen where she found Nate and Robby sitting at the table together, hovered over a piece of paper.

Sydney dropped her keys on the table and peered down at them. "Is that math homework?" she asked.

Nate looked up. "Hey, Syd," he said as if it were totally regular for him to be sitting at the table with her son. "Yes," he answered finally. "Robby texted me so I came over to help."

"You texted?" she asked her son.

"He told me to text any time," Robby said.

"He told you to text any time," she repeated for clarity she knew she wouldn't get. "And you texted him on your emergency cell phone that I got you?"

"It *was* an emergency. I had five word problems tonight. They're really hard and Uncle Hank didn't know how to do them either." Robby had had a tutor for the summer, after falling behind in school a little bit last school year. She came over once a week to review with him and then she usually left him a few assignments to complete. With Sydney having so much on her plate with moving back to Firefly Beach and taking care of Uncle Hank and the cottage, and her mother being a lost cause at math, Uncle Hank had been stepping in as much as he could. But sometimes, given his health, he just wasn't up for it.

Sydney shifted her attention to Nate. "You gave Robby your number?"

"I gave it to the whole team," he said, pointing to the football team roster that she, herself, had pinned to the fridge with a magnet after the informational night.

"Look," Robby said, turning the homework paper around. "Nate knew how to do them all."

"But do *you* know how to do them all?" she asked.

"Yeah, Nate is a really good teacher! He even made me two new problems to solve on my own and I did it!" He grinned fondly at Nate. "Are we done now?"

"If you feel like you've got it," Nate said, reaching down to rub Beau's head as the dog sat up in response to Robby climbing off his chair.

"Okay," Robby replied. "I'm gonna go out on the porch with Uncle Hank and everybody."

"Wait, don't you want some dinner?" she asked.

"I already ate," he said. "Nate made us all burgers on the grill." Robby ran over to the door and let himself out, taking Beau with him.

"*You* hungry?" Nate asked once they were alone.

"I'll just make a sandwich," she said.

"Nonsense. I've got a bunch of food left." He stood up and walked over to the fridge, like he owned the place, pulling out a plate of burgers covered in plastic wrap.

Sydney wrestled with the two sides of her mind. Part of her wanted to sit down with Nate, asking him about what Mary Alice had said, and the other half wanted to get him out of their kitchen and on his merry way.

"I really just want a sandwich," she said, her fear of letting him back into their lives winning out.

"Okay, I'll make you a sandwich." He slid the burgers back into the refrigerator.

"I don't want you to make me a sandwich," she stated, taking the loaf of bread from the pantry and setting it on the counter, her frustration with herself getting the best of her. She couldn't deny the fizzle of happiness that had shot through her when she saw him at the table tonight, and she should be stronger than that. "I've got it," she said, snatching the pack of cheese that he'd just gotten out of the refrigerator drawer.

He held up his hands in playful surrender. "I come in peace." When she didn't return his lighthearted banter, he added, "I have no other motive than to help Robby with his homework. *He* called *me*, remember?"

Sydney tried to unscrew the lid on the mayo to give her fingers an outlet for the nervous energy pulsing through her, but she struggled to get it open. "And you just decided to make an entire dinner for the family while you were here." She twisted with all her might, the whole situation heating her face.

"Your mom bought hamburger patties at the grocery store earlier and Uncle Hank needed help starting the grill to cook them. She asked if I'd help him." He eyed her struggle with the mayo and held out his hand, but she kept the jar pinned against her as she continued to twist unsuccessfully. Finally, her shoulders relaxed in concession.

"I'm sorry I snapped at you on the boat," Nate said. "I was aggravated with myself; it wasn't directed at you." He gently took the jar from Sydney and opened the lid, handing it back to her. "Look, I know it's been a very long time… I've been coming on pretty strong since I've been back… You've moved on, and rightfully so."

He stopped talking as if he were giving her one more chance to deny it, to tell him he was the one, and she'd been waiting for him to show up, but she wasn't about to say a thing. She didn't trust herself to open her mouth. She would inevitably follow her heart, and that hadn't worked very well for her in the past. She turned back to her sandwich, twirling the knife around in the jar of mayonnaise.

"I'd like to wipe the slate clean."

Sydney looked up at him, honesty swimming around in those blue eyes of his, making her curious. "And how do you propose to do that?"

"I can't change the past," he said, looking into her eyes. "And I can't predict the future. But I have *this* moment in unspoiled clarity, and I don't want to mess it up. It's perfect exactly the way it is, so why don't we just *be* for a little while? No expectations, no consequences."

"That sounds like something Aunt Clara would say… And the start of a song idea," she said, thawing toward him.

He raised his eyebrows. "Maybe it will be. Hurry up with that sandwich and you can help me write it." He grinned. In that one look, the Nathan Carr persona was completely gone, as if Firefly Beach had worn it off him the way the tide smoothes a seashell. His jagged edges were softer now.

"I can't," she said. "I'd like to spend some quality time with Robby—I haven't seen him all day. Then I have work to do."

His face lit up. "How *is* the new job going?"

She dared not tell him that she'd gotten interest from *NY Pulse*. "It's going great," she said. Why had she just done that? She knew why. She didn't want Nate to know that she might blow her first ever chance at writing full-time professionally.

Nate was staring at her as if he were assessing something.

"What?" she asked, turning back to the sandwich to avoid eye contact. He could see through her; he always could. She laid a piece of cheese and a few cold cuts onto the bread and set the sandwich on a plate, carrying it over to the table.

Nate plopped down beside Sydney, not taking his eyes off her. "Is the job not what you thought?" he asked, a clear attempt to decipher her inner turmoil. "I always pictured you writing about specific topics of interest…"

Sydney buried her insecurity deeper and lifted her chin. "What are you talking about? I said it's going great."

"Yes, but you're blinking more than usual, and that means that you are completely lying..." he said with a grin.

He was clearly making light of the situation but hitting a nerve instead. He'd tapped right into her self-doubt. What if she failed at this? She swallowed the lump that was forming in her throat, fighting the tears as they surfaced.

"Oh, Syd," Nate said, his face sobering, wrapping his protective arms around her like he used to when she was upset. "It's okay," he soothed.

She closed her eyes and buried her face in his chest, inhaling the familiar scent of him, drawing her back in time. A wave of calm engulfed her for an instant, but then she thought about the magazine and wondered if she was completely out of her league.

"Tell me," he urged her softly.

Nate was the only person she'd ever been able to be vulnerable with, the only one whom she'd open up to. Perhaps it was the old feeling that came back being in his arms or she was finally having some sort of breakdown, but she blurted, "I was given the opportunity to write a few pieces to see if I'd be a good fit for a magazine in New York." Tears surfaced unexpectedly as the fear became all too real.

Nate lifted her chin and wiped her tears, smiling down at her. "*This* is the girl I remember," he said fondly.

Confused, she waited for more explanation.

"The girl who gets upset when she hasn't built an empire by her first day on the job," he said, huffing out an affectionate laugh. "It's only a couple of pieces. The people reading them will know that your comfort level will build as you go. You'll get there. And I think they'll see the potential. Your writing is incredible, Syd."

His encouraging tone was like finally catching her breath after being under water.

"Do you know what the difference is between you and all the people who fail?"

Sydney shook her head, drinking in his reassurance.

"Motivation."

"Lots of people are motivated," she countered. "You put too much faith in me."

"Yes, people are, but they don't have the level of motivation you have. Look at you: you're in tears before you've even written the pieces. And you think it's because you aren't qualified, for some ridiculous reason, but I think, deep down, it's because you *want* it. And I know you. You won't sleep at night until you get it. Those wheels will turn relentlessly," he said, tapping his temple, "until you get an idea that satisfies you. Remember that little exercise you used to do to help me think?"

"The messages on trees?"

"Yes. It worked because I need to move and I'm visual. But you're introspective. Look inside yourself and break it down one thing at a time."

"If I'm breaking it down one thing at a time, it isn't just the *NY Pulse* job. I have to come up with a cover for Mary Alice's magazine, and I'm having a little trouble with it too."

"Tell me what you're thinking."

She told him about her idea for a couple on the cover, and the more she said her ideas out loud, the more vibrant they became. No one could tap into her frequency like Nate could. She'd forgotten how great he was at pulling ideas out of her, and she could always do the same for him. They were great together. *Were*, she reminded herself.

"I don't have anyone to do the shoot for the cover photo, though," she said. "I've contacted a few modeling agencies and talent agencies, and I've seen some headshots, but finding someone close enough to Firefly Beach who can live up to my visual image is tough. Do you think there's any way we could get Juliana to agree to do the shoot, or would it bring back too many painful memories?"

"I think it's worth explaining it to her," he said. "This would be more informal than her typical shoots, right?"

"Yes. I've emailed the local photographer Gavin Wilson and he's agreed to do the shoot. We'd use mostly natural light, and the beach, so the set would be minimal. I was hoping to have the two of you, hand-in-hand, walking down the beach." She threw in that last bit just to be indulgent.

"You want me to be in it?"

"The back of you, yes."

"So you and I would work together?" There was a playful suggestiveness in his eyes when he said it.

"For that *one* day." She wasn't going to totally give in to his charm.

"I like the sound of that," he said. "We'll ask Juliana. Want me to text her right now?" He pulled out his phone.

Sydney put her hand on his to stop him, and her gesture worked because his movements became still. He let go of his phone and twisted his hand under hers, peering down at her fingers as if they were some sort of delicate seashell that might break if he handled it incorrectly. The tips of his fingers stroked her palm before she pulled her hand away, her heart thumping like crazy.

"Right," he said, on an inhale, and then cleared his throat. "Work. What's the first topic?"

"Sorry?" she asked, trying to regain her focus.

"The first topic you have to write for the magazine? We're trying to work through your problems, right?"

"I'm not sure yet," she said. "I wish I could talk to someone who's done this sort of thing to pick their brain on structure and length before I start writing."

Nate picked his phone back up and began to scroll through his contacts, stopping on one. "I must have someone who can give you a quick pep-talk." He studied the screen, scrolling up. "If not, I've got a massage therapist…" He gave her a smirk, scrolling again because he obviously knew it was a stretch.

Sydney rolled her eyes and leaned over to look with him. When she did, she caught sight of Mary Alice's name in his phone—no last name, just her first name as if she were one of his close friends. *How odd*, Sydney thought. It wasn't *that* odd. They'd known each other since childhood, but they hadn't been close growing up. The phone contact, coupled with what she'd just learned about him talking Mary Alice into moving back to Firefly Beach, gave Sydney pause.

"See anyone interesting?" he asked, his brows pulling together as he looked at her. Only then did she realize she'd been staring at his phone.

Curious or not, it wasn't any of her business. It was better just to let it go.

Startling her, Nate's phone came to life. "One sec," he said, standing up and walking over to the doorway. "Hello?" His broad shoulders were hunched just slightly as he leaned forward to take the call. "You're kidding…" He began pacing slowly, a smile crawling across his face. "When does he want me there? …Absolutely. Talk soon." Nate ended the call and came back over to the table. "I've got a pretty big writing retreat to go to."

"Writing retreat?"

"Yeah. When an artist wants to make an album, sometimes they might ask a few songwriters to collaborate. We all go to a specific location together for a week or so and hash out a bunch of songs. This time, it's Malibu."

"California?" she asked, more so out of disbelief. Nate's reality was that he found it completely normal to leave suddenly and head to Malibu for a couple of weeks—all in the name of work.

"Yep. It's for a major country music star who's coming out of retirement, but it's sort of under wraps, I was told, so I'd better not say." Nate mimed zipping his lips. "I have to leave tonight."

"You're just going to drop everything and go?"

"I've gotten pretty good at managing schedules on the road," he said. "I'm totally used to this sort of thing. I do it all the time."

"Just like that? Will Juliana be okay? What if that photographer comes back while you're gone?" she asked. "If we call you, will you come home?"

"I have to silence my phone when I'm writing. I completely go off the grid. But Juliana knows how to handle herself with the press."

"That guy Seth wouldn't come to Firefly Beach to find her, would he?" Sydney fretted.

Nate shook his head. "I doubt it. He's a busy man and he doesn't strike me as the type that would spend his energy chasing people around. I won't let anything happen. And if she needs support, Malory's here, and Mary Alice will help her through any issues until I can get back."

"And when will that be?" she asked.

"I'm not sure. Probably whenever we have enough songs written. Sometimes we can get on a roll and be done in a few days; it just depends."

Robby ran past the window and a stab of fear shot through Sydney. What would Nate do if he had to leave during football season this fall? Certainly, he couldn't just disappear for an unspecified amount of time with absolutely no contact. Had he given any thought to this at all? Living in Firefly Beach wasn't the same as the big cities he'd become accustomed to. Here, if he wanted to be a part of the community, people would count on him to be there when they needed him.

"You look worried," he said, pulling her out of her thoughts. "If anyone needs anything, I have an assistant named Cameron Ross. He'll be coming into town in about two days to oversee the building on my lot while I'm working. I'll text him and ask him to come earlier."

The mental image of Nate sending his assistant to Robby's game when he couldn't make it slid into her consciousness and suddenly, when Sydney looked at Nate, all she could see was Nathan Carr. "That won't be necessary," she eventually said.

"No, really. He'd be okay with it."

"I'm sure he would." Sydney stood up and tipped her plate, sending her sandwich into the trash.

Nate followed her with his gaze as she dumped the plate into the sink. "You didn't eat," he said slowly, something brewing in that brain of his.

"I'm not very hungry anymore. I'm going to go out with Robby and the family."

"I haven't finished helping you with the magazine," he said.

"I don't need any help."

She would do this on her own because that was what she'd become great at doing. She hadn't needed Nate in the years he'd been gone, and she didn't need him now. He was right: the only clarity she had was this moment, and this moment wasn't any different than the other moments she'd had with Nate since he'd been back. They had become two very different people.

Chapter Eighteen

Sydney took in the picturesque view through the French doors of the living room this morning as she sat on the sofa with her coffee. The gulf was striped in bright aquamarine and electric blue, and the sun beamed while the palms danced in a light breeze. Sydney couldn't wait to get ready for the day and head to work.

She'd slept like a baby. But this morning, the uneasiness of Nate's absence settled upon her when she looked at the clock and guessed he'd already left for Malibu. He'd stayed an incredibly long time last night, playing with Robby and talking with Uncle Hank about some options for Starlight Cottage, none of which did she want to hear unless they involved stopping the development and maintaining the land surrounding them. To avoid any more lengthy conversations, she'd stayed out on the porch with her mother, and then she'd run into town to get a few things her mother had forgotten at the store, until she knew he'd be gone. Any later, and he'd miss his flight.

She'd fallen asleep with Robby while tucking him in and blindly made it to her room sometime in the middle of the night. It wasn't until she'd come back into her bedroom and raised the blinds that she'd seen the note that had stopped her cold. She walked over to the dresser and picked up the plastic ring with the purple stone that sat on top of the paper. Hesitantly, she slid the little band onto her finger and peered down at it. So many dreams had been wrapped up in that toy ring. But that wasn't what was bothering her right now. What was eating away at her was the message on the paper beside it. In Nate's familiar writing, the note simply said:

When I get back, I need to tell you something.
Love you, Nate

No, no he didn't. He didn't need to tell her anything. He needed to just let her move on already. Too much had changed between them. And every time she considered her feelings for him, they were all based on what she knew of the past, not what she saw in front of her now. But she couldn't ignore the niggling curiosity of what it was he had to say. She looked down at the ring, the memories surrounding it assaulting her. What could he have to tell her that hadn't already been said?

"Hey, Mama," Robby said from the doorway, rubbing his sleepy eyes.

"Good morning." Sydney walked over to him and wrapped her arms around his tiny frame. "Did you sleep well?"

"Mm hmm," he said, before a yawn engulfed him. When he finally opened his eyes, he touched the ring on her finger. "I showed that to Nate last night."

"You did?"

"Yeah. We were playing that word game that Uncle Hank has. When it was my go, I got a really hard word so I ran to Uncle Hank and asked him to explain what it was. I was trying to get Nate to say 'costume jewelry' and Uncle Hank said that was pretend jewelry that was less expensive than real jewelry. I wasn't allowed to talk, so I remembered you had that ring! Wasn't that good thinking?"

"Yes, it was!" she replied with forced enthusiasm. "Did Nate guess the word?" she asked carefully, mortified that he'd seen the ring and dying to know Nate's reaction after she'd told him she didn't have it anymore.

"He looked at it really weird for a long time and then he guessed the word was 'love.'" Robby squeezed his eyes shut and shook his head, giggling. "You *could* give someone a ring if you love them, but gross." He wrinkled his nose at the idea, making her laugh.

Sydney slipped the ring off her finger and set it down on top of Nate's note. "Come on," she said, "let's get you some breakfast."

Sydney sat at her desk in the old sewing room. The sewing room used to double as an extra bedroom, but in the renovation of Starlight Cottage, Sydney had replaced the twin bed with a soft, seashell-colored cream sofa and rearranged the furniture, keeping Aunt Clara's sewing machine that she'd used to make some of the pieces she'd designed for her company Morgan and Flynn as a focal point on one wall while adding a small desk in the center of the room. She stared at her computer screen.

This was what she knew: Nate dropped everything to run off and write—it was his job to do that. He said he did it all the time, and, being an incredibly successful songwriter, he probably had to. The magazines reported that he never stayed in one location for very long, and, given what Sydney knew of his attention span, they were most likely correct. He lived a life where he was followed by photographers and hounded by the press…

Sydney tapped her pen against her bottom lip. She wanted to run into his arms when he got back, but everything in her brain told her she needed to get over him once and for all or he'd haunt her for the rest of her life. What could she do to take her mind off him, though? Here she was at her desk at work, needing to get a move on with figuring out this magazine, and he was filling her head. She had to have something else to think about…

Slowly, she looked down at her handbag on the floor, leaning against her desk, and an idea came to her. In that instant, she realized that Nate kept trying because deep down, she still had hope that they could be what they were, and she allowed him to have glimpses of it. As much as it would hurt, she had to give Nate a solid message that he needed to stop. It was the only way that she could get him out of her head so she could move forward in life.

Sydney grabbed her cell phone and pulled up Logan's number on a text screen. She typed:

Hi. This is Sydney. I was wondering if you want to get together again sometime.

She stared at the message, considering, and the more she thought about it, the more she knew she had to do it. She hit send.

The word "read" appeared at the bottom of her message, alerting her that Logan had seen the message, and a cold shiver coursed through her. *He seemed nice*, she told herself. *He was funny.*

Logan's text came in:

Love to. Today work?

Yes, she answered. She could take a late lunch and meet him in town.

How about 1:00 at The Fruity Fish?

She hadn't been to the local juice bar called The Fruity Fish in ages. It would be nice to stop back in. Maybe she could even grab a take-out menu to see if Robby would like any of their smoothies.

Logan came back to her:

See you then!

Logan emerged through the throng of vacationers strolling through town and met her in front of The Fruity Fish. He was much more casual than he'd been when she'd seen him last, wearing a T-shirt and sunglasses, his thick crop of dark hair attractively messier than it had been before. He broke into a gorgeous smile when he saw her.

"Hey," he said, greeting her with a friendly hug. "It's great to see you."

"Shall we go inside?" she asked.

In response, Logan opened the door for her and allowed her to enter, the cool air welcoming after being in the midday heat. Every table was occupied. As usual, the place was crawling with tourists, wide-eyed and buzzing over the selection of beverages listed above the juice bar, their arms full of Fruity Fish mugs and T-shirts that said "Eat your veggies" with a cartoon smoothie bending at the side, a smile stretching across the cup.

The owner, Sanders McCoy, waved to them between juice cup flips and straw catches. He was known for his acrobatics when making juice drinks. In fact, Aunt Clara had tried to get her and Nate a job there after they'd shown her their lemon-juggling routine.

They joined the line to put in their orders.

"Do you see an open seat?" she asked Logan. He was taller than she was, so perhaps he could get a better view over the crowd.

He took off his sunglasses and tipped his head up, scanning the room. "Nothing." He looked down at her, the corners of his eyes creasing with his smile. "Where can you get the worst food in town?" he asked.

She smiled. "Even there, it'll be full of tourists this time of year." She really should've thought this through a little better, but her mind had been on Nate instead of planning a great spot. Her tummy growled.

"Was that your stomach? You're hungry," he said.

"A little," she replied, trying not to let on that she was absolutely starving.

"I'm not trying to be creepy, but my place is just a couple minutes' drive. I could make you lunch. And I *do* have coffee."

Sydney had to be back at work in an hour. And going to Logan's house was a little more involved than grabbing a cup of coffee with him. She froze with indecision.

"Did I mention that I'm Ben's sound designer? I have a summer house here that's been in our family for years. It's on the beach in the next village." He held up his hands. "I promise I'm not a crazy person or anything. In fact, my mother is visiting at the moment, so she'll be there too."

It sounded better by the second.

Logan pulled to a stop in front of a cedar-shingled bungalow that sat on stilts in the powdery white sand. It had a modest but elegant front porch with two rocking chairs on either side of a bright orange front door displaying a wreath made of seashells and starfish.

"When you were getting in the car at the coffee shop, I texted my mom to tell her we were coming," he said as they got out and headed up the steps of the cottage. "Fingers crossed she's dishing us up her famous chicken salad."

Logan slipped his key into the lock and let Sydney inside. The small space was open and airy, decorated in the classic beach style: lots of white and nautical blue. She eyed the small wicker bench in the entryway and ran her fingers over the navy blue and white striped pillows propped up on it. Like a smaller version of Starlight Cottage, the kitchen was along the back, and a wall of windows afforded a view of the stretch of white sand, dotted with dark blue umbrellas, which didn't disappoint.

"Oh my stars! Logan found a friend," teased a smartly dressed woman with a gray bob of hair and a friendly smile as she greeted them. The woman swished forward in her flowing linen trousers and loosely belted shirt. Her delicate jade bracelets jingled on her wrist as she held out her hand to introduce herself. "I'm so happy to meet you. I'm Delilah Hayes, Logan's mother."

"It's nice to meet you," Sydney said, already enjoying the lift she felt being with someone who had no ties to her past. Like Nate's suggestion to live in the present moment—it certainly was a comfortable place to be. Even Sydney's ex-husband had grown up with her, and there was always the element of shared experiences that could be a blessing but at times, also a curse. Whether this meeting between herself and Logan went anywhere from today was yet to be seen, but this was a clean slate from which to build.

"Logan never brings girls to the house," Delilah said, beckoning them into the kitchen where she had plates made already with croissant sandwiches and fresh pineapple garnish.

"Maybe it's because I never had your chicken salad to offer them," he said with a wink.

"Yes," Sydney said, playing along. "I was actually just walking by, minding my own business, when Logan came up to me and offered me chicken salad. I completely changed my plans."

Delilah laughed and patted his shoulder, handing him a plate.

"Mom, are you hungry? You should join us," Logan offered.

"Yes, please do," Sydney replied.

"I'd hate to intrude," Delilah said, wiping the crumbs from the counter with a dishrag.

Logan silently consulted Sydney and she offered her consent. It would be nice to have someone else to take some of the pressure off.

"Nonsense," Logan said. "We're just having lunch."

Delilah whipped up another sandwich and sat down with the two of them at the small farmhouse-style distressed wood table. She scooted a bowl of lemons to the side so they could all talk. "How do you two know each other?" she asked.

"Sydney was at Ben's wedding," Logan told her.

"Ah, Ben. I adore him." Delilah handed Sydney a paper napkin, still getting settled but not wasting a minute of conversation time. It reminded Sydney of Aunt Clara. She used to be just like that, talking and genuinely listening as she puttered around the house. "Life is too short not to have conversation. We're built to be with one another, not alone," she said once.

"I'm Ben's new sister-in-law," Sydney explained. "But I've known him since we were kids."

"Oh!" Her eyebrows rose in interest. "So that makes you one of Hank and Clara Eubanks's nieces?"

"Yes," Sydney said.

"How lovely. I never knew them, but I've heard what wonderful people they are. I know how much Clara has done for the community of Firefly Beach. And I've also seen Starlight Cottage in all the magazines—it's incredible! Your Aunt Clara was so talented."

"Yes, she was."

"I'd heard they're planning to put in that public beach access right beside the cottage. How does your family feel about that?"

"We're all really upset about it." Sydney picked up her sandwich. "My Uncle Hank attended the last meeting and he's going to the one today."

Delilah shook her head. "Logan, don't you know someone who could help change their minds?" She leaned forward, as a thought clearly came to her. "What about that guy from the music business—the famous guy on the board of supervisors for Firefly Beach—the one that I pointed out in the local paper this morning? Do you know him at all? Couldn't you bend his ear a little?"

"Nathan Carr? I don't know him… And I doubt I could change his mind anyway. I think he's heading up the whole thing."

All the blood rushed out of Sydney's face.

"Ben knows him… And *you* were talking to Nathan at the wedding, right?" Logan said to Sydney. Logan's voice plunged through the fog that had filled Sydney's mind. She struggled to pull herself back into the conversation.

"Uh, yes. I know him."

"Maybe you could talk to him?"

Sydney could kick herself. She'd let Nate in, allowed him to manipulate her thoughts, and her worst fears were confirmed: Nate had only come back into her life because he wanted something. He was hoping to convince Sydney and the family to sell Starlight Cottage so he could put in the beach access. Everything was coming together—the empty lot where he'd leveled his parents' cottage that sat vacant because it was in the line of houses that needed to be torn down for the beach access. The fact that he was building his new house further out so he wouldn't have to be near the mess he was going to cause with the influx of tourists. Was that what he wanted to tell her when he got back?

"It's just an idea," Logan said, tearing her away from her complete panic at the thought that Nate had deceived her. She'd never have thought he'd stoop so low.

Sydney forced herself back into the moment and forced a smile. "Yes, I could definitely talk to him," she said. Oh, she certainly would talk to him. She planned to give him a piece of her mind and push him out of her life once and for all.

"You okay?" Logan asked, concern written on his face.

Sydney scrambled to gain composure. "Yes. I'm totally fine. It just makes me so sad that Starlight Cottage is facing this, you know?"

"I can't imagine," he said with a compassionate shake of his head. "I'll tell you what. There's a little ice cream shop down the road, and I'll bet it isn't nearly as busy as the one in Firefly Beach." He raised his eyebrows in suggestion. "We can't fix the big things in life sometimes, but we can take a second to free our minds of them. Wanna go after lunch?"

Sydney was grateful for Logan's kindness. "I can't think of anything better."

Chapter Nineteen

Juliana walked up the steps to Starlight Cottage, sitting down in the rocking chair beside Sydney's and crossing her legs.

"Thank you for coming," Sydney said. "I didn't know who else to call."

Now in the shade of the porch, Juliana pushed her sunglasses up on her head. "What is it?" she asked, her eyes wide.

"Remember the magazine I'm working on? I need someone great for the cover," she said. "It would be a very informal shoot…"

"I am sorry," Juliana said with a frown. "I do not want to work in this field anymore. It has too many bad memories for me… I am sure you can find someone else to do it."

She'd thought about asking Logan if he'd do the shoot. He definitely had the right build. She just needed a partner for him. "I don't know anyone else," Sydney admitted.

"Yes, you do. *You* do it."

Sydney laughed, the idea completely taking her by surprise. "I wouldn't be natural at modeling, I'm afraid."

"What if I coached you?" Juliana offered. "I can show you how to use the sunlight, the way your limbs should move when you walk so the shot is clean, if you're doing an action shot. I can position you and the other person to be sure you're at the best angle."

"I don't look the part…"

Juliana chuckled. "I will style you. You're gorgeous! I will do your hair and make-up."

This magazine cover was sure to be a complete disaster if she didn't take charge right now. "I need it to look professional."

"Why don't you let me do your hair and make-up and dress you in something elegant? Then you will see."

Sydney deliberated. She wished she had Aunt Clara to ask about these sorts of things. She wasn't any good at this. She put her forearms on the arms of the chair and started to rock it, thinking. *What would Aunt Clara do?* She would hustle. Aunt Clara used to always say, "Real success comes from a good hustle, and when something you really want doesn't go your way, you don't pout about it; you make it happen—you just have to get creative and hustle a little more than you expected."

"Okay," Sydney said.

"I am so happy!" Juliana said. "We could also call your photographer to do some shots."

"Great idea. I'll give Gavin a call." She felt a swell of excitement, and tried not to think about how long the road still was to getting this publication ready. *Baby steps*, she told herself. "What time can I come over?"

Juliana twisted the watch on her thin wrist around to view the time. "Want to do it now?"

"My mom and Uncle Hank took Robby to a movie so we'll have a few hours to work."

"Perfect!"

When Juliana said, "Let me grab my make-up bag," Sydney hadn't been ready for the suitcase-sized tote that Juliana loaded into Sydney's car at Malory's. Juliana lumped it on Sydney's bed next to where she was sitting. She then set up a circular tripod with white lighting and shined it on Sydney's face.

"You need all this for a shot of two people holding hands?" Sydney asked, peeking into the bag. It was filled with different combinations of make-up colors, nail polishes, hairstyling kits—everything anyone could ever need and then some.

Juliana scooted the bag over and sat down beside Sydney. "The shot is only one element of a great image," she said. "Before we put anything on your face at all, we need to know what we are painting."

"What do you mean?"

"What is the product you're trying to sell?"

Sydney tied her hair back with a rubber band. "The wellness magazine."

"What emotion or question do you want from your reader when he or she sees this cover? What will make them pick it up?"

Sydney contemplated this for a second. She'd been so consumed with the minutiae of each of the pieces that she realized she hadn't given thought to the overarching theme of the whole thing. "I'm not sure if it's a question per se," Sydney said, thinking out loud, "but more of a curiosity. I want people dying to know what's inside that will better their lives."

Juliana sighed a long, luscious exhalation of happiness. "You think like a writer," she said. "You are an emotional thinker. I love that. We need to tap into it."

Sydney had never really considered that her thought pattern was any different than anyone else's. She'd just gotten used to pondering things in this way from being around Nate. She hadn't really dissected the "why" of things in a long time. Perhaps it was the fact that, since Nate had left, she hadn't had anyone ask the right questions.

"I have only known one other person who thinks that deeply about everything he does," Juliana said.

Her comment made Sydney feel exposed, and her cheeks heated right up. "Well, if it's Nate, let's move along," she said. "He's a colossal distraction, and I need to focus on the magazine right now."

"Yes, you are right. Let us focus." She pulled a curling iron out of her bag and plugged it in, setting it on the dresser. "What is the title of the magazine?"

"It's called *A Better You*."

"So my interpretation of this is clean lines, simplistic, stripping away all the baggage—nothing but fresh, youthful happiness. We need a visual representation of mindfulness, wellbeing, and joy. Minimal make-up, loose hair that allows the sunlight to flow through it, lightweight clothing, perhaps bare feet. How does that sound?"

Sydney was surprised at how much more there was to Juliana's creativity and spirit than what she put out in the public eye. "I love how you work," she said.

"Thank you."

Juliana gave her a meek smile that was different than the vivacious looks she'd offered the cameras over the years.

Juliana rooted around in her bag and pulled out a wide tray of varying colors. "I'm thinking we will play up the colors that you already have naturally. With your auburn curls, we want cinnamons and coppers for your eyes, a light, shiny nutmeg for your lips." She dabbed her finger in one of the colors and swiped it on the back of her hand. "Like this."

"That's beautiful," Sydney said. "These decisions seem to come naturally for you. In seconds, you can choose the right colors. It would take me hours of discussion at the make-up counter in town."

Juliana smiled and motioned for her to close her eyes. "I could do it in my sleep," she said as she applied Sydney's eyeshadow.

As Juliana worked on Sydney's face, her brushes and sponges moving effortlessly, various creams and powders dabbed on the back of Juliana's hand, Sydney said with a little laugh, "It takes a lot to look natural, doesn't it?"

"Yes," Juliana said, returning the amusement in her words. "At the end of the day, it is like art: we play with colors and textures and light…" She dragged a wide brush across Sydney's forehead. "What we want to do is give your natural skin the texture and color it needs to look just as beautiful on camera as you do in real life. But to do that, we have to speak the language of the lens in terms of reflection and shape."

"You sound like my friend Gavin. He's the photographer for the shoot, and he has an art gallery in town. Have you been there yet?"

Juliana shook her head.

"He's incredibly kind, and I think you two would have a lot to talk about. Of course you'll meet him soon anyway if he comes to take those shots you suggested."

Juliana seemed happy at the thought of meeting someone else in Firefly Beach.

"Do you like it here?" Sydney asked out of the blue.

In this moment, Juliana had relaxed so much that she was nearly unrecognizable from the images she posted on her social media feeds. Her hair was in a loose ponytail at the back of her neck, her face naturally youthful and glowing without any make-up. She had on an unassuming white T, the front hem tucked into the waistband of her faded jeans. She was still incredibly beautiful, but her mannerisms were relaxed and small, as if the bubble of fame that encapsulated her had deflated over her time here, leaving just the raw beauty of her. At her heart, she, too, was just a small-town girl, trying to make her way.

"I love it here."

"What do you love about it?" Sydney asked, curious.

Juliana got out a small brush and plunged it into a tube of lip-gloss. "I love that people are kind when they have no ulterior motive. They are kind simply in the hope that you will be friendly in return. I feel valued here. In that way, it reminds me of my home." She unwound the cap on a tube of mascara. "Look up for me."

Sydney couldn't deny the tiny seed of hope that Firefly Beach would have the same effect on Nate. Maybe over the years, the sea would wash that big image right off him, diluting Nathan Carr, and he'd be the boy who'd looked into her eyes with all that love so many years ago. That is, if he didn't completely ruin Starlight Cottage before then, she thought, her blood boiling. She decided that it would be too much to ask even the heavens for Nate to come around.

Juliana got to work on Sydney's hair, twisting and curling large pieces of it. "I envy you," she said as she unclipped a curl, the lock bouncing down Sydney's cheek.

"*Me*?" Sydney asked. "Why?"

"You know what you want. He loves that about you. He thinks the world of you."

"How could he?" she said in a knee-jerk reaction. "You don't betray people you care about."

"Betray?" she asked.

Sydney shook her head. "He… It isn't important," she lied.

"Nate tells me you are a very talented writer. He said he never imagined you doing anything but writing. And here you are, working on the magazine for the wellness center and he tells me you are also writing for a column."

Just like her view of Juliana—things weren't always as they seemed. "I don't know if I'm cut out for the job yet."

Juliana's face crumpled in concern. "How could you not be?" She ran her fingers through Sydney's hair to comb it out.

"I was given the opportunity to apply for a magazine position that would be pretty close to my dream job. But at times, I feel like I'm shooting too high for a girl who's spent most of her time as a mom, doing part-time work to pay the bills. I don't have the clout I need to pull it off."

Juliana's hands stilled as she turned inward, thoughtful. "You know, I would never have believed I would leave my little village in Argentina for the bright lights of Los Angeles. That was something of movies, not real life. On my first shoots, I was not performing the way they'd hoped, and another model pulled me aside and gave me some advice. She said, '*None* of us belong here. We just pretend like we do until it becomes who we are.'"

Sydney grinned. "Fake it till you make it."

"That's right. But it is more than that. You have to believe that at some point, you *will* belong. You just have to be creative with how to build yourself up from the bottom."

"You know what? You're exactly right."

Juliana turned Sydney around in front of the mirror and Sydney's jaw nearly dropped to the floor.

"Oh my gosh," she said as she viewed the stranger in her reflection.

"You are beautiful."

"How did you do that? I don't even look like myself. Well, I do, but it's like some heavenly version of me. You are so talented… You know, you wouldn't have to model to work in the business. You could do something behind the scenes. You could teach people how to model, teach them about color and light."

"I wouldn't know where to begin," Juliana said.

"Fake it till you make it."

Both women laughed at Sydney's comment, but Sydney could see a sparkle in Juliana's eye at the possibilities.

"Mama, is that you?" Robby asked when he and Jacqueline entered the cottage and slid their flip-flops off at the door. Sydney was still wearing the make-up Juliana had put on her.

Uncle Hank came in behind them and shut the door while Sydney's mother pushed the shoes to the side to get them out of his path. "You could win the Miss Firefly Beach pageant looking like that."

"Yes, she certainly could," Jacqueline said, her eyes round.

Sydney bent down to give Robby a hug. "Juliana thinks I should be on the cover of the wellness magazine. She did my make-up so I could see if it would work."

After Juliana left, Sydney was so energized by their conversation that she was ready to take charge of her life. She texted Logan to ask if he would be interested in doing the shoot with her. He was beyond excited, and he invited her to dinner after the shoot tomorrow. Sydney had said she'd go; but Nate's deceit weighed heavily on her mind, casting a cloud over everything. No matter how hard she tried to push it out of her mind, it wouldn't budge.

Chapter Twenty

Sydney and her family waited to cross the intersection at the over-crowded traffic signal, beachgoers flooding the center of town. When the walk sign finally flashed, Sydney guided Robby across the street and then entered the town hall through the double front doors, following her mother, Lewis, and Uncle Hank, along with the gathering of others opposing the public beach access. The building they were in was a historical landmark, part of it having been the first permanent structure of the village. The old wood floors creaked beneath their feet as they all headed deeper into the cool air-conditioned space.

Uncle Hank's smile was replaced by a serious expression of concentration, his eyes fixed on the door at the end of the hallway where they were all going. The family had decided, along with the other residents that would be affected by the public beach access, that everyone should attend to show their disagreement. As they took their seats, Sydney tried to overlook the fact that, even with them all present, their numbers weren't terribly overwhelming. What she also hadn't had the heart to tell Uncle Hank and her family was that Nate was behind the plans. The icy cold feeling that had pelted her over and over in the early days after he'd left Firefly Beach slithered back in at the thought of his betrayal. It was nearly more than she could bear.

An older woman by the name of Sheila Fox lowered herself warily into one of the three chairs on the small stage and tapped her microphone, causing it to squeal in protest.

"I thought the entire board would be here tonight," Sydney whispered to Uncle Hank as board members filled the other two chairs on stage. The idea that Nate would head this thing up and not even bother to attend any of the meetings sent a bitter taste through Sydney's mouth. How convenient that he would disappear for the final discussion before the vote to essentially ruin Starlight Cottage.

"As Firefly Beach grows, there seems to be less and less personal interaction," Uncle Hank said under his breath. "And I think the board members are just doing this so we feel like we have a voice."

Sheila stood up to the clearing of throats and shifting in chairs. "Thank you for joining us tonight," she said into the microphone, her amplified voice echoing in the church-like room full of empty chairs, only the first few rows sparsely occupied. "If you'll bear with us, we'd like to inform you all of our considerations for the project at length before we take any of your questions." Sheila opened a hand toward the man in the chair at her right. "Forrest Baker will mention the current state of affairs regarding traffic through Firefly Beach, leading to the proposal by the board," she said, before turning to her left, "and Joyce Powell will give you the impact on your wallets with the suggested tax increase as well as the projected revenue the project will provide."

The crowd sat, hushed and waiting, some with arms folded, others with eyes clamped on Sheila, chests filling with air in anticipation of the next part.

"I will begin with an overview…"

What if, for some unknown reason, Sydney wasn't meant to stay in Firefly Beach? It certainly seemed like the odds were against her: Nate's constant presence would only drive her crazy, the future of Starlight Cottage was in jeopardy, and, even though she'd managed to look on the bright side, the magazine for Mary Alice still wouldn't have gotten off the ground were it not for Juliana's help. She wondered if she should go back to her old paralegal job in Nashville, where she'd been just fine before.

"There will always be forward movement," Sheila's voice filtered back into Sydney's consciousness. "We have to prepare for it, whether we like it or not. Change is inevitable and, at times, uncomfortable. But we *must* move forward." Sheila paused dramatically to the silent staring eyes of the crowd surrounding Sydney. With a hesitant breath over the speakers, she said, "I'm going to turn the microphone over to Forrest who will give you the breakdown of traffic through the main thoroughfare as well as the proposal for how to alleviate that traffic."

Forrest Baker walked over and took the microphone from a relieved Sheila and began pacing the stage, his long, thin strides making him look as though he were gliding. "Last meeting, we discussed the proposed zoning for the project. With that now cemented, it's time to look forward to the project at hand: alleviating the overcrowding on our main street while building up the area with more shopping surrounding the new public beach access..."

"I'm bored," Robby whispered to Sydney. "I wish Nate was here so we could draw."

A pinch caught in the back of her shoulder. "What about Ben?" she asked.

Robby grinned up at her, nodding. "He'd be fun too, but Nate likes *all* the stuff I like."

Sydney leaned close to Robby's ear. "I'm not sure Nate will be around a lot," she said, ignoring the churning in her stomach. "Maybe

I can draw with you." She dug around quietly in her handbag for a pen and a scrap of paper.

"What do you mean?" Robby looked up at her with concern in his little eyes.

"Well, he travels a lot, and I'm not sure how long he'll be in Firefly Beach."

"But he said—"

She shook her head and waved him quiet with a kind smile, hating Nate for the pain he would cause her son. "We'll talk about it later, okay?" She drew a tic-tac-toe board on the back of an old receipt and handed him the pen. "You go first."

Joyce Powell gave them all the financial breakdown while Sydney played games with Robby. The entire time, the fear kept creeping in that Robby was going to be devastated when Nate was no longer welcome. There was no way she was going to let him back in to their lives after this. Now, all the kindness he'd shown was in question. Had it all been to sway them to sell their property? Would they knock it down to build shops like the ones that surrounded the current public beach? She scanned the faces in the crowd, noticing that Malory wasn't there. She remembered now that he was building something for her on his land.

"Once the final two residents agree to sell, the project *will* move forward," Joyce said. "I hope that after tonight, you have some buy-in as to the positive economic and aesthetic impact the public beach access will have on Firefly Beach. It will essentially give us our streets back. Now, we will all take your questions."

"Are we one of the remaining two?" Jacqueline asked Uncle Hank, clearly worried.

He shook his head. "We've been approached to sell, but we aren't in the actual development line. We'll lose our view, but we can stay."

"Who approached you to sell?" Jacqueline asked.

"I got a letter from the board."

An icy thorn of anger poked Sydney's insides. Nate wanted them to sell, didn't he? It seemed pretty darn obvious now.

Attempting to ease Jacqueline's nerves, Uncle Hank replied, "They probably just heard that I'd been asking around for real estate agents and thought I was interested."

"And are you?" Jacqueline asked. "Are you *really* interested in abandoning the dream that Aunt Clara built for us all?"

Sydney feared that her mother's emotion would upset Uncle Hank, but she knew Mama wasn't snapping at him. She was just making sure that he understood what he was considering. Starlight Cottage was a part of their history, an extension of Aunt Clara, and the only legacy left by her in Firefly Beach.

"Nate offered to sell us a piece of his property," Uncle Hank said, clearly considering this as the words left his mouth. "We'll talk about it later." He shifted his focus back to the stage.

A tingling sensation crawled over Sydney's skin. She did *not* want to be any closer to Nate than she had to be, and once Uncle Hank and her family found out about Nate's involvement in the—

Sydney's thoughts were interrupted by a buzzing wave of noise from the crowd.

Joyce put the microphone to her lips. "I'm delighted that we could get our intentions across with this meeting. With the two of you agreeing to sell tonight," she said, her gaze on the owners of the final two cottages on Sydney's street, "we will be able to move forward. Our board will be preparing a step-by-step guide of the process that will be online to keep you informed as we go."

"What just happened?" Sydney said to Uncle Hank.

Uncle Hank had also missed the conversation while they'd been whispering back and forth, but unlike Sydney, his level-headedness had kept him from panicking, and he'd been able to jump right back into the conversation. "Looks like it's a go," he said. He tipped his head back, searching the ceiling, as if he were trying to find Aunt Clara up there.

They all needed her help right now.

The crowd was restless and Tom McCoy, the owner of the old fruit stand and one of the final two cottages to sell, got up on the stage and took the microphone in an obvious attempt to calm any fears. "I was approached by a board member a few days ago," he said into the microphone, his eyes suddenly finding Sydney. Why was he looking at her? "He gave me a price I can't refuse, and also let me know that it would be in my best interest to sell. I've known him since he was a boy and while I'm nervous about the change, I have to trust him."

Sydney had to close her gaping mouth. The only person on the board that Tom knew like that was Nate. Fire coursed through her veins and her hand shot up into the air.

A look of surprise washed over Tom's face. "Yes?" he asked.

Sydney stood up, ignoring her mother's confused glances. She called out over the two rows of chairs separating them: "And what stake does this board member have in the project?" Her eyes narrowed.

Tom shrugged, helpless, his shoulders slumping as he shook his head in surrender.

"*How* is this in your best interest, Tom?" she nearly pleaded.

He just shook his head, mute.

Sydney felt like she was moving down a dark tunnel, the room closing in on her. She hadn't gotten this feeling since seeing Nate's truck driving away from her that day. Once again, Nate had managed to take all her joy with him. She'd tried her best not to let him hurt her again but he just had. He'd torn her heart out. Her anger withering to sadness, she sank back down into her chair in silence.

After Robby had had his bath, Sydney tucked him into bed and kissed his forehead.

"When is Nate coming back?" he asked her.

Sydney took in a deep breath of air to keep her shoulders from tensing. "Ben will be home in two days," she suggested instead, praying that he would refocus his attention on the man who would never hurt him.

Robby broke into a smile. "I miss him. And Beau misses him too."

Sydney nodded. "We all miss him. I miss Aunt Hallie a lot."

Robby's tired eyes grew round as a thought entered his mind. "Isn't Ben friends with Nate? Maybe when Ben gets back, the three of us could go fishing!"

"Maybe," she said, trying to soothe him to sleep. She couldn't tell him outright that she never planned to let him near Nate again. He had no regard for anyone's feelings.

"You look sad, Mama," he said. "You can go fishing with us if you want to."

She ran her fingers through the strands of hair on his forehead, brushing them back affectionately. Robby would be devastated if he knew that Nate was no longer going to be in his life, and the idea of yet another man leaving him would make things worse.

"Ben has another friend named Logan. Maybe he could go fishing with you all," she heard herself say. She had no idea why she uttered Logan's name, except for perhaps her hope that Robby could like someone who couldn't hurt him. The more she considered this, the stronger the idea became. Ben would eventually be wrapped up in the family he would start with Hallie, and Nate would be out of the picture.

Logan was kind and funny. Maybe he could be a role model for Robby.

"Who's Logan?" he asked.

"I met him at the wedding," she said. "He doesn't know a lot of people here. Maybe you should include him. He'd probably like that."

Robby's gaze was cautious.

"Maybe you could meet him first," she suggested. "You and Ben could show him all the good fishing spots."

"And Nate," he corrected her.

She smiled to cover her worry. "It was just an idea. We can talk more about it later." She kissed his cheek and tucked the blankets around his little body. "I love you."

"Love you too," he said, closing his eyes.

"Sleep tight."

Sydney turned off the lamp by Robby's bed and let herself out of the room, the uncertainty of the situation settling heavily on her. Before she joined her family, she had an idea. It was time to give Logan a quick call.

"Sydney, it's nice to hear from you," Logan said as Sydney closed herself into her bedroom and lowered herself down on the four-poster bed. She smoothed her hand over Aunt Clara's sand-colored linens.

"I had an idea," she said to him.

"Tell me." His voice was gently eager to hear what she had to say.

"When we have dinner tomorrow night, how about we do a picnic instead?"

"A storm's coming in, so the temperature will drop a little by tomorrow night. It would be perfect."

"One more request," she said. "I'd like to bring my son, Robby."

"Oh?" He didn't sound taken aback, which was good. He was more curious.

"I've been so busy this week, and I don't want to leave him with my mom again. She's done so much for me since I've gone back to work—she needs a break, even though she'd never say so, and I need some quality time with Robby. You could come to Starlight Cottage and we could go down to the beach once the fireflies are out, maybe do some fishing."

Her shoulders relaxed when she could almost hear his smile on the other end of the line. "That would be fantastic. I'll gather up all my fishing supplies."

"Thank you so much," she said, relieved.

"I can't wait. … and maybe when Robby goes to bed, we can grab a drink somewhere?"

"That sounds great." For the first time in a while, a quiet optimism settled over her.

Sydney said her goodbyes, and then settled in, under her covers, leaning against the headboard with her laptop balanced on her legs. She stared at the email she'd opened and viewed her two topics for *NY Pulse*. The first one was titled "A Love Letter." She opened a blank document and rested her fingers on the keys, pulling into herself to think of possible angles for this topic. There were so many people she could write a love letter to—she even thought of Mel and his lost love—but the more she thought about it, the more she realized that she needed to write one to herself. She started typing.

To the girl who wonders

To the girl who wonders where she went wrong, sometimes there's no right or left, only forward. To begin the journey you want, all it requires of you is to take the first step. To the girl who wishes things could be different, ask yourself, "Different from what?" Different from the empty space and time in which you live, the void yearning to be filled with your dreams? It can be different. Look up at the stars, find your light, and pull it into your void. To the girl who wonders if there's love out there…

She took a deep breath and tried to collect her thoughts. This was a tough one. How did she really feel about love? As she considered this, her phone pinged with an email from mel4221. She opened it.

Hi Ms. Flynn,

I was wondering what you thought about my last statement that I was going to show the person I love how much I love her. Do you think that's a good idea?

Mel

Goodness. What should she say to this? Maybe she should just be honest with him.

Hi there,

I was just pondering the idea of love for an article I'm writing. I was wondering if, for those of us who love people we can't be with, are there others out there for us who can make us happy? Is the idea of "the one" something we've made up? Perhaps there are many people we could be with?

Ms. Flynn

She got an immediate response.

I believe in "the one." And the reason is because I think we're wired that way. I'm a pretty regular guy. I'm rational at work, in my friendships, with people I meet. But she makes me irrational. She makes me want to give her whatever she needs to understand how much I care about her. How can we feel so strongly for one person if we were built to simply let our love go and find someone else?

Sydney could definitely relate. What she didn't write to mel4221 was that when she'd typed the words "to the girl who wonders if there's love out there," all she could think about was Nate and the disappointment he'd caused her. She yearned for things to be different because it would be so easy to love him. She already did. But he'd betrayed her in the worst way, and there was no coming back from that.

I don't know…

She hit send, the whole conversation making her feel lost and confused. The truth was that Sydney *had* found someone else. She'd gotten married and started a life with that person, but she'd never really let her love for Nate go. Her phone lit up.

If you don't know—sorry to ask such a personal question, but I'm curious—does that mean you still feel you could have something with him? I guess I'm hoping that my theory about The One is true…

Sydney didn't want to give this person false hope. She typed back:

How long were you two together?

Mel answered.

Four years… So, is he still special to you?

That was definitely enough time to know if he loved her. She knew that much from being with Nate. However, Sydney wasn't going to get into her issues regarding Nate with a total stranger. The thing was that no matter what he'd done in the present, she'd had four amazing years with Nate, and he'd changed her for the better. She responded.

He'll always be special. I really hope you figure out what to do about your own situation. I wish you luck.

Her phone lit up with one last email.

Thanks. I'm gonna need it. One day soon, I'll tell her everything.

Chapter Twenty-One

"Thank you for agreeing to do this," Sydney said to Logan as he stood, holding a slew of fishing rods and a tackle box while simultaneously appearing more groomed than she'd seen him since the wedding. His hair was freshly washed and perfectly combed, and his outfit matched the specifics that Juliana had given him over the phone this morning for the photo shoot.

He stared at her as if he were speechless for a while before finally saying, "Wow. You look..."

He lost his words again, making her feel self-conscious in all the make-up. Juliana had been meticulous with her makeover, taking all morning to get it just right. Sydney nervously pushed a perfectly curled tendril out of her face.

"Gavin's out back," she said.

"Oh, you two look gorgeous in those outfits," Juliana said, as she strode up to them from the hallway. She'd chosen the white sundress that Sydney had worn to the Easter church service last spring and dressed it down with a pair of wedge sandals and dangly shell earrings from Sydney's jewelry box. Juliana had explained to him on the phone that the color for the shoot was going to come mostly from the gulf, and everything else should be muted and color-coordinated in the same shade as the sand. Gavin had agreed with this completely because the soft colors of their clothing against the shoreline would give her a lot of options for text overlay on the photo once it was formatted for the cover.

Juliana had struck up a conversation with Gavin almost immediately, both of them talking a mile a minute about camera angles. He invited her to have a look at his gallery downtown, and she laughed, telling him she'd already been in. Gavin's art and photography gallery had gotten so popular with the tourists that he'd hired two people to work for him, which allowed him more time to do things like this. But it also meant that he missed moments in the shop like Juliana Vargas browsing around, looking at his work.

"Let us go outside," Juliana said, starting back down the hallway while beckoning them to come along. "We'll want to get our shots. A storm is brewing off shore."

Juliana had been soft-spoken around Sydney most of the time she'd known her, but when she was working, she was an entirely different person. She was in her element. Her hair was pulled back from her face in a ponytail secured by a silk scarf, and she had a camera around her neck. She'd told Sydney this morning that she planned to take some shots herself to get a feel for how the outside lighting affected the make-up, and her hair would blow across the lens were it not for the ponytail.

When they got outside, Logan leaned his fishing rods against a tree near the pier and they all walked over to the area of the shore where Gavin had set up a small set.

Gavin threw up his hand in greeting. "Hey there," he said when they'd approached. He shook hands with Logan, introducing himself. "I'll be shooting the cover of Sydney's fantastic new magazine today," he said with a smile, always encouraging.

Sydney shook her head, her modesty coming through. Or perhaps it was the rampant imposter syndrome she felt taking on this project. "It's only a small magazine," she said, "for the wellness center patrons."

Gavin's smile widened. "We have to start somewhere. One day, we'll all look back on this moment and say, 'Remember when…'"

"I don't know," she said teasingly, but really simply expressing her insecurity.

Juliana cut in. "From what Nate tells me, you are an incredibly talented writer. He still reads over old writings of yours that he has."

That was the old Nate, Sydney thought. But Juliana's comment did strike something within her: she didn't believe in herself anymore. Gavin was right: we all have to start somewhere.

"Will you have them walk this way?" Juliana asked, getting right to work, swinging her arm along an imaginary path and bringing Sydney's attention back to the photo shoot. "It might be good light from the sun if it hits them at the side—it would create depth, I think."

"It would be easy to shoot too," Gavin agreed. "We'll just have to watch how the shadows fall on their faces."

"We can tilt your speedlight out of the shot but toward their faces," she suggested.

"Brilliant." Gavin tilted the large screen toward them to shield some of the direct sun.

Juliana put her camera to her eye and peered through the lens, taking a shot. She pulled back to view the screen. "Oh!" she called out. "It's exquisite. The lighting is perfect." She guided Sydney, leading her over to the spot she wanted. "If you can stand here, face the wind so your gorgeous hair flows behind you, that would be perfect. Logan, come over beside her and take her hand."

Logan stepped up beside Sydney and lightly touched her fingertips before clasping her hand. She looked up at him, and before she could process anything at all, the camera went off, causing spots in her eyes.

Gavin peered down at his camera. "That's a great shot," he said. "Sorry." He beamed over at Sydney. "You two just looked so perfect in that moment that I stole a photo. Just perfect."

Juliana laughed. "Those are the best shots," she said.

"The cloud cover from the storm coming in is also allowing fantastic lighting," Gavin said.

This creative process was sort of like Sydney's writing. It was all about forming ideas and emotion around parameters. Her parameters were written language, but both Juliana's and Gavin's were light, wind, and movement. She could see how certain expressions and lighting would affect the overall feel of the picture just like her choice of words did.

"When you walk, Logan," Juliana said, "turn your other hand to the side and relax your fingers like this. She demonstrated the position she wanted. "It feels unnatural but actually looks more normal on film than your regular pose…"

The entire time they worked, Gavin moved around them snapping photos. The freedom to think outside the normal day-to-day that Sydney felt as the shoot progressed gave her a buzzing need to start writing. She couldn't wait to get back into the house. Tonight, once everyone had turned in, she was going to write the remaining piece and send it to *NY Pulse*.

Robby sat on the dock quietly between Sydney and Logan, his feet swinging above the water, his eyes on the spot where the fishing line met the water's surface. He wasn't as open with Logan, but he'd agreed to come out and fish with them, which was encouraging.

"I've got some homemade raspberry lemonade in a cooler in the truck," Logan said, reeling in and setting his rod on the dock. Ben's dog Beau, who had been lounging beside them, stirred and his ears perked up. "My mom made sure she didn't leave me empty-handed before she headed back home to North Carolina. She packed a whole bunch of snacks." He leaned in to Robby's view. "Including her famous chocolate chip cookies. I asked her to be sure to leave some behind so I could bring them for you."

Robby's gaze slid over to Logan.

"Want me to go get them?" he asked.

Robby nodded.

Logan was so kind, and thoughtful. His mother seemed lovely, and it was clear that she'd raised a wonderful man in Logan. But something held Sydney back. Her feelings were totally cut off. Her head told her that he was a great catch, and he seemed interested in her, but any time she tried to stir up affection for him, it just felt forced. She couldn't deny the comparison to Nate. Even with everything against them, it was easy for her to love Nate. More importantly, she reminded herself, perhaps it was because she knew deep down that she needed to focus on herself.

Beau wandered over to Sydney and dropped down at her feet. "One more day," she told him. He looked up at her as if he knew that she was talking about Ben's return. His head popped up and turned to the side, then he got to his feet.

Robby handed his fishing rod to Sydney, scrambling up the dock toward Logan. But her heart slammed around in her chest when he ran past Logan to Nate, who'd just come over the hill. Logan turned around and they greeted each other, walking together toward Sydney. She reeled in Robby's line and got up to face them. Nate had a new football in his hand.

"Robby, go long!" he said, and he tossed it into the air. "I brought that back for you. All the way from Malibu." Robby ran up to him and he tousled Robby's hair before throwing it again as her son sprinted across the yard to catch it.

"Hey," Nate said when he reached Sydney, but his gaze devoured her. She realized then that she still had her hair and make-up done from the photo shoot today. He seemed to be assessing the situation, his gaze darting from her hair to Logan and the blanket they'd spread out on the grass, the cooler in Logan's hand…

"Hi," she said, not wanting to make a scene. The last thing she wanted to do was to make Logan feel uncomfortable.

"You're… going somewhere?" Nate asked, clearly trying to make sense of her appearance.

"Juliana got a hold of me," she said, allowing a smirk. "I had the photo shoot with Logan today and he's staying for a dinner date tonight."

Nate's jaw clenched just slightly, as he regarded Logan. Sydney suddenly felt a rush of empowerment. She was making him uncomfortable. Having Logan there was evidently spoiling his plan of sweet-talking her into thinking she was doing something wonderful by selling Starlight Cottage and moving in on his land. Perhaps she wouldn't set things straight at all about Logan, and Nate would give up and go back to LA where he came from.

"You're back so soon?" she asked.

He clamped his eyes on her and the pain in them almost made her falter, taking her back to long summer drives next to him with the windows down and the ache in her heart that she felt when she was headed back to school, away from him… She stood her ground, lifting her chin.

"I wrote four songs for them," he said. "But then I told them I had to get back. I had important business to attend to."

Like convincing my family to give up Starlight? she wanted to say, but it wasn't the time.

Logan set the cooler down on the blanket and beckoned Robby over. "Here are the cookies I promised," he said with added excitement for Robby's benefit.

Robby set the ball down in the grass and took the cookie from him, kneeling down beside him, nibbling.

"Good, right?"

"Mm hmm," Robby said.

Nate stepped into Sydney's view. "Can we talk?" he asked, that hurt she'd seen on his face now clear in his words. He gave Logan a discreet look of appraisal.

"I can't," she replied, forcing herself to be strong. "I have company."

He nodded, his gaze fluttering over to Logan, his jaw clenching again as a cloud pushed its way in front of the sun. "I'm sorry to interrupt. Maybe you can come over later?"

"Logan and I are going out for drinks."

"Tomorrow, then."

"Hallie and Ben come home tomorrow, so I'm sure I'll want to see them and hear all about their honeymoon."

He took in a deep breath and let it out slowly. Sydney knew she couldn't put off talking to him forever, and she did want to give him a piece of her mind, as well as find out why in the world he would do this to Starlight Cottage. But she also needed time to figure out how to approach the situation. The last thing she wanted to do was to break down and cry the way she felt like doing every time she thought about it.

"Syd..." he said in a quiet plea, playing on her emotions, but this time, she wouldn't allow him to get the better of her. "I need to tell you something," he said into her ear.

"It's clear that you do," she replied. "But whatever it is, I don't want to hear it." She took a step back. "We're being rude to Logan. He's here to spend time with me and Robby, and I'm being a terrible hostess." She didn't give him time to reply, turning away from him and sitting down on the blanket. But she did allow herself one quick glance over her shoulder to see him slowly walking away.

Chapter Twenty-Two

"Glad to see you," Wes said over his shoulder as he led Sydney and Logan through the throngs of tourists.

The beach-goers surrounding them were the same every summer: they had settled in for a good seafood meal before their sleepy-eyed jaunts along the main street, dipping in and out of candy and souvenir shops before finally turning in for the night, sunburned and exhausted. All of them were seemingly oblivious to the clouds that were rolling in. The wind picked up, signaling the calm before a quick summer storm. The harsh weather warnings promised for this evening that they'd been reporting on the news hadn't materialized yet but Sydney had lived along the coast long enough to know that the strip of gray on the horizon moving quickly toward them would not remain silent before it blew over. "How's Uncle Hank?" Wes asked.

"He's doing well, apart from the public beach access that is going in down the road from us."

"I'd heard," Wes said, offering a chair to Logan. Their table sat at the edge of the outside deck of Wes and Maggie's restaurant, close enough to feel the coastal breeze as it gently danced across the gulf between gusts that blew in sporadically. The red flags had been raised on the beach, alerting swimmers to potentially rough waters. "Rumor has it that someone's bought all the lots around the public beach access and the plan is to build commercial retail shops. It's supposed to bring in high-end merchants."

"The purchase didn't go through the board? I assumed the county acquired them."

Wes frowned. "I'm not sure." He leaned in to keep the conversation between just them. "It's all being kept hush-hush because people are going to be upset when they find out that our little village is going to be overrun by tourists. I like the business—don't get me wrong—but we can hardly keep up *now*."

Sydney knew only one person whose description included the words "high-end" and "hush-hush." And pounding at her temples was the realization that the one in question was also now on the board of supervisors…

"I definitely need your Passion Punch," Sydney told Wes as she took a seat across from Logan. She clarified for him: "It's got rum, strawberry daiquiri mix, and a splash of pineapple and coconut. It's divine."

"Great memory!" Wes said, waiting expectantly for Logan's order.

"Make it two," Logan told him. When Wes left to fill their drink requests, Logan leaned forward, putting his forearms on the table between them. "Judging by your drink order and the way you closed right up after seeing Nathan Carr today, I'd venture to say something is bothering you. Want to tell me what it is?"

"Not really," she said, shaking her head.

Wes brought them their drinks: large hurricane glasses with painted umbrellas sporting starfish and brightly colored flip-flops stabbed through maraschino cherries.

She leaned back in her chair and smiled kindly, honing in on the shushing of the waves as they lapped up on the beach behind them to give her calm. Even at their harshest, gulf waves were like little angry children stomping their feet in a storm. But the gray clouds on the horizon that were creeping closer were another matter.

"I certainly don't want to pull you in to Nathan Carr's drama," Sydney said. "He doesn't deserve our time. You and I had an amazing photo shoot, and we need to celebrate that." When he didn't seem convinced, she let her smile fall. "I'm sorry if I wasn't myself after Nate showed up at the house. He's really upset me," she told Logan honestly. "But I don't want it to impact tonight."

"Might be too late," Logan replied, looking over her head.

Sydney turned around to find Juliana and Nate walking up to them. The trouble with this town was that Nate would have a pretty good idea of where Sydney would be. Didn't he have the decency to let her enjoy her night?

"I'm so sorry to interrupt," Nate said.

"Well, you definitely have," she snapped quietly so as not to sound totally awful to poor Logan.

She eyed Juliana for help, but Juliana shrugged as if to say she'd already tried. Sydney took a large gulp of her drink, the alcohol zinging down her throat. She needed to calm herself down before she said something to Nate that no one else would need to hear. She'd known when he'd gotten here that he was a self-centered, selfish man. She should've listened to her gut.

"I need just one minute of your time and then Juliana and I will go have dinner," he said, nodding a second apology to Logan. A gust of wind whipped through the deck, rustling the light items on tables, and a few paper napkins went somersaulting through the air as a man dropped his fork to catch them. Vacationers were starting to catch on, an unsettling buzz pushing through the crowd as another gust of coastal wind blew in.

Sydney gritted her teeth and wriggled up from her chair against her will. “I’m so sorry,” she said to Logan. “I’ll be right back.”

“Logan and I can talk about the shoot today,” Juliana said as she sat in Sydney’s seat, clearly trying to lighten the mood.

Sydney mouthed a thank-you, her cheeks burning with irritation, and then followed Nate down the restaurant stairs at the back of the deck leading to the boardwalk that stretched over the dunes and down to the gulf. Nate walked all the way to the water’s furiously foaming edge, and Sydney kicked off her flip-flops, joining him.

“What is so important that it couldn’t wait for me to have a drink?” she asked, raising her voice above the wind picking up.

He turned to her, his face full of emotion, the wind rippling his white cotton shirt as he folded his arms. “Why didn’t you tell me you still had the ring?”

“What?” She was getting more irritated by the second. “I was having drinks with someone, Nate! You can’t just interrupt my night over some stupid toy ring that I happen to still have!” She turned away, ready to stomp back up the beach when he caught her arm, spinning her around.

“I couldn’t let you go a third time,” he said, a crease forming between his eyes with his emotion.

She stared at him. “Third time? What are you talking about?”

“Robby said you were on a date, and I nearly fell apart. I haven’t had enough time to make things right, and I can’t lose you again.”

“Robby?” she asked, taken completely off guard, totally forgetting his comment about letting her go three times. “I thought he was asleep.”

"He had a bad dream and your mom told him you were out with someone and you'd be back soon. He tried to text you, but he didn't get you, so he texted me. He was worried you were on a date. To calm him down, I promised to play football with him tomorrow."

Stunned, Sydney pulled her phone out of her pocket and realized her ringer was off. She had three missed texts. Guilt ran rampant inside her, knotting her stomach. She quickly texted Robby back, even though she knew that he was probably asleep by now, and put her phone back into her pocket. Another explosion of wind blew off the gulf, whipping her hair into her face. She pushed her hair back.

"You are *not* playing football with Robby tomorrow," she said. "I'll put his mind at ease about my night out." The dark clouds had completely filled the sky above them, plunging them into an early dimness that usually didn't fall upon the coast for several more hours, but she barely noticed.

"I know Hallie and Ben are coming back. I wouldn't get in your way. It might be nice to have someone play with Robby so you and your sister can catch up."

"Okay," she said, closing her eyes in a feeble attempt to alleviate her growing frustration. "I'm having drinks right now. Or I'm supposed to be. Yet I'm out on the beach with you instead. You said you needed *one* minute. You've already used your time." She turned around to walk back toward Logan, mortified that she'd left him as long as she had.

"Okay!" Nate said, running ahead and getting in front of her. "One minute."

"No!" Sydney replied, now completely exasperated. She'd told herself she wouldn't allow him to distract her and here she was, right back with him. "You had your minute. And all the minutes between the day you pulled out of town and now. I've given you more minutes than any human being should ever give someone who leaves someone they love like that," she said, her voice cracking under her emotion. "And I'm done, Nate." If she wanted him totally out of her life, now was her chance. Using her momentum, she'd drive the nail in the coffin. "You know why I still have that ring? Because it reminds me every day of a life I don't ever want."

There. She'd finally said it out loud: she would never love Nathan Carr. He had to know that because the truth of the matter was that he couldn't go back to being Nate Henderson again—no matter how hard she wished it would happen.

Nate's arms fell limp at his sides, her words wiping his face clean of all emotion except for the glassiness in his eyes and the shock that had turned his skin pale. He suddenly looked broken, like the life had been sucked out of him. Seeing him like that made her want to wrap her arms around him and tell him how much she still cared for him but she reminded herself that it wasn't Nathan Carr she was still in love with.

A crack of thunder sounded above them. She'd been so involved in their conversation that she hadn't noticed how quickly the storm was coming in. Lightning flashed, reaching a jagged finger to the sea.

He slowly sat down in the sand. "Go ahead," he nearly whispered, either oblivious or indifferent to the incoming weather. "I need a minute." He wiped a tear that spilled from his eye, ripping her heart out. Why did things have to be so complicated? She wished they could go back to the day before he left; she wished he'd have chosen to do a lot of things differently. But he hadn't. And they both had to live with that.

"Nate, what did you expect? Your choices in life are completely opposed to mine. At every turn, I disagree with them. You make me frustrated and upset all the time. You *have* to let me move on."

He looked up at her. "Is it the way I left all those years ago? Because I was just a kid, and there were reasons… But I've even messed *that* up."

He wasn't making any sense.

"I wish I could go back to that day…" He shook his head once and closed his eyes, as if to hurl the thought from his mind. "Everything I do pushes you away. I just wish I could show you how much you mean to me. I wish you could know how *I* see you."

What did he mean that he wished he could go back to that day? His motives had been pretty clear. Sydney recounted everything that had been burned in her memory that day: how he wouldn't even look at her, the way he brushed her off, telling her there was more to life than Firefly Beach, how he never once looked back. She wanted to believe that he was sincere, but the fact that he was on the board kept coming back into her mind, challenging her feelings and screaming at her to use her head. She opened her mouth to confront him about it, but Logan was waiting and with the roll of thunder and the biting wind from the storm that was coming, it was time to call it a night. She needed to get back, and nothing they said right now could alter reality.

"I need to get back," she said, her tone softer now. Despite her anger it hurt her to see him in pain.

She didn't only need to get back to Logan, she needed to get out of the past and back to her life. And she had to make the decision to separate her feelings from the boy she once loved and the man right in front of her now.

Chapter Twenty-Three

"What in the world are you doing?" Sydney called out her bedroom window. In the light of early morning, Uncle Hank was on the beach, banging away on some sort of wood contraption. Her head still pounding from the emotion of last night, she squeezed her eyes shut with another *bang*.

With the rush of the tide, and a boat going by, he didn't hear her, so she shut her window, slipped on her flip-flops, and went out in her pajamas to see what exactly it was that he was doing. He'd woken her up from a sound sleep and she didn't want him to wake up Robby and the rest of the house.

"What are you making?" she asked, hopping over a piece of drift-wood to get to Uncle Hank.

The occasional blowing clouds made the lighthouse behind him look as though it were swaying. The storm had gone as quickly as it had arrived last night, leaving a crisp blue sky behind scattered hazy clouds that drifted past now and again.

"I'm making a birdhouse," he said with another slam of his hammer. He'd constructed an enormous box of wood and he was nailing the last piece onto the front. It had holes drilled in it to fit against the grid of wood that he'd built inside. "Clara had always wanted one and I'd never gotten around to building it for her." He picked up another nail and lined it up, with focused determination.

"How come you aren't building this in the woodshed?" she asked.

He looked up, out of breath slightly from bending over, small beads of sweat on his forehead. "Your Aunt Clara used to draw out her designs while sitting on this beach, so I wanted to build it out here where she could give me inspiration. I did the cuts in the woodshed but then I carried it all out to the sand—this was her place."

She couldn't help herself. "And why are you deciding to build it now?"

"I didn't sleep last night," he said, his voice heavy. "At all. The bed felt emptier than it has in a long time. I'm failing her by giving up Starlight Cottage." He lifted the large box and set it upright. "This is old wood from when we had the gazebo built all those years ago. It had been the one place in the house she and I designed together, and, through the years, it was there that we went whenever we wanted to talk. I wanted to put it up out there, so the birds would fill it." Uncle Hank stood back and took a look at the birdhouse, brushing a bit of sand off the top. "She loved the sound of birds in the morning. Putting this up would bring life to the gazebo again. When I sit out there, it's so quiet now. Her humming is gone. Her little chatter about whatever was on her mind is absent."

Sydney could hear Aunt Clara now. She'd told her once, "The birds singing are a constant reminder of life outside our walls, of a whole world out there, and the peace it can have if we all slow down enough to recognize our strengths. You'll never find an anxious bird, worried about where its next worm will come from. They just get up every morning singing and then do what they do best. And they're always fed. That's really all any of us should do."

"If I fill the silence with birds, then I won't feel so alone. I'm hoping to feel like she's with me."

Sydney looked out at the end of the pier where the gazebo sat as if it were suspended above the water. It was the place she'd first found a broken Uncle Hank a year ago, when they'd all arrived to finish carrying out Aunt Clara's wishes. Now it made sense as to why he'd been out there that day.

"So you've made the decision to sell?" she asked, fear swimming around as she waited for the answer.

"It's not a decision," he said, frowning. "My hand has been forced. If I stay, I'll be staring at a parking lot. All the property between us and the main road has now been bought up—the rezoning signs are posted. I saw them this morning on my walk. It's happening whether we like it or not." He peered down at one of the boards and inspected where it met another. "I want to hang it up in the gazebo and then take it with me when I move so that wherever I go, I'll have something left of Starlight Cottage."

"Where will we go?" she asked, feeling the emotion rising in her throat.

"I'm going to ask Nate about his land," he said.

She still hadn't told Uncle Hank about Nate's involvement in all this. "I need to talk to you about something," she said, taking a deep breath, steeling herself.

Uncle Hank's hands stilled and he turned to her.

"You might not want to live on Nate's land, once you hear this. Why don't we go over and sit down on the pier… Nate's on the board of supervisors," she said once they'd reached it. "He's also the one who bought all the lots surrounding the public beach access. I'm wondering if it was because he had more money than the county to offer the sellers. He wanted to make it a sure thing."

Disbelief slid across Uncle Hank's face as he sat on the edge of the pier, needing to steady himself. He looked wounded by the news rather than angry, his gaze submitting to the hurt and dropping to his folded hands in his lap.

"My guess is that Nate's moved back to Firefly Beach to invest in all those shops that are going up around the public beach access."

"He's not a developer," Uncle Hank said, clearly trying to make sense of this.

"No, but he grew up here. Who was his childhood best friend? Do you remember?"

"Colin Ferguson." Uncle Hank's eyes grew round. "The contractor who built the new waterfront hotel down the road."

"Yep." The whole thing gave her a bad taste in her mouth. She'd have never thought that he'd stoop this low. "I'm thinking he's offering us a spot on his land to relocate us so he can get us out of the way to build with Colin. I don't know for sure, of course, and I plan to give him a piece of my mind and find out what's going on, from his mouth, but I can't see any other reason for him to do this."

Uncle Hank put an unsteady hand against his face, and rubbed the white stubble on his cheek in thought. "I just can't believe this."

"I can't either."

The pain she'd seen on Nate's face last night had been etched into her mind. It was so confusing. What was also baffling was the intense ache that she felt at the finality of that moment on the beach. As angry as she was with him, there was a tiny irrational part of her that adored seeing him.

She missed him so much it hurt. Sydney pondered the undeniable pull she had toward him despite her attempts to drag herself away. What was becoming abundantly clear was that the reason she hadn't really been able to make the kind of life she really wanted for herself was because she'd always imagined Nate in it. Nothing had ever felt as right as the two of them together. It was her coping mechanism to hide her absolute sorrow that she wouldn't ever get the future she'd always hoped for.

She wanted to believe that he was the same wonderful man he'd been when they were together, and that there was some other reason for his actions, but her head told her there couldn't be another motive. There was no Nate Henderson. Why else would he be doing all this?

Sydney's mind was still swimming about Nate and the way he had deceived them all. There was a part of her that felt like she needed to get some closure on all this, but she didn't know how. She sat on the bed in her bedroom, staring at the view of the palms through her window, thinking. Her gaze slid down the panel curtain to her handbag on the floor, the napkin with Logan's number peeking out from it. Already having his number in her phone, she got up and plucked the napkin from her bag, dropping it into the trash. When she did, something occurred to her: she was still heartbroken about Nate, searching for closure she'd never gotten. Not even now.

One thing was certain: she couldn't move forward until she got over Nate, and she needed to be honest with Logan about that. She grabbed her cell and called him.

"Hey," he said, recognizing her call.

"Hi," she returned.

"I'm glad you called. I was wondering if you wanted to grab some dinner. But I'll cook. I think we should find something preferably inside and in a location where we won't be interrupted."

She could feel his smile on the other end of the line, making this more difficult but definitely necessary.

"About that interruption last time," she began.

His voice became serious. "You don't have to say anything," he said. "I wondered… Things aren't finished with you and Nate, are they?"

"Oh, they're finished," she said. "But it's complicated. I just don't want to drag you into the middle of everything. You deserve better than that. I just need some time to figure out what I want and where I'm going, you know?"

"I totally get it," he said, as kind as ever. "But if you ever want to get that dinner, it's a standing offer."

"Thank you for being amazing," she said.

When Sydney got off the phone call, she needed to take her mind off everything, deciding to help Uncle Hank install the birdhouse at the end of the gazebo. It was so big that they'd almost needed help, but eventually they'd managed it. Her biceps and shoulders ached from holding it up so long, but she also wondered if the pinched nerve she felt now was exacerbated by the stress of thinking about Nate. Even though she'd tried to push it out of her mind, his involvement in the public beach access had gone round and round in her head the entire time she'd been helping Uncle Hank.

Her inner thoughts were interrupted by the sound of a truck pulling into the driveway and Beau racing across the yard. Hallie got out of the truck and yanked her large suitcase from the vehicle, the thing landing with a thud onto the driveway. Ben got out the driver's side and ran around to greet an ecstatic Beau, who was alternating between whimpering and jumping up to Ben's face.

Hallie put a hand up to assist her pink visor in shielding the sun and caught sight of Sydney and Uncle Hank. She came jogging down to them, her slim frame tanned under her brightly colored T-shirt and shorts. She threw her arms around both of them, squeezing Sydney and Uncle Hank into a bear hug.

"I'm so happy to see you!" Sydney told her, giving her an enormous embrace.

"I missed you so much," Hallie said, her cheeks rosy from too much sun. She let them go, completely ignoring the fact that Sydney was still in her pajamas. "We had so much fun, Syd! We went snorkeling and we took a speedboat ride to this amazing restaurant right on the water…" She threw her hand to her chest dramatically. "The pool had personal cabanas with their own wait staff, and everything was included!"

"I knew I should've hidden out in your suitcase," Sydney teased.

"I've brought a little bit of it home with me," she said, waving her hands in the air in excitement. "I brought goodies! Who cares that I've been up since 4:30 for my flight home; I'm still in an island frame of mind! I've got piña colada mix in my bag and lots of presents for everyone. Let's go inside. Where's Mama?"

"That sounds amazing! And I need to check on Robby anyway. He should be up by now, and if he isn't, I'm going to wake him up so he can see you," she said as they walked, on either side of Uncle Hank, linking arms with him. "Hey, Ben!"

Ben raised his hand, a big smile on his face. He picked up their bags and took them inside.

Robby, who was having breakfast at the kitchen table when they came in, jumped up at the sight of Hallie and Ben and ran over to them.

"Hey, buddy!" Ben said, ruffling his hair and giving him a big hug. "Whatcha been doing while I was gone?"

Robby looked up at him, an enormous grin on his face. "Football and fishing and drawing and school work! Lots of stuff!"

"Sounds like you've had a busy week. Did Uncle Hank do all those things with you?" Ben took a seat at the table while Hallie ran over to give Mama a hug.

"No, I was with Nate! Isn't he your friend?"

Curiosity consumed Ben's face, and then he looked oddly excited. "Nate Henderson?" he asked, looking over at Sydney with suggestive delight.

"You mean Nathan Carr," Sydney corrected. "And yes."

"Sooo…" Ben said, clearly dying to know the details.

Sydney discreetly shook her head to let him know that there was no news with the Sydney-Nate situation, which seemed to confuse him. Strangely, he looked down at her hand and then made eye contact again. What was that all about?

"Have you talked to Nate at all, Syd?" he asked her.

"Plenty," she answered.

"Aaaand did he tell you…?" He eyed her as if she could read his mind.

"How he feels? Yes." She didn't want to get in to this in front of everyone.

"And what did you think about that?"

At this point, Ben and Sydney had Uncle Hank, Lewis, Hallie, *and* Jacqueline's attention.

"I'll tell you later," she replied. "Hallie said she has piña coladas."

They'd all left the kitchen table littered with empty piña colada glasses and scattered gift bags, their gifts of seashell necklaces, straw hats, and key chains sitting by their places, while they sat outside on the porch watching Beau run into the surf, shaking himself off and diving in again, clearly delighted his human was home. Ben and Robby were in the yard, and Jacqueline, Hallie, and Sydney had been catching up on everything.

"Where's Uncle Hank?" Hallie asked.

He'd gone in for a second and Sydney just now realized he'd been gone for a while. "Maybe he fell asleep after Lewis went home," she said. "I'll go in and check on him."

Sydney went inside. "Uncle Hank?" she called into the empty downstairs. "Uncle Hank?" she walked into the front sitting room and peered through the window to the porch—nobody was there. Where was he? "Hello-o!" she said, to no answer. She looked out at the road to see if he'd perhaps gone out to get the mail and had gotten stuck chatting with Lewis or something, but it was empty. She climbed the stairs to check up there.

When she got to the top, she heard a whimper in Uncle Hank's bedroom. She rushed down the hallway and knocked on his door, pushing it open. "What's the matter?" she asked, coming over to him and taking his hand. He sat on the bed, hunched over, his head hanging low while his back heaved with sobs.

"With Hallie and Ben home, it just hit me."

"What hit you?"

"I've already lost Clara. I can't lose Starlight Cottage too. It belongs in our family. Where will we all gather together once it's gone?" He took in a jagged breath. "And I'm worried they're going to level it if we let it go." His lip trembled. "I've tried to act like it's no big deal, but I'm losing the last bit of myself. I'm too old to start a new life somewhere. I should be slowing down and basking in all the memories of this gorgeous place."

The sound of Robby's voice outside the window cut through their conversation. A car had pulled into the drive. Sydney tipped her head up to see Nate—he'd come over in some sort of ridiculously expensive luxury car. This was all *his* fault. And he didn't seem to be bothered at all by the fact that he was disrupting the lives of everyone who used to support him in this house.

"I'll be right back," she said with determination. This was it. She was going to tell him once and for all, get everything out into the open right now. Sydney marched downstairs and out the front door, breezing right past Ben and Hallie. She poked her finger into Nate's chest. "We need to talk," she snapped.

"Hey, Robby," Ben said, clearly gauging the situation. "Let's go play football."

"Okay!" Robby ran over to Ben and the two of them went over to the yard. Hallie followed them, but she didn't leave without first giving a look of question to her sister. Sydney brushed it off kindly and then turned her dagger-of-a-stare back to Nate.

Opening the door to his shiny black Mercedes SUV, Nate gestured for her to get in. Without a word, she slid into the seat, her lips set in a pout. He got into the driver's side and shut the door.

"I know just where we can talk," he said. With a rev of the engine, he pulled out of the drive.

Chapter Twenty-Four

Sydney sat silently while Nate drove. They must have driven for at least twenty minutes, but she didn't notice. She was too busy seething. She'd absolutely had it. As soon as they got wherever he was going, she was ready to lay into him. He couldn't do this to her family.

Nate pulled onto a long, winding gravel road, propelling them deep into the woods. He put the windows down, allowing the earthy scent and the warm wind to fill up the car. Sydney's hair blew into her face and she tucked a tendril behind her ear. When they'd made it far enough down the path that the main road was no longer visible, he stopped the car right in the middle of the road and got out. She followed him to a small patch of grass that had formed in a natural clearing. A few beams of sunlight slid through the opening in the canopy of trees, illuminating the area. Nate sat down on the ground and patted the space beside him.

She wanted to ask where they were, but it didn't matter. This was about Starlight Cottage and Nate's selfish act to take it away. She sat down across from him instead.

"Why are you *really* back in Firefly Beach, Nate?" she clipped.

He stared at her.

It was obvious that she'd put him on the spot. "Cat got your tongue?"

"I've tried to tell you," he said.

"No, Nate. You haven't."

The skin between his eyes wrinkled in a way that she'd always found adorable whenever he didn't understand something, but she forced herself to push whatever fondness she had for him aside.

"Why don't you start by telling me about the lots?"

"The lots?" He looked deeply into her eyes as if he were trying to figure out how much she knew. Well, she knew it all.

"Yeah. The lots. How's Colin Ferguson these days?"

His initial confusion slid off his face, replaced by a cautious interest. "He's good," Nate said guardedly.

"Anything you want to tell me? Maybe, say, how you and Colin are about to rob me and my family of our home for your financial gain?"

The confusion was back again.

"How could you, Nate?" She stood up to hide her emotion. He came up behind her and put his hands on her shoulders. Usually, she'd flinch, but she didn't have the energy anymore. A tear fell down her cheek.

He turned her around and offered her a tender smile. "Come with me," he said gently into her ear. The fact that he wasn't even the least bit defensive had her questioning his reaction, so she walked back to his vehicle. He opened the door and she got in.

Another few minutes down the gravel road led them to another clearing, but this one was outlined by turquoise coast, and sitting right in the middle of it was a brand new white farmhouse with a porch that wrapped all the way around the structure, rocking chairs on painted gray decking, enormous windows showing off the stylish beach décor inside, and an incredible view of the glistening gulf, its water lapping lazily onto the bright sand, a white sailboat bobbing out on the horizon. It was literally the house she'd always dreamed of.

Nate shut off the engine and went around to her side to open her door. She stepped out and tipped her head up to view the massive house. "Is this yours?" she asked, her curiosity getting the better of her.

"For now," he said.

She regarded him with questions in her eyes. It would be just like him to build something beautiful like this only to go back to LA, but his demeanor was telling her something else that she couldn't decipher.

"Let's go in." He held out his hand, but she didn't take it, so he gestured for her to lead the way to the massive glass-paned double door, reaching around her to open it once they had climbed the porch stairs.

The décor of whitewashed wood and textured fabrics was just as she would've chosen for herself, but then again, Nate had always had wonderful taste. They used to talk about what their life together would look like once the two of them had made it big.

"I want to give you a big, white farmhouse," he'd said back then, rolling onto his belly, grabbing her wrists and pinning them gently to the grass she was lying on. He kissed her. "With a big porch going all the way around it for all of our kids," he told her, playfully. He broke her hold, wrapping his arms around her waist and nuzzled her neck, making her flinch and giggle.

"Not until I have a big, fat diamond on my hand. You'd better make an honest woman of me first," she'd said, giggling as he tickled her. "And we'll be famous, so I want more than that."

He looked into her eyes, that familiar smirk on his lips. "Whatever you want," he said softly. "Tell me."

"It has to sit right on the beach, with rocking chairs so we can grow old together there."

"I can't wait to grow old with you." He rolled her over so that she hovered above him. He ran his finger softly down her face and kissed her again.

"And we should have a giant barn for parties. I want to get married on the beach and have our reception in the barn."

"I'll do anything you want," he said lovingly.

Both of them were silent, speaking volumes with their eyes.

They'd never questioned it; it had always been a "when" rather than an "if." From the look of this house, he hadn't changed his mind about what he wanted.

"Would you like something to drink?" he asked, tearing her away from the past, and the memories that hurt her to relive. Nate crossed the driftwood-colored hardwoods to the expansive kitchen that overlooked a rustic living area.

It was all so beautiful that she'd forgotten for a second why she was there. "No, thank you," she replied, but he went to the fridge anyway and poured two glasses of iced tea.

"Please," he said, offering her one and pulling out a chair at the oversized bar that separated the space between the kitchen and living room.

Sydney sat down, wanting to move things along.

Nate lowered himself on a barstool beside her and wrapped his hand around his iced tea. "Would you like to tell me why you think I want to take Starlight Cottage from you?"

She turned toward him. "I know you're on the board, Nate. Stop trying to avoid this."

A small smile twitched around his lips. "Is that why you're so angry with me?"

Was he serious right now? She hopped off her barstool and cut her eyes at him. "Yes, Nate," was all she could get out for fear she'd reach over and shake him by the shoulders. Frustrated beyond belief, she walked over to the large glass doors that overlooked the pearly white sand and the restless waters beyond.

Nate came up behind her, looking over her head at the view. Then suddenly, his voice was at her ear, causing goose bumps down her arm. "I *am* on the board," he said softly. "And I've bought all the lots for the public beach access, which I will be donating to the county."

She felt the prick of tears. Finally, he'd admitted it. But even worse than the realization of the truth, was the fact she knew there was no more Nate Henderson left. He was now entirely Nathan Carr, because Nate Henderson would never have done this to her. She wiped a tear away quickly, but Nate turned her around before she could clear the emotion from her face.

"You asked me why I came back to Firefly Beach," he said, wiping another of her tears. "In order to truly answer that, I have to explain why I'd ever left in the first place." He took her hand and walked her over to the sofa, gently pulling her down beside him. "If you'll give me your time right now, I want to tell you everything. I've been trying but I haven't gotten it right. I need you to give me this. You don't owe it to me, but I'm asking you. Let me tell you everything."

"Okay," she finally said, literally praying that some miracle would fall from the sky and make everything better.

"You are an incredible writer," he said. "You got that writing opportunity to travel the U.S., remember?"

She nodded, hanging on his every word. She wanted to know why he'd left, in his own words.

"But what about the chance you didn't explore? Your professor gave you two opportunities that year: the one in the U.S., but also one to live in Africa for two years, and you never filled out the paperwork."

What did any of this have to do with why Nate left? "I couldn't leave Firefly Beach," she said with a disbelieving laugh.

"I know that—you told me. But why? What was the reason you didn't want to go?"

She didn't want to admit it now, after everything. He had to know the answer to that already. But she needed him to be honest with her, so she decided she should be too. "It meant that I had to spend two years away from you." She stared at him as she said it, driving home the fact that she hadn't wanted to spend even two years away, let alone a decade. He needed to know how much he'd hurt her.

He leaned in, his fingers brushing hers. "I couldn't allow you to give up your dreams because of me. I never expected to be the successful writer of the two of us. Going to LA was my cover for removing myself from your life so that you could go on and do amazing things without me holding you back."

This revelation hit her like a ton of bricks. All these years, she'd thought he saw her as lesser when really he thought she was more. A tidal wave of emotions flooded Sydney as she sat in front of Nate, completely exposed. "When you left, you never even looked back. Not once," she challenged him, brushing a tear away. "I waited, staring at your rear-view mirror for just one tiny indication that you cared at all that you were tearing my heart out as your truck headed down the drive. You never. Looked. Back."

Nate leaned into her personal space, peering down at her, his hand resting on her arm, his eyes brimming with emotion. "There was a moment where I didn't know if I could make it out of the drive. I had to force my foot to stay on the gas, because I knew that I'd never feel for anyone else the way I felt for you." His touch moved down her arm until his fingers found hers and finally came to rest intertwined in her own the way they used to do without even thinking about it, all those years ago. "If I'd have looked back, I would've faltered." He bowed his head as if the memory of it had stolen his breath and he needed a minute to recover. "I thought I was doing the right thing, giving you the space you needed to be great."

"I didn't need space to be great, Nate. I needed *you*."

"I thought I was in your way." He shook his head. "You're the best writer I've ever known. Why didn't you continue, Syd?"

"I couldn't do it without you," she said, the ache burning her chest like it had the day he'd left.

"That's not true. You don't need me to be great."

"But I have to be happy to write, and you made me the happiest."

"I was just a boy from Firefly Beach. I never really expected to be anything more than that. And I knew how much you wanted to stay with me. It terrified me because your talent overwhelmed me. I didn't want you to wake up one day, stuck in this little town, wishing your life could've been different. I knew the only way to make you move forward was to cut ties. In my young brain, I'd thought it had been the right thing to do. But the more I tried living without you, the more I wanted to prove myself, to prove that I was worthy enough to be with you. When I looked at you, I knew I needed to be something great. For you."

"This doesn't make any sense," she said, breathless.

"I've been walking around quietly heartbroken, missing you for years. I stayed quiet when I wanted to speak. I stayed away when I wanted to run to you." He lightly ran his thumb over her hand. "You said you kept our ring to remind you of what you don't want, and all my fears came true." He hung his head and took in a deep breath before letting it out. When he looked back up at her, his eyes glistened with tears. He cleared his throat.

"That's not… I didn't mean it."

His eyes found hers. "This house, the boat outside, the truck that we used to ride in—it's all for you. I came back for you. I thought I lost you when you married Christian. I even called you, but I felt awful for meddling in your life when you'd moved on… I lost you once when we were young, and again when you married Christian. I wanted to give it everything I had this time. I wanted to do it right."

Sydney swam out of her feelings, trying to keep her head in check. "Then why in the world would you get on the board of supervisors and put Starlight Cottage in jeopardy?"

"I got on the board to talk some sense into them. I talked Colin out of building in the area, and I bought all the lots myself so that they would be forced to listen to me. The empty lots are going to be a natural preserve. There will be parking, but it will be inconspicuously placed. The view from Starlight Cottage won't change. I've been working with the county on hiking trails and water access for kayaking, planting trees, and landscaping out to the road. I've been calling people about it since the wedding. I didn't want to say anything in case I couldn't make it happen, but it passed with a vote of fifteen to two."

Sydney stood up and clasped a hand over her mouth in utter shock. It felt like a ten-year weight had been lifted, as if she were waking up from a terrible nightmare. How could she have gotten it so wrong: it had been Nathan Carr who'd been the imposter all along.

"I wish you'd have said something all those years ago…"

He nodded. "It was the worst decision of my life. I had to go to therapy for years just to stop the stress of it from eating me alive. That's how I was in touch with Mary Alice. I needed someone I could trust. I had run into her after college, and we'd shared what we were doing at the time, so when I needed a therapist, she was the one I turned to because I knew she would keep it from the press. She urged me to call you, and I tried, but I just didn't know if you'd want me in your life after what I'd done to us."

Sydney looked around the room, processing all of this. *That's* why Mary Alice's name was on his phone…

He rose and put his face right in front of hers. "I did it all because I'm totally in love with you."

"Nate, I'm so sorry," was all she could get out. She felt terrible that she'd misjudged him. All those times she'd thought he was being awful and selfish… Then all of a sudden, she noticed his frown and the disappointment on his face and she realized he thought she was apologizing for not feeling the way he did about her. "No," she said, taking his hands. "I'm sorry it took me so long to understand."

His face lifted and he squeezed her hands in his.

"I haven't stopped missing you since the day you left," she said.

With a *whoop*, Nate scooped her up into his arms, laughing with happiness. Then he looked into her eyes and pulled her close. "I've been wanting to do this for a long damn time." Agonizingly slowly, he pressed his lips to hers, and in that one kiss, he made up for all their lost time. His lips moved urgently on hers, his hands unstill, finding all the places they used to roam the last time his fingers had been set free upon her. She reached up, and ran her fingers through the back of his hair, the feel of him better than anything in the world.

Gently, Nate pulled back, the effort clearly quite difficult for him. He took his phone out of his pocket and typed something. Then, as he set his phone down on the counter, hers buzzed to life. Suspiciously, she pulled her phone from her back pocket and peered down at the email push notification.

I told her everything.

Love, Mel

She looked up from her phone, confused.

"I wanted to talk to you when you weren't so angry. I wanted to hear what your real thoughts were…"

"Mel?" she asked.

"Short for Melody, the name we wanted for our little girl."

She swallowed. "And what's the significance of 4221 in your email address?"

He lifted his eyes to the ceiling, and then shifted his gaze around the room. "It's the address of our new house," he said, spreading his arms wide.

"*Our* new house? Nope, I'm not shacking up with anyone who hasn't made an honest woman out of me," she teased, recalling their old memory. "My ring is back at Starlight Cottage."

Nate grabbed his phone again, and started typing something, his action jarring and pulling her out of the moment. Was he responding to something in the middle of their conversation? The fear that Nathan Carr was still present came rushing back, despite everything.

"Come outside with me?" he asked suddenly. "Let's take a walk."

He grabbed a pad of paper and a marker from the drawer and led her through the floor-to-ceiling glass doors that opened up, exposing the entire room to the beach. The warm breeze blew in like an old friend as he took her hand and led her across the deck and down the stairs to the sand.

"Where are we going?" she asked.

"You'll see." He led her around the house and down the path they'd driven, into the mass of trees. The brush had all been cleared and shade-grass planted, the tops of it cool against the sides of her feet as she walked in her flip-flops.

"What was the message you sent from your phone just before we left?" she asked casually.

He stopped and faced her, looking down at her with a grin on his face. "It was nothing," he replied. He leaned down and kissed her.

"Then why won't you tell me?" she pressed playfully as she got up on her toes and looked him square in the eye. "You'd better tell me," she said when he laughed instead of answering her. "I'm small but I'm feisty! I can take you down." She hit her best karate pose, making him laugh even harder.

"You have nothing on me," he said, tossing his notebook and pen into the grass. He grabbed her around the waist, lifting her up and making her squeal.

She wrapped her legs around his torso to hold on while she tickled his sides, causing him to collapse from the weight of her, both of them tumbling together onto the soft grass.

"I know your weakness," she said, still giggling. She reached out and tickled him again.

Taking her hands, he trapped them across her chest so she couldn't move. "I can still defend myself." He then pulled her hands around him as he hovered over her. "I don't want to, though," he said tenderly. "I'm all yours…"

Abruptly, he looked at his watch and stood up, grabbing her hands and pulling her to a standing position.

"What's going on?" she asked.

He took her hands again. "I need you to close your eyes. Will you trust me?"

She nodded, almost unable to follow his command because of the way he was drinking her in like he used to do. Finally, she closed her eyes.

"Okay, don't move or look until I tell you to. Promise?"

"I promise." She didn't move a muscle, all of her other senses on high alert. She took in the clean cotton scent of him when he kissed her forehead, the warmth of the sun on her skin, the rustle of the palm trees in the coastal wind. She could feel him rushing around her, breezing past her.

And then finally, he said, "Open your eyes." She allowed her blurred vision to sharpen on Nate. He was a ways from her, still holding the marker and the pad of paper. But as her scope widened, she started to notice little pieces of white paper stuck beneath the triangular bark of the palms between them. "Start there," he said, pointing to the tree closest to her.

Slowly, she paced over to it. Nate had written a message on it like they used to do at Starlight Cottage. Sydney plucked the paper from the bark and read, "I love you." She looked out at him and smiled as he stared at her with that adoring look that melted her in an instant. He pointed to the next tree.

Another note: "I never want to live another day without you."

Nate gestured toward the next tree. Holding both the pages in her hand, Sydney went to the third note. "Everything that you achieve in life, I promise from this day forward to be by your side to cheer you on." Sydney's eyes clouded with tears and she blinked them away to go to the next tree. She read the next one. "I want you with me for every sunset and every sunrise for the rest of my life." There was one more tree between Sydney and Nate and he stepped up beside her as she read the last message. It said simply, "Take my hand." Nate held out his hand and Sydney placed hers in his.

"Follow me," he said, leading her toward the back of the house. When they got to the beach, he kissed her. "Wait right here." Then he nearly sprinted across the yard and up the steps, rushing into the cottage. She caught sight of a white van, driving away around front just as he came back down to the shore out of breath. He took a minute and then smiled at her. "Ready to go inside?"

Sydney took his hand and walked beside Nate, climbing the steps where she got the first glimpse inside. She gasped, throwing her hand over her mouth. Every surface of the entire open area was filled with red roses, gardenias, and flickering candles. "What's going on?" she asked, breathless, as he led her into the center of the room, the fragrance filling her. "How did you do all this?"

"I've had the florist on standby since the wedding. All I had to do was text him and he'd be ready."

"You've had this planned since Hallie and Ben's wedding?" she asked, looking around at all the stunning bouquets.

"Somehow, I was going to get you back. Even if I spent the rest of my life trying. This house is yours whenever you want to move in. And as for making an honest woman of you…" He reached into his pocket and gripped a small black velvet box while taking her hand with his other. He got down on one knee. "Sydney Marie Flynn, will you marry me?" He opened the box to reveal an emerald-cut solitaire that was big enough to blind someone if she went out in the sunshine wearing it.

"Yes," she said, tears pricking her eyes. "It's incredible."

"I asked you to wear the plastic ring until I could get you the best ring money could buy. This is it." He took it out of the case and slipped it onto her finger, the weight of it substantial, but at the same time, like it was meant to be there. Then he stood up and gazed into her eyes. "Mrs. Nate Henderson. I like it."

"Not Mrs. Carr?" she questioned.

He shook his head, placing his hands on her face. "Definitely not. Just the real me and the real you." He leaned in and pressed his lips to hers. "I love you," he said into her ear. "I'm madly in love with you!" Nate scooped her up, spinning her around.

All of a sudden, when he set her down, something came to her: she remembered how Ben had looked at her hand when he'd come home. "Does Ben know about this?" she wriggled her finger with the solitaire.

"Yeah," he said with a grin. "I told him all about it when I came home for the wedding. I already texted him too. Everyone's coming over. They'll be here in just a few minutes."

"Everyone?"

"Yep. Your whole family, Malory, and Juliana. Ben's explained everything to them. He's telling them about my involvement with the board and the *real* reason I came back." He trailed his hand down her cheek. "He's rounding them up now."

"Where will they stand with all the flowers?" she giggled.

He leaned in and nibbled her neck, clearly unable to keep his hands off her. "Let's get in the truck," he said, taking her hand and moving toward the front door. "I've got something else to show you."

Nate locked up behind them and led her to the old truck she'd spent so many days in. He opened her door. "After you, my dear," he said dramatically. He kissed the top of her hand and ran around to his side, getting in. As she sat in his truck now, it felt just like it had all those years ago, all the pain associated with it leaving her like a grain of sand in the wind.

They left the beach and started down a narrow gravel path through the woods in the other direction.

"Are you kidnapping me?" she teased as they pushed on further into the middle of nowhere.

"Absolutely." He gave her a wink, leaning his elbow on the open window like he always had, his other hand resting on the top of the steering wheel. "I'm never letting you go again." She scooted over so that she was right next to him on the old bench-style seat. He eyed her with a suggestive look on his face. "I should've thought this whole family gathering out… I want you all to myself."

"There's plenty of time to be by ourselves," she said, kissing him on the cheek.

He nodded. "We have our whole life ahead of us."

She put her head on his shoulder.

When the truck came to a stop, next to a line of familiar cars belonging to her family and friends, they were outside of an enormous red barn with white trim. Nate got out and opened her door before running up to the barn and sliding the large panel to open the space. Inside, it was finished with hardwood floors and an enormous chandelier hanging from the vaulted A-line ceiling. "What is this?" she asked, coming up beside him and waving to everyone inside.

Lewis was there and Uncle Hank. Mama and Robby were both grinning like crazy, and Hallie had her hand on her heart lovingly as she stood by Ben and Malory. Juliana was grinning from ear to ear.

"Well, by day, it's a whiskey distillery. And by night, it's a private concert venue… I thought we could get married on the beach and have our reception here, if that's what you still want to do."

Robby ran forward and put his arms around them both. "Hey, buddy," she said, her two realities colliding. "I want to tell you about Nate," she said.

"Ben told me!" Robby said excitedly.

"Oh?" she asked. "What did he tell you?"

"He said that Nate loves the two of us very much and that he's going to take care of us and play all the football I want!"

Nate and Sydney both laughed, their attention moving over to Ben, who shrugged with a guilty smile.

"He's right," Nate said. "Football all day, every day! But right now, we have a party to go to."

As they went inside the barn, Sydney noticed a table full of boxes of pizza and bottles of soda. She looked at Ben questioningly.

"It's the best I could do on short notice. I know you've never been a big planner, Nate, but thirty minutes would be difficult for anyone," he said with a laugh. "The rest of town should be here in about an hour. Fingers crossed they can find the place. But I do have a surprise." He pointed to the corner of the barn, and Uncle Hank pushed a lever on the wall illuminating a small stage. The back door opened and one of Ben's super-groups that he produced, Sylvan Park, a band that recently had been selling out whole stadiums, walked in and took their places on stage.

Sydney clapped a hand over her mouth. "How did you manage this?" she asked through her fingers.

"They're on vacation down the road in Seaside at the moment, and they owed Nate and me a favor."

The lead singer tapped his microphone, the amplifiers on the walls thumping. "This is a song that Nate wrote for Sydney. It's on our next album. You all are the first to hear it live. I hope you enjoy it. It's called 'It Was Always You.'"

Rest your head tonight
In your bed tonight,
Close your eyes
And think of me
I'm out here all alone
Hoping you hear me,
Wishing you knew
It was always you…

Nate took Sydney's hand and walked her out under the chandelier to dance with her. As they moved to the music, he whispered in her ear, "It was always you." And Sydney danced with Nate Henderson for the rest of the song, and forever.

Epilogue

"You know I don't like you flying to New York in your state," Nate said to Sydney, kissing her as they sat together on the porch swing at their cottage. "*NY Pulse* will have to wait for our little Abigail to make her appearance."

They'd decided to name their baby girl Clara Abigail after Aunt Clara instead of their original choice of Melody. Abigail and Robby were going to grow up in Firefly Beach, and it was only fitting that the next woman in the family carry Aunt Clara's name. Abigail would have her whole life ahead of her to choose what she wanted to do, but one thing was for sure: Clara Abigail Henderson would be born into a strong line of creative and innovative women. And Nate and Sydney would be right there with her to help her along the way.

Sydney waved to Robby, who was chasing their new cocker spaniel mix they'd named Bentley down the beach. Bentley was their gift to Robby to celebrate the fact that he was going to be a big brother. Nate pulled Robby aside. "You know, I was a big brother, and there's a lot of responsibility that comes with taking care of your sister," he'd said. "I think you might need some practice with that. Wait right here." While Robby waited in the front yard of their new home, Nate let Bentley out of his crate and opened the door. The little puppy went racing across the grass toward Robby, his big red bow flapping in the wind, tackling him and knocking him over with puppy kisses.

Sydney set her laptop aside. "I have just a few meetings to wrap up before I stop completely. But I don't have to fly to New York this time. Amanda is coming to me. She didn't want me flying either when I'm due in two weeks." Sydney rubbed her belly fondly, her wedding band and solitaire sparkling in the summer light.

Only a week after her engagement to Nate, she'd gotten a call from Amanda Rains of *NY Pulse* magazine, offering her the content editor position. She'd been able to work remotely, and her work had been so successful that over the last year, she'd been promoted to Senior Content Editor.

"Should we go?" she asked, standing up as Nate folded down her laptop to take it inside. She called Robby and the puppy Bentley, beckoning them back up to the house.

"Juliana's flown in for the baby shower," Nate said, peering down at his phone. "Your mom just texted to say they're home from the airport."

"Oh my goodness!" Sydney hadn't seen Juliana in a year and she couldn't believe she'd come all the way from Argentina just to see her.

After her contract had ended, Juliana had gone back home to her family farm, away from the paparazzi, where she'd opened a small studio for aspiring models. Before she left, she'd gone to the media about Seth, causing a firestorm. He would never work again. Between losing so many models over the last year after Juliana's admission and his legal fees, he barely had a cent to his name. Before going home, she'd told Sydney that what was most important to her was making sure that the girls she worked with knew that they were worth more than just their faces. She explained her new approach to modeling, where they would get instruction in how to pose and walking techniques, but also self-esteem classes and information on what best practices looked like in the industry. She was loving the work, feeling more fulfilled than ever.

"And Uncle Hank has made a key lime pie." Nate eyed her.

Sydney threw her head back, laughing. Uncle Hank and Lewis had taken a culinary class focusing on desserts. Uncle Hank had truly enjoyed it, and he'd been making pies for the last eight months or so.

"Hallie said not to worry; she'd had her team decorate in lime green anyway."

Hallie and Ben were expecting their first adoptive child to arrive in mere months. And the birth mother had just told them she was having a girl. Hallie and Ben decided to name her Violet. Both cousins Violet and Abigail would be born in the same year, and Sydney and Hallie were having a joint baby shower for the two of them.

"Nate!" Robby said, out of breath, his bare feet sandy and a football in his hand. "Will we be able to bring this?" He tossed it into the air.

"Absolutely," Nate said, catching it above Robby's head before Robby could reach it. "There's only so much cake one man can eat in a day…" He winked at Robby. "Go long!"

A Letter from Jenny

Thank you for reading *The House on Firefly Beach*. I hope it got you longing for those endless summer days, ocean views, and the sound of island music and fresh-fruit cocktails!

If you'd like me to drop you an email when my next book is out, you can sign up here:

www.ItsJennyHale.com/email-signup

I won't share your email with anyone else, and I'll only email you when a new book is released.

If you did enjoy *The House on Firefly Beach*, I'd love it if you'd write a review. Getting feedback from readers is amazing, and it also helps to persuade other readers to pick up one of my books for the first time.

If you enjoyed this story, you can read about Hallie and Ben in my novel *Summer at Firefly Beach*. And if you'd like even a little *more* summertime on the beach, do check out my other summer novels: *The Summer House* and *Summer by the Sea*.

Until next time!
Jenny

Acknowledgments

To my husband Justin, for his steadfast support, as he listens to all my wild ideas, I am forever grateful.

To my friends and family, I am thankful from the bottom of my heart for all the positivity and encouragement they provide. I am so appreciative of the creative people I've met here in Nashville, and delighted that I was welcomed into their circles. I am continually inspired by the people who surround me in this business.

Thanks to the folks at Bookouture. An enormous thank you to my editor Christina Demosthenous, who jumped right in and never missed a beat with me. To Oliver Rhodes, I am eternally grateful. I am so thankful for everything he's given me.

About the Author

Jenny Hale is a *USA Today* bestselling author of romantic women's fiction. Her novels *Coming Home for Christmas* and *Christmas Wishes and Mistletoe Kisses* have been adapted for television on the Hallmark Channel. Her stories are chock-full of feel-good romance and overflowing with warm settings, great friends, and family. Grab a cup of coffee, settle in, and enjoy the fun!

You can learn more at:
ItsJennyHale.com
Twitter @JHaleAuthor
Facebook.com/JennyHaleAuthor
Instagram @JHaleAuthor

me as the name of the mountain where I was born. A free life, released from all responsibilities!

Sickness is the only way we have to obtain peace of mind.

I think: I wish they would all die. But nobody dies. I think: I wish they would all be my enemies. But nobody shows me any special enmity, and my friends all pity me.

Why am I loved? Why can't I hate anyone from the heart? To be loved is an insufferable insult.

But I am tired! I am a weakling!

For just a year, for even a month,
Even a week, even three days will do,
God, if you exist, God!
I have just one wish, that you
Will break down my body somewhere.
It doesn't matter if it hurts, make me sick
Oh, make me sick.

I want to sleep
On pure white, soft, and
Gently enveloping my whole body
Cushions, where I feel as though I am sinking
All the way into the bottom of a valley of peace, no
On the worn mat of a home for the aged will do,
Not thinking of anything (so that even if I die,
I don't care) to sleep a long time.
To sleep so soundly that I won't know
If someone comes and steals my hands and feet.

How's that for a feeling? Ah—
Just the thought makes me sleepy.

If I could tear off and throw away
This garment I am wearing now,
This heavy, heavy garment of obligation (ah, I grow drowsy).
My body would become light as hydrogen,

And perhaps I would fly, high, high into the great sky,
And everyone below would say, perhaps, a lark!

Death! Death! My wish
Is for this alone.

Ah, will you really kill me? Wait just a bit,
Merciful God, oh, just a little while!

Just a bit, just enough to buy some bread,
Five, five cents will do,
If you have enough mercy to kill me!

A tepid wind heavy with rain is blowing this evening. In the distance the croaking of the frogs. At three in the morning the rain came splashing down.

11th, Sunday

Today I had to go to a poetry gathering at Yosano's house.[2] Naturally, there was no likelihood of anything amusing taking place. Hiraide was telling what a big success last night's "Devotees of Pan"[3] had been. Yoshii, who came in late, was saying, "Last night when I got drunk and pissed from Eitai Bridge, a policeman bawled me out." Everybody seems to have been drunk and had a wild time.

As usual we wrote poems on given themes. It must have been about nine o'clock when the selection of poems was completed. Recently I haven't felt like writing serious *uta,* and as usual turned out some mock verses. Here are a couple:

When I wear shoes
That make a squeak

[2] Yosano Tekkan (1873-1935), a leading poet of the day. For poetry by his wife Akiko, see pp. 202-3, 206.

[3] An artistic and literary club—1908-1912—led by the poets Kitahara Hakushū and Yoshii Isamu. The club stood for both European literature and the art of the Tokugawa period.

I feel unpleasant, as if
I tread upon a frog.

Your eyes must have
The mechanism of
A fountain pen—
You are always shedding tears.

The man
Whose hands tremble and voice breaks
At sight of a woman
No longer exists.

Akiko suggested that we sit up all night composing poetry. I made some silly excuse and left.

Another precious day wasted. Suddenly a feeling of regret surged up within me. If I was going to look at the cherry blossoms, why didn't I go by myself and look at them as I wanted? A poetry gathering! Of all the stupid things!

I am a person who delights in solitude, a born individualist. I feel as if the time I have spent with others, at least when I haven't been fighting with them, has been so much emptiness. It seems quite natural that when I spend an hour with two or three or more people, the hour, or at least half of it, is so much emptiness.

I used to enjoy people's visits, and tried to send guests away as happy as possible so that they would come again. What a stupid thing to have done! Now I am not so pleased when people come. The only ones I'm glad to see are those who are likely to lend me money when I am broke. But I try not to borrow unless I have to. How happy I would be if I could make a living without being helped in anything because I am pitied! This doesn't necessarily refer only to money. Then I could live without listening to anybody's talk.

I have thought what a pointless way I am living, but the thoughts after that have frightened me. My desk is in a mess. I haven't anything to read. At the moment the most pressing thing is to write a letter to my mother, but that also frightens me. I always think: I wish I could comfort those poor people by writing them something, anything at all. And since the beginning of the year I've sent them exactly one letter and one postcard. This month, it was at the beginning of the month, I had a letter saying that they had only twenty sen to spend on Kyōko. I borrowed in advance even more than usual from the firm, with the intention of sending them fifteen yen. But I put it off from day to day, disliking to write a letter. Ah—

I fell asleep immediately.

12th, Monday

Today was just as beautiful as yesterday. The cherry blossoms, enjoying their three days of life under a windless sky, have yet to fall. The cherry tree under my window is sprouting pale leaves above the blossoms.

Down the hill on the right-hand side of the street, just at the corner of Tamachi, is a shoemaker's shop. When I passed there, suddenly a happy, gay voice entered my ears, as if from a fond memory. A wide grassy field floated up before my eyes—a skylark was singing in a cage at the shoemaker's. For a minute or so I remembered my dead cousin, with whom I used to go shooting in the fields near his house.

When I think of it, I have left my old—yes, old—friends, and the time has come for me to build a house for myself. The "old friends" I have are, or were, actually the newest friends I have made. Naturally I don't think of Yosano as an elder brother or as a father. He is simply a person who has helped me. The relations between one who helps and one who is helped can continue only while the former is more important a person than the latter, or while the two are traveling different roads, or if the former is no longer as great as the latter. When they are traveling the same road and there is rivalry between them, the friendship ends. I do not now have special respect for Yosano. We are both writers, but I somehow feel that we are traveling different roads.

I have no desire to be any closer to Yosano, but at the same time I do not feel any necessity of making a break with him. If an occasion comes, I should like to thank him for all he has done for me.

It is different with Akiko. I sometimes do think of her as an elder sister . . . the two of them are quite different.

Most of the other friends I have made through the New Poetry Society are very different from the Yosanos. I have already quarreled with Hirano. Yoshii is a second-rate lascivious daydreamer who frightens people by wearing a devil's mask—a pitiable second-rater. If their so-called literature is the same thing as my literature, I won't hesitate to throw away my pen forever. The others are not even worth mentioning.

No, such things have no use. However I think of it, they don't amount to anything.

To do only what I want, go where I want, follow all my own needs. . . .

Yes, I want to do as I please.

That is all! All of all!

Do not be loved by others, do not accept their charity, do not promise anything. Do nothing which entails asking forgiveness. Never talk to anyone about yourself. Always wear a mask. Always be ready for a fight—be able to hit the next man on the head at any time. Don't forget that when you make friends with someone you are sooner or later certain to break with him.

13th, Tuesday

Early this morning I opened my eyes, momentarily wakened by the noise of the maid opening the shutters. Hearing nothing else, I dozed off again, the unconscious sleep of spring. It is a cloudy calm day. All over the city the blossoms are gradually beginning to fall.

A sad letter came from my mother.

> "Dear Mr. Ishikawa,
>
> I was so happy with the letter you sent to Mr. Miyazaki. I have been waiting every day since, hoping word would come from you, and now it is April already. I am taking care of Kyōko and feeding her, which I have never done before. She is getting bigger every day, and is almost too much for me.

Can't you send for her? I beg the ravor of a reply.[4] On the sixth and seventh there was a terrible rainstorm. The rain leaked in and we had nowhere to stay. Kyōko was so upset she couldn't sleep. She caught a cold on the second of April and is still not better. Setsuko [5] leaves for work every morning at eight o'clock and doesn't return until five or six. It's so hard for me when she is not here. There's no more household money left. Even one yen will be appreciated. I beg you kindly to send something soon. When do you think we will be able to go to Tokyo? Please let me know. If we don't get an answer from you, it's all over with us. We are all coming, so please make preparations.

Katsu"

My mother's letter, in shaky characters, full of spelling mistakes! I don't suppose very many people besides myself could read it. They say Mother was the best student at school when she was a girl. But in forty years of married life with my father, she probably never once wrote a letter. The first one I received from her was two summers ago. I had left Mother alone in Shibutami. She couldn't stand that dreadful town any longer, and she had written out of loneliness, searching in her memory for the completely forgotten characters. Today was the fifth letter I have received since coming to Tokyo. There are fewer mistakes, and the characters are better formed. How sad—my mother's letter!

14th, Wednesday

I decided to take off today and tomorrow, and started a story. I'm calling it "The Wooden Horse."

Inspiration in writing seems to be something like sexual desire. The man from the lending library came today and offered me some "unusual" books. Somehow I wanted to read them, and I borrowed two. One is called *The Misty Night in the Blossoms,* the other

[4] The letter is written in a combination of common, dialectal speech and old-fashioned phrases redolent of epistolary manuals.

[5] Takuboku's wife.

The Secrets of Love. I wasted three hours copying out in Romaji *The Misty Night.*

At night Nakajima came here, together with a minor poet named Uchiyama. Uchiyama's nose has the most extraordinary shape! It looks as if a deformed sweet potato had been stuck in the middle of his face, with a few parings and flattenings here and there. An endless flow of chatter comes from him: he's like one of those unshaven beggars one sees clowning in the streets. On top of everything else, he is practically a midget. I have never seen anyone quite so pathetic-looking. A truly pitiful, farcical innocent—excessively so, perhaps: I felt a strange impulse to smash him in the face. Every serious utterance he makes sounds funny, and when he says something humorous with a sniff of his grotesque nose, he looks as if he is crying.

It started to rain a little before ten. Nakajima professes to be a Socialist, but his is a very aristocratic socialism—he left in a rickshaw. Uchiyama—the poet is a real Socialist—went home under a borrowed umbrella. He really looked a poet.

I wrote three pages of "The Wooden Horse." I longed for Setsuko —not because of the lonely patter of the rain, but because I had been reading *The Misty Night in the Blossoms.*

15th, Thursday

No! Does my need for Setsuko arise simply out of sexual desire? No! No!

My love for her has cooled. That is a fact, a not surprising fact— regrettable but inescapable.

Love is only a part, not the entirety of human life, a diversion, something like a song. Everyone wants at times to sing, and it is a pleasant thing to do. But man cannot spend his whole life in song, and to sing the same tune all the time, however joyous it may be, is sating.

My love has cooled; I am tired of singing that song—it's not that I dislike it. Setsuko is really a good woman. Is there in all the world another such good, gentle, sensible woman? I cannot imagine a better wife than Setsuko. Sometimes, even while I was actually sleeping with Setsuko, I have hungered for other women. But what has that to do with Setsuko? I was not dissatisfied with her. It is simply that men have complex desires.

I have not changed in my love for Setsuko. She was not the only woman I loved, but the one I loved most. Even now, especially during the last few days, I often think of her.

The present marriage system—the whole social system—is riddled with errors. Why must I be tied down because of parents, a wife, or a child? Why must they be victimized because of me? But that, naturally, is quite apart from the fact that I love my parents, Setsuko, and Kyōko.

16th, Friday

What an idiotic thing! Last night I stayed up until three copying in my notebook that pornographic old novel *The Misty Night in the Blossoms.* Ah, me!

I could not control my craving for that intense pleasure!

When I woke about ten this morning I felt a strange mental fatigue. I read the letter from Miyazaki.

Will they all please die, or must I? It's one or the other! I really thought that as I sat down to write an answer. I assured Miyazaki that I am now able to make a living, and said that all I need is the money to move from these lodgings, to rent a house, and to pay the traveling expenses for my family! When I finished writing, I wished I were dead.

I finally got off the one yen to my mother. Out of dislike for writing, out of fear, I have neglected to send it until today. I enclosed it in the letter to Miyazaki.

Tonight Kindaichi [6] came to my room. He talked about all kinds of things, hoping to stir up some literary inspiration in me. I didn't answer—instead, I indulged in a variety of absurd pranks which eventually drove Kindaichi away. I took up my pen immediately. Half an hour went by. I was obliged to give serious consideration again to my inability to write a novel and to the fact that my future

[6] Kindaichi Kyōsuke, the distinguished philologist and student of the Ainu, was a close friend of Takuboku's, and lived in the next room during this period.

is devoid of hope. I went to Kindaichi's room and performed my whole repertory of silly tricks. I painted a huge face on my chest and made all kinds of grimaces, whistled like a thrush, and, in conclusion, took out my knife and acted out the part of the murderer in a play. Kindaichi fled from the room! I certainly must have been thinking something horrible!

I had switched off the light in his room, and stood in the doorway brandishing my knife.

Later, back in my room, we looked at each other in dismay at what had happened. I thought that suicide could not frighten me.

Then, at night, what did I do? *Misty Night in the Blossoms!*

It is about two o'clock. Somewhere off beyond Koishigawa there is a fire, a single dull red line of smoke climbing perpendicularly into the black sky.

A fire!

17th, Saturday

I did not go to work today because I was sure I would be able to write—no, it was because I wanted to take the day off that I decided to write. I attempted to describe last night's thoughts about suicide. I wrote three pages and couldn't think of another line.

I tried to correct some poems, but just spreading out the paper was enough to make me sick.

I thought of writing a story about a man who is arrested by a policeman for sleeping in a vacant house, but couldn't find the energy to lift my pen.

I said to myself, "I positively will give up my literary career."

"If I give up literature, what shall I do?"

Death! That's the only answer.

Either I must have money or else be released from all responsibilities.

Probably this problem will haunt me until I die—I'll think about it in bed!

19th, Monday

The abominable treatment I receive at my lodgings has reached a limit. I got up about nine. No fire, even after I finished washing. I put away the bedding myself. While I impatiently smoked a cigarette, a child went by in the hall. I told him to get me fire and some hot water. Twenty minutes later they brought breakfast. Nothing to eat it with. I rang the bell. Nobody came. I rang again. Nobody came. After what seemed hours the maid brought a spoon, which she flung down without a word on the table. The soup had become stone cold.

Under my window an elderbush is in blossom. Long, long ago, when I was still living in Shibutami, I often used to make pipes from elder branches.

I always think when the maid and the others are rude to me, "Damn them! I can just imagine how they'll fawn on me when I pay the bill!" But, I wonder, will such a day ever come?

21st, Wednesday

The cherry trees are in full leaf. When I opened the window this morning, a smoky color of young leaves met my eyes. Yesterday I saw two people in summer hats. It's summer!

At nine o'clock I went to the public bath in Daimachi. I often used to go there when I first came to Tokyo last year. Nothing has changed, except that the seventeen-year-old girl-attendant, the one who seemed fond of me, is no longer there. I could see through the window the shadows of young leaves in the fresh morning sunlight. I returned to all my feelings of a year ago. Then the memory of the dreadful Tokyo summer came back with painful vividness, that summer I spent in lodgings. I was in terrible financial straits, but happy to be escaping even briefly the responsibility of providing for my family. Yes, I was enjoying the sensation of being a "semi-bachelor." I soon abandoned the woman with whom I was having an affair at the time. She's now a geisha in Asakusa. A great deal has changed. I have made a number of new friends and discarded them.

As I scrubbed my body, healthier than it was then, I lost myself in recollections—a year of terrible struggle! *The dreadful summer is coming again on me—the penniless novelist! The dreadful summer!*

alas! with great pains and deep sorrows of physical struggle, and, other young with the bottomless rapture of hand, Nihilist!

As I come out of the gate of the bathhouse, the expressful faced woman who sold me the soap yesterday said to me 'Good morning' with something calm and favourable gesture.

The bath and the memories bring me some hot and young lightness. I am young, and, at last, the life is not so dark and so painful. The sun shines, and moon is calm. If I do not send the money, or call up them to Tôkyô, they—my mother and wife will take other manner to eat. I am young, and young, and young: and I have the pen, the brain, the eyes, the heart and the mind. That is all. All of all. If the inn-master take me out of this room, I will go everywhere —where are many inns and hotels in this capital. To-day, I have only one piece of 5rin-dôkwa:[7] *but what then? Nonsence! There are many, many writers in Tokyo. What is that to me? There is nothing. They are writing with their finger-bones and the brush: but I must write with the ink and the G pen! That is all. Ah, the burning summer and the green-coloured struggle!*

TRANSLATED BY DONALD KEENE

[7] A small copper coin, half a sen.

THE WILD GOOSE

[Gan, IX-XI, 1911-1913] by Mori Ōgai (1862-1922)

Mori Ōgai was one of the leading literary figures of the early twentieth century. After his graduation from the Tokyo University Medical Department he spent several years studying in Germany, and returned to Japan to lead a double career as a writer and doctor. Some of his most famous works are translations from the German, and others describe his experiences in Europe as a young man.

Among Mori Ōgai's original writings the novel The Wild Goose, *published serially in 1911-1913, probably retains the greatest appeal. It is the story of Otama, a girl who, after a false marriage with a bigamous police officer, becomes the mistress of another man. Later in the novel she falls in love with a medical student who passes her house every day, but he leaves for Germany before she can confess her love. The following excerpts deal with her life immediately after she becomes the mistress of Suezō.*

•

Otama, who had never before been separated from her father, often thought of going to see how he was getting along. She was afraid, however, that Suezō, who came every day, might be annoyed if she were out when he called, and thus it was that her plan to visit her father was put off from one day to the next. Suezō never stayed until morning, and often he left as early as eleven. At other times, explaining that he had business that evening, he would stay only long enough for a moment's smoke by the fire. Yet there was no day on which Otama could be sure that he would not come. She might have gone to her father's in the daytime, but Ume, the maid, was such a child that it was impossible to trust her to do anything alone, and in any case, Otama did not wish to leave the house when the neighbors could see her. At first she had gone without thought to the public bath at the foot of the hill, but now she generally sent the maid down to make sure it was empty before quietly slipping out to take her bath.

On the third day after she moved, Otama, who was prone to take fright at almost anything, had had an experience that quite took her courage away. On the day of her arrival, men from the grocer's and the fish store had come with their order-books to request her patronage, but that morning the fishmonger failed to call, and she sent the maid out to buy a slice of fish for lunch. Otama had no desire to eat fresh fish every day; her father had always been satisfied with any sort of simple dinner, and she had become accustomed to making do with whatever happened to be in the house. But she had heard how people talk of "poverty-stricken neighbors who never eat fresh food," and she was afraid that the same thing might be said of her, bringing shame on a master who had been most generous. She accordingly sent the maid to the fish store at the foot of the hill, mainly so that she might be seen.

Ume found a shop and went in, only to discover that it was not the same one whose man had come for orders. The proprietor was out, and his wife was tending the counter. From the heaps of fish laid out on the racks, Ume selected a small mackerel that looked fresh, and asked the price. "I don't believe I've seen you before," said the fishwife. "Where do you come from?" Ume described the house on the hill in which she lived, whereupon the woman suddenly looked very displeased. "Indeed!" she said. "I'm sorry, then, but you had better run along. We have no fish here to sell to a moneylender's mistress!" With this she turned away and went on smoking, not deigning to pay any further attention to the girl. Ume, too upset to feel like going to any other shop, came running back and, looking very wretched, repeated in disconnected scraps what the fishwife had said.

As Otama listened her face turned pale, and for some time she stood silent. In the heart of the naive young woman a hundred confused emotions mingled in chaos, nor could she herself have untangled their knotted threads. A great weight pressed down upon her heart, to which now the blood from throughout her body flowed, leaving her face blanched and a cold sweat over her back. Her first conscious thought was that, after such an incident, Ume would no longer be able to remain in the house.

Ume gazed at the pale, bloodless face of her mistress, sensing merely that she was in great distress, without comprehending the cause. She had returned in anger from the store, but now she realized that there was still nothing for lunch, and she could hardly leave things as they were. The purse which her mistress had given her for the shopping remained thrust into the sash of her kimono. "I've never seen such a horrid old woman," she said in an effort to be comforting. "I don't know who would buy her fish, anyway! There's another store down by the Inari Shrine. I'll run down there and get something, shall I?" Otama felt a momentary joy that Ume had declared herself her ally, and her face reflected a weak smile as she nodded approval. Ume bounded off with a clatter.

Otama remained for a while without moving. Then her taut nerves began gradually to relax, and tears welled up in her eyes. She drew a handkerchief from her sleeve to press them back. In her heart was only one thought—how dreadful! Did she hate the fishwife for not selling her anything, or was she ashamed or unhappy that she was the sort of person that shops would not sell to? No, it was not that sort of feeling. Nor was it that she hated Suezō, the man to whom she had given herself and whom she now knew to be a moneylender. Nor indeed did she feel any particular shame or regret that she had given herself to such a man. She had heard from others that moneylenders were unpleasant, frightening people whom everybody detested; but her father had never borrowed money from one. He had always gone to the pawnshop, and even when the clerk had hardheartedly refused to give him as much as he asked for a pledge, the old man would never express any resentment over the clerk's unreasonableness, but would merely shake his head sadly. As a child fears ghosts or policemen, Otama counted moneylenders among the things to be afraid of, but with no vivid or personal emotion. What, then, upset her so?

In her mortification there was very little hatred for the world or for people. If one were to ask what in fact she resented, the answer was, perhaps, her own fate. Through no fault of her own she had been made to suffer persecution, and this was what she found so painful. She had first felt this mortification when she was deceived and abandoned by the police officer, and recently, again, when she realized that she must become someone's mistress. Now she learned that she was not only a mistress but the mistress of a despised money-lender, and her despair, that had been ground smooth between the teeth of time and washed of its color in the waters of resignation, assumed once more in her heart its stark and vivid outline.

After a while Otama got up, took from the cupboard a calico apron and, tying it on, went with a deep sigh into the kitchen. She was now quite calm again. Resignation was the mental process she had most often experienced, and if she directed her mind toward that goal, it operated with the accustomed smoothness of a well-oiled machine.

. . .

At first when Suezō came in the evenings, Otama would spread a mat for him by the side of the large square brazier, where he would sit at his ease, smoking and gossiping. She herself, at a loss to know what to do with her hands, would sit on her side, drumming on the edge of the brazier or playing with the fire tongs, and answer him shyly. After they had chatted a while, she would become more voluble, speaking mostly of the minor joys and sorrows that she had known during the years with her father. Suezō paid little attention to the content of her discourse, but listened rather as to a cricket in a cage whose engaging chirps brought a smile to his face. Then Otama would suddenly become aware of her own garrulousness and, blushing, would break off her story and return to her former silence. Her words and actions were so guileless that to Suezō's ever observant eyes they appeared as transparent as clear water in a bowl. Her companionship brought a refreshing delight that to him was a totally new experience; in his visits to the house he was like a wild animal introduced for the first time to the ways of human society.

Some days later, when Suezō was sitting as usual before the brazier, he noticed that Otama, for no apparent reason, kept moving restlessly around the room without settling down. She had always been slow to answer and shy, but her behavior tonight had about it a new and unusual air.

"What are you thinking about?" he asked as he filled his pipe.

Otama pulled the drawer at the end of the brazier halfway out and, although she was not looking for anything, peered intently into it. "Nothing," she said, turning her large eyes to his face.

"What do you mean, 'nothing'? You're thinking, 'What shall I do, what shall I do?'—it's written all over your face," he retorted.

Otama flushed and for a moment remained silent while she considered what to say. The workings of the delicate apparatus of her mind became almost visible. "I've been thinking that I ought to go visit my father," she said. Tiny insects that must forever be escaping more powerful creatures have their protective coloring; women tell lies.

Suezō laughed and spoke in a scolding voice. "Come now! Your father living by the pond not ten minutes' walk from here, and you haven't gone to see him yet? You can go now if you like. Or, better still, tomorrow morning."

Otama, twirling the ashes with the fire tongs, stole a glance at Suezō. "I was just wondering whether it would be all right—"

"There's no need to worry about a thing like that. How long will you stay a child?" This time his voice was gentle.

Suezō was vaguely aware that there was still something in Otama's heart that she was hiding, but when he tried to discover what it was she had given him that childish, trivial answer. Still, as he left the house somewhat after eleven and walked slowly down the hill, he knew that there was something. She had been told something that had aroused in her a feeling of uneasiness, he surmised. But what she had heard, or from whom, he could not tell.

. .

When Otama arrived at her father's house by the pond the next morning, he had just finished breakfast. Otama, who had hastened there without even taking time to put on any powder, wondered if she might not be too early; but the old man, accustomed to early rising, had already swept the gate and sprinkled water about to settle the dust. He was now just finishing his lonely morning meal.

The gates of the neighboring houses were still shut, and in the early morning the surroundings seemed unusually quiet. From the low windows of the house one could see through the pine boughs a weeping willow trembling in the breeze, and beyond, the lotus leaves that covered the surface of the pond. Here and there among their green shone the pink dots of blossoms newly opened in the morning sun.

From the time Otama was old enough to think for herself she had dreamt of all the things she would do for her father, should fortune ever come her way, and now, when she saw before her eyes the house that she had provided for him, she could not but feel joyful. Yet in her joy there was mingled a drop of bitterness. If it were not for that, how great her joy would be at meeting her father today, but, as she thought with irritation, one cannot have the world quite as one wishes it.

There had as yet been no visitors to the old man's house. When he heard the sound of someone at the gate, he put down the cup of tea he was drinking and glanced in surprise toward the entrance hall. Then, while she was still hidden by the hall screen, he heard Otama's voice calling, "Papa!" He restrained his impulse to jump up in greeting, and sat where he was, considering what to say. "It was so good of you to remember your old father," he thought of saying in spite, but when his beloved daughter suddenly appeared by his side, he could not utter the words. Disgruntled as he was, he only gazed in silence at her face. Against his will his expression softened.

Otama had thought only of how much she wanted to see her father again, but now was unable to find words for all the things she had planned to say.

The maid poked her head in from the kitchen and asked in her country dialect, "Shall I remove the tray?"

"Yes, take it away and bring some fresh tea. Use the green tea on the shelf," said the old man, pushing the tray away from him.

"Oh, please don't bother to make special tea!" Otama protested.

"Nonsense! I have some biscuits here, too." The old man rose and brought back some egg biscuits from a tin in the cupboard and put them on the table.

While the two drank their tea they chatted as if they had never been apart. Suddenly the old man asked in a rather embarrassed tone, "How are things coming along? Does your master come to see you sometimes?"

"Yes," said Otama, and for a moment she seemed unable to answer more. It was not "sometimes" that Suezō came, but every night without fail. Had she just been married, she might have replied with great cheerfulness to an inquiry as to whether she was getting along well with her husband, but in her present position the fact that her master came every night seemed almost shameful, and she found it difficult to mention. She thought for a moment, and then replied, "Things seem to be going all right, Papa. There is nothing at all for you to worry about."

"That's good," he said, though he felt at the same time a certain lack of assurance in his daughter's answer. An evasiveness had come into their speech. They who up until now had always spoken with complete freedom, who had never had the slightest secret from each other, found themselves forced, against their will, to address each other like strangers and to maintain a certain reserve. In the past, when they had been deceived by the fraudulent police officer, they had been ashamed before their neighbors, but they had both of them known in their hearts that the blame lay with him, and they had discussed the whole terrible affair without the slightest reserve. But now, when their plans had turned out successfully and they were comfortably established, a new shadow, a sadness, lay over their conversation.

The old man was anxious to have a more concrete answer. "What sort of man is he?" he began again.

"Well—" said Otama thoughtfully, inclining her head to one side and speaking as though to herself, "I surely don't think he is a *bad* person. We haven't been together very long, but so far he has never used any harsh language or anything like that."

"Oh?" said the old man with a look of dissatisfaction. "And is there any reason to suppose that he *is* a bad person?"

Otama looked quickly at her father and her heart began to pound. If she was to say what she had come to say, now was the time to say it. But the thought of inflicting a new blow on her father, now that she had at last brought him peace of mind, was too painful. She resolved to go away without revealing her secret, and at the crucial moment she turned the conversation in another direction. "They said he was a man who had done all sorts of things to build a fortune for himself. I didn't know what to expect, and I was rather worried. But he's—well, what would you say—chivalrous. Whether that is his real nature I can't say, but he is certainly making an effort to act that way. As long as he tries to be chivalrous, that's enough, don't you think, Papa?" She looked up at her father. For a woman, no matter how honest, to hide what is in her heart and talk of something else is not so difficult as it is for a man. It is possible that in such a situation the more volubly she speaks the more honest she really is.

"Perhaps you are right. But somehow you speak as though you don't trust the man," her father said.

Otama smiled. "I've grown up, Papa. From now on I don't intend to be made a fool of by others. I intend to be strong."

The old man, suddenly sensing that his daughter, usually so mild and submissive, was for once turning the point of her remarks at him, looked at her uneasily. "Well, it's true, as you know, that I've gone through life pretty consistently being made a fool of. But you will feel a good deal better in your heart if you are cheated by others than if you are always cheating them. Whatever business you are in, you must never be dishonest, and you must remember those who have been kind to you."

"Don't worry. You always used to say that I was an honest child, and I still am. But I've been thinking quite a bit lately. I want no more of being taken in by people."

"You mean that you don't trust what your master says?"

"Yes, that's it. He thinks I'm just a child. Compared to him, perhaps I am, but I am not as much of a child as he thinks."

"Has he told you anything that you've discovered to be untrue?"

"Indeed he has! You remember how the old go-between kept saying that his wife had died and left him with the children, and that if I accepted his favors it would be just as though I were a proper wife? She told us that it was just to keep up appearances that he couldn't let me live in his own home. It happens that he *has* a wife. He said so himself, just like that. I was so surprised that I didn't know what to do."

The father's eyes widened. "So, she was just trying to make it sound like a good match—"

"Of course, he has to keep everything about me a strict secret from his wife," Otama continued. "He tells her all kinds of lies, so I hardly expect him to speak nothing but the truth to me. I intend to take anything he says with a grain of salt."

The old man sat holding the burnt-out pipe he had been smoking, and looked blankly at his daughter. She seemed suddenly to have grown so much older and more serious. "I must be getting back," she said hurriedly, as though she had just remembered something. "Now that I've come and seen that everything is all right, I'll be visiting you every day. I had hesitated because I thought that I'd better get his permission first, but last night he finally told me I might come. Now I must run on and see how things are at home."

"If you got permission from him to come, why don't you stay for lunch?" the old man asked.

"No, I don't think I should. I'll come again very soon, Papa. Good-bye!" Otama got up to leave.

"Come again when you can," said the old man without rising, "and give my kindest regards to your master."

Otama pulled a little purse from her black satin sash, took out a few bills, and gave them to the maid. Then she went out to the gate. She had come intending to bare the bitterness in her breast and share her misfortune with her father, but to her own surprise she now found herself leaving almost in good spirits. With a cheerful face she walked along the edge of the pond. Although the sun, now risen high above Ueno Hill, was beating down fiercely, lighting the vermilion pillars of the Benten Shrine, Otama carried her little foreign-style parasol in her hand without bothering to put it up.

TRANSLATED BY BURTON WATSON

A TALE OF THREE WHO WERE BLIND

[*Sannin no Mekura no Hanashi, 1912*] *by Izumi Kyōka (1873-1939)*

Izumi Kyōka is known as a "romantic," and his best work derives from the erotic and fantastic literature of the Edo period. He is much admired as a stylist.

•

"One moment . . . you, sir."

At the voice, a chill shot down Sakagami's back—though not as at a voice he remembered and disliked. From the foot of the hill he had seen them creeping down toward him from Yotsuya, appearing and disappearing, floating up and falling back again, in the mist that huddled in motionless spirals halfway up the slope. He could hardly hear the sound of their feet; and then, as they passed, that voice.

They were nothing to him, and yet he knew that something must happen before he would be allowed to pass. They would call him, they would stop him—he was strangely sure that somehow he must hear a voice. It might be as when a traveler hears the cry of a raven or the scream of a night heron and cannot be sure, even if he is quite alone, that the call has been at him; but Sakagami knew that he would have to hear that unpleasant, that odious voice.

Three blind ones in single file.

In the center was a woman, perhaps in her middle years, white throated, thick haired, her shoulders thin and slight. The long sleeves, falling down from her folded arms, were of a darkness that seemed to sink through to the thin breasts beneath, and their trailing edges gave way to a like darkness in the obi. Was the slapping from her sandals?—but the long skirt brushed the ground and hid her feet.

The man in front wore a limp, loose garment, gray perhaps, in the darkness almost like the night mist itself spun and woven. His brimless cap shot into the air, a veritable miter. His gaunt body swayed as he drew near—and passed.

The other man, slender and of no more than medium height, clung to the woman as if he meant to hide in the shadow of her hair. Though Sakagami had had no clear view of any of them, the third had been the most obscure of all.

And yet Sakagami knew immediately that he had been stopped by this shadowy one.

"Are you speaking to me?" Sakagami looked back. His shoulders were hunched in the sudden chill, and his answer was like a curse flung at a barking dog.

"I am speaking to you." The voice was low. It was indeed the slight man in the rear. He seemed to straighten up as he spoke to Sakagami, who was two or three paces up the hill from him. He held his staff at an angle, an oar with which to row his way through the mist.

The other two—the long head in front; and the high Japanese coiffure (Sakagami could not be sure what style), like a wig on an actor's wig stand, suspended upside-down—stood diagonally down the slope with their backs to their companion.

Sakagami turned on his heels to stare at the man.

"And what do you want?"

"I should like to talk to you." Whether he was very sure of himself, or out of breath, his slowness seemed wrong in the cold of the late winter night.

2

"What is it?"

Coming toward him in the mist, they had seemed like two grave markers, a tall one and a low one, blown in by a last gust of the autumn winds from some cemetery on the moors, the dead tufts of grass white in the earth still clinging to their bases.

But his tone became more gentle as he saw that the three, groping their way along this shabby, deserted street as through the caves on the Musashino Plain, were only three blind ones who made their living by massaging and who had set out together, who would blow the flutes that were the sign of their trade, as thin and high in the winter night as the sound of a mosquito in January, and who would presently disappear behind the lantern of a poor rooming house.

"I have little to say. But I should like to know where you are going. Where? Where? Where?" There was a touch of derision in the nasal tone. His head cocked to one side, the man looked up at Sakagami. He raised his hand as if to scratch his ear, and tapped at the head of the staff.

"It makes no difference," said Sakagami testily. He was going to meet a woman who had been forbidden to see him. "Does it matter where I'm going?"

"It does. I am sorry, sir, but it does." There was a strength in the voice that kept Sakagami fixed to the spot.

"And why?" Sakagami turned and started down toward the man; but he pulled back as the mist clutched at his face.

"It is late." The voice was suddenly strong. The head bowed heavily toward the earth.

Long Head, in front, turned slowly to face the bank above the road.

The woman seemed to sink into the earth as she sat down disconsolately on her heels. The tip of her staff was white against the dark hair.

Seeing that the three meant to stay, Sakagami resigned himself to being delayed; but at the thought of what lay ahead his chest rose and fell violently, as if poison were being forced in through his mouth. A rising, a rush of blood, and a collapse with an angry tremor of the flesh.

Banks rose on both sides like mountain slopes. Against the sky, over the bank toward which Long Head faced, one or two barracks-style houses stood like tea huts on a mountain pass, tight and dark. Not a sliver of light escaped from them. On the bank, dead grass, blanketed by the mist as by a frost.

On the side of the road where the three had stopped, the bank had slid away, exposing the roots of trees and the retaining stakes.

Trees sent up their skeleton forms above. Here and there the mist clung to the branches like dirty moonlight. There were no stars. The bottom of a defile in Yotsuya, like the bottom of a mountain ravine, at one o'clock in the morning.

Only the racing in the chest. "Is it wrong to be so late?" The words themselves seemed to be weighted down by the heavy air.

"You were certain to say that." The man slapped the back of the hand that held the staff. "It is wrong, very wrong indeed."

"I am not to go on then?" Perhaps this oracle could tell him something of the meeting that was to come.

"If you will go on, whatever I say, let that be the end of it. But I must stop you for a moment. I alone—or that gentleman too."

Long Head coughed faintly as the other brought his staff upright.

3

"And what if I have to go?" Sakagami's breath came faster. "What if my father is dying, or a friend is ill? How can you know? You speak as though I were doing something wrong."

The man bent his head as though to rub his cheek against the staff, and laughed unpleasantly. "I know where you are going. And that gentleman says I must speak. . . . Shall I tell you? It will be no trouble. And you will tell me I am right. You go to meet a woman."

Sakagami did not answer.

"She has duties and ties. There are obstacles and complications. But you have pushed and slashed, and broken down fences and walls. . . . You have pressed her with an urgency that would tear her very breast open, and she will meet you at the risk of her life. You are on your way to meet her. I knew from your footsteps as you came up, and met us, and passed. I knew a man rushing along, out of his senses.

"Dew falls, frost falls. The moon clouds over, the stars are dark. In the wide skies too there are shadows. The shadows are gentle. But the breast is blocked and the breath is tight. See the lightning and the thunderclap after the darkness.

"In the heart of man, nothing is strange.

"I think as you do, I put myself in your place, and everything is clear, even to a blind man, as clear as this hand itself." The man brought his hand up to cover his face.

Sakagami could see in the dim light that the other two were nodding deeply, as if on a signal.

"You are fortunetellers, are you? I was in a hurry, and perhaps I was rude." Sakagami heaved a sigh. "She left home barefoot. . . . It is some distance from here, but she is waiting in the woods alone. She cannot move until I come.

"I had a telephone call from her just now, so short that it was no more than a signal, and I hardly know what I am about. Can I help going? Do you say I shouldn't go?"

"I thought as much. . . . No, you were right to admit everything like a man. It will be sad for both of you. But how very dangerous." The man clutched his staff to his chest with both hands, and stood in silence for a moment. "I shall ask you a question. Along this bank where we are gathered there is a row of gaslights. How many of them are lighted, and how many are dark? Tell me, please. Tell me." He nodded as he spoke, and his head fell to his chest.

Sakagami followed the line from the bottom of the hill behind the three. It was not the first time he had taken this road. Below the cliff, on one side, the gaslights stood at intervals of about two yards, put up by a nearby movie theatre for the safety of passers-by.

The lamps were white and cold as frost needles. The glass chambers, like windows in the face of the cliff, were dark as far as his eye reached. They drank at the mist and sucked it in, and at intervals spewed out an ashen breath.

Like a devil's death mask shaped from cotton wadding, the mist clung to the nearest lamp and became a great earth spider, sending out horrible threads on that ashen breath, into the sky and down to the ground. Was that why the mist seemed to clutch so at the face?

4

"They will all be out," the man said as Sakagami looked up and down the row.

"They are all out." The darkness of the night closed in more tightly.

"They will all be out. And now, you will see that one lamp up the hill from here is still burning. You see it? How many lamps away is it?"

"I see it." There was one feeble, wavering flame, about to float off on the mist. "But I can't tell you how many lamps away it is."

"Not far away. When the traveler sees a night crane in the pines along a lonely road, it is always in the fifth pine away. . . . The lamp will be the fifth up the hill from you.

"If I am wrong, that gentleman will tell me so. He says nothing. I am right. Count them for yourself, count them for yourself. One . . ." He tapped twice with his staff.

"One."

"Two." Tap, tap, tap.

"Three. Four. Five. It is the fifth."

"As I said."

"But why?"

"You see us, and this bank, and these dark lamps, all because of that one light. But for it, you would not see me if I were to pinch your nose."

He did indeed see the dim figures by the light of that one lamp. By that faint light, even the row of dark lamps down the slope sent out an occasional flicker of light—and Sakagami stood dim and uncertain in the breathing mist.

"What does it mean?"

"And can you see nothing under the fifth lamp, the lamp that is burning?"

"I beg your pardon?" Sakagami's voice shook.

"And can you see nothing?"

"Nothing."

"Nothing?"

"Not a thing."

"That is not as it should be. If you will but go up and look, you will see. It is for that that I have stopped you. Listen, if you will."

He twisted and bent forward a little, and rattled his staff in the stones that lay at the base of a gas lamp. The sound was drunk up in the mist.

"Let me make the point clear: The gaslight under which we stand—it has moved not one step ahead of us and not one step behind us since I stopped you—is the nineteenth in the row from the bottom of the hill.

"If I am wrong, the master there will correct me.

"Three years ago, on a different night indeed, but in this same November, at this same hour, this happened to me too.

"I was not then the blind man you see now."

He turned squarely toward Sakagami, but his head was still bowed.

"I was going to meet a woman as you are, and I was climbing this hill.

"But I passed only one blind man. That is the whole of the difference."

Long Head faced squarely down the hill away from Sakagami, and started to walk off—and was still again.

5

And the woman: still sitting on her heels, she turned to hear the story. The knee of her kimono and the obi at her waist were folded one against the other. Her throat was white.

The man's voice was firm. "He called me from behind, as I called you, and, at the nineteenth lamp, the fifth below the lighted lamp, he said to me what I have said to you.

"I have but repeated it.

"And why should I not go to meet the woman, I retorted as you did. He answered. . . ."

Sakagami somehow knew that "he" was Long Head here.

" 'There is a strange creature under the fifth lamp ahead, the lamp that is still lighted. . . . A demon that takes the shadows of men, snatches them, devours them.

" 'He sucks at a shadow, and the man grows thin; licks the shadow with his tongue, and the man languishes; tramps on the shadow, and the man is ill; snuffs it quite away, and the man dies.

" 'The demon is always about, in the sunlight and the moonlight, to suck, to lick, to trample, and in time the man dies. Terrible though that is, it is more terrible when, under just such a light as we have here, he opens his mouth . . .' "

The blind man's gaping mouth.

" '. . . and swallows the shadow. That is all. The man dies. You are not to pass by here again.'

"That is what he said.

"But I was young and hotheaded. What was he talking about? I retorted. In the first place, what sort of monster was it? He did not smile. 'Very well, very well, I shall tell you. It is like a lizard with a fez. It is like a white dog spread-eagled, and on its head a biretta.'

"Seeing was quicker than hearing, I said. Let the thing have my shadow—I had believed nothing. I climbed to that fifth light, kicking up the gravel as I went. I found nothing there.

"The blind man, scraping at the gravel with his staff, sprang up the hill after me. 'Have you gone mad? You are too brave for your own good. It is no use talking to one who believes nothing I say, but the demon will not be after your shadow for a time.

" 'He has long been after the shadow of the woman, the woman you are going to meet. I tell her through you to be forever careful, not for a moment to be off her guard.'

"That is what he said."

6

"And why should he be giving advice—did he know the woman, I asked. 'A housewife in my block saw her just this evening. They were at the bath together. The skin like snow, patted and rounded —one wondered why it did not melt in the steam. Over it, scarlet satin, and a pale yellow sash—scarlet that seemed to glide and flow from the breasts. A kimono for good autumn weather, a latticework of indigo and dark-blue stripes. A black damask obi, and a scarlet cord. An azure ribbon to bind the hair. An ear, faint through hair aglow like falling dew. And the rich swell of the neck and shoulders. Woman though she was, the housewife I speak of stood fascinated. She moved around to the front, and stared at the back, and peered at the naked form in the mirror. And she described everything to me, down to the mole on the white skin at the base of the left breast.'

" 'It will be this woman you are going to see.'

"That is what he said."

Sakagami was trembling. Not only because the faint image of the woman, now looking away, came to him as that of the woman being described—the same kimono, the same obi.

But because of the woman he was going to meet tonight. He expected her to have on *that* obi, and *that* kimono—but what if she should have on the everyday black obi and the latticed kimono that had so become a part of his life?

His blood ran cold, and an instant later he flushed.

" 'Am I right? The kimono, the obi, the scarlet beneath . . . am I right about the woman you are going to meet?' It made no difference about the black damask, or about the indigo and blue, or about the white skin. But imagine, if you will, how it was to be told even of the mole on the breast.

"It was as though I could see before my eyes—fearsome thing—the figure lying naked, the kimono open, here in this Yotsuya Valley.

"The demon, said the blind man, was after the woman, to lick her shadow, to suck at it, to take it, to trample it, to devour it. 'Tell her, if you please, that she is to be careful.' But I was not listening. I flew off in a dark cloud. I was not to be stopped by iron gate or stone door, and I went to meet that small, defenseless woman.

"I had seen a demon that would take her shadow, would suck at her shadow, would lick at her shadow. I had seen it in the light of the gas lamp.

"The woman's house was very near here.

" 'It will be after you day and night. You are not looking well, your shadow is thin already. Watch for it.' That, sir, is what I said.

"An unhappy woman, whom labor and anguish had already so devastated that her obi, however tightly bound, could not be tight enough—into the head of this unhappy woman I drove my words as with a hammer.

"In my anger that she had shown herself naked to another. She fell upon my knee, and in a voice that trembled asked whom I had met and what I had heard along the way. Look to your own conscience—I said; and I did not tell her I had heard the story from a blind man.

"A tragic mistake. It was the blind man himself who clung to the woman like her very shadow. It was the blind man himself who might have been taken for a lizard in the gaslight, who hovered about the back fence, the well, the hedge, face livid, eyes red, lips pale and tight, waiting for the woman to come in or go out.

"Had she known it was the blind man, she would not have been so haunted by the story."

7

"Thereafter I saw the woman less often.

"She seemed to avoid me.

"I thought of killing her and myself; but presently, as I heard the details, I learned that she was avoiding everyone. She had a strange longing to be hidden.

"And finally, like the splittailed cat who has taken the shape of a beautiful woman, she came to hate the light of the sun. Whether it was night or day, she closed the doors and the shutters, and lay hidden behind two and three screens.

"I forced my way through, and saw her. Her very kimono seemed moldering and musty, and she only knelt looking at the floor, so slight and wraithlike that it seemed she must quite disappear.

"I raised her face. The eyes were destroyed. I beg your pardon? No, the woman's eyes, both the woman's eyes.

"I heard her story. She had not been able even for an instant to take her eyes from her shadow.

"If she went into the kitchen it was on the window, if she went to the veranda it was on the doorstep or behind her on the door, the wall, the screen.

"And wherever the shadow was, there was the demon, to suck at it, to lick, trample, rub, embrace, cover.

"In the light of the moon, the light of the sun, the light of the lamp, the faint light of the snow or of trees in blossom, there was always that shadow. And with the shadow: discomfort, revulsion—terror and loathing.

"Finally, darkness. But even when she could not see the palm of her own hand, there was the shadow. When all the lights were out.

"In the alcove, on the lintel, on the ceiling, on the doorframe, the floor, now here and now there—the shape of a lizard with something slapped down on its head, weirdly white, the body long, the legs writhing—now clinging, now curling into a ball, now crawling along stretched out its full length.

"She would scream when she saw it, and it would flit away—how quickly! But a moment later it would come creeping back again.

"She tried desperately not to see. But she saw because she had eyes. Lying back on her pillow, her hair pulled tightly back, she dropped medicine into her eyes, and was blind.

"Darkness, over the heart too. I took her hand, and for the first time told her that I had heard the story of the demon who eats shadows from a certain blind man halfway up the hill. I told her how old he seemed to be, and described his appearance, and the woman gasped as though her eyes had suddenly been opened, and began weeping bitterly.

"Frustrated in love, the blind man had put his curse on her.

"I clutched at the flesh of my face and wept tears of anger, chagrin, exation—and finally of pity. I determined that I would be with her, nd with this hand I drove a needle into both my eyes.

"A bond from one life lasts through three. Enlightenment has ome to us, and penitence, and release from the appetites of the world. We take our staffs, that blind man with us, and, ashamed of the daylight, go out into the night.

"We have met you along the way.

"I have troubled you; but as our sleeves brushed in the mist, I knew, and I spoke to you. It is for you to take my advice or throw it away.

"I have nothing more to say. If you will, I shall leave you."

Forlorn and graceful, the woman rose to her feet. Her weeping had sounded below the narrative.

Led by Long Head, the three of them groped their way down the hill. Three staffs, three phantoms in the fading gaslight.

The bit of silk pressed to the eyes by that white hand as the woman had arisen seemed to linger on, a scarlet butterfly cutting its way in and out of the mist.

TRANSLATED BY EDWARD SEIDENSTICKER

SANCTUARY

[from Gin no Saji, 1911-1912] by Naka Kansuke (born 1885)

Naka Kansuke has spent his life outside the main stream of literary activity in Japan, and has never attained fame commensurate with his genius as a writer. His first novel, The Silver Spoon *(of which the concluding section is given here), is an extraordinarily beautiful evocation of the world of childhood, which retains its freshness today.*

•

The year I was sixteen I spent my vacation alone at a friend's summer house. Its heavily thatched roof was nestled in the foothills along the shore of a beautiful, lonely peninsula which I had once visited with my brother. An old woman who sold flowers came in to take care of the house. She was from the same province as my dead aunt, and somehow—if only in age and in the way she talked—reminded me of her. Since I knew the dialect too, and had heard a great deal about that part of the country, we were soon on very good terms. . . .

One afternoon as I was climbing toward a huge pine at the top of a mountain behind the house I lost my bearings and went off into a wild ravine. Elbowing blindly through the tall underbrush, lashed by dense branches and tripped by what looked like fan-vines, I clambered out of its choking depths up to a ridge. The ridge was shaped like an ox, its head thrust down the middle of a deep valley that opened out to the sea. I picked my way along its back toward the plump, bulging shoulders. Dried-up little pines were clinging desperately to places where reddish granite powder had hardened into a sharkskin-like crust; here and there lay the droppings of birds that had come to eat the pine cones. Clutching the coarse rock to keep from sliding down into the valley, I crawled up the hump that made the ox's shoulders. The sun leapt brilliantly into a sky full of dazzling light. Then I went along the gently sloping neck for about a hundred yards, as both sides of the ridge fell away more and more sharply and the valley became deeper and deeper, until at last, across a small level space that was the muzzle, I came to the edge of a sheer cliff.

I was on one of the many spurs reaching to the sea from the chain of rugged mountains, as high as two thousand feet, that extended seven or eight miles along this coast. Here, though, the middle one of three such spurs had been eroded at the base, so that it looked like a wedge driven between the other two. Screened in by the peak behind it and by the still higher rock cliffs on either side of the valley, under a vault of blue sky, it made a strange sanctuary. Now and then the hawks screeching shrilly overhead would swoop down, skim past my eyes, and soar into the sky again. Below, in the valley to my right, a road threaded the thick black forest, between the mountains, down toward the village on the other side. Through a narrow pass I could see mountain after mountain, red, pink, purple, faintly purple, with rows of clouds along them, going on in endless folds and layers. Full of joy and admiration, mingled with a kind of terror, I began to sing. An echo! My song was repeated as clearly as if someone hiding behind the mountain had mimicked it. Enticed by the unseen singer, I strained my voice to its highest pitch. The other voice, too, sang at that pitch. I spent the rest of the day singing there happily, with a primitive delight in that sure reply. By the time I reached our hedge gate the summer sun was sinking into the ocean.

I walked around to the bathroom to wash my feet, and then remembered the bath would be ready. The water was just right, so I got in the tub and soaked, stretching my tired legs luxuriously. Where the hot water circled my chest I felt as if I were lightly enlaced in threads. As I leaned back and held my buoyant body afloat, or breathed on my warm skin, I enjoyed the day's pleasures over again. I named the place Echo Peak. That I had found it by losing my way, which meant no one else knew about it, and that it could only be reached by scrambling across a dangerous ridge—these things made me all the more happy. Meanwhile I peered down through the shifting surface of the water . . . and noticed, barely visible, a pale oily glint. Had someone already taken a bath? Evidently another guest had come. I became extremely uneasy. To me, strangers were unbearable. Then, as I was feeling disappointed, my pleasure completely spoiled, the old woman hurried in to help me wash. She apologized for not having changed the water, and told me 'the young mistress from Tokyo' had arrived. It didn't sound like anyone in my friend's family. But I had heard of an elder sister in Kyoto who would be in Tokyo this summer—perhaps she was the one. In that case I would have to put up with it, I decided. Hopeless.

Lowering her voice dramatically, the old woman added, "Now there's a handsome young lady for you!" And she went out.

Later I slipped back to my own room like a fugitive, and sat leaning against the alcove pillar, utterly downcast. Meeting someone for the first time was an ordeal: the strain of being polite to an unfamiliar person bound me with invisible cords, till my forehead narrowed into a frown and my shoulders were burning hot. And now, it seemed, someone was in the guest cottage beyond the garden. The sister had not sounded too unpleasant; even so, I worried about what might be expected of me. Then I heard soft footsteps come down the veranda—to my door.

I left the pillar and went over to sit at my desk, just as a calm, gentle feminine voice asked, "May I trouble you for a moment?" As if impelled by that voice, the door slid smoothly open. "Oh dear," I heard, "you haven't been brought a lamp yet!" A white face was set in clear relief against the rectangle of dim light.

"How do you do?" She introduced herself as my friend's elder sister. "I'm afraid I'll be disturbing you for two or three days."

"Oh." I sat there like a criminal awaiting sentence.

"Do you suppose you'll like these?" Gracefully she offered me a dish of sweet-scented foreign confections . . . and all at once a grave, cool sculpture had become a beautiful woman, smiling shyly. Then, "I'll bring a lamp." And there was only the sculpture again, disappearing into the darkness.

I gave a sigh of relief. Filled with shame at my own wretchedness, I tried to remember how she had looked, but it was like groping for a dream. Yet when I shut my eyes tight, a sharp image drifted up as if I had suddenly gone out into a lighted place. A large round chignon in the style of a married woman. Black, black hair. Vivid black eyes sparkling under clear-cut eyebrows. So distinct was the entire outline that it gave me a curious feeling of coldness; even the somewhat pouting lips, which were painfully beautiful, seemed carved out of icy coral from the ocean depths. But when those lips curved up charmingly, parting to allow a glimpse of lovely teeth, that cool smile softened the whole image, and a tinge of color came into the white cheeks. The carved figure had turned into a beautiful woman.

After that I found myself trying to avoid her. Of course it was impossible not to meet now and then, though I would go off to Echo Peak in the morning and purposely come back too late for dinner. But when I went to the peak I refused to sing a note . . . like a bird out of season. And I stared vacantly at the deep colors of the mountains beyond the pass.

One evening, rather late, I was standing in the garden watching the moon rise over the mountain. Insects were singing everywhere, a fresh breeze carried the scent and murmur of the ocean across the fields. The round window of the guest cottage was still glowing, and in the lotus basin in front of it I could see the closed flowers, dimly white, and leaves beaded with moisture from a late afternoon shower. Sunk in the deepest and most obscure of all my thoughts, I stood there gazing at the moon, every night diminished a little further . . . and as I gazed I became aware that my friend's sister was standing beside me in the garden. The moon and flowers vanished—as the reflections in a pond vanish when a waterfowl sweeps down and alights on it, and there is only the white shape floating casually. . . .

In confusion I tried to say something. "The moon . . ." But she had discreetly begun to walk away. I flushed. It was my nature to be terribly ashamed of a trifle like that, of a little slip in speech or an awkwardness of any kind.

She went calmly on around the garden a little way, and then, as she was coming back to me, tactfully finished off my words: "It *is* beautiful, isn't it?" I was very grateful.

The next day I went to the cottage to return a newspaper, and found her combing her hair before a mirror. Her long hair was hanging loose, flowing smoothly down her back in rich waves. As I left, the hand that held the comb paused a moment, and the face in the mirror smiled. "I'll be going tomorrow," she said; "so I wondered if we couldn't have dinner together."

Again I went off to climb Echo Peak, and spent half the day, silent, in that sanctuary where only the soaring hawks could see me. The echo was silent too, but I thought of its friendly voice.

That evening the dinner table was spread with a pure white cloth; the old woman sat at one side, the sister and I facing each other. I felt shy, pleased, lonely, and sad, all at the same time.

"Won't you begin?" She bowed her head slightly. "The cook hasn't much experience, though. . . . I'm not sure you'll care for this." Smiling, she glanced over at my plate a little hesitantly. A square of homemade bean curd lay quivering there, so white it looked as if it would take up the indigo pattern of the plate. She grated citron for me, and I sprinkled on the pale-green powder. When I dipped the almost melting cake into its sauce, once, twice, it turned a reddish brown. Slowly I slipped it onto my tongue. There was the delicate savor of the citron, the sharp taste of soy sauce, and a cold, slippery feeling. I rolled it around in my mouth a few times and it was gone, leaving only a faint starchy flavor. Another dish held a neat row of tiny mackerel, their tails cocked up. The side-markings were chestnut-colored, the backs blue, the bellies a glittering silver—and there was the usual delicate aroma of this fish. When I pulled off a morsel of the firm flesh, dipped it in sauce, and ate it, it had a rich taste.

Later, fruit was served. The sister picked out a large, sweet-looking pear, and began to peel it. Setting the heavy fruit firmly in the circle of her long, arched fingers, she turned it round and round, as a strip of yellow peel curved over her pale hand and down in a loose spiral. Then she said she was not especially fond of pears, and put it, dripping with juice, on a dish for me. While I sliced and ate it, I watched her take a beautiful cherry, hold it lightly between her lips, and then glide it deftly in with the tip of her tongue. Her soft rounded chin moved deliciously.

She seemed unusually gay. The old woman became very jolly too, and announced she was going to guess how many teeth I had. So she hid her face like a child, pondered a long time, and declared: "Twenty-eight, not counting wisdom-teeth!"

"Everybody has twenty-eight."

But she wouldn't hear it. "What do you mean! Don't they say the Lord Buddha had forty odd?" Across the table I saw those lips part in a lovely smile.

After that our conversation somehow got around to birds. The old woman told us the mountains in her province were full of snowy herons. Wild geese and ducks came too, and flocks of cranes; a pair of white-naped cranes was sure to come every year, an event that had to be reported to the castle. Storks turned their heads to scream, and wove basket-like nests of twigs in the huge cedars of the local shrine. . . . On and on she went in her excitement, till we asked how long ago all that had been.

"When I was a child."

"Then they'd be gone now."

"But there were lots of them!" she insisted. "And they had little ones every year!" Again I saw that lovely smile.

My friend's sister was supposed to leave the next morning, but for some reason stayed till evening. When I came out of the bath at dusk, my room was dark and the old woman had gone off somewhere, so I decided to go out to the garden.

Just then I heard the sister call to me from the round window of the cottage. "I borrowed your lamp for a moment." And she came to say good-bye, bringing a tray of peaches.

"I hope you'll be all right. Do come to see us whenever you're in Kyoto."

I went down and sat in the garden by the flowers, and watched the stars wheeling on endlessly toward the ocean. There was only the sky, the cries of insects, the distant murmur of the waves. . . . The old woman came back with a rickshawman. I saw the sister, beautifully dressed and ready to leave, hurrying to my room to return the lamp. Finally, after her luggage had been taken out, she went down the veranda toward the entrance hall, and made a little bow to me as she passed.

"Good-bye!" she called. But I pretended not to hear.

"Good-bye! Good-bye!"

Silently I bowed my head there in the dark. The creak of the rickshaw died away, and I heard the gate being shut. Hidden among the flowers, I brushed at my streaming tears. Why had I kept silent? Why couldn't I have said good-bye? I stayed in the garden till I was cold, and at last, when the now slender moon hung over the mountain, went back to my room. Propping both elbows listlessly on the desk, I cupped my hands tenderly around a peach—a peach with a tinge of color, like a cheek, and with the smooth curve of a softly rounded chin—and pressed it to my lips. And as I sniffed the fragrance subtly diffused through its fine-textured skin, my tears began to fall once again.

TRANSLATED BY HOWARD HIBBETT

HAN'S CRIME

[Han no Hanzai, 1913] by Shiga Naoya (born 1883)

Shiga Naoya is one of the most important and influential writers of modern Japan. In his writings a style of exceptional beauty is joined to delicate perceptivity. Some of his stories are purely fictional, but his most characteristic works, such as At Kinosaki, *with its meditations on death, are largely autobiographical. Shiga's immense success encouraged many other writers to turn to the "I" novel, which occupies so prominent a place in twentieth-century Japanese literature.*

•

Much to everyone's astonishment, the young Chinese juggler, Han, severed his wife's carotid artery with one of his heavy knives in the course of a performance. The young woman died on the spot. Han was immediately arrested.

At the scene of the event were the director of the theatre, Han's Chinese assistant, the announcer, and more than three hundred spectators. There was also a policeman who had been stationed behind the audience. Despite the presence of all these witnesses, it was a complete mystery whether the killing had been intentional or accidental.

Han's act was as follows: his wife would stand in front of a wooden board about the size of a door, and from a distance of approximately four yards, he would throw his large knives at her so that they stuck in the board about two inches apart, forming a contour around her body. As each knife left his hand, he would let out a staccato exclamation as if to punctuate his performance.

The examining judge first questioned the director of the theatre.

"Would you say that this was a very difficult act?"

"No, Your Honor, it's not as difficult as all that for an experienced performer. But to do it properly, you need steady nerves and complete concentration."

"I see. Then assuming that what happened was an accident, it was an extremely unlikely type of accident?"

"Yes indeed, Your Honor. If accidents were not so very unlikely, I should never have allowed the act in my theatre."

"Well then, do you consider that this was done on purpose?"

"No, Your Honor, I do not. And for this reason: an act of this kind performed at a distance of twelve feet requires not only skill but at the same time a certain—well, intuitive sense. It is true that we all thought a mistake virtually out of the question, but after what has happened, I think we must admit that there was always the possibility of a mistake."

"Well then, which do you think it was—a mistake or on purpose?"

"That I simply cannot say, Your Honor."

The judge felt puzzled. Here was a clear case of homicide, but whether it was manslaughter or premeditated murder it was impossible to tell. If a murder, it was indeed a clever one, thought the judge.

Next the judge decided to question the Chinese assistant, who had worked with Han for many years past.

"What was Han's normal behavior?" he asked.

"He was always very correct, Your Honor; he didn't gamble or drink or run after women. Besides, last year he took up Christianity. He studied English and in his free time always seemed to be reading collections of sermons—the Bible and that sort of thing."

"And what about his wife's behavior?"

"Also very correct, Your Honor. Strolling players aren't always the most moral people, as you know. Mrs. Han was a pretty little woman and quite a few men used to make propositions to her, but she never paid the slightest attention to that kind of thing."

"And what sort of temperaments did they have?"

"Always very kind and gentle, sir. They were extremely good to all their friends and acquaintances and never quarreled with anyone. But . . ." He broke off and reflected a moment before continuing. "Your Honor, I'm afraid that if I tell you this, it may go badly for

Han. But to be quite truthful, these two people, who were so gentle and unselfish to others, were amazingly cruel in their relations to each other."

"Why was that?"

"I don't know, Your Honor."

"Was that the case ever since you first knew them?"

"No, Your Honor. About two years ago Mrs. Han was pregnant. The child was born prematurely and died after about three days. That marked a change in their relations. They began having terrible rows over the most trivial things, and Han's face used to turn white as a sheet. He always ended by suddenly growing silent. He never once raised his hand against her or anything like that—I suppose it would have gone against his principles. But when you looked at him, Your Honor, you could see the terrible anger in his eyes! It was quite frightening at times.

"One day I asked Han why he didn't separate from his wife, seeing that things were so bad between them. Well, he told me that he had no real grounds for divorce, even though his love for her had died. Of course, she felt this and gradually stopped loving him too. He told me all this himself. I think the reason he began reading the Bible and all those sermons was to calm the violence in his heart and stop himself from hating his wife, whom he had no real cause to hate. Mrs. Han was really a pathetic woman. She had been with Han nearly three years and had traveled all over the country with him as a strolling player. If she'd ever left Han and gone back home, I don't think she'd have found it easy to get married. How many men would trust a woman who'd spent all that time traveling about? I suppose that's why she stayed with Han, even though they got on so badly."

"And what do you really think about this killing?"

"You mean, Your Honor, do I think it was an accident or done on purpose?"

"That's right."

"Well, sir, I've been thinking about it from every angle since the day it happened. The more I think, the less I know what to make of it. I've talked about it with the announcer, and he also says he can't understand what happened."

"Very well. But tell me this: at the actual moment it did happen, did it occur to you to wonder whether it was accidental or on purpose?"

"Yes, sir, it did. I thought . . . I thought, 'He's gone and killed her.' "

"On purpose, you mean?"

"Yes, sir. However the announcer says that he thought, 'His hand's slipped.' "

"Yes, but he didn't know about their everyday relations as you did."

"That may be, Your Honor. But afterwards I wondered if it wasn't just because I did know about those relations that I thought, 'He's killed her.' "

"What were Han's reactions at the moment?"

"He cried out, 'Ha.' As soon as I heard that, I looked up and saw blood gushing from his wife's throat. For a few seconds she kept standing there, then her knees seemed to fold up under her and her body swayed forward. When the knife fell out, she collapsed on the floor, all crumpled in a heap. Of course there was nothing any of us could do—we just sat there petrified, staring at her. . . . As to Han, I really can't describe his reactions, for I wasn't looking at him. It was only when the thought struck me, 'He's finally gone and killed her,' that I glanced at him. His face was dead white and his eyes closed. The stage manager lowered the curtain. When they picked up Mrs. Han's body she was already dead. Han dropped to his knees then, and for a long time he went on praying in silence."

"Did he appear very upset?"

"Yes, sir, he was quite upset."

"Very well. If I have anything further to ask you, I shall call for you again."

The judge dismissed the Chinese assistant and now summoned Han himself to the stand. The juggler's intelligent face was drawn and pale; one could tell right away that he was in a state of nervous exhaustion.

"I have already questioned the director of the theatre and your assistant," said the judge when Han had taken his place in the witness box. "I now propose to examine you."

Han bowed his head.

"Tell me," said the judge, "did you at any time love your wife?"

"From the day of our marriage until the child was born I loved her with all my heart."

"And why did the birth of the child change things?"

"Because I knew it was not mine."

"Did you know who the other man was?"

"I had a very good idea. I think it was my wife's cousin."

"Did you know him personally?"

"He was a close friend. It was he who first suggested that we get married. It was he who urged me to marry her."

"I presume that his relations with her occurred prior to your marriage."

"Yes, sir. The child was born eight months after we were married."

"According to your assistant, it was a premature birth."

"That is what I told everyone."

"The child died very soon after birth, did it not? What was the cause of death?"

"He was smothered by his mother's breasts."

"Did your wife do that on purpose?"

"She said it was an accident."

The judge was silent and looked fixedly at Han's face. Han raised his head but kept his eyes lowered as he awaited the next question. The judge continued,

"Did your wife confess these relations to you?"

"She did not confess, nor did I ever ask her about them. The child's death seemed like retribution for everything and I decided that I should be as magnanimous as possible, but . . ."

"But in the end you were unable to be magnanimous?"

"That's right. I could not help thinking that the death of the child was insufficient retribution. When apart from my wife, I was able to reason calmly, but as soon as I saw her, something happened inside me. When I saw her body, my temper would begin to rise."

"Didn't divorce occur to you?"

"I often thought that I should like to have a divorce, but I never mentioned it to my wife. My wife used to say that if I left her she could no longer exist."

"Did she love you?"

"She did not love me."

"Then why did she say such things?"

"I think she was referring to the material means of existence. Her home had been ruined by her elder brother, and she knew that no serious man would want to marry a woman who had been the wife of a strolling player. Also her feet were too small for her to do any ordinary work."

"What were your physical relations?"

"I imagine about the same as with most couples."

"Did your wife have any real liking for you?"

"I do not think she really liked me. In fact, I think it must have been very painful for her to live with me as my wife. Still, she endured it. She endured it with a degree of patience almost unthinkable for a man. She used to observe me with a cold, cruel look in her eyes as my life gradually went to pieces. She never showed a flicker of sympathy as she saw me struggling in agony to escape into a better, truer sort of existence."

"Why could you not take some decisive action—have it out with her, or even leave her if necessary?"

"Because my mind was full of all sorts of ideals."

"What ideals?"

"I wanted to behave towards my wife in such a way that there would be no wrong on my side. . . . But in the end it didn't work."

"Did you never think of killing your wife?"

Han did not answer and the judge repeated his question. After a long pause, Han replied,

"Before the idea of killing her occurred to me, I often used to think it would be a good thing if she died."

"Well, in that case, if it had not been against the law, don't you think you might have killed her?"

"I wasn't thinking in terms of the law, sir. That's not what stopped me. It was just that I was weak. At the same time I had this overmastering desire to enter into a truer sort of life."

"Nevertheless you did think of killing your wife, did you not—later on, I mean?"

"I never made up my mind to do it. But, yes, it is correct to say that I did think about it once."

"How long was that before the event?"

"The previous night. . . . Or perhaps even the same morning."

"Had you been quarreling?"

"Yes, sir."

"What about?"

"About something so petty that it's hardly worth mentioning."

"Try telling me about it."

"It was a question of food. I get rather short-tempered when I haven't eaten for some time. Well, that evening my wife had been dawdling and our supper wasn't ready when it should have been. I got very angry."

"Were you more violent than usual?"

"No, but afterwards I still felt worked up, which was unusual. I suppose it was because I'd been worrying so much during those past weeks about making a better existence for myself, and realizing there was nothing I could do about it. I went to bed but couldn't get to sleep. All sorts of upsetting thoughts went through my mind. I began to feel that whatever I did, I should never be able to achieve the things I really wanted—that however hard I tried, I should never be able to escape from all the hateful aspects of my present life. This sad, hopeless state of affairs all seemed connected with my marriage. I desperately wanted to find a chink of light to lead me out of my darkness, but even this desire was gradually being extinguished. The hope of escape still flickered and sputtered within me, and I knew that if ever it should go out I would to all intents and purposes be a dead person.

"And then the ugly thought began flitting through my mind, 'If only she would die! If only she would die! Why should I not kill her?' The practical consequence of such a crime meant nothing to me any longer. No doubt I would go to prison, but life in prison could not be worse—could only be better—than this present existence. And yet somehow I had the feeling that killing my wife would solve nothing. It would have been a shirking of the issue, in the same way as suicide. I must go through each day's suffering as it came, I told myself; there was no way to circumvent that. That had become my true life: to suffer.

"As my mind raced along these tracks, I almost forgot that the cause of my suffering lay beside me. Utterly exhausted, I lay there unable to sleep. I fell into a blank state of stupefaction, and as my tortured mind turned numb, the idea of killing my wife gradually faded. Then I was overcome by the sad empty feeling that follows a nightmare. I thought of all my fine resolutions for a better life, and realized that I was too weakhearted to attain it. When dawn finally broke I saw that my wife also, had not been sleeping. . . ."

"When you got up, did you behave normally towards each other?"

"We did not say a single word to each other."

"But why didn't you think of leaving her, when things had come to this?"

"Do you mean, Your Honor, that that would have been a solution of my problem? No, no, that too would have been a shirking of the issue! As I told you, I was determined to behave towards my wife so that there would be no wrong on my side."

Han gazed earnestly at the judge, who nodded his head as a sign for him to continue.

"Next day I was physically exhausted and of course my nerves were ragged. It was agony for me to remain still, and as soon as I had got dressed I left the house and wandered aimlessly about the deserted parts of town. Constantly the thought kept returning that I must do something to solve my life, but the idea of killing no longer occurred to me. The truth is that there was a chasm between my thoughts of murder the night before and any actual decision to commit a crime! Indeed, I never even thought about that evening's performance. If I had, I certainly would have decided to leave out the knife-throwing act. There were dozens of other acts that could have been substituted.

"Well, the evening came and finally it was our turn to appear on the stage. I did not have the slightest premonition that anything out of the ordinary was to happen. As usual, I demonstrated to the audience the sharpness of my knives by slicing pieces of paper and throwing some of the knives at the floor boards. Presently my wife appeared, heavily made up and wearing an elaborate Chinese costume; after greeting the audience with her charming smile, she took up her position in front of the board. I picked up one of the knives and placed myself at the distance from her.

"That's when our eyes met for the first time since the previous evening. At once I understood the risk of having chosen this particular act for that night's performance! Obviously I would have to master my nerves, yet the exhaustion which had penetrated to the very marrow of my bones prevented me. I sensed that I could no longer trust my own arm. To calm myself I closed my eyes for a moment, and I sensed that my whole body was trembling.

"Now the time had come! I aimed my first knife above her head; it struck just one inch higher than usual. My wife raised her arms and I prepared to throw my next two knives under each of her arms. As the first one left the ends of my fingers, I felt as if something were holding it back; I no longer had the sense of being able to determine the exact destination of my knives. It was now really a matter of luck if the knife struck at the point intended; each of my movements had become deliberate and self-conscious.

"I threw one knife to the left of my wife's neck and was about to throw another to the right when I saw a strange expression in her eyes. She seemed to be seized by a paroxysm of fear! Did she have a presentiment that this knife, that in a matter of seconds would come hurtling towards her, was going to lodge in her throat? I felt dizzy, as if about to faint. Forcing the knife deliberately out of my hand, I as good as aimed it into space. . . ."

The judge was silent, peering intently at Han.

"All at once the thought came to me, 'I've killed her,'" said Han abruptly.

"On purpose, you mean?"

"Yes. Suddenly I felt that I had done it on purpose."

"After that I understand you knelt down beside your wife's body and prayed in silence."

"Yes, sir. That was a rather cunning device that occurred to me on the spur of the moment. I realized that everyone knew me as a believer in Christianity. But while I was making a pretense of praying, I was in fact carefully calculating what attitude to adopt."

"So you were absolutely convinced that what you had done was on purpose?"

"I was. But I realized at once that I should be able to pretend it had been an accident."

"And why did you think it had been on purpose?"

"I had lost all sense of judgment."

"Did you think you'd succeeded in giving the impression it was an accident?"

"Yes, though when I thought about it afterwards it made my flesh creep. I pretended as convincingly as I could to be grief-stricken, but if there'd been just one really sharp-witted person about, he'd have realized right away that I was only acting. Well, that evening I decided that there was no good reason why I should not be acquitted; I told myself very calmly that there wasn't a shred of material evidence against me. To be sure, everyone knew how badly I got on with my wife, but if I persisted in saying that it was an accident, no one could prove the contrary. Going over in my mind everything that had happened, I saw that my wife's death could be explained very plausibly as an accident.

"And then a strange question came to my mind: why did I myself believe that it had *not* been an accident? The previous night I had thought about killing her, but might it not be that very fact which now caused me to think of my act as deliberate? Gradually I came to the point that I myself did not know what actually had happened! At that I became very happy—almost unbearably happy. I wanted to shout at the top of my lungs."

"Because you had come to consider it an accident?"

"No, that I can't say: because I no longer had the slightest idea as to whether it had been intentional or not. So I decided that my best way of being acquitted would be to make a clean breast of everything. Rather than deceive myself and everyone else by saying it was an accident, why not be completely honest and say I did not know what happened? I cannot declare it was a mistake; on the other hand I can't admit it was intentional. In fact, I can plead neither 'guilty' nor 'not guilty.' "

Han was silent. The judge, too, remained silent for a long moment before saying softly, reflectively, "I believe that what you have told me is true. Just one more question: do you not feel the slightest sorrow for your wife's death?"

"None at all! Even when I hated my wife most bitterly in the past, I never could have imagined I would feel such happiness in talking about her death."

"Very well," said the judge. "You may stand down."

Han silently lowered his head and left the room. Feeling strangely moved, the judge reached for his pen. On the document which lay on the table before him he wrote down the words, "Not guilty."

TRANSLATED BY IVAN MORRIS

AT KINOSAKI

[Kinosaki ni te, 1917] by *Shiga Naoya*

•

I had been hit by a train on the Tokyo loop line and I went alone to Kinosaki hot spring to convalesce. If I developed tuberculosis of the spine it could be fatal, but the doctor did not think I would. I would be out of danger in two or three years, he said, and the important thing was to take care of myself; and so I made the trip. I thought I would stay three weeks and more—five weeks if I could stand it.

My head was still not clear. I had taken to forgetting things at an alarming rate. But I had a pleasant feeling of quiet and repose as I had not had in recent years. The weather was beautiful as the time came to begin harvesting the rice.

I was quite alone. I had no one to talk to. I could read or write, I could sit in the chair on the veranda and look out absently at the mountains or the street, and beyond that I could go for walks. A road that followed a little stream gradually up from the town was good for walking. Where the stream skirted the base of the mountain it formed a little pool, which was full of brook salmon. Sometimes, when I looked carefully, I could find a big river crab with hair on its claws, still as a stone. I liked to walk up the road just before dinner in the evening. More often than not I would be sunk in thought as I followed the blue little stream up that lonely mountain valley in the evening chill. My thoughts were melancholy ones. And yet I felt a pleasant repose. I thought often of my accident. But a little more and I would be lying face up under the ground in Aoyama cemetery. My face would be green and cold and hard, and the wounds on my face and my back would be as they were that day. The bodies of my grandfather and my mother would be beside me. Nothing would pass between us. —Those were the things I thought. Gloomy thoughts, but they held little terror. All this would come sometime. When would it be? —Much the same thoughts had come to me before, but that "when" had seemed distant then and beyond knowing. Now, however, I felt I really could not tell when it might be here. I had been saved this time, something had failed to kill me, there were things I must do. —I remembered reading in middle school how Lord Clive was stirred to new efforts by thoughts like these. I wanted to react so to the crisis I had been through. I even did. But my heart was strangely quiet. Something had made it friendly to death.

My room was on the second floor, a rather quiet room with no neighbors. Often when I was tired I would go out and sit on the veranda. The roof of the entranceway was to one side below me, and it joined the main building at a boarded wall. There seemed to be a beehive under the boards. When the weather was good the big tiger-striped bees would work from morning to dark. Pushing their way out from between the boards they would pause on the roof of the entranceway. Some would walk around for a moment after they had arranged their wings and feelers with their front and hind legs, and immediately they too would spread their slender wings taut and take off with a heavy droning. Once in the air they moved quickly away. They gathered around the late shrubs in the garden, just then coming into bloom. I would hang over the railing when I was bored and watch them come and go.

One morning I saw a dead bee on the roof. Its legs were doubled tight under it, its feelers dropped untidily over its head. The other bees seemed indifferent to it, quite untroubled as they crawled busily around it on their way in and out. The industrious living bees gave so completely a sense of life. The other beside them, rolled over with its legs under it, still in the same spot whenever I looked at it, morning, noon, night—how completely it gave a sense of death. For three days it lay there. It gave me a feeling of utter quietness. Of loneliness. It was lonely to see the dead body left there on the cold tile in the evening when the rest had gone inside. And at the same time it was tranquil, soothing.

In the night a fierce rain fell. The next morning it was clear, and the leaves of the trees, the ground, the roof were all washed clean. The body of the dead bee was gone. The others were busy again, but that one had probably washed down the eaves trough to the ground. It was likely somewhere covered with mud, unmoving, its legs still tight beneath it, its feelers still flat against its head. Probably it was lying quiet until a change in the world outside would move it again. Or perhaps ants were pulling it off. Even so, how quiet it must be—before only working and working, no longer moving now. I felt a certain nearness to that quiet. I had written a short story not long before called "Han's Crime." A Chinese named Han murdered his wife in his jealousy over her relations with a friend of his before they were married, the jealousy abetted by physical pressures in Han himself. I had written from the point of view of Han, but now I thought I wanted to write of the wife, to describe her murdered and quiet in her grave.

I thought of writing "The Murdered Wife of Han." I never did, but the urge was there. I was much disturbed that my way of thinking had become so different from that of the hero of a long novel I was writing.

It was shortly after the bee was washed away. I left the inn for a walk out to a park where I could look down on the Maruyama River and the Japan Sea into which it flows. From in front of the large bathhouse a little stream ran gently down the middle of the street and into the river. A noisy crowd was looking down into the water from one spot along its banks and from a bridge. A large rat had been thrown in and was swimming desperately to get away. A skewer some eight or ten inches long was thrust through the skin of its neck, so that it projected about three or four inches above the head and three or four below the throat. The rat tried to climb up the stone wall. Two or three children and a rickshawman forty years old or so were throwing stones at it. They were having trouble hitting their mark. The stones struck against the wall and bounced off. The spectators laughed loudly. The rat finally brought its front paws up into a hole in the wall. When it tried to climb in, the skewer caught on the rocks. The rat fell back into the stream, trying still to save itself somehow. One could tell nothing from its face, but from its actions one could see how desperate it was. It seemed to think that if it could find shelter somewhere it would be safe, and with the skewer still in its neck it turned off again into the stream. The children and the rickshawman, more and more taken with the sport, continued to throw stones. Two or three ducks bobbing for food in front of the laundry place stretched their necks out in surprise. The stones splashed into the water. The ducks looked alarmed and paddled off upstream, their necks still astretch.

I did not want to see the end. The sight of the rat, doomed to die and yet putting its whole strength into the search for an escape, lingered stubbornly in my mind. I felt lonely and unhappy. Here was the truth, I told myself. It was terrible to think that this suffering lay before the quiet I was after. Even if I did feel a certain nearness to that quiet after death, still the struggle on the way was terrible. Beasts that do not know suicide must continue the struggle until it is finally cut short by death. What would I do if what was happening to the rat were happening to me now? Would I not, after all, struggle as the rat was struggling? I could not help remembering how near I was to doing very much that at the time of my accident. I wanted to do what could be done. I decided on a hospital for myself. I told how I was to be taken there. I asked someone to telephone in advance because I was afraid the doctor might be out and they would not be ready to operate immediately. Even when I was but half-conscious my mind worked so well on what was most important that I was surprised at it afterward myself. The question of whether I would die or not was moreover very much mine, and yet, while I did consider the possibility that I might, I was surprised afterward too at how little I was troubled by fear of death. "Is it fatal? What did the doctor say?" I asked a friend who was at my side. "He says it isn't," I was told. With that my spirits rose. I became most animated in my excitement. What would I have done if I had been told it would be fatal? I had trouble imagining. I would have been upset. But I thought I would not have been assailed by the intense fear I had always imagined. And I thought that even then I would have gone on struggling, looking for a way out. I would have behaved but little differently indeed from the rat. Even now, I decided, it would be much the same—let it be. My mood at the moment, it was clear, could have little immediate effect. And the truth lay on both sides. It was very good if there was such an effect, and it was very good if there was none. That was all.

One evening, some time later, I started out alone from the town, climbing gradually up along the little river. The road grew narrow and steep after it crossed the railroad at the mouth of a tunnel, the stream grew rapid, the last houses disappeared. I kept thinking I would go back, but each time I went on to see what was around the next corner. Everything was a pale green, the touch of the air was chilly against the skin. The quiet made me strangely restless. There was a large mulberry tree beside the road. A leaf on one branch that protruded out over the road from the far side fluttered rhythmically back and forth. There was no wind, everything except the stream was sunk in silence, only that one leaf fluttered on. I thought it odd. I was a little afraid even, but I was curious. I went down and looked at it for a time. A breeze came up. The leaf stopped moving. I saw what was happening, and it came to me that I had known all this before.

It began to get dark. No matter how far I went there were still corners ahead. I decided to go back. I looked down at the stream. On a rock that sloped up perhaps a yard square from the water at the far bank there was a small dark object. A water lizard. It was still wet, a good color. It was quite still, its head facing down the incline as it looked into the stream. The water from its body ran dark an inch or two down the dry rock. I squatted down and looked at it absent-mindedly. I no longer disliked water lizards. I was rather fond of land lizards. I loathed the horny wall lizard more than anything else of its sort. Some ten years before, when I was staying in the mountains not far from Tokyo, I had seen water lizards gathered around a drain from the inn, and I had thought how I would hate to be a water lizard, what it would be like to be reborn one. I did not like to come on water lizards because they always brought back the same thought. But now I was no longer bothered by it. I wanted to startle the lizard into the water. I could see in my mind how it would run, clumsily twisting its body. Still crouched by the stream, I took up a stone the size of a small ball and threw it. I was not especially aiming at the lizard. My aim is so bad that I could not have hit it had I tried, and it never occurred to me that I might. The stone slapped against the rock and fell into the water. As it hit, the lizard seemed to jump five inches or so to the side. Its tail curled high in the air. I wondered what had happened. I did not think at first that the rock had struck home. The curved tail began quietly to fall back down of its own weight. The toes of the projecting front feet, braced against the slope with knee joints cut, turned under and the lizard fell forward, its strength gone. Its tail lay flat against the rock. It did not move. It was dead.

What had I done, I thought. I often enough kill lizards and such, but the thought that I had killed one without intending to filled me with a strange revulsion. I had done it, but from the beginning entirely by chance. For the lizard it was a completely unexpected death. I continued to squat there. I felt as if there were only the lizard and I, as if I had become the lizard and knew its feelings. I was filled with a sadness for the lizard, with a sense of the loneliness of the living creature. Quite by accident I had lived. Quite by accident the lizard had died. I was lonely, and presently I started back toward the inn down the road still visible at my feet. The lights at the outskirts of the town came into view. What had happened to the dead bee? Probably it was carried underground by that rain. And the rat? Swept off to sea, probably, and its body, bloated from the water, would be washing up now with the rubbish on a beach. And I who had not died was walking here. I knew I should be grateful. But the proper feeling of happiness refused to come. To be alive and to be dead were not two opposite extremes. There did not seem to be much difference between them. It was now fairly dark. My sense of sight took in only the distant lights, and the feel of my feet against the ground, cut off from my sight, seemed uncertain in the extreme. Only my head worked on as it would. It led me deeper and deeper into these fancies.

I left after about three weeks. It is more than three years now. I did not get spinal tuberculosis—that much I escaped.

TRANSLATED BY EDWARD SEIDENSTICKER

THE MADMAN ON THE ROOF

[Okujō no Kyōjin, 1916] by Kikuchi Kan (1888-1948)

•

Characters

KATSUSHIMA YOSHITARO, the madman, twenty-four years of age
KATSUSHIMA SUEJIRO, his brother, a seventeen-year-old high school student
KATSUSHIMA GISUKE, their father
KATSUSHIMA OYOSHI, their mother
TOSAKU, a neighbor
KICHIJI, a manservant, twenty years of age
A PRIESTESS, about fifty years of age

PLACE: A small island in the Inland Sea
TIME: 1900

The stage setting represents the backyard of the Katsushimas, who are the richest family on the island. A bamboo fence prevents one from seeing more of the house than the high roof, which stands out sharply against the rich greenish sky of the southern island summer. At the left of the stage one can catch a glimpse of the sea shining in the sunlight.

Yoshitaro, the elder son of the family, is sitting astride the ridge of the roof, and is looking out over the sea.

GISUKE (*speaking from within the house*): Yoshi is sitting on the roof again. He'll get a sunstroke—the sun's so terribly hot. (*Coming out.*) Kichiji! —Where is Kichiji?

KICHIJI (*appearing from the right*): Yes! What do you want?

GISUKE: Bring Yoshitaro down. He has no hat on, up there in the hot sun. He'll get a sunstroke. How did he get up there, anyway? From the barn? Didn't you put wires around the barn roof as I told you to the other day?

KICHIJI: Yes, I did exactly as you told me.

GISUKE (*coming through the gate to the center of the stage, and *looking up to the roof*): I don't see how he can stand it, sitting on that hot slate roof. (*He calls.*) Yoshitaro! You'd better come down. If you stay up there you'll get a sunstroke, and maybe die.

KICHIJI: Young master! Come on down. You'll get sick if you stay there.

GISUKE: Yoshi! Come down quick! What are you doing up there, anyway? Come down, I say! (*He calls loudly.*) Yoshi!

YOSHITARO (*indifferently*): Wha-a-at?

GISUKE: No "whats"! Come down right away. If you don't come down, I'll get after you with a stick.

YOSHITARO (*protesting like a spoiled child*): No, I don't want to. There's something wonderful. The priest of the god Kompira is dancing in the clouds. Dancing with an angel in pink robes. They're calling to me to come. (*Crying out ecstatically.*) Wait! I'm coming!

GISUKE: If you talk like that you'll fall, just as you did once before. You're already crippled and insane—what will you do next to worry your parents? Come down, you fool!

KICHIJI: Master, don't get so angry. The young master will not obey you. You should get some fried bean cake; when he sees it he will come down, because he likes it.

GISUKE: No, you had better get the stick after him. Don't be afraid to give him a good shaking-up.

KICHIJI: That's too cruel. The young master doesn't understand anything. He's under the influence of evil spirits.

GISUKE: We may have to put bamboo guards on the roof to keep him down from there.

KICHIJI: Whatever you do won't keep him down. Why, he climbed the roof of the Honzen Temple without even a ladder; a low roof like this one is the easiest thing in the world for him. I tell you, it's the evil spirits that make him climb. Nothing can stop him.

GISUKE: You may be right, but he worries me to death. If we could only keep him in the house it wouldn't be so bad, even though he is crazy; but he's always climbing up to high places. Suejiro says that everybody as far as Takamatsu knows about Yoshitaro the Madman.

KICHIJI: People on the island all say he's under the influence of a fox-spirit, but I don't believe that. I never heard of a fox climbing trees.

GISUKE: You're right. I think I know the real reason. About the time Yoshitaro was born, I bought a very expensive imported rifle, and I shot every monkey on the island. I believe a monkey-spirit is now working in him.

KICHIJI: That's just what I think. Otherwise, how could he climb trees so well? He can climb anything without a ladder. Even Saku, who's a professional climber, admits that he's no match for Yoshitaro.

GISUKE (*with a bitter laugh*): Don't joke about it! It's no laughing matter, having a son who is always climbing on the roof. (*Calling again.*) Yoshitaro, come down! Yoshitaro! —When he's up there on the roof, he doesn't hear me at all—he's so engrossed. I cut down all the trees around the house so he couldn't climb them, but there's nothing I can do about the roof.

KICHIJI: When I was a boy I remember there was a gingko tree in front of the gate.

GISUKE: Yes, that was one of the biggest trees on the island. One day Yoshitaro climbed clear to the top. He sat out on a branch, at least ninety feet above the ground, dreaming away as usual. My wife and I never expected him to get down alive, but after a while, down he slid. We were all too astonished to speak.

KICHIJI: That was certainly a miracle.

GISUKE: That's why I say it's a monkey-spirit that's working in him. (*He calls again.*) Yoshi! Come down! (*Dropping his voice.*) Kichiji, you'd better go up and fetch him.

KICHIJI: But when anyone else climbs up there, the young master gets angry.

GISUKE: Never mind his getting angry. Pull him down.

KICHIJI: Yes, master.

(*Kichiji goes out after the ladder. Tosaku, the neighbor, enters.*)

TOSAKU: Good day, sir.

GISUKE: Good day. Fine weather. Catch anything with the nets you put out yesterday?

TOSAKU: No, not much. The season's over.

GISUKE: Maybe it *is* too late now.

TOSAKU (*looking up at Yoshitaro*): Your son's on the roof again.

GISUKE: Yes, as usual. I don't like it, but when I keep him locked in a room he's like a fish out of water. Then, when I take pity on him and let him out, back he goes up on the roof.

TOSAKU: But after all, he doesn't bother anybody.

GISUKE: He bothers us. We feel so ashamed when he climbs up there and shouts.

TOSAKU: But your younger son, Suejiro, has a fine record at school. That must be some consolation for you.

GISUKE: Yes, he's a good student, and that is a consolation to me. If both of them were crazy, I don't know how I could go on living.

TOSAKU: By the way, a Priestess has just come to the island. How would you like to have her pray for your son? —That's really what I came to see you about.

GISUKE: We've tried prayers before, but it's never done any good.

TOSAKU: This Priestess believes in the god Kompira. She works all kinds of miracles. People say the god inspires her, and that's why her prayers have more effect than those of ordinary priests. Why don't you try her once?

GISUKE: Well, we might. How much does she charge?

TOSAKU: She won't take any money unless the patient is cured. If he is cured, you pay her whatever you feel like.

GISUKE: Suejiro says he doesn't believe in prayers. . . . But there's no harm in letting her try.

(*Kichiji enters carrying the ladder and disappears behind the fence.*)

TOSAKU: I'll go and bring her here. In the meantime you get your son down off the roof.

GISUKE: Thanks for your trouble. (*After seeing that Tosaku has gone, he calls again.*) Yoshi! Be a good boy and come down.

KICHIJI (*who is up on the roof by this time*): Now then, young master, come down with me. If you stay up here any longer you'll have a fever tonight.

YOSHITARO (*drawing away from Kichiji as a Buddhist might from a heathen*): Don't touch me! The angels are beckoning to me. You're not supposed to come here. What do you want?

KICHIJI: Don't talk nonsense! Please come down.

YOSHITARO: If you touch me the demons will tear you apart.

(*Kichiji hurriedly catches Yoshitaro by the shoulder and pulls him to the ladder. Yoshitaro suddenly becomes submissive.*)

KICHIJI: Don't make any trouble now. If you do you'll fall and hurt yourself.

GISUKE: Be careful!

(*Yoshitaro comes down to the center of the stage, followed by Kichiji. Yoshitaro is lame in his right leg.*)

GISUKE (*calling*): Oyoshi! Come out here a minute.

OYOSHI (*from within*): What is it?

GISUKE: I've sent for a Priestess.

OYOSHI (*coming out*): That may help. You never can tell what will.

GISUKE: Yoshitaro says he talks with the god Kompira. Well, this Priestess is a follower of Kompira, so she ought to be able to help him.

YOSHITARO (*looking uneasy*): Father! Why did you bring me down? There was a beautiful cloud of five colors rolling down to fetch me.

GISUKE: Idiot! Once before you said there was a five-colored cloud, and you jumped off the roof. That's the way you became a cripple. A Priestess of the god Kompira is coming here today to drive the evil spirit out of you, so don't you go back up on the roof.

(*Tosaku enters, leading the Priestess. She has a crafty face.*)

TOSAKU: This is the Priestess I spoke to you about.

GISUKE: Ah, good afternoon. I'm glad you've come—this boy is really a disgrace to the whole family.

PRIESTESS (*casually*): You needn't worry any more about him. I'll cure him at once with the god's help. (*Looking at Yoshitaro.*) This is the one?

GISUKE: Yes. He's twenty-four years old, and the only thing he can do is climb up to high places.

PRIESTESS: How long has he been this way?

GISUKE: Ever since he was born. Even when he was a baby, he wanted to be climbing. When he was four or five years old, he climbed onto the low shrine, then onto the high shrine of Buddha, and finally onto a very high shelf. When he was seven he began climbing trees. At fifteen he climbed to the tops of mountains and stayed there all day long. He says he talks with demons and with the gods. What do you think is the matter with him?

PRIESTESS: There's no doubt but that it's a fox-spirit. I will pray for him. (*Looking at Yoshitaro.*) Listen now! I am the messenger of the god Kompira. All that I say comes from the god.

YOSHITARO (*uneasily*): You say the god Kompira? Have you ever seen him?

PRIESTESS (*staring at him*): Don't say such sacrilegious things! The god cannot be seen.

YOSHITARO (*exultantly*): I have seen him many times! He's an old man with white robes and a golden crown. He's my best friend.

PRIESTESS (*taken aback at this assertion, and speaking to Gisuke*): This is a fox-spirit, all right, and a very extreme case. I will address the god.

(*She chants a prayer in a weird manner. Yoshitaro, held fast by Kichiji, watches the Priestess blankly. She works herself into a frenzy, and falls to the ground in a faint. Presently she rises to her feet and looks about her strangely.*)

PRIESTESS (*in a changed voice*): I am the god Kompira!

(*All except Yoshitaro fall to their knees with exclamations of reverence.*)

PRIESTESS (*with affected dignity*): The elder son of this family is under the influence of a fox-spirit. Hang him up on the branch of a tree and purify him with the smoke of green pine needles. If you fail to do what I say, you will all be punished!

(*She faints again. There are more exclamations of astonishment.*)

PRIESTESS (*rising and looking about her as though unconscious of what has taken place*): What has happened? Did the god speak?

GISUKE: It was a miracle.

PRIESTESS: You must do at once whatever the god told you, or you'll be punished. I warn you for your own sake.

GISUKE (*hesitating somewhat*): Kichiji, go and get some green pine needles.

OYOSHI: No! It's too cruel, even if it is the god's command.

PRIESTESS: He will not suffer, only the fox-spirit within him. The boy himself will not suffer at all. Hurry! (*Looking fixedly at Yoshitaro.*) Did you hear the god's command? He told the spirit to leave your body before it hurt.

YOSHITARO: That was not Kompira's voice. He wouldn't talk to a priestess like you.

PRIESTESS (*insulted*): I'll get even with you. Just wait! Don't talk back to the god like that, you horrid fox!

(*Kichiji enters with an armful of green pine boughs. Oyoshi is frightened.*)

PRIESTESS: Respect the god or be punished!

(*Gisuke and Kichiji reluctantly set fire to the pine needles, then bring Yoshitaro to the fire. He struggles against being held in the smoke.*)

YOSHITARO: Father! What are you doing to me? I don't like it! I don't like it!

PRIESTESS: That's not his own voice speaking. It's the fox within him. Only the fox is suffering.

OYOSHI: But it's cruel!

(*Gisuke and Kichiji attempt to press Yoshitaro's face into the smoke. Suddenly Suejiro's voice is heard calling within the house, and presently he appears. He stands amazed at the scene before him.*)

SUEJIRO: What's happening here? What's the smoke for?

YOSHITARO (*coughing from the smoke, and looking at his brother as at a savior*): Father and Kichiji are putting me in the smoke.

SUEJIRO (*angrily*): Father! What foolish thing are you doing now? Haven't I told you time and time again about this sort of business?

GISUKE: But the god inspired the miraculous Priestess . . .

SUEJIRO (*interrupting*): What nonsense is that? You do these insane things merely because he is so helpless.

(*With a contemptuous look at the Priestess he stamps the fire out.*)

PRIESTESS: Wait! That fire was made at the command of the god!

(*Suejiro sneeringly puts out the last spark.*)

GISUKE (*more courageously*): Suejiro, I have no education, and you have, so I am always willing to listen to you. But this fire was made at the god's command, and you shouldn't have stamped on it.

SUEJIRO: Smoke won't cure him. People will laugh at you if they hear you've been trying to drive out a fox. All the gods in the country together couldn't even cure a cold. This Priestess is a fraud. All she wants is the money.

GISUKE: But the doctors can't cure him.

SUEJIRO: If the doctors can't, nobody can. I've told you before that he doesn't suffer. If he did, we'd have to do something for him. But as long as he can climb up on the roof, he is happy. Nobody in the whole country is as happy as he is—perhaps nobody in the world. Besides, if you cure him now, what can he do? He's twenty-four years old and he knows nothing, not even the alphabet. He's had no practical experience. If he were cured, he would be conscious of being crippled, and he'd be the most miserable man alive. Is that what you want to see? It's all because you want to make him normal. But wouldn't it be foolish to become normal merely to suffer? (*Looking sidewise at the Priestess.*) Tosaku, if you brought her here, you had better take her away.

PRIESTESS (*angry and insulted*): You disbelieve the oracle of the god. You will be punished! (*She starts her chant as before. She faints, rises, and speaks in a changed voice.*) I am the great god Kompira! What the brother of the patient says springs from his own selfishness. He knows if his sick brother is cured, he'll get the family estate. Doubt not this oracle!

SUEJIRO (*excitedly knocking the Priestess down*): That's a damned lie, you old fool.

(*He kicks her.*)

PRIESTESS (*getting to her feet and resuming her ordinary voice*): You've hurt me! You savage!

SUEJIRO: You fraud! You swindler!

TOSAKU (*coming between them*): Wait, young man! Don't get in such a frenzy.

SUEJIRO (*still excited*): You liar! A woman like you can't understand brotherly love!

TOSAKU: We'll leave now. It was my mistake to have brought her.

GISUKE (*giving Tosaku some money*): I hope you'll excuse him. He's young and has such a temper.

PRIESTESS: You kicked me when I was inspired by the god. You'll be lucky to survive until tonight.

SUEJIRO: Liar!

OYOSHI (*soothing Suejiro*): Be still now. (*To the Priestess*): I'm sorry this has happened.

PRIESTESS (*leaving with Tosaku*): The foot you kicked me with will rot off!

(*The Priestess and Tosaku go out.*)

GISUKE (*to Suejiro*): Aren't you afraid of being punished for what you've done?

SUEJIRO: A god never inspires a woman like that old swindler. She lies about everything.

OYOSHI: I suspected her from the very first. She wouldn't do such cruel things if a real god inspired her.

GISUKE (*without any insistence*): Maybe so. But, Suejiro, your brother will be a burden to you all your life.

SUEJIRO: It will be no burden at all. When I become successful, I'll build a tower for him on top of a mountain.

GISUKE (*suddenly*): But where's Yoshitaro gone?

KICHIJI (*pointing at the roof*): He's up there.

GISUKE (*having to smile*): As usual.

(*During the preceding excitement, Yoshitaro has slipped away and climbed back up on the roof. The four persons below look at each other and smile.*)

SUEJIRO: A normal person would be angry with you for having put him in the smoke, but you see, he's forgotten everything. (*He calls.*) Yoshitaro!

YOSHITARO (*for all his madness there is affection for his brother*): Suejiro! I asked Kompira and he says he doesn't know her!

SUEJIRO (*smiling*): You're right. The god will inspire you, not a priestess like her.

(*Through a rift in the clouds, the golden light of the sunset strikes the roof.*)

SUEJIRO (*exclaiming*): What a beautiful sunset!

YOSHITARO (*his face lighted by the sun's reflection*): Suejiro, look! Can't you see a golden palace in that cloud over there? There! Can't you see? Just look! How beautiful!

SUEJIRO (*as he feels the sorrow of sanity*): Yes, I see. I see it, too. Wonderful.

YOSHITARO (*filled with joy*): There! I hear music coming from the palace. Flutes, what I love best of all. Isn't it beautiful?

(*The parents have gone into the house. The mad brother on the roof and the sane brother on the ground remain looking at the golden sunset.*)

TRANSLATED BY YOZAN T. IWASAKI AND GLENN HUGHES

THE TIGER

[*Tora, 1918*] *by Kume Masao (1891-1952)*

•

As was his custom, Fukai Yasuke, the Shimpa[1] actor, did not awaken until it was nearly noon. With a rather theatrical blink of his sleep-laden eyes, he looked out at the blue sky of a cloudless autumn day, and surrendered himself to a huge, deliberate stretch. But, with a sudden realization that this performance was somewhat overdone, even for him, he darted a furtive glance about the room and smiled sheepishly at the thought of how much a part of him the grandiose gestures of the stage had become. He was, even for an actor, a born exaggerator: the very essence of his acting style lay in his ability to create farcical effects through the overuse of the bombastic and the grandiloquent. He was the best known comic actor of the Shimpa.

Fukai had started life as the dashing young man of a fish market down by the river; but when he heard that Kawakami, the founder of the Shimpa Theatre, was rounding up a collection of bit-players, Fukai had gone at once to apply for a job, ignoring the caustic comments of his friends. When it at last came Fukai's turn to undergo his stage test, Kawakami had taken one hard look at the young fishmonger with his close-cropped head, and said in tones of undisguised contempt, "You'll never make an actor, I can see."

Fukai had poured forth in his defense every argument he could muster, but Kawakami only smiled and paid him no further attention. Even this experience did not chasten Fukai. The next time he shaved every last hair from his head, and went in disguise to take another test. It so happened that one theatre needed a large number of players, and Fukai, by mingling in with the other applicants evaded Kawakami's watchful eye long enough to get himself hired.

[1] The "New School," a late nineteenth-century development in Kabuki, founded by Kawakami Otojirō.

Once he entered the company, however, Kawakami noticed him immediately.

"So! You've finally wormed your way in!" Kawakami said in considerable surprise.

"That's right. I'm a thickheaded fellow," Fukai replied, knocking on his shaven pate.

Kawakami laughed. "It can't be helped, I suppose. Now that you're in, let's see you buckle down and work hard." It had occurred to him that such a man might possibly have his uses, and there was no reason not to let him into the company gracefully.

Such was Fukai's initiation into the theatre. Since then he had become an outstanding player of comic parts, and having weathered the various vicissitudes of Shimpa, he had eventually succeeded in making himself indispensable. His salary was quite a handsome one; he would every now and then, in true actor's fashion, take up with some woman; there was no doubt but that he had made quite a success of himself.

That did not mean, however, that he was satisfied with his present lot. He was already over thirty-five. Had he followed one of the more usual vocations, at this time of life he would have been at the height of his powers and his capacity to work, but as things stood with him now, his sole function was to play the clown on the stage. He had never had a single straight part. He served merely to give the audience a good laugh, or to liven them to the proper pitch for some other actor. It was obvious even to Fukai that this was no better than being the comic assistant in some juggler's act. Obvious, but there was nothing he could do about it. At the prime of life, he was still continuing in the same old way.

Fukai had a son nearly eight years old. Last year the boy had made his debut on the stage, and like his father—or rather, with much more confidence than his father—could look forward to a future as a Shimpa actor. Fukai had no intention of letting his son play comic parts. No, he was determined to see to it that, unlike himself, the boy was given the chance to play serious roles.

At the moment Fukai still lay indolently in bed, thinking about the part he had been assigned the day before. Yesterday at the

Kabuki Theatre there had been a reading of the script of the forthcoming production *The Foster Child,* and he had been assigned the part of "the tiger." This was not the name of a character: it was the beast itself, and *that* was his whole part.

Play a tiger! He was disgusted at the thought, but it had struck him as so amusing that he could not bring himself to complain. He had played a cat once. He had also pranced around in front of the curtain in the role of a dog. People had dubbed him "the animal actor." What, then, was so strange in his being cast as a tiger? On the contrary, it would have been really hard to understand if the part had *not* devolved upon him.

Still it saddened him a little to think that there was nothing unusual about his playing a tiger. Long years of experience had accustomed him to this disappointment: he knew it was the way he earned his living, and he was, after all, a comedian. And yet it seemed as if the "humanity" in him were being affronted. He even felt a moment of anger.

At the reading of the script the day before, all eyes had automatically turned his way when the author paused and said, with a glance that took in the whole company, "I thought I'd change the old plot here a bit, and bring out Tamae's extravagance by having him keep a tiger on his front porch. The tiger's a savage brute from Malaya, and at the end of the scene he goes wild and turns on Tamae. How does that strike you?"

"Sounds all right to me," the head of the company had answered. "That gives us a chance to fit in a part for Fukai here. I take it he won't turn it down?"

Once more everyone had looked his way, and this time Fukai could sense in their expressions a kind of mocking contempt. Nevertheless, when Kawahara, the leading actor of female roles, remarked, "It's a sure hit! That act will be devoured by Fukai's tiger!", he too had joined in the laughter. He had even felt a glow of pride.

"Well, anyhow," he thought, still lying in bed, "I've got to play the part of the tiger, and play it well. It's nothing to be ashamed of. . . . Just so long as you do a part well, whether it's a beast or a bird, you're a good actor. Besides, when all's said and done, I'm the only actor in the whole of Japan that can play a tiger. I'll do a tiger for them that'll make the audience stand up and shout. And I'll give the other actors a good kicking around. If I'm to go on making my living, that's the only thing I *can* do."

He jumped out of bed, called to his wife downstairs, and got dressed. This accomplished, he went down with a cheerful countenance. His late morning meal was waiting for him on a tray covered with a yellow cloth. After a cursory brushing of his teeth, he applied himself eagerly to the food.

His son Wataru was lying on the veranda, idly leafing through the pages of an old issue of *Theatre Arts Illustrated,* no doubt an issue—one of the very rare ones—with a tiny photograph of Fukai on the first page, printed out of pity for him. He felt—it was nothing new—an embarrassment before his son. What kind of image of him as an actor was reflected in his son's eyes? And to what extent did this conflict with the boy's impression of him as a father? —These were some of the vague thoughts that ran through his head as he mechanically ate his meal.

Wataru called to him, "Father! Haven't you a rehearsal today?"

"No—at least I don't have to go to the theatre."

As he said this, his chagrin at being cast as a tiger, without a single word of dialogue to memorize, returned to him in full force. This time there was no necessity even for working out his cues with the other actors. All he had to do was decide in his own mind the most tiger-like manner in which to jump around the stage.

But come to think of it, just how *did* a tiger spring upon its victim? He had seen paintings of tigers, of course, and knew how tigers were represented in old-fashioned plays. But he had only the haziest notion what real tigers were like. When it actually came to playing the part of one, even Fukai, "animal actor" that he was, was ignorant of their special qualities. One thing was sure—they belonged to the cat family. He probably could not go too far wrong if he thought of them as huge, powerful cats. Still, if he failed to do any better than behave like a cat in one of those cat fights of the old plays, some malicious critic might say that Fukai had literally come on a tiger and exited a cat, which would be very irritating indeed.

"Do you have to go see anybody about anything?" Wataru, unaware of his father's troubled thoughts, persisted with his interrogation, his voice taking on that wheedling tone that children affect when they want to get something out of their parents.

"Let's see. No, I suppose not. But what are you asking me for, anyway?"

"I thought if you hadn't anything to do, maybe you'd take me to Ueno today. It's such a nice day. Please take me."

"Why do you want to go to Ueno? There's nothing to interest you. A kid your age wouldn't get anything out of the art museum. . . ."

"But I want to go to the zoo! I haven't been there once since last year!"

"The zoo?" Fukai repeated the word mechanically. Various ideas fluttered through his mind. Ought he to regard his child's words as a kind of divine revelation and be duly thankful? Or should he take them as an irony of fate, to which the proper response was a bitter smile? It was hard to know how to react. But even assuming that the gods were manifesting their contempt for him through the child, his long professional experience told him that his first concern should be to make good use of this opportunity for finding out how a tiger really behaves.

"They've got a hippopotamus at the zoo now, Father! Come on, take me, please."

He turned to his wife and said, as if in self-explanation, "Shall Wataru and I go to see the hippopotamus and the tiger?"

"Why don't you, if you haven't anything else to attend to? You never can tell—it might prove more of a distraction than going somewhere else," agreed his wife, showing by the special emphasis she placed on the words "somewhere else" that her mind was on quite a different subject than the tiger.

He was by no means impervious to the irony of her remark, but knew how to parry the thrust by taking it lightly. "I see. I suppose that would give you less to worry about than if I went to see a 'cat' somewhere!" His laugh was intentionally loud.

"Let's get started, Father, shall we?"

"All right! All right!"

Unashamedly he had leapt at this Heaven-sent opportunity, but somewhere deep inside him there still lurked an uneasiness which made him feel embarrassed before the child. However, he told himself, it was, after all, his job; cheered by this thought, he lightheartedly abandoned all compunctions. He had become once more the true son of Tokyo, who consoles himself by laughing at his own expense.

Less than half an hour later, he and Wataru boarded a streetcar headed for Ueno. Like most actors, he hoped when on a streetcar or in some other public place, to enjoy by turns the pleasure of elaborate efforts to remain unrecognized, and the agreeable sensation of being noticed and pointed out, despite his precautions. Decked out in a kimono of a pattern garish enough to attract anyone's attention, and with Wataru dressed in one of those kimonos with extra-long sleeves that are the mark of a child actor, Fukai sat down in a corner of the car, his elbows close to his sides, as if to appear as inconspicuous as possible. True, he did not especially wish to have any of his acquaintances catch sight of him on the way to the zoo; still, it would be amusing to meet someone unexpectedly and tell him with a straight face about his strange errand, making the whole business into a good joke.

At Suda-chō a man got on who filled the bill to perfection: the drama critic from the J newspaper, with whom Fukai had a casual acquaintance. Fukai recognized him instantly from under the felt hat pulled low over his brow, and sat with bated breath, waiting for it to dawn on the other man who he was. The critic presently discovered him and came over. With a conspiratorial, friendly air, he tapped Fukai silently on the shoulder.

Fukai looked up eagerly. "Is that you, sir? What an unexpected place to run into you!"

"I seem to be sharing the same car with a strange fellow! That's what makes riding these spark-wagons such an adventure."

"Where are you heading for? Are you on the way to her house or on your way back?"

"Which answer should I choose, I wonder? You might say I was on my way there, and then again you might say I was on my way back."

"That's because you've reached the point where you don't remember anymore where your real home is, I suppose."

"I'm not so much of a man about town as all that! But what about you? Where are you off to?"

"Me? Oh, a really fashionable place! —Look for yourself! I'm with my little millstone." He pointed with his chin at the child, whom the critic had not noticed up to this point.

"Is that you, Wataru? So you're keeping your father company today, are you? Or is your father keeping *you* company?"

"That's it, that's what makes me so stylish today—I'm being dragged off to Ueno by the kid!"

"What? To the exhibition at the art museum? Sounds pretty impressive!"

"Oh no, we wouldn't go to such an unrefined place. It's the zoo for us," he said, adding hastily, "to see the hippopotamus."

"The zoo?" The drama critic raised his eyebrows. Then his face lighted into a broad smile, and he slapped his knee. "I get it! But I'll bet it's not the hippopotamus you're going to see! You're off to see the tiger. I've heard all about the plot of the new play. They say the big boss himself thought up that idea. He's a smart man."

"Is that right? It's news to me. Here I've been furious at the leading man all along, thinking it was one of his tricks. I see I had better take the part more seriously. I've got to keep on the good side of the boss, you know."

"Now you've confessed it! But if you want to see a tiger, you needn't go to all the trouble of making a trip to the zoo."

"You mean a couple of quarts will make anybody a tiger?" [2]

"How about it? What do you say we have a look at one of those tigers?"

"No, can't do it. After all, I can't just ditch this fellow here," said Fukai, glancing once more at the child.

[2] In Japanese slang a boisterous drunken man is called a "tiger."

"You're getting old, aren't you?" the critic said casually, looking fixedly at Wataru.

At these words, like cold water dashed in his face, Fukai became serious again. He felt moreover profoundly ashamed that he had carried on this tiresome prattle without the least regard for his son's feelings. But his whole training had been much too frivolous for him to let the conversation drop, even at this juncture.

"I may be getting along in years, but they still treat me like a child as far as my parts are concerned. A tiger is more than even I can put up with."

"The other parts are just as bad. Who knows? The tiger may in the long run bring you more credit. It could easily turn out to be the hit of the show."

"That's what I keep telling myself, and that's why I have every intention of doing my best."

"Of course you will! We're all looking forward to your tiger."

"You overwhelm me!" Fukai smiled ironically, but secretly derived considerable solace from the critic's words.

The streetcar by this time had arrived at Ueno, and prodded impatiently by his son, Fukai hurriedly got off, taking an unceremonious leave of the critic.

The trees in Ueno Park had turned their bright autumn colors, and streams of people were moving along the broad gravel walks, with here and there a parasol floating in their midst. For Fukai, who was used to being indoors all the time, to be out under the blue sky at once raised his spirits. They made straight for the zoo.

Once inside the wicket, Wataru started to skip off happily. Fukai restrained him. "I'll be looking at the tiger, and after you've seen everything, come back and meet me there."

Wataru was in too much of a hurry to ask why his father was so interested in the tiger. Rejoicing in this release from parental authority, he bounded off gaily, and was soon lost in the crowd of children before the monkeys' cage.

Fukai for his part was also glad to be free of the child. Relying on his vague memories of the layout of the zoo from a previous visit years ago, he slowly walked in search of the cages where they kept the dangerous animals. He found the tiger almost immediately.

He had a queer feeling as he stopped in front of the cage. Inside the steel bars crouched the tiger that he sought, its forelegs stretched out indolently. When Fukai first noticed its dirty coat and lackluster eyes, glimmering like two leaden suns, he felt a certain disappointment—it was too unlike the fierce power of the beast he had hitherto imagined. But as he intently observed the tiger, a feeling of sympathy gradually came over him. He felt pity for the tiger, but that was not all—a strange affection welled up. Shut up in a dank cage on this brilliant autumn day, robbed of all its savage powers, forced to crouch there dully, not so much as twitching under the curious stares of people: Fukai felt the wild beast's circumstances much resembled his own. But just wherein the resemblance lay was not clear, even to himself.

Deeply moved by these emotions, which remained nevertheless vague and unformulated, he stood in rapt contemplation before the cage, forgetting that he was to play the part of this tiger, forgetting to note the tiger's posture or the position of the legs.

The tiger and Fukai were both absolutely motionless. For a long time the man and the beast stared at each other. In the end, Fukai felt as if he were experiencing the same feelings as the tiger, as if he were thinking the tiger's thoughts.

Suddenly the tiger contorted its face strangely. At the same instant, it opened its jaws ringed with bright silver whiskers, and gave vent to an enormous yawn. The inside of its gaping mouth was a brilliant scarlet, rather like a peony, or rather, a rose in full bloom. This action took less than a minute, after which the tiger lapsed back into its silent apathy.

Startled out of his trance, Fukai summoned back to mind the nearly forgotten purpose on which he had come. The tiger, after demonstrating only that single yawn, remained immovable as a tree in some primeval forest, but Fukai was content. It seemed to him that, having penetrated this far into the tiger's feelings, he would be able to improvise the pouncing and roaring and all the rest.

"Yes, I'll really do the tiger! I can understand a tiger's feelings a whole lot better than those of a philandering man about town," he cried to himself.

Presently his son rejoined him, and taking the boy's hand, Fukai walked out the gate of the zoo, with a lighter step than when he had come.

The following day he happened to glance at the gossip column called "A Night at the Theatre" in the J newspaper. There, in unadorned terms, appeared the following paragraph:

> *Fukai Yasuke, well known as a popular actor of animal roles, has recently severed the last of his few tenuous connections with the human species. He devours his lunch in seclusion, emitting weird meows and grunts. He is still intent enough on getting his salary to stand up on his hind legs and beg for it, but now that he finally seems to have won a part in the forthcoming production at the Kabuki Theatre, he is so pleased with his role as a tiger that he spends his days going back and forth to the zoo to study.*

This was the drama critic he had met the day before, giving free rein to his pen. A feeling of resentment rose up in Fukai when he read the article. However, that quickly vanished, and an embarrassed smile took its place, to be followed in turn by an expression of contentment. "After all, that's what my popularity depends on."

Viewed in that light, it seemed more important than ever that he should make a success with the role of the tiger. Now, whether smoking a cigarette or eating his lunch or lying in bed, his thoughts were completely absorbed with the actions of tigers.

Opening day arrived at last. The play developed through its various scenes, and soon it was time for the third act, in which he was to appear as the tiger. There was no trace of a smile on his features as he put on the tiger costume. He stretched out on the balcony of Tamae's villa, just as the wooden clappers announced the beginning of the act.

The curtains parted. No one else was on stage. The tiger raised itself slightly, as if it had finally awakened from its long midday slumber, and uttered a few low growls. At that moment five or six voices called out, "Fukai! Fukai!", from up in the top gallery. Fukai felt considerable gratification.

The principal actor and Kawahara, the female impersonator, came on stage. But the shouts of recognition from the gallery when they made their entrances were certainly no more enthusiastic than those that had greeted him. "Look at that!" he thought, feeling more and more pleased with himself.

The play advanced. As he listened to the dialogue, he was waiting only for the instant when he would spring into action. The play reached its climax. The moment for him to act was here at last.

He stretched himself once, with a movement that might have been that of a cat just as well as a tiger. He growled lazily once or twice. Then, as Tamae began to tease him, he made a sudden savage lunge straight at Tamae's chest. The chain by which he was fastened sprang taut with a snap as he bounded fiercely about.

The audience was in an uproar. "Fukai! Fukai!" voices shouted all over the theatre. Fukai was almost beside himself as he pounced and leapt. He had no complaints now. Nor any resentment. His depression and shame had vanished. All that remained in his ecstatic heart was an indescribable joy.

The curtains closed just as he was executing the most daring and savage leap of all. The applause of the audience echoed through the theatre. He was utterly content. Still dressed in his costume, he withdrew triumphantly. In the dark shadows of the wings someone unexpectedly caught his hand. He turned his head, somewhat startled, and looked through the peepholes in his mask. There stood his son, Wataru. "Father!" he said.

With sickening suddenness, Fukai plunged from the heights of pride to the depths of shame. He blushed as he stood before his son. But when he looked down once more into the boy's eyes, there was no hint of reproach in them for the role his father had played. Their expression was tearful, as if he could have wept in sympathy with his father.

"Wataru!" exclaimed Fukai, clasping the boy tightly in his arms.

The tears fell in big drops and trickled along the stripes in the tiger costume. . . .

Thus the tiger and the human child stood for a while, weeping together in the shadows of the dark scenery.

TRANSLATED BY ROBERT H. BROWER

KESA AND MORITŌ

[Kesa to Moritō, 1918] by Akutagawa Ryūnosuke (1892-1927)

The reinterpretations of traditional Japanese tales, chiefly of those contained in the thirteenth-century Tales from the Uji Collection, *form the most brilliant part of the writings of Akutagawa Ryūnosuke. In this unusual presentation of the affair between the lady Kesa and the soldier Moritō—treated also by Kikuchi Kan in his* "Gate of Hell"—*Akutagawa's particular genius for the macabre is splendidly displayed.*

•

Night. Moritō gazes at the new-risen moon, as he walks through dead leaves lying outside a wall. He is lost in thought.

There's the moon. I used to wait for it, but now its brightness fills me with horror. When I think that I'll be a murderer before the night is over, I can't help trembling. Imagine these two hands red with blood! How evil I'll seem to myself then! Yet if I had to kill a hated enemy, my conscience wouldn't trouble me this way. Tonight I must kill a man I do not hate.

I've known him by sight for a long time . . . Wataru Saemon-no-jō. Though his name's still new to me, I can't remember how many years ago I first saw that fair, slightly too handsome face. Of course I was jealous when I found he was Kesa's husband, but my jealousy has completely disappeared. So even if he's a rival in love, I don't feel any hatred or resentment toward him. No, you might say I'm sympathetic. When Koromogawa told me how hard he worked to win Kesa, I actually thought very kindly of him. Didn't he go so far as to take lessons in writing poetry, merely to help his courtship? I find myself smiling a little to think of the love poems written by that simple, honest samurai. Not a scornful smile: it seems rather touching that he went to such lengths to please her. Perhaps his passionate eagerness to please the woman I love gives me, her lover, a kind of satisfaction.

But can I really say that I love Kesa? Our love affair has had two phases: past and present. I was already in love with her before she married Wataru. Or I thought I was. Now that I recall, my feelings were scarcely pure. What did I want from Kesa, at that time when I'd never had a woman? Obviously I wanted her body. I'm not far wrong in saying my love was only a sentimental embellishment of that desire. For example, it's true I didn't forget her during the three years after we broke off—but would I have stayed in love if I'd already slept with her? I admit I haven't the courage to say yes. A good deal of my later love was regret that I'd never had her. So I brooded on my discontent, till at last I fell into this relationship that I'd feared, and yet longed for. And now? Let me ask myself again. Do I really love Kesa?

When I happened to see her three years later at the dedication of the Watanabe Bridge, I began trying everything I could think of to meet her in secret. And after about half a year I succeeded. Not only that, I made love to her just as I'd dreamed. Yet what dominated me then was not the regret that I hadn't slept with her. Meeting Kesa there in Koromogawa's house, I noticed my regret had already faded. No doubt it was weakened because I'd had other women—but the real reason is that she was no longer beautiful. What had become of the Kesa of three years ago? Now her skin was lusterless; her smooth cheeks and neck had withered; only those clear, proud, black eyes . . . and there were dark rings around them. The change in her had a crushing effect on my desire. I remember how shocked I was: face to face with her at last, I had to look away.

Then why did I make love to a woman who seemed so unattractive? In the first place, I felt a strange urge to make a conquest of her. There sat Kesa, deliberately exaggerating how much she loved her husband. But to me it had only a hollow ring. She's vain of him, I thought. Or again: She's afraid I'll pity her. Every moment I became more anxious to expose her lies. Why did I think she was lying? If anyone told me conceit had something to do with my suspicion, I couldn't very well deny it. Nevertheless, I believed she was lying. I still believe it.

But it wasn't only the urge to conquer her that possessed me. Even more—and I feel myself blush to think of it—I was driven by sheer lust. Not the regret that I'd never slept with her. It was a coarse lust-for-lust's-sake that might have been satisfied by any woman. A man taking a prostitute wouldn't have been so gross.

Anyway, out of such motives I finally made love to Kesa. Or rather I forced myself on her. And now when I come back to my first question—no, there's no need for me to go on wondering whether or not I love her. Sometimes I hate her. Especially when it was all over and she lay there crying . . . as I pulled her up to me she seemed more disgusting than I was. Tangled hair, sweat-smeared make-up—everything showed her ugliness of mind and body. If I'd been in love with her till then, that was the day love vanished forever. Or, if I hadn't, it was the day a new hatred entered my heart. To think that tonight, for the sake of a woman I don't love, I'm going to murder a man I don't hate!

And, really, I have only myself to blame. I boldly suggested it. "Let's kill Wataru!" . . . When I think of whispering those words into her ear, I begin to doubt my own sanity! But I whispered them, though I knew I shouldn't have, and set my teeth against it. Why did I want to? Looking back at it now, I can't imagine. If I have to decide, I suppose the more I despised and hated her, the more I felt I had to bring her some kind of shame. What could be better than saying we should kill Wataru—that husband she made so much of—and forcing her to consent? And so, like a man in a nightmare, I pressed her to agree to this murder I didn't want to commit. If that's not a sufficient motive, I can only say that some unknown power—call it an evil spirit—lured me astray. Anyhow, I grimly went on whispering the same thing over and over into Kesa's ear.

After a little while she looked up at me—and meekly consented. But it wasn't just how easily I'd persuaded her that surprised me. Then, for the first time, I saw a curious gleam in her eye. . . . Adulteress! A sudden despair awakened me to the horror of my dilemma. How I detested that foul, repulsive creature! I wanted to take back my promise. I wanted to thrust that treacherous woman down into the depths of shame. Then, even if I'd satisfied myself with her, my conscience could have hidden behind a display of indignation. But it was impossible. While she looked into my eyes her expression changed, as if she knew exactly what I was thinking . . . I confess it frankly: the reason I found myself fixing the day and hour to kill Wataru was the fear that, if I refused, Kesa would have her revenge. Yes, and this fear still holds its relentless grip on me. Never mind those who would laugh at my cowardice—they didn't see Kesa at that moment! In despair I watched her dry-eyed weeping, and thought: If I don't kill him she'll make sure I'm the victim somehow, so I'll kill him and get it over with. And after I made the vow, didn't I see her pale face dimple with a smile as she lowered her gaze?

Now, because of this evil promise I'm going to add murder to all my other crimes! If I break this promise that hangs over my head tonight. . . . But I can't. For one thing, there's my vow. For another, I said I was afraid of her revenge. And that's certainly true. But there's something more. . . . What? What is the power that drives me, a coward like me, to murder an innocent man? I don't know. I don't know, though possibly. . . . But that couldn't be. I despise the woman. I'm afraid of her. I detest her. And yet . . . perhaps it's because I love her.

Moritō wanders on, silent. Moonlight. A voice is heard singing a ballad.

Darkness enshrouds the human heart
In an illimitable night;
Only the fires of earthly passion
Blaze and die with life.

2

Night. Kesa sits outside gauze bed curtains, her back to a lamp. She nibbles at her sleeve, lost in thought.

Will he come or not, I wonder. Surely he will, yet the moon is already sinking and there isn't a footstep. He may have changed his mind. If he doesn't come. . . . Oh, I'll have to lift up my wicked face to the sun again, like any prostitute. How could I be so brazen? I'd be like a corpse left by the roadside—humiliated, trampled on, and then shamelessly exposed to light. And I'd have to keep silent. If that happened, even my death wouldn't be the end of it. But no, he'll come. When I looked into his eyes before we parted that day, I knew he would. He's afraid of me. He hates and despises me, and yet he's afraid of me. Of course, if I had to rely only on myself, I couldn't be sure he'd come. But I rely on him. I rely on his selfishness. Yes, I rely on the disgusting fear that his selfishness creates. And so I can be sure of him. He'll come stealing in. . . .

But what a pitiful thing I am, now that I've lost confidence in myself! Three years ago I depended above all on my own beauty Perhaps it would be truer to say till that day—the day I met him at my aunt's house. One glance into his eyes and I saw my ugliness mirrored in them. He pretended I hadn't changed, and talked as seductively as if he really wanted me. But how can such words console a woman, once she knows her own ugliness? I was bitter . . . frightened . . . wretched. How much worse, even, than the ominous uneasiness I felt as a child in my nurse's arms when I saw the moon eclipsed! He had destroyed all my dreams. And then loneliness enveloped me like a gray, rainy dawn. Shivering with that loneliness, at last I yielded my corpselike body to the man—to a man I don't even love, a lecherous man who hates and despises me! Couldn't I bear the loneliness of mourning my lost beauty? Was I trying to shut it out that delirious moment when I buried my face in his arms? Or, if not, was I myself stirred by his kind of filthy lust? Even to think so is shameful to me! shameful! shameful! Especially when he let me go, and my body was free again, how loathsome I felt!

I tried not to weep, but loneliness and anger kept the tears welling to my eyes. I wasn't just miserable because I'd been unfaithful. I had been unfaithful, but worst of all I was despised, I was hated and tormented like a leprous dog. What did I do then? I have only a vague, distant memory. I recall that, as I was sobbing, I thought his mustache grazed my ear . . . and with his hot breath came the soft whispered words: "Let's kill Wataru!" Hearing them I felt an odd exhilaration, such as I'd never known before. Exhilaration? If moonlight may be called bright, I felt exhilarated—but it was far from an exhilaration like strong sunlight. Yet didn't those dreadful words comfort me, after all? Oh, to me—to a woman—is there still joy in being loved even if it means killing your own husband?

I went on crying for a while, out of my strange, moonlit-night feelings of loneliness and exhilaration. And after that? When did I finally promise to help him in this murder? Only then did I think of my husband. Yes, only then. Until that instant I was obsessed with my own shame. And then the thought of my husband, my gentle, reserved husband . . . no, it wasn't the thought of him, but the vivid image of his smiling face—smiling as he told me something. In that instant the plan occurred to me. I was ready to die . . . and I was happy.

But when I stopped crying and looked up into *his* eyes, my ugliness was still mirrored in them. I felt the happiness dissolve away . . . again I think of the darkness of that eclipse I saw with my nurse . . . it was as if all the evil spirits lurking beneath my joy had been set free at once. Was it really because I love my husband that I wanted to die in his place? No, it was a pretext—I wanted to make up for the sin of giving my body to that man. I haven't the courage to commit suicide, and I'm miserably worried about what people will think. All this might still be forgiven, but it's even more disgusting—much more ugly. On the pretext of sacrificing myself for my husband, didn't I really want revenge for the man's hatred of me, for his scorn, for his blind, evil lust? Yes, I'm sure of it. Looking into his face I lost that queer moonlight exhilaration and my heart froze with grief. I'll not die for my husband—I'll die for myself. I'll die from bitterness for my wounded feelings, from resentment for my tainted body. Oh, I didn't even have a decent cause for dying!

Yet how much better to die that unworthy death than to go on living! So I forced a smile and promised over and over to help kill my husband. He's clever enough to guess what I'll do if he fails me.

He even swore to it, so he'll surely come stealing in. . . . Is that the wind? When I think all these torments will end tonight, I feel an immense relief. Tomorrow the chilly light of dawn will fall on my headless corpse. When he sees it, my husband—no, I don't want to think of him. He loves me but I can't return his love. I have loved only one man, and tonight my lover will kill me. Even the lamplight is dazzling . . . in this last sweet torture.

Kesa blows out the light. Soon, the faint sound of a shutter opening. And a shaft of pale moonlight strikes the curtains.

TRANSLATED BY HOWARD HIBBETT

HELL SCREEN

[Jigokuhen, 1918] by Akutagawa Ryūnosuke

•

I doubt whether there will ever be another man like the Lord of Horikawa. Certainly there has been no one like him till now. Some say that a Guardian King appeared to her ladyship his mother in a dream before he was born; at least it is true that from the day he was born he was a most extraordinary person. Nothing he did was commonplace; he was constantly startling people. You have only to glance at a plan of Horikawa to perceive its grandeur. No ordinary person would ever have dreamt of the boldness and daring with which it was conceived.

But it certainly was not his lordship's intention merely to glorify himself; he was generous, he did not forget the lower classes; he wanted the whole country to enjoy itself when he did.

There is the story about the famous Kawara Palace at Higashi Sanjō. It was said that the ghost of Tōru, Minister of the Left, appeared there night after night until his lordship exorcised it by rebuking it. Such was his prestige in the capital that everyone, man, woman, and child, regarded him, with good reason, as a god incarnate. Once, as he was returning in his carriage from the Feast of the Plum Blossoms, his ox got loose and injured an old man who happened to be passing. But the latter, they say, put his hands together in reverence and was actually grateful that he had been knocked over by an ox of his lordship.

Thus, there are the makings of many good stories in the life of his lordship. At a certain banquet he made a presentation of thirty white horses; another time he gave a favorite boy to be the human pillar of Nagara Bridge. There would be no end if I started to tell them all. Numerous as these anecdotes are, I doubt if there are any that match in horror the story of the making of the Hell Screen, one of the most valuable treasures in the house. His lordship is not easily upset, but that time he seemed to be startled. How much more terrified, then, were we who served him; we feared for our very souls. As for me, I had served him for twenty years, but when I witnessed that dreadful spectacle I felt that such a thing could never have happened before. But in order to tell this story, I must first tell about Yoshihide, who painted the Hell Screen.

2

Yoshihide is, I expect, remembered by many even today. In his time he was a famous painter surpassed by no contemporary. He would be about fifty then, I imagine. He was cross-grained, and not much to look at: short of stature, a bag of skin and bones, and his youthful red lips made him seem even more evil, as though he were some sort of animal. Some said it was because he put his reddened paint brush to his lips, but I doubt this. Others, more unkind, said that his appearance and movements suggested a monkey. And that reminds me of this story. Yoshihide's only daughter, Yūzuki, a charming girl of fifteen, quite unlike her father, was at that time a maid in Horikawa. Probably owing to the fact that her mother had died while she was still very small, Yūzuki was sympathetic and intelligent beyond her years, and greatly petted by her ladyship and her attendants in consequence.

About that time it happened that someone presented a tame monkey from Tamba. The mischievous young lord called it Yoshihide. The monkey was a comical-looking beast, anyway; with this name, nobody in the mansion could resist laughing at him. But they did more than that. If he climbed the pine tree in the garden, or soiled the mats, whatever he did they teased him, shouting, "Yoshihide, Yoshihide."

One day Yūzuki was passing along one of the long halls with a note in a twig of red winter plum blossom when the monkey appeared from behind a sliding door, fleeing as fast as he could. Apparently he had dislocated a leg, for he limped, unable, it seemed, to climb a post with his usual agility. After him came the young lord, waving a switch, shouting, "Stop thief! Orange thief!" Yūzuki hesitated a moment, but it gave the fleeing monkey a chance to cling to her skirt, crying most piteously. Suddenly she felt she could not restrain her pity. With one hand she still held the plum branch, with the other, the sleeve of her mauve kimono sweeping in a half-circle, she picked the monkey up gently. Then bending before the young lord, she said sweetly, "I crave your pardon. He is only an animal. Be kind enough to pardon him, my lord."

But he had come running with his temper up; he frowned and stamped his foot two or three times. "Why do you protect him? He has stolen some oranges."

"But he is only an animal." She repeated it; then after a little, smiling sadly, "And since you call him Yoshihide, it is as if my father were being punished. I couldn't bear to see it," she said boldly. This defeated the young lord.

"Well, if you're pleading for your father's skin, I'll pardon him," he said reluctantly, "against my better judgment." Dropping the switch, he turned and went back through the sliding door through which he had come.

3

Yūzuki and the monkey were devoted to each other from that day. She hung a golden bell that she had received from the Princess by a bright red cord around the monkey's neck, and the monkey would hardly let her out of his sight. Once, for instance, when she caught cold and took to her bed, the monkey, apparently much depressed, sat immovable by her pillow, gnawing his nails.

Another strange thing was that from that time the monkey was not teased as badly as before. On the contrary, they began to pet him, and even the young lord would occasionally toss him a persimmon or a chestnut. Once he got quite angry when he caught a samurai kicking the monkey. As for his lordship, they say that when he heard his son was protecting the monkey from abuse, he had Yūzuki appear before him with the monkey in her arms. On this occasion he must have heard why she had made a pet of the monkey.

"You're a filial girl. I'll reward you for it," he said, and gave her a crimson ceremonial kimono. Whereupon the monkey with the greatest deference mimicked her acceptance of the kimono. That greatly tickled his lordship. Thus the girl who befriended the monkey became a favorite of his lordship, because he admired her filial piety—not, as rumor had it, because he was too fond of her. There may have been some grounds for this rumor, but of that I shall tell later. It should be enough to say that the Lord of Horikawa was not the sort of person to fall in love with an artist's daughter, no matter how beautiful she was.

Thus honored, Yoshihide's daughter withdrew from his presence. Since she was wise and good, the other maids were not jealous of her. Rather she and her monkey became more popular than ever, particularly, they say, with the Princess, from whom she was hardly ever separated. She invariably accompanied her in her pleasure carriage.

However, we must leave the daughter a while and turn to the father. Though the monkey was soon being petted by everybody, they all disliked the great Yoshihide. This was not limited to the mansion folk only. The Abbot of Yokogawa hated him, and if Yoshihide were mentioned would change color as though he had encountered a devil. (That was after Yoshihide had drawn a caricature of the Abbot, according to the gossip of the domestics, which, after all, may have been nothing more than gossip.) Anyhow, the man was unpopular with anyone you met. If there were some who did not speak badly of him, they were but two or three fellow-artists, or people who knew his pictures, but not the man.

Yoshihide was not only very repellent in appearance: people disliked him more because of his habits. No one was to blame for his unpopularity except himself.

4

He was stingy, he was bad-tempered, he was shameless, he was lazy, he was greedy, but worst of all, he was arrogant and contemptuous, certain that he was the greatest artist in the country.

If he had been proud only of his work it would not have been so bad, but he despised everything, even the customs and amenities of society.

It was in character, therefore, that when he was making a picture of the Goddess of Beauty he should paint the face of a common harlot, and that for Fudō[1] he should paint a villainous ex-convict. The models he chose were shocking. When he was taken to task for it, he said coolly, "It would be strange if the gods and buddhas I have given life with my brush should punish me."

His apprentices were appalled when they thought of the dreadful fate in store for him, and many left his studio. It was pride—he imagined himself to be the greatest man in Japan.

In short, though exceptionally gifted, he behaved much above his station. Among artists who were not on good terms with him, many maintained that he was a charlatan, because his brushwork and coloring were so unusual. Look at the door-paintings of the famous artists of the past! You can almost smell the perfume of the plum blossom on a moonlit night; you can almost hear some courtier on a screen playing his flute. That is how they gained their reputation for surpassing beauty. Yoshihide's pictures were reputed to be always weird or unpleasant. For instance, he painted the "Five Aspects of Life and Death" on Ryugai Temple gate, and they say if you pass the gate at night you can hear the sighing and sobbing of the divinities he depicted there. Others say you can smell rotting corpses. Or when, at the command of his lordship, he painted the portraits of some of his household women, within three years everyone of them sickened as though her spirit had left her, and died. Those who spoke ill of Yoshihide regarded this as certain proof that his pictures were done by means of the black art.

Yoshihide delighted in his reputation for perversity. Once, when his lordship said to him jokingly, "You seem to like the ugly," Yoshihide's unnaturally red lips curled in an evil laugh. "I do. Daubers usually cannot understand the beauty of ugly things," he said contemptuously.

[1] The third of the Five Great Kings, guarding the center. In his right hand he holds a sword to strike the demons, in his left, a cord to bind them.

But Yoshihide, the unspeakably unscrupulous Yoshihide, had one tender human trait.

5

And that was his affection for his only child, whom he loved passionately. As I said before, Yūzuki was gentle, and deeply devoted to her father, but his love for her was not inferior to her devotion to him. Does it not seem incredible that the man who never gave a donation to a temple could have provided such kimono and hairpins for his daughter with reckless disregard of cost?

But Yoshihide's affection for Yūzuki was nothing more than the emotion. He gave no thought, for instance, to finding her a good husband. Yet he certainly would have hired roughs to assassinate anyone who made improper advances to her. Therefore, when she became a maid at Horikawa, at the command of his lordship, Yoshihide took it very badly; and even when he appeared before the daimyo, he sulked for a while. The rumor that, attracted by her beauty, his lordship had tasted her delights in spite of her father, was largely the guess of those who noted Yoshihide's displeasure.

Of course, even if the rumor were false it was clear that the intensity of his affection made Yoshihide long to have his daughter come down from among his lordship's women. When Yoshihide was commanded to paint Monju, the God of Wisdom, he took as his model his lordship's favorite page, and the Lord of Horikawa, highly pleased—for it was a beautiful thing—said graciously, "I will give you whatever you wish as a reward. Now what would you like?" Yoshihide acknowledged the tribute; but what do you think was the bold request that he made? That his daughter should leave his lordship's service! It would be presumptuous to ask that one's daughter be taken in; who but Yoshihide would have asked for his daughter's release, no matter how much he loved her! At this even the genial daimyo seemed ruffled, and he silently watched Yoshihide's face for a long moment.

"No," he spat out, and stood up suddenly. This happened again on four or five different occasions, and as I recall it now, with each repetition, the eye with which his lordship regarded Yoshihide grew colder. Possibly it was on account of this that Yūzuki was concerned for her father's safety, for often, biting her sleeves, she sobbed when she was in her room. Without doubt it was this that made the rumors that his lordship had fallen in love with Yoshihide's daughter become widely current. One of them had it that the very existence of the Hell Screen was owing to the fact that she would not comply with his wishes, but of course this could not have been true.

We believe his lordship did not dismiss her simply because he pitied her. He felt sorry for her situation, and rather than leave her with her hardened father he wanted her in the mansion where there would be no inconvenience for her. It was nothing but kindness on his part. It was quite obvious that the girl received his favors, but it would have been an exaggeration to say that she was his mistress. No, that would have been a completely unfounded lie.

Be that as it may, owing to his request about his daughter, Yoshihide came to be disliked by his lordship. Then suddenly the Lord of Horikawa summoned Yoshihide, whatever may have been his reason, and bade him paint a screen of the circles of hell.

6

When I say screen of the circles of hell, the scenes of those frightful paintings seem to come floating before my very eyes. Other painters have done Hell Screens, but from the first sketch Yoshihide's was different. In one corner of the first leaf he painted the Ten Kings[2] and their households in small scale, the rest was an awful whirlpool of fire around the Forest of Swords which likewise seemed ready to burst into flames. In fact, except for the robes of the hellish officials, which were dotted yellows and blues, all was a flame color, and in the center leapt and danced pitch-black smoke and sparks like flying charcoal.

The brushwork of this alone was enough to astonish one, but the

[2] Judges of the underworld.

treatment of the sinners rolling over and over in the avenging fire was unlike that of any ordinary picture of hell. From the highest noble to the lowest beggar every conceivable sort of person was to be seen there. Courtiers in formal attire, alluring young maidens of the court in palace robes, priests droning over their prayer beads, scholars on high wooden clogs, little girls in white shifts, diviners flourishing their papered wands—I won't name them all. There they all were, enveloped in flame and smoke, tormented by bull- and horse-headed jailers: blown and scattered in all directions like fallen leaves in a gale, they fled hither and yon. There were female fortunetellers, their hair caught in forks, their limbs trussed tighter than spiders' legs. Young princes hung inverted like bats, their breasts pierced with javelins. They were beaten with iron whips, they were crushed with mighty weights of adamant, they were pecked by weird birds, they were devoured by poisonous dragons. I don't know how many sinners were depicted, nor can I list all their torments.

But I must mention one dreadful scene that stood out from the rest. Grazing the tops of the sword trees, that were as sharp as an animal's fangs—there were several souls on them, spitted two or three deep—came falling through space an ox-carriage. Its blinds were blown open by the winds of hell and in it an emperor's favorite, gorgeously attired, her long black hair fluttering in the flames, bent her white neck and writhed in agony. Nothing made the fiery torments of hell more realistic than the appearance of that woman in her burning carriage. The horror of the whole picture was concentrated in this one scene. So inspired an accomplishment was it that those who looked at her thought they heard dreadful cries in their ears.

Ah, it was for this, it was for this picture that that dreadful event occurred! Without it how could even Yoshihide have expressed so vividly the agonies of hell? It was to finish this screen that Yoshihide met a destiny so cruel that he took his own life. For this hell he pictured was the hell that he, the greatest painter in the country, was one day to fall into. . . .

I may be telling the strange story of the Hell Screen too hastily;

I may have told the wrong end of the story first. Let me return to Yoshihide, bidden by his lordship to paint a picture of hell.

7

For five or six months Yoshihide was so busy working on the screen that he was not seen at the mansion at all. Was it not remarkable that with all his affection, when he became absorbed in his painting, he did not even want to see his daughter? The apprentice to whom I have already referred said that when Yoshihide was engaged on a piece of work it was as though he had been bewitched by a fox. According to the stories that circulated at that time Yoshihide had achieved fame with the assistance of the black art because of a vow he had made to some great god of fortune. And the proof of it was that if you went to his studio and peered at him unbeknownst you could see the ghostly foxes swarming all around him. Thus it was that when once he had taken up his brushes everything was forgotten till he had finished the picture. Day and night he would shut himself up in one room, scarcely seeing the light of day. And when he painted the Hell Screen this absorption was complete.

The shutters were kept down during the day and he mixed his secret colors by the light of a tripod lamp. He had his apprentices dress in all sorts of finery, and painted each with great care. It did not take the Hell Screen to make him behave like that: he demanded it for every picture he painted. At the time he was painting the "Five Aspects of Life and Death" at Ryugaiji, he chanced to see a corpse lying beside the road. Any ordinary person would have averted his face, but Yoshihide stepped out of the crowd, squatted down, and at his leisure painted the half-decayed face and limbs exactly as they looked.

How can I convey his violent concentration? Some of you will still fail to grasp it. Since I cannot tell it in detail, I shall relate it broadly.

The apprentice, then, was one day mixing paints. Suddenly Yoshihide appeared. "I'd like to take a short nap," he said. "But I've been bothered a lot by bad dreams recently."

Since this was not extraordinary the apprentice answered briefly but politely, "Indeed, sir," without lifting his hand from his work. Whereupon the artist said, with a loneliness and diffidence that were strange to him, "I mean I would like to have you sit by my pillow while I rest." The apprentice thought it unusual that he should be troubled so badly by dreams, but the request was a simple one and he assented readily. Yoshihide, still anxious, asked him to come back in at once. "And if another apprentice comes, don't let him enter the room while I am sleeping," he said hesitantly. By "room" he meant the room where he was painting the screen. In that room the doors were shut fast as if it were night, and a light was usually left burning. The screen stood around the sides of the room; only the charcoal sketch of the design was completed. Yoshihide put his elbow on the pillow like a man completely exhausted and quietly fell asleep. But before an hour was out an indescribably unpleasant voice began to sound in the apprentice's ears.

8

At first it was nothing more than a voice, but presently there were clear words, as of a drowning man moaning in the water. "What . . . you are calling me? Where? Where to . . . to hell? To the hell of fire . . . Who is it? Who is your honor? Who is your honor? If I knew who . . ."

Unconsciously the apprentice stopped mixing the colors; feeling that he was intruding on privacy he looked at the artist's face. That wrinkled face was pale; great drops of sweat stood out on it, the lips were dry, and the mouth with its scanty teeth was wide open, as though it gasped for air. And that thing that moved so dizzily as if on a thread, was that his tongue!

"If I knew who . . . Oh, it is your honor, is it? I thought it was. What! You have come to meet me. So I am to come. I am to go to hell! My daughter awaits me in hell!"

At that moment a strange, hazy shadow seemed to descend over the face of the screen, so uncanny did the apprentice feel. Immediately, of course, he shook the master with all his might, but Yoshihide, still in the clutch of the nightmare, continued his monologue, unable, apparently, to wake out of it. Thereupon the apprentice boldly took the water that stood at hand for his brushes and poured it over Yoshihide's face.

"It is waiting: get in this carriage. Get in this carriage and go down to hell." As he said these words Yoshihide's voice changed, he sounded like a man being strangled, and at length he opened his eyes. Terrified, he leapt up like one pierced with needles: the weird things of his dream must still have been with him. His expression was dreadful, his mouth gaped, he stared into space. Presently he seemed to have recovered himself. "It's all right now. You may leave," he said curtly.

As the apprentice would have been badly scolded had he disobeyed, he promptly left the room. When he saw the good light of day, he sighed with relief like one awakening from a bad dream.

But this was not the worst. A month later another apprentice was called into the back room. As usual Yoshihide was gnawing his brushes in the dim light of the oil lamp. Suddenly he turned to the apprentice. "I want you to strip again."

Since he had been asked to do this several times before, the apprentice obeyed immediately. But when that unspeakable man saw him stark naked before him, his face became strangely distorted. "I want to see a man bound with a chain. I want you to do as I tell you for a little while," he said coldly and unsympathetically. The apprentice was a sturdy fellow who had formerly thought that swinging a sword was better than handling a brush, but this request astonished him. As he often said afterwards, "I began to wonder if the master hadn't gone crazy and wasn't going to kill me." Yoshihide, however, growing impatient with the other's hesitation, produced from somewhere a light iron chain a-rattle in his hand; and without giving him the opportunity of obeying or refusing, sprang on the apprentice, sat on his back, twisted up his arms and bound him around and around. The pain was almost intolerable, for he pulled the end of the chain brutally, so that the apprentice fell loudly sideways and lay there extended.

9

He said that he lay there like a wine jar rolled over on its side. Because his hands and feet were cruelly bent and twisted he could move only his head. He was fat, and with his circulation impeded, the blood gathered not only in his trunk and face but everywhere under his skin. This, however, did not trouble Yoshihide at all; he walked all around him, "a wine jar," making sketch after sketch. I do not need to elaborate on the apprentice's sufferings.

Had nothing occurred, doubtless the torture would have been protracted longer. Fortunately—or maybe unfortunately—something like black oil, a thin streak, came flowing sinuously from behind a jar in the corner of the room. At first it moved slowly like a sticky substance, but then it slid more smoothly until, as he watched it, it moved gleaming up to his nose. He drew in his breath involuntarily. "A snake! A snake!" he screamed. It seemed that all the blood in his body would freeze at once, nor was it surprising. A little more and the snake would actually have touched with its cold tongue his head into which the chains were biting. Even the unscrupulous Yoshihide must have been startled at this. He dropped his brush, bent down like a flash, deftly caught the snake by its tail and lifted it up, head downward. The snake raised its head, coiled itself in circles, twisted its body, but could not reach Yoshihide's hand.

"You have made me botch a stroke." Complaining offensively, Yoshihide dropped the snake into the jar in the corner of the room and reluctantly loosed the chain that bound the apprentice. All he did was to loose him; not a word of thanks did the long-suffering fellow get. Obviously Yoshihide was vexed that he had botched a stroke instead of letting his apprentice be bitten by the snake. Afterwards they heard that he kept the snake there as a model.

This story should give you some idea of Yoshihide's madness, his sinister absorption. However, I should like to describe one more dreadful experience that almost cost a young apprentice his life. He was thirteen or fourteen at the time, a girlish, fair-complexioned lad. One night he was suddenly called to his master's room. In the lamplight he saw Yoshihide feeding a strange bird, about the size of an ordinary cat, with a bloody piece of meat which he held in his hand. It had large, round, amber-colored eyes and feather-like ears that stuck out on either side of its head. It was extraordinarily like a cat.

10

Yoshihide always disliked anyone sticking his nose into what he was doing. As was the case with the snake, his apprentices never knew what he had in his room. Therefore sometimes silver bowls, sometimes a skull, or one-stemmed lacquer stands—various odd things, models for what he was painting—would be set out on his table. But nobody knew where he kept these things. The rumor that some great god of fortune lent him divine help certainly arose from these circumstances.

Then the apprentice, seeing the strange bird on the table and imagining it to be something needed for the Hell Screen, bowed to the artist and said respectfully, "What do you wish, sir?" Yoshihide, as if he had not heard him, licked his red lips and jerked his chin towards the bird. "Isn't it tame!"

While he was saying this the apprentice was staring with an uncanny feeling at that catlike bird with ears. Yoshihide answered with his sneer, "What! Never seen a bird like this? That's the trouble with people who live in the capital. It's a horned owl. A hunter gave it to me two or three days ago. But I'll warrant there aren't many as tame as this."

As he said this he slowly raised his hand and stroked the back of the bird, which had just finished eating the meat, the wrong way. The owl let out a short piercing screech, flew up from the table, extended its claws, and pounced at the face of the apprentice. Panic-stricken, the latter raised his sleeve to shield his face. Had he not done so he undoubtedly would have been badly slashed. As he cried out he shook his sleeve to drive off the owl, but it screeched and, taking advantage of his weakness, attacked again. Forgetting the master's presence, the lad fled distracted up and down the narrow room; standing, he tried to ward it off, sitting, to drive it away. The sinister bird wheeled high and low after its prey, darting at his eyes, watching for an opening. The noisy threshing of its wings seemed to evoke something uncanny like the smell of dead leaves, or the spray of a waterfall. It was dreadful, revolting. The apprentice had the feeling that the dim oil lamp was the vague light of the moon, and the room a valley shut in the ill-omened air of some remote mountain.

But the apprentice's horror was due not so much to the attack of the horned owl. What made his hair stand on end was the sight of the artist Yoshihide. The latter watched the commotion coolly, unrolled his paper deliberately, and began to paint the fantastic picture of a girlish boy being mangled by a horrible bird. When the apprentice saw this out of the corner of his eye, he was overwhelmed with an inexpressible horror, for he thought that he really was going to be killed for the artist.

II

You could not say that this was impossible to believe. Yoshihide had called the apprentice deliberately that night in order to set the owl after him and paint him trying to escape. Therefore the apprentice, when he saw what the master was up to, involuntarily hid his head in his sleeves, began screaming he knew not what, and huddled down in the corner of the room by the sliding door. Then Yoshihide shouted as though he were a little flustered and got to his feet, but immediately the beating of the owl's wings became louder and there was the startling noise of things being torn or knocked down. Though he was badly shaken, the apprentice involuntarily lifted his head to see. The room had become as black as night, and out of it came Yoshihide's voice harshly calling for his apprentices.

Presently one of them answered from a distance, and in a minute came running in with a light. By its sooty illumination he saw the tripod lamp overturned and the owl fluttering painfully with one wing on mats that were swimming in oil. Yoshihide was in a half-sitting position beyond the table. He seemed aghast and was muttering words unintelligible to mortals. This is no exaggeration. A snake as black as the pit was coiling itself rapidly around the owl, encircling its neck and one wing. Apparently in crouching down the apprentice had knocked over the jar, the snake had crawled out, and the owl had made a feeble attempt to pounce on it. It was this which had caused the clatter and commotion. The two apprentices exchanged glances and simply stood dumbfounded, eying that remarkable spectacle. Then without a word they bowed to Yoshihide and withdrew. Nobody discovered what happened to the owl and the snake.

This sort of thing was matched by many other incidents. I forgot to say that it was in the early autumn that Yoshihide received orders to paint the screen. From then until the end of the winter his apprentices were in a constant state of terror because of his weird behavior. But towards the end of the winter something about the picture seemed to trouble Yoshihide; he became even more saturnine than usual and spoke more harshly. The sketch of the screen, eight-tenths completed, did not progress. In fact, there did not seem to be any chance that the outlines would ever be painted in and finished.

Nobody knew what it was that hindered the work on the screen and nobody tried to find out. Hitherto the apprentices had been fascinated by everything that happened. They had felt that they were caged with a wolf or a tiger, but from this time they contrived to keep away from their master as much as possible.

12

Accordingly, there is not much that is worth telling about this period. But if one had to say something, it would be that the stubborn old man was, for some strange reason, easily moved to tears, and was often found weeping, they say, when he thought no one was by. One day, for instance, an apprentice went into the garden on an errand. Yoshihide was standing absently in the corridor, gazing at the sky with its promise of spring, his eyes full of tears. The apprentice felt embarrassed and withdrew stealthily without saying a word. Was it not remarkable that the arrogant man who had used a decaying corpse as model for the "Five Aspects of Life and Death" should weep so childishly?

While Yoshihide painted the screen in a frenzy incomprehensible to the sane, it began to be noticed that his daughter was very despondent and often appeared to be holding back tears. When this happens to a girl with a pale modest face, her eyelashes become heavy, shadows appear around her eyes, and her face grows still sadder. At first they said that she was suffering from a love affair, or blamed her father, but soon it got around that the Lord of Horikawa wanted to have his way with her. Then suddenly all talk about the girl ceased as if everybody had forgotten her.

It was about that time that late one night I happened to be passing along a corridor. Suddenly the monkey Yoshihide sprang out from somewhere and began pulling the hem of my skirt insistently. As I remember it, the night was warm, there was a pale moon shining, and the plum blossoms were already fragrant. The monkey bared his white teeth, wrinkled the tip of his nose, and shrieked wildly in the moonlight as though he were demented. I felt upset and very angry that my new skirts should be pulled about. Kicking the monkey loose, I was about to walk on when I recalled that a samurai had earned the young lord's displeasure by chastising the monkey. Besides his behavior did seem most unusual. So at last I walked a dozen yards in the direction he was pulling me.

There the corridor turned, showing the water of the pond, pale white in the night light, beyond a pine tree with gently bending branches. At that point what sounded like people quarreling fell on my ears, weird and startling, from a room nearby. Except for this everything around was sunk in silence. In the half-light that was neither haze nor moonlight I heard no other voices. There was nothing but the sound of the fish jumping in the pond. With that din in my ears, I stopped instinctively. My first thought was "Some ruffians," and I approached the sliding door quietly, holding my breath, ready to show them my mettle.

13

But the monkey must have thought me too hesitant. He ran around me two or three times, impatiently, crying out as though he were being strangled, then leapt straight up from the floor to my shoulder. I jerked back my head so as not to be clawed, but he clung to my sleeve to keep from falling to the floor. Staggering back two or three steps, I banged heavily into the sliding door. After that there was no cause for hesitation. I opened the door immediately and was about to advance into the inner part of the room where the moonlight did not fall. But just then something passed before my eyes—what was this?—a girl came running out from the back of the room as though released from a spring. She barely missed running into me, passed me, and half-fell outside the room, where she knelt gasping, looking up at my face, and shuddering as though she still saw some horror.

Do I need to say she was Yūzuki? That night she appeared vivid, she seemed to be a different person. Her big eyes shone, her cheeks flamed red. Her disordered kimono and skirt gave her a fascination she did not ordinarily possess. Was this really that shrinking daughter of Yoshihide's? I leaned against the sliding door and stared at her beautiful figure in the moonlight. Then, indicating the direction where the alarmed footsteps had died away, "What was it?", I asked with my eyes.

But she only bit her lips, shook her head, and said nothing. She seemed unusually mortified. Then I bent over her, put my mouth to her ear, and asked, "Who was it?" in a whisper. But the girl still shook her head; tears filled her eyes and hung on her long lashes; she bit her lips harder than ever.

I have always been a stupid person and unless something is absolutely plain I cannot grasp it. I did not know what to say and stood motionless for a moment, as though listening to the beating of her heart. But this was because I felt I ought not to question her too closely.

I don't know how long it lasted. At length I closed the door I had left open and, looking back at the girl, who seemed to have recovered from her agitation, said as gently as possible, "You had better go back to your room." Then, troubled with the uncomfortable feeling that I had seen something I should not have, embarrassed though no one was near, I quietly returned to where I had come from. But before I had gone ten steps, something again plucked the hem of my skirt, timidly this time. Astonished, I stopped and turned around. What do you think it was? The monkey Yoshihide, his gold bell jingling, his hands together like a human, was bowing most politely to me, again and again.

14

About two weeks later Yoshihide came to the mansion and asked for an immediate audience with the Lord of Horikawa. He belonged to the lower classes but he had always been in favor, and his lordship, ordinarily difficult of access, granted Yoshihide an audience at once. The latter prostrated himself before the daimyo deferentially and presently began to speak in his hoarse voice.

"Some time ago, my lord, you ordered a Hell Screen. Day and night have I labored, taking great pains, and now the result can be seen: the design has almost been completed."

"Congratulations. I am content." But in his lordship's voice there was a strange lack of conviction, of interest.

"No, congratulations are not in order." With his eyes firmly lowered Yoshihide answered almost as if he were becoming angry. "It is nearly finished, but there is just one part I cannot paint—now."

"What! You cannot paint part of it!"

"No, my lord. I cannot paint anything for which a model is lacking. Even if I try, the pictures lack conviction. And isn't that the same as being unable to paint it?"

When he heard this a sneering sort of smile passed over his lordship's face. "Then in order to paint this Hell Screen, you must see hell, eh?"

"Yes, my lord. Some years ago in a great fire I saw flames close up that resembled the raging fires of hell. The flames in my painting are what I then saw. Your lordship is acquainted with that picture, I believe."

"What about criminals? You haven't seen jailers, have you?" He spoke as though he had not heard Yoshihide, his words following the artist's without pause.

"I have seen men bound in iron chains. I have copied in detail men attacked by strange birds. So I cannot say I have not seen the sufferings of criminals under torture. As for jailers—" Yoshihide smiled repulsively, "I have seen them before me many times in my dreams. Cows' heads, horses' heads, three-faced six-armed demons, clapping hands that make no noise, voiceless mouths agape—they all come to torment me. I am not exaggerating when I say that I see them every day and every night. What I wish to paint and cannot are not things like that."

His lordship must have been thoroughly astonished. For a long moment he stared at Yoshihide irritably; then he arched his eyebrows sharply. "What is it you cannot paint?"

15

"In the middle of the screen I want to paint a carriage falling down through the sky," said Yoshihide, and for the first time he looked sharply at his lordship's face. When Yoshihide spoke of pictures I have heard that he looked insane. He certainly seemed insane when he said this. "In the carriage an exquisite court lady, her hair disordered in the raging fire, writhes in agony. Her face is contorted with smoke, her eyebrows are drawn; she looks up at the roof of the carriage. As she plucks at the bamboo blinds she tries to ward off the sparks that shower down. And strange birds of prey, ten or twenty, fly around the carriage with shrill cries. Ah, that beauty in the carriage. I cannot possibly paint her."

"Well, what else?"

For some reason his lordship took strange pleasure in urging Yoshihide on. But the artist's red lips moved feverishly, and when he spoke it was like a man in a dream. "No," he repeated, "I cannot paint it." Then suddenly he almost snarled, "Burn a carriage for me. If only you could . . ."

His lordship's face darkened, then he burst out laughing with startling abruptness. "I'll do entirely as you wish," he said, almost choking with the violence of his laughter. "And all discussion as to whether it is possible or not is beside the point."

When I heard this I felt a strange thrill of horror. Maybe it was a premonition. His lordship, as though infected with Yoshihide's madness, changed, foam gathered white on his lips, and like lightning the terror flashed in the corners of his eyes. He stopped abruptly, and then a great laugh burst from his throat. "I'll fire a carriage for you. And there'll be an exquisite beauty in the robes of a fine lady in it. Attacked by flames and black smoke the woman will die in agony. The man who thought of painting that must be the greatest artist in Japan. I'll praise him. Oh, I'll praise him!"

When he heard his lordship's words, Yoshihide became pale and moved his lips as though he were gasping. But soon his body relaxed, and placing both hands on the mats, he bowed politely. "How kind a destiny," he said, so low that he could scarcely be heard. Probably this was because the daimyo's words had brought the frightfulness of his plan vividly before his eyes. That was the only time in my life that I pitied Yoshihide.

16

Two or three days after this his lordship told Yoshihide that he was ready to fulfill his promise. Of course the carriage was not to be burned at Horikawa, but rather at a country house outside the capital, which the common people called Yukige. Though it had formerly been the residence of his lordship's younger sister, no one had occupied Yukige for many years. It had a large garden that had been allowed to run wild. People attributed its neglect to many causes: for instance, they said that on moonless nights the daimyo's dead sister, wearing a strange scarlet skirt, still walked along the corridors without touching the floor. The mansion was desolate enough by day, but at night, with the plashing sounds of the invisible brook and the monstrous shapes of the night herons flying through the starlight, it was entirely eerie.

As it happened, that night was moonless and pitch black. The light of the oil lamps shone on his lordship, clad in pale yellow robes and a dark purple skirt embroidered with crests, sitting on the veranda on a plaited straw cushion with a white silk embroidered hem. I need not add that before and behind, to the left and to the right of him, five or six attendants stood respectfully. The choice of one was significant—he was a powerful samurai who had eaten human flesh to stay his hunger at the Battle of Michinoku, and since then, they say, he has been able to tear apart the horns of a live deer. His long sword sticking out behind like a gull's tail, he stood, a forbidding figure, beneath the veranda. The flickering light of the lamps, now bright, now dark, shone on the scene. So dreadful a horror was on us that we scarcely knew whether we dreamed or waked.

They had drawn the carriage into the garden. There it stood, its heavy roof weighing down the darkness. There were no oxen harnessed to it, and the end of its black tongue rested on a stand. When we saw its gold metalwork glittering like stars, we felt chilly in spite of the spring night. The carriage was heavily closed with blue blinds edged with embroidery, so that we could not know what was inside. Around it stood attendants with torches in their hands, worrying over the smoke that drifted towards the veranda and waiting significantly.

Yoshihide knelt facing the veranda, a little distance off. He seemed smaller and shabbier than usual, the starry sky seemed to oppress him. The man who squatted behind him was doubtless an apprentice. The two of them were at some distance from me and below the veranda so that I could not be sure of the color of their clothes.

17

It must have been near midnight. The darkness that enveloped the brook seemed to watch our very breathing. In it was only the faint stir of the night wind that carried the sooty smell of the pine torches to us. For some time his lordship watched the scene in silence, motionless. Presently he moved forward a little and called sharply, "Yoshihide."

The latter must have made some sort of reply, though what I heard sounded more like a groan.

"Yoshihide, tonight in accordance with your request I am going to burn this carriage for you."

His lordship glanced sidelong at those around him and seemed to exchange a meaningful smile with one or two, though I may have only imagined it. Yoshihide raised his head fearfully and looked up at the veranda, but said nothing and did not move from where he squatted.

"Look. That is the carriage I have always used. You recognize it, don't you? I am going to burn it and show you blazing hell itself."

Again his lordship paused and winked at his attendants. Suddenly his tone became unpleasant. "In that carriage, by my command, is a female malefactor. Therefore, when it is fired her flesh will be roasted, her bones burnt, she will die in extreme agony. Never again will you find such a model for the completion of your screen. Do not flinch from looking at snow-white skin inflamed with fire. Look well at her black hair dancing up in sparks."

His lordship ceased speaking for the third time. I don't know what thoughts were in his mind, but his shoulders shook with silent laughter. "Posterity will never see anything like it. I'll watch it from here. Come, come, lift up the blinds and show Yoshihide the woman inside."

At the daimyo's word one of the attendants, holding high his pine torch in one hand, walked up to the carriage without more ado, stretched out his free hand, and raised the blind. The flickering torch burned with a sharp crackling noise. It brightly lit up the narrow interior of the carriage, showing a woman on its couch, cruelly bound with chains. Who was she? Ah, it could not be! She was clad in a gorgeously embroidered cherry-patterned mantle; her black hair, alluringly loosened, hung straight down; the golden hairpins set at different angles gleamed beautifully, but there was a gag over her mouth tied behind her neck. The small slight body, the modest profile—the attire only was different—it was Yūzuki. I nearly cried aloud.

At that moment the samurai opposite me got to his feet hastily and put his hand on his sword. It must have been Yoshihide that he glared at. Startled I glanced at the artist. He seemed half-stunned by what he now saw. Suddenly he leapt up, stretched out both his arms before him, and forgetting everything else, began to run toward the carriage. Unfortunately, as I have already said, he was at some distance in the shadow, and I could not see the expression on his face. But that was momentary, for now I saw that it was absolutely colorless. His whole form cleaving the darkness appeared vividly before our eyes in the half-light—he was held in space, it seemed, by some invisible power that lifted him from the ground. Then, at his lordship's command, "Set fire," the carriage with its passenger, bathed in the light of the torches that were tossed on to it, burst into flames.

18

As we watched, the flames enveloped the carriage. The purple tassels that hung from the roof corners swung as though in a wind, while from below them the smoke swirled white against the blackness of the night. So frightful was it that the bamboo blinds, the hangings, the metal ornaments in the roof, seemed to be flying in the leaping shower of sparks. The tongues of flame that licked up from beneath the blinds, those serried flames that shot up into the sky, seemed to be celestial flames of the sun fallen to the earth. I had almost shouted before, but now I felt completely overwhelmed and dumbfounded; mouth agape, I could do nothing but watch the dreadful spectacle. But the father—Yoshihide. . . .

I still remember the expression on his face. He had started involuntarily toward the carriage, but when the fire blazed up he stopped, arms outstretched, and with piercing eyes watched the smoke and fire that enveloped the carriage as though he would be drawn into it. The blaze lit his wrinkled face so clearly that even the hairs of his head could be seen distinctly: in the depths of his wide staring eyes, in his drawn distorted lips, in his twitching cheeks, the grief, dread, and bewilderment that passed through his soul were clearly inscribed. A robber, guilty of unspeakable crimes and about to be beheaded, or dragged before the court of the Ten Kings, could hardly have looked more agonized. Even that gigantic samurai changed color and looked fearfully at the Lord of Horikawa.

But the latter, without taking his eyes off the carriage, merely bit his lips or laughed unpleasantly from time to time. As for the carriage and its passenger, that girl—I am not brave enough to tell you all that I saw. Her white face, choking in the smoke, looked upward; her long loosened hair fluttered in the smoke, her cherry-patterned mantle—how beautiful it all was! What a terrible spectacle! But when the night wind dropped and the smoke was drawn away to the other side, where gold dust seemed to be scattered above the red flames, when the girl gnawed her gag, writhing so that it seemed the chains must burst, I, and even the gigantic samurai, wondered whether we were not spectators of the torments of hell itself, and our flesh crept.

Then once more we thought the night wind stirred in the treetops of the garden. As that sound passed over the sky, something black that neither touched ground nor flew through the sky, dancing like a ball, leaped from the roof of the house into the blazing carriage. Into the crumbling blinds, cinnabar-stained, he fell, and putting his arms around the straining girl, he cried shrill and long into the smoke, a cry that sounded like tearing silk. He repeated it two or three times, then we forgot ourselves and shouted out together. Against the transparent curtain of flames, clinging to the girl's shoulder, was Yoshihide, Yoshihide the monkey, that had been left tied at the mansion.

19

But we saw him only for a moment. Like gold leaf on a brown screen the sparks climbed into the sky. The monkey and Yūzuki were hidden in black smoke while the carriage blazed away with a dreadful noise in the garden. It was a pillar of fire—those awful flames stabbed the very sky.

In front of that pillar Yoshihide stood rooted. Then, wonderful to say, over the wrinkled face of this Yoshihide, who had seemed to suffer on a previous occasion the tortures of hell, over his face the light of an inexpressible ecstasy passed, and forgetful even of his lordship's presence he folded his arms and stood watching. It was almost as if he did not see his daughter dying in agony. Rather he seemed to delight in the beautiful color of the flames and the form of a woman in torment.

What was most remarkable was not that he was joyfully watching the death of his daughter. It was rather that in him seemed to be a sternness not human, like the wrath of a kingly lion seen in a dream. Surprised by the fire, flocks of night birds that cried and clamored seemed thicker—though it may have been my imagination—around Yoshihide's cap. Maybe those soulless birds seemed to see a weird glory like a halo around that man's head. If the birds were attracted, how much more were we, the servants, filled with a strange feeling of worship as we watched Yoshihide. We quaked within, we held our breath, we watched him like a Buddha unveiled. The roaring of the fire that filled the air, and Yoshihide, his soul taken captive by it, standing there motionless—what awe we felt, what intense pleasure at this spectacle. Only his lordship sat on the veranda as though he were a different sort of being. He grew pale, foam gathered on his lips, he clutched his purple-skirted knee with both hands, he panted like some thirsty animal. . . .

20

It got around that his lordship had burnt a carriage at Yukige that night—though of course nobody said anything—and a great variety of opinions were expressed. The first and most prevalent rumor was that he had burnt Yoshihide's daughter to death in resentment over thwarted love. But there was no doubt that it was the daimyo's purpose to punish the perversity of the artist, who was painting the Hell Screen, even if he had to kill someone to do so. In fact, his lordship himself told me this.

Then there was much talk about the stony-heartedness of Yoshihide, who saw his daughter die in flames before his eyes and yet wanted to paint the screen. Some called him a beast of prey in human form, rendered incapable of human love by a picture. The

Abbot of Yokogawa often said, "A man's genius may be very great, great his art, but only an understanding of the Five Virtues [3] will save him from hell."

However, about a month later the Hell Screen was completed. Yoshihide immediately took it to the mansion and showed it with great deference to the Lord of Horikawa. The Abbot happened to be visiting his lordship at the time, and when he looked at it he must have been properly startled by the storm of fire that rages across the firmament on one of the leaves. He pulled a wry face, stared hard at Yoshihide, but said, "Well done," in spite of himself. I still remember the forced laugh with which his lordship greeted this.

From that time on, there was none that spoke badly of Yoshihide, at least in the mansion. And anyone who saw the screen, even if he had hated the artist before, was struck solemn, because he felt that he was experiencing hell's most exquisite tortures.

But by that time Yoshihide was no longer among the living. The night after the screen was finished he hanged himself from a beam in his studio. With his only daughter preceding him he felt, no doubt, that he could not bear to live on in idleness. His remains still lie within the ruins of his house. The rains and winds of many decades have bleached the little stone that marked his grave, and the moss has covered it in oblivion.

TRANSLATED BY W. H. H. NORMAN

[3] The Five Virtues of Confucius: Humanity, Justice, Propriety, Wisdom and Fidelity.

THE CANNERY BOAT

[*Kani Kōsen, 1929*] *by Kobayashi Takiji (1903-1933)*

The Cannery Boat *is the story of the voyage of a floating cannery in the waters off Kamchatka. The ship is manned by rough sailors, students from the universities, who have been tricked into believing the work is a desirable summer job, and boys from the farms of northern Japan. The descriptions of the life aboard ship are powerful and convincing, but what gives this book its characteristic flavor is the Marxist philosophy underlying it. The boss, Asakawa, is a fiend, and he represents an organization of cold-blooded monsters to whom the loss of sailors' lives means nothing. The only cheerful moments come when, in the extract given here, some sailors hear of the deliverance afforded by communism.* The Cannery Boat, *for all its gross imperfections, is considered to be the masterpiece of the "proletarian literature" movement. The author later died in prison of torture.*

•

In the afternoon the sky changed. There was a mist so light as to seem almost unreal. Myriads of three-cornered waves sprang up across the great cloth of sea. Suddenly the wind began to howl through the masts. The bottoms of the tarpaulins covering the cargo flapped against the deck.

The crests of the triangular waves were soon flinging their white spray over the whole surface of the sea, for all the world like thousands of rabbits scampering over a vast plain. This was the herald of one of Kamchatka's sudden storms. All at once the tide began to ebb quickly.

The ship started to swing round on herself. Kamchatka, which until now had been visible on the starboard side, suddenly appeared on the port side. There was great excitement among fishermen and sailors. Above their heads sounded an alarm whistle. They all stood looking up at the sky. The funnel shook and rattled. Maybe because they were standing directly under it, it seemed incredibly wide, like a huge bathtub, sloping away out backwards. The piercing note from the alarm whistle had something tragic in it. Warned by its prolonged blowing, the boats out fishing far from the main ship returned home through the storm.

Early that morning the boss had received warning of the storm from another ship which was anchored about ten miles away. The message also stated that if the boats were out they should be recalled immediately. Asakawa had said, "If we're going to take notice of every little thing that comes along, do you think we'll ever get finished with this job we came all the way to Kamchatka to do?" This information had leaked out through the radio operator.

The first sailor to hear this had started to roar at the operator as if he had been Asakawa. "What does he think human lives are, anyway?"

"Human lives?"

"Yes."

"But Asakawa never thinks of us as human beings."

Toward evening there was a great shouting from the bridge. The men below rushed up the companionway two steps at a time. Two boats had been sighted, drawing near. They had been lashed together with ropes. They came very close, but, just as if they were at one end of a seesaw with the ship at the other, the big waves lifted them up and down by turns. One after another immense roaring waves rose up between them. Although so near, they made no progress. Everyone felt the tension. A rope was thrown from the deck, but it did not reach. It only fell on the water with a vain splashing. Then, twisting like a water snake, it was hauled back. This was repeated several times. From the ship all shouted in one voice, but no answer came. Faces were like masks, with eyes immobile. The whole scene, with its unbearable grimness, seared every heart.

By dusk all the boats except two had got safely back. As soon as the fishermen came on deck they lost consciousness. One of the boats, having become full of water, had been anchored and its crew transferred to another boat. The other one together with its crew was missing.

The boss was fuming with rage. He kept on going down into the fishermen's cabin and then up again. The men cast sullen glances at him throughout this performance.

The next day, partly to search for the missing boat, partly to follow up the crabs, it was decided that the ship should move on. The loss of the carcasses of five or six men was nothing, but it would be a pity to lose the boat. . . .

When the lost boat did not return, the fishermen gathered together the belongings of the missing men, looking for the addresses of their families and getting everything ready in case worse came to worst. It wasn't the pleasantest of jobs. As they worked they had the feeling that they were examining their own remains. Various parcels and letters addressed to women relatives were discovered in the missing men's baggage. Among one man's things there was a letter written in crudely formed script, obviously with a frequently licked pencil. This was passed from one rough sailor's hand to another's. Each one spelled the words out to himself laboriously, but with intense interest, and shaking his head passed it on to his neighbor. It was a letter from the man's child.

One man raised his head from the page and whispered, "It's all because of Asakawa. When we know for sure this poor fellow is dead we'll revenge him." The speaker was a big, hefty man who had a past behind him. In a still lower voice one young round-shouldered fisherman said, "I expect we could beat up Asakawa."

"Ah, that letter was no good; it's made me homesick," said another man.

"Look here," the first speaker said, "if we don't look out the swine will get us. We've got to look out for ourselves."

One man who had been sitting in the corner with his knees up, biting his thumbnails and listening to every word, remarked, "Leave it to me. When the time comes, I'll lay into the swine!"

They were all silent, but they felt relieved.

Three days later the *Hakkō Maru* returned to her original position and the missing boat came back. Everyone on board was safe and sound.

Because of the storm they had lost control of their boat. They were more helpless than babes strung up by the neck, and were all prepared for death. Fishermen must always be ready for death.

Their boat had been washed up on the coast of Kamchatka, and they were rescued by some Russians living near. The Russians were a family of four. Thirsty as they were for a "home" with women and children in it, this place held an indescribable attraction for the sailors. Added to that, everyone was kind, offering all kinds of help. Still, at first the fact that their rescuers were foreigners, with different colored hair and eyes, using incomprehensible words, made the sailors feel rather strange. The thought soon occurred to them, however, that after all these were just human beings like themselves.

Hearing of the wreck, many people from the village gathered. The place was a long way off from the Japanese fishing waters.

They stayed there two days recovering and then started back. "We didn't want to come back. Who would, to a hell like this?"

Their story didn't end there. There was another interesting thing which they were hiding.

Just on the day they were to leave, as they were standing round the stove, putting on their clothes and talking, four or five Russians entered, and with them was a Chinese. One Russian, with a large face and a short brown beard, burst into a flood of loud talking and gesticulations. In order to let him know that they could not understand Russian the sailors waved their hands in front of their faces. Then the Russian said a single sentence and the Chinese, who was watching his lips, started to speak in Japanese. It was strange Japanese, with the order of the words all mixed up. Word after word came reeling out drunkenly.

"You, for sure, have no money."

"That's right."

"You are poor men."

"That's right too."

"So you proletarians. Understand?"

"Yes."

The Russian, smiling, started to walk around. Sometimes he would stop and look over at them.

"Rich man, he do this to you" (gripping his throat). "Rich man become fatter and fatter" (swelling out his stomach). "You no good at all, you become poor. Understand? Japan no good. Workers like this" (pulling a long face and making himself look like a sick man). "Men that don't work like this" (walking about haughtily).

The young fishermen were very amused at him. "That's right, that's right," they said and laughed.

"Workers like this. Men that don't work like this" (repeating the same gestures). "Like that no good. Workers like this!" (this time just the opposite, swelling out his chest and walking proudly). "Men that don't work like this!" (looking like a decrepit beggar). "That very good. Understand? That country, Russia. Only workers like this!" (proud). "Russia. We have no men who don't work. No cunning men. No men who seize your throat. Understand? Russia not at all terrible country. What everyone says only lies."

They were all vaguely wondering whether this wasn't what was called "terrible" and "Red." But even if it was "Red" one part of them couldn't help feeling that it sounded very right.

"Understand? Really understand?"

Two or three of the Russians started to jabber something among themselves. The Chinese listened to them. Then in a stuttering kind of way he began to speak again in Japanese: "Among men who no work, many make profit. Proletariat always like this" (a gesture of being gripped by the throat). "This no good! You proletarians, one, two, three, a hundred, a thousand, fifty thousand, a hundred thousand, all of you, all like this" (swinging his hands like children do when walking together). "Then become strong. It safe" (tapping the muscles of his arm). "You no lose. Understand?"

"Yes."

"Japan no good yet. Workers like this" (bending and cringing). "Men who no work like this" (pretending to punch and knock over his neighbor). "That no good! Workers like this" (straightening up his body in a threatening way and advancing; then pretending to knock his neighbor down and kick him). "Men who no work like this" (running away). "Japan only workers. Fine country. Proletarians' country! Understand?"

"Yes, yes, we understand."

The Russian raised a strange voice and began a kind of dance.

"Japan workers, act!" (straightening himself and making to attack). "Very glad. Russia all glad. Banzai! . . . You go back to ship. In your ship men who no work like this" (proud). "You, proletariat, do this!" (pretending to box, then swinging hands as before, and then advancing). "Very safe. You win! Understand?"

"We understand." The young fishermen, who before they knew it had become very much excited, suddenly shook the Chinese's hand. "We'll do it . . . we'll certainly do it."

The head sailor thought all this was "Red," that they were being egged on to do terrible things. Like this, by such tricks, Russia was making a complete fool of Japan, he thought.

When the Russian had finished he shouted something and then pressed their hands with all his might. He embraced them and pressed his bristly face to theirs. The flustered Japanese, with their heads pushed back, did not know what to do.

The sailors in the hold listening to this story were eager to hear more, in spite of occasional glances toward the door. The fishermen went on telling them many other things about the Russians. Their minds lapped it all up as if they were blotting paper.

"Hey, there, that's about enough!" The head sailor, seeing how impressed they all were by these tales, tapped the shoulder of one young fisherman, who was talking for all he was worth.

TRANSLATED ANONYMOUSLY

TIME

[*Jikan, 1931*] *by Yokomitsu Riichi (1898-1947)*

Yokomitsu Riichi was one of the most brilliantly gifted of modern Japanese writers. His name is associated with a number of literary schools of the twenties and thirties, but he was essentially an independent. He disagreed both with the advocates of "proletarian" literature and the writers of autobiographical fiction, affirming his own belief in the purely artistic values of literature. European influences are detectable in his works, but in "Time" and some of his other stories we find not only the psychological insights characteristic of European writing, but an essentially Buddhist concern with the hell that man creates for himself on earth.

•

The manager of our troupe failed to return for a whole week after stepping out one evening. Takagi decided to open the suitcase he had left behind. It was empty. Then we were really at our wits' end. When the truth dawned on us—our manager had run off, leaving us without a penny—we were all too dumbfounded to make any suggestion as to how to deal with the room and board bill. I was finally chosen as delegate for the group to face the landlord. I asked him please to allow us to continue as we were for the time being, and assured him that remittances would be forthcoming from our families. I earned us thus a temporary reprieve. Two or three money orders did in fact come, and each time we acclaimed them with joyous shouts. What happened, however, was that the money which arrived was the exclusive possession of the man receiving it, and it simply led to his making off immediately with whichever actress of the company he liked best.

Finally there were twelve of us left—eight men and four women:

six-feet tall, amply built Takagi, who assumed as a matter of course that women had eyes for no one but him; Kinoshita, who liked gambling better than three meals a day and whose every thought was directed towards inventing a means of seeing dice through the box; pale, gentle Sasa, whom everyone called Buddha, and who, mysteriously enough, licked the windowpanes when he was drunk; Yagi, who was a little peculiar, and collected women's underwear; Matsugi, a champion at hand and foot wrestling, always on the lookout for billiard parlors in whatever town we went to; Kurigi, who was forever forgetting and mislaying his belongings, and whose only talent was for losing whatever came into his hands; Yashima, who, miser that he was, hated to return borrowed articles; and myself—eight men, plus the four women, Namiko, Shinako, Kikue, and Yukiko. In our cases it was not so much that remittances were unconscionably slow in arriving, as that little or no possibility existed of any money coming to us. Knowing this all along, we had placed our hopes on the money of others more likely to receive it.

The landlord's looks turned unfriendly, as he too began to doubt whether he would see his money, however much longer he waited. His surveillance over the remaining twelve of us was eagle-eyed, to say the least. For our part, we each felt that it was preferable for no money to arrive at all than to have some come to any one of us—whoever received it was sure to sneak off by himself, and make the burden on those who remained all the heavier. Our suspicions grew so strong that soon we were spying on one another secretly, wondering who would be the next to run off. But it was only at the beginning that we could afford the luxury of this mutual spying. Before long we had more pressing matters on our minds than who would be the next to escape—the landlord stopped giving us even one meal a day. We gradually turned pallid and unwell, and our days were spent drinking water to fill our stomachs and discussing interminably what we should do. At length we reached agreement: we would all escape together. If, as we reasoned, we escaped in a group, we would have little to worry about even if a couple of men were sent in pursuit of us. There lurked also in our minds the specter of the fate which lay in store for anyone who happened by mischance to be the last left behind. These considerations led us to swear up and down to make a joint escape. However, if we were simply to make a wild break for it, or in any way attract the attention of the local bullies in the landlord's employ, we would have no chance of success. We decided therefore to take advantage of our visits to the public bath, the one freedom we were allowed, and some rainy night when the watch over us was least strict to make our escape. We would have to follow the road along the coast rather than an easier route, for unless the way we took was the most difficult and unlikely, we were certain to be caught. With these matters settled by way of preliminaries, we resolved to await a rainy night.

In the room next to the one where our escape plans were being discussed, Namiko lay all alone. She had suffered a severe attack of some female sickness during a performance, and was still unable to move from her bed. Whenever the question of what to do with her arose, we all fell silent. On this one topic, no one had a word to say. It was quite clearly—if tacitly—understood that we had no alternative but to abandon her. As a matter of fact, I was also of the opinion that we would have to sacrifice Namiko for the sake of the eleven others of us, but after we had finished our discussion I happened to pass through her room. She suddenly thrust out her arms and seized my foot. She begged me in tears to take her along, insisting that she must escape when we did. I managed eventually to extricate my foot by promising to discuss the matter with the others.

I called everyone together again to reopen our discussion. They were all perfectly aware of my reason for summoning them. In their eyes flashed repeated warnings not to propose anything foolish. I asked if they would not consent to taking Namiko along. First of all, I explained, she was passionately anxious to escape with the rest of us. There was also the sentimental consideration that, after all, she had shared rice from the same pot with us for such a long time. Yukiko, who was standing next to me, capitulated first. She declared that she didn't feel right about leaving Namiko behind. She had once received a pair of stockings from her. Shinako remembered that she had been given some lace cuffs, and Kikue had been given a comb. The women thus were at least not opposed to taking Namiko along. Not one of the men spoke openly. Instead, one after another they took me aside to urge that I drop the subject. "Come on," I said, in an attempt to persuade them, "let's take her. Something good is bound to come of it." They began for the first time to come around to my point of view, and finally agreed that we might as well take her.

When we actually reached the point of making our escape, we faced the necessity of following a trail over the cliffs along the sea for some fifteen or twenty miles before we could get through the pass. The thought of carrying a sick woman on our backs loomed as a staggering undertaking. In order to fool that scoundrel of a landlord we would have to leave the rooming house one by one, swinging our towels as part of the pretense of visiting the public bath in a storm. If we took too much time over our departure we would have no chance to eat, and would be obliged to set out with empty stomachs. In that case we would have no choice but to risk making our way, under cover of darkness, to the next station.

I asked Namiko to try and stand, as a test of her ability to walk. She made an effort, but immediately collapsed limply over the bedding, moaning that her eyes felt as if they were swimming in her head. She seemed utterly without bones. I, who in a moment of sympathy had urged the others to take Namiko along, now could not help thinking that in her condition it would be best for all of us to leave her behind. "Wouldn't you really prefer to remain here by yourself?" I said. "I can't imagine that the landlord would do anything bad to a sick person like yourself. We promise to send you money." Namiko burst into tears. "I'd rather you killed me than left me here alone." She persisted, and I could do nothing to change her mind. After having convinced the others to take Namiko along, I could not bring myself to be so irresponsible as to propose now that we abandon her. So, I too began to wait for the next rainy night. I made no mention of Namiko again. But even waiting for the rain was not easy for us. Anyone who went to the public bath would always pawn an article of clothing and buy buns to be shared with the rest of us. We realized, however, at this rate we might use up the money needed for our train fare, and then face real disaster. We stopped smoking altogether, and limited ourselves to only one bun a day. The whole time was spent lolling around, drinking water to keep ourselves going. There was nothing else to do. Fortunately, the autumn rains began to fall a few mornings later, and by late afternoon an increasingly violent storm had developed. We determined to stage our escape that night, and each of us completed whatever preparations were necessary. We waited for the dark. One thought obsessed me—assuming that we all managed to reach the railway station safely, which man would eventually go off with which woman. The fact that eight men had remained behind with the four women was not only because they had no money. Each of the women had had relations with two or even three of the men, I rather suspected, which made separation extremely difficult. I felt certain that sooner or later, somewhere, there would be trouble. However, no one betrayed any presentiment of this as night approached and the time set for our escape drew upon us. Soon, one or two at a time, the members of the troupe began going out, towels in hand. It crossed my mind that, unknown to me, the matter of which man would go with which woman had already been decided. My share of the escape preparations consisted merely of bundling together changes of clothes for all of us and throwing the bundles over the wall to the others waiting on the opposite side. I was conscious of the danger that, if I was the last to leave, since it had been my idea to take Namiko along, I might well be left to figure out an escape for the two of us. Were such a proposal to be made, the others were only too likely to agree with it. I therefore contrived that Takagi should be the last to leave. With my towel slung over my shoulder I took Namiko on my back and set out in the rain for the bamboo thicket where I was to join the others.

There were about ten of us huddled together in the thicket, protected only by three oil-paper umbrellas. We waited for the others. Kinoshita, who had taken our bundles to the pawnshop, did not appear. No one actually voiced anything, but an expression of uneasiness gradually crept over our faces, as much as to say, "Kinoshita has run off with the money." We stood in silence, staring at each other. Soon, Kinoshita returned with ten yen in his hand. Our next problem was to eat before we started. Takagi was the last to arrive and suggested we all go together to a restaurant. Matsugi pointed out that it would be best to go one at a time, since we were sure to be discovered if we went in a crowd. We agreed to this. We decided to divide the money, but all we had was a ten yen bill. We could have sent someone to change it, but the unspoken fear that anyone who went for change might run off with the money prevented us from letting the money out of our sight. Someone said, "Having the money is just the same as not having it. What are we going to do?" For a while there was silence, then another remarked that if we delayed any longer people from the rooming house would catch up with us. And still another voice: "What could we do if they really came after us? I'm too hungry to move." When we reached this impasse Yashima suggested that the money be turned over to me, since I was the one person who could not run away or hide, what with a sick woman on my back. To this everyone assented. However, I knew that if I were entrusted with the money the others would constantly be spying on me, and this would be extremely disagreeable. I thought it would be better if in front of everybody I gave the money to Namiko. As guardian of our money, she would certainly, at least for the time being, be carefully protected. I thrust the bill into her kimono. With this, the sick woman, who up until now had been treated as a disgusting nuisance, suddenly became an object of value, a reassuringly dependable safe-deposit vault. Automatically we began to formulate regulations around her. First of all, the men in the group were to take turns carrying Namiko on their back, each one taking a hundred steps. The women were not required to carry the burden, but to take turns counting. Next we settled the order of carrying her, while the women laughingly watched and backed one or another of us in our choosing games. Those of us who were to go in front began to walk out of the bamboo thicket.

There were only three umbrellas for the twelve of us, and the rain whipped by a gale beat headlong into our faces. We struggled forward in single file, four to an umbrella, and drenched by the rain. In the middle was Namiko, guarded like a holy image in procession, immediately behind her the women, and farther back some of the men. Sasa, who was near the middle, suddenly called out, "We seem to have forgotten all about eating." There were cries of assent, and again the column came to a halt. But there was hardly time now for eating: if we were overtaken we would be finished. Several favored making a desperate attempt to cross the pass tonight in the hope that tomorrow would be safe, and by tacit consent our column began to wriggle caterpillar-like ahead in the darkness. The starch had drained from the women's felt hats, which began to make a loud spattering noise. At first we thought in terror that it might be the sound of pursuers. From time to time, as if by a prearranged signal, we all would turn to look behind us. But as Kurigi said, even supposing that the landlord discovered what had happened and sent people out after us, they would never choose this terrible road at first. This observation was reassuring, but the fact remained that none of us had ever traveled on the road before. We had not the least idea what lay ahead, not even whether we were to pass through cultivated land or barren desolation. The road, from which the sand had been washed by the rain to expose frequently the raised heads of stones, was only dimly visible at our feet. Uneasiness akin to desperation mounted steadily within us. Only Kinoshita, who chattered on with his usual socialistic talk, displayed any energy. "The next time I meet that damned manager who's responsible for all our suffering, I will really give him a beating," he swore, and at his words the hatred of the group for the already half-forgotten manager suddenly flared up again. "Beat him? I'll shove him in the ocean!" shouted someone else; and another voice chimed in, "The ocean's too good for him! I'll split his head open with a rock." "I'll stick burning hot prongs down his throat!" "Burning hot prongs are too good for him," another man was saying when the sick woman, who up until that moment had not uttered a sound, suddenly burst into loud wails. Yagi, who was carrying her on his back, stopped in his tracks. There were cries from behind. "What's the matter? Can't you move any faster?" Namiko was weeping convulsively, and she began now to beg us to go on without her. At first we were at a loss to tell what had caused this outburst, when we discovered that she was losing blood. We stood there in the rain, bewildered and helpless. I suggested that the women be left to deal with this female disorder, and one of the women thereupon said that a dry cloth was needed immediately. I felt obliged to offer my undershirt. The sick woman felt sorry for us, and all the while that Matsugi, whose turn was next, was carrying her, she begged him in tears again and again to go on without her. Matsugi finally lost his temper and threatened to leave her then and there if she kept whining, and this only made her wail all the more hysterically. Uppermost in our minds, however, was the fear of being overtaken. Finally we reached a point where even that ceased to worry us, when thoughts of our hunger assailed us. "Tomorrow," began one of us, "when we get to a town the first thing I'm going to do is eat pork cutlets." "I'll take fish." "I'd rather have eels than fish." "I'd like a steak." Then we all started to talk about food, not listening to what anyone else had to say, but elaborating on what we liked to eat and places where we had once had a good meal. We were becoming like voracious beasts.

I was as desperate as the others, at least as far as hunger was concerned. I looked for something to eat along the road, but ever since we had emerged from the bamboo thicket we had not passed a single cultivated field. There was hardly much point in searching here: to the right was a wall of sheer rock, and to the left, at the foot of a cliff that dropped several hundred feet, we could hear the sound of waves. It was all we could do to avoid a misstep from the path, which was a bare four feet wide. We lurched ahead tied to one another with our belts, following whichever way the umbrella in front led. The road twisted up and down. Sometimes the rain unexpectedly swept up on us from below, and before we knew it we would be pasted against the edge of the rock face. Our column staggered ahead over the endless cliff, now stretching out, now contracting, and we began to collide with each other: we obviously could not allow stories of food to dull our faculties. Presently the pleasant remembrances of food turned into grim reminders of the fact that we had nothing to eat. One after another of us dropped out of the discussion. Then we were silent, and all that could be heard between the roar of the waves and the sound of the wind was the monotonous voice of the woman counting the number of paces. There were no sighs now, nor even so much as a cough. The silence which pressed on every one of us, the mute fear of what would happen if things continued this way much longer, was almost tangible enough to touch. At this juncture Namiko's losses of blood became severe. The confusion of removing our undershirts and the wailing of Namiko restored our animation, and with it talk about food. Some protested that so much talk about food worked up our appetites all the more, but the others answered that talk was now the only means at our disposal for blunting our hunger. Water was better than nothing, and some began to lick the drops of rain which trickled from the umbrellas, or else to chew on pine needles pulled from the stunted trees along our way. We looked like so many ravenous demons, but this occasioned no laughter. My clothes were soaked through and through, but my throat was parched. When the rain blew against me I would turn my head away from the umbrella into the rain with my mouth open. And when it came my turn to carry Namiko again, however much I tried to remind myself that the weight on my back was a woman, I was so hungry that I could scarcely keep my feet moving. Everything grew misty before my eyes as I ran more and more out of breath. My arms became numb, and my legs trembled under me. I could go on only by biting my tongue and leaning my head into the back of the man in front of me who carried the umbrella. By the time that the woman had counted up to about ninety, I felt like tossing Namiko over the edge, but I steeled myself against betraying any emotion, for I knew that if she detected it she would start her screeching again. My eyelids became so stiff that when I opened them I heard a click. Even though the burden was eventually shifted to the next man, it came back every eight hundred yards, after each man had performed his stint, and there was pitiful little time to recuperate from the strain. To make matters worse, every minute increased my hunger, and with it the sick woman on my back became heavier. This was unbearable enough, but Namiko took it into her head to insist that we carry her at the front of the column because she couldn't bear being sandwiched in the middle. This was probably more agreeable to Namiko, for it reduced her fear of being abandoned, but we who were doing the carrying were additionally fatigued by the constant pushing from behind. I recalled that everyone was being made to suffer simply because I had brought the sick woman along, and I resolved that if ever we became so exhausted as to reach the verge of collapse, I would either hurl Namiko into the ocean or remain with her and ask the others to go on without us.

But in point of fact we had already reached the "verge of collapse" and such thoughts obviously served no useful purpose. Our faces were livid and stained with a greasy sweat, our eyes had begun to glaze, and there were some who after protracted yawns would suddenly let out strange, unnerving cries. When one of us, as if broken by the wind, collapsed over a projecting ledge of the rock wall, Namiko again began to weep and beg us to leave her there. Water was streaming from the women's hair and clothes, and they walked like specters, with their wet hair plastered over their faces. The color of their underwear had seeped through and stained their kimonos. By the time water had soaked their compacts and purses, a heavy calm fell over them. Kikue said, "We're going to die soon, anyway; I wish it were all over." "Why don't you jump over the edge then? It'd be perfectly simple," snapped Yagi. This crude joke apparently got on the nerves of Kurigi, who was already at the end of his tether. He snarled, "What do you mean by joking when people are suffering?" and closed in on Yagi. Yagi drew himself up, as if startled at being so unexpectedly threatened, and blurted out, "You needn't get so angry, no matter how much I joke with Kikue. You may be in love with her, but you haven't got a chance—I've seen her with Takagi myself." Gentle Sasa, who up to now had kept absolutely silent, suddenly pulled a knife from his pocket and lunged at Takagi. Takagi deftly avoided the point of Sasa's knife, and made a headlong dash along the cliff. Sasa ran in pursuit, lurching heavily. Kurigi, who for a while had remained dumbfounded by this development, now realizing that his enemy was actually not Yagi but rather Takagi and Sasa, ran off after them.

Dimly visible through the dark beside me, I could see and hear Kikue, sobbing that it was all her fault. "Go at once," I said, "and stop the fight." But she answered, "Unless you go too I can't stop them." Then, and this came as an entirely unexpected event, Namiko suddenly thrust out her arms and, fastening herself on the neck of the weeping Kikue, began to gnash her teeth. Apparently she had realized for the first time that her lover—whichever one of the three he was—had been taken from her. Soon even Yagi, who had caused the quarrel, was in a rage, and I was amazed to see him drag Shinako to the ground and demand that she reveal her lover's name. It was obvious that the fight could soon involve us all, and if anyone got hurt and could not proceed farther, we were all without question doomed. I was appalled at our horrible plight; my only comfort came from the fact that nobody around me had a weapon. But one of the men up the road had a knife, and I could not very well leave things at that. Shaking all over, I ran along the black cliff, shouting again and again, "Wait! Wait!" When I had gone about two hundred yards I saw the three of them lying motionless by the side of the road, flat on their backs. I thought that they must be dead, but I noticed then that they were all staring at my face, their eyes popping from their sockets. I asked what had happened. "We decided that to get hurt fighting over a woman in a place like this wouldn't do us any good, and we stopped. But don't make us talk for a while—we're so exhausted that breathing is painful."

"You are very wise," I said, and returned to the sick woman. There the fight seemed just beginning. Yagi and Kinoshita were grappling and snarling on the road near the shrieking Namiko. Even the women had evidently lost all track of who had stolen their man and whose man they themselves had stolen. They were in such a state of bewilderment that they did not even bother to ask me what had happened in the fight up the road. The fights had not actually come as a great surprise to me, but I never imagined that they would explode with such violence here. The detached calm with which I had contemplated the quarrels was now rudely shattered by the realization that our progress might be halted because of them. Yagi and Kinoshita had long been on bad terms and rivals in love.

There was not much likelihood therefore that they would separate even if I tried to force my way in and stop the fight. In any case, it was certainly pleasanter for them to be lying on the ground hitting each other than to be on their feet walking and obliged to carry a sick woman. They seemed in fact to be hitting each other merely in order to rest their grappling legs. I thought that the best plan was to let them fight all they could, as long as they did not cause each other any real harm. I sat on the ground to rest myself while the two of them continued to wrestle weakly. As I watched, suddenly both Yagi and Kinoshita ceased moving altogether, both apparently utterly exhausted, and capable now only of panting furiously. This, I thought, was a good point to intervene. I said, "You can't go on lying there indefinitely. If you want to fight, go ahead and fight. If you've had enough, break it up now, and let's get moving again. The three of them up the road have had the sense to realize that nothing is so stupid as fighting over a woman, and now they've made up." Yagi and Kinoshita slowly got to their feet and began to walk.

When our procession joined the three men up the road, the sick woman was shifted to another back. There were no more undershirts left among us to wipe her bleeding, and now as we walked along peacefully, our shorts one by one were used. In spite of the fact that the result of the immorality of the women had been to excite violent quarrels among the men, when the various relations had become so excessively complicated as to upset all judgments, a balance was restored, and a kind of calm monotony ensued. This to me was at once fascinating and terrifying. But soon afterwards, as hunger began to assail us more fiercely than ever, our peace was turned into a bestial stupor from which all individuality had been stripped. I became incapable of speech. The skin of my abdomen stuck to my spine. There was no saliva left in my mouth. Sour juices welled up from my stomach, bringing with them a griping pain. The rims of my eyes burned. My incessant yawns reeked of bitter tobacco. No doubt as a result of our exhaustion from the scuffles, not a word was said as we proceeded in the soaking rain, with our heads down. Our helplessness was so manifest, that Namiko, now weeping quietly to herself, began to appear the strongest of us. We were plunged into despair and doubted we could ever manage to cross the cliff which extended limitlessly before us in the dark. We could no longer think in terms so remote as hope or a happier future. Our heads held no other thoughts but of the moments of time that kept pressing in on us, one after another: what would our hunger be like in another two minutes, how could we last out another minute. The time which I could conceive of came to be filled entirely with sensations of hunger, and I began to feel as if what was trudging forward in the endless darkness was not myself but only a stomach. I could feel already that time as far as I was concerned was nothing but a measure of my stomach.

We must have walked ten or twelve miles since nightfall. Just about when the men were turning over the last of their underclothes to the sick woman, we discovered a small hut on the rock face somewhat above the road. Those who were in the lead could not be sure at first whether it was a boulder or a hut. While they were still arguing, we saw that it was an abandoned water mill. We decided that it would be a good idea to rest there a bit, if only to escape from the rain, and we went in. It was evident that no human being had made his way here for a very long time: cobwebs that crisscrossed the hut clung to our faces. There was space enough to shelter us from the rain, a musty little room into which the twelve of us squeezed. "There must be water somewhere, this is a mill. I'm going to look," Yagi said, and wandered outside the hut. But the pipes which should have carried water had rotted into pieces, and the blades of the water wheel were covered with white mold. It was impossible to find any water here. The sweat on our skins turned icy, and the dampness in our clothes made us shiver. To our fatigue and hunger now was added the biting cold of the late autumn night, so sharp that anyone who separated himself from the others could not have endured it. We wished to make a fire, but no one had matches. The best we could do was remove our coats, spread them out on the floor, and arrange ourselves together so as to share one another's warmth. The sick woman was placed in the center with the three other women around her, and the men spread their arms around the women making an effect something like an artichoke. But such measures did not suffice. The cold assaulted us even more keenly. Then our teeth began to chatter so badly that we could not form words but only stammer. Tears came but not a sound from the lips. We were shaking like jellyfish in the water. Soon the sick woman in the center lost even the strength to shiver, and in the midst of our trembling she lay shrunken and motionless. One of the women moaned, "When I die, please cut off my hair and send it to my mother. I can't stand any more." Then another voice cried, "I'm finished too. When I die, cut off my thumb and send it home." "Send back my glasses." Even while they spoke our knees grew numb, our thighs grew numb, and soon the pain reached our heads. Kurigi suddenly burst out, "I'm being punished now because when I was a boy I threw stones at the village god." And Takagi said, "I'm being punished for having deceived so many women," a remark which seemed to transfix men and women alike. They joined in with affirmative exclamations amidst their tears. The extreme mercilessness they all displayed rather amused me, but at the same time I could not detach myself from the conviction that we would die there. I was sitting on a wooden support next to the millstone, and I wondered when the next disaster would strike us. It proved to be something which we might have foreseen: an insidious drowsiness began to overtake us. Our shivering imperceptibly had died away. I realized with a shock that if we once permitted ourselves to fall asleep the end would come. I began to shout, to shake people's heads, to strike them. I told them if we fell asleep we were finished; I urged them to hit at once anyone who dozed. What made our struggle so difficult against the strange enemy was that the very consciousness we were losing was the only weapon we could employ in our defense. Even as I exhorted the others, I felt myself growing increasingly drowsy, and my thoughts wandered to reveries on the nature of sleep. I dimly realized that soon I too would be dropping off. But that thought itself made me leap up, ready to kick that thing, whatever it was, that was trying to steal my consciousness. Then I came face to face with something even stranger—in the midst of this frantic shuttling between life and death I sensed time, milder than ever I had experienced it, and I felt that I should like to go that one step further and peep at the instant of time when my consciousness was extinguished. Abruptly I opened my eyes and looked around me. In front the others were all dropping off to sleep, their heads hanging lifelessly.

I rushed from one to another, striking violently, and shouting warnings to wake up. Each opened his vacant eyes, some only again to lean senselessly against the person next to them, others, aware suddenly of the mortal danger threatening them, gazed around in bewilderment, blinking their eyes. Still others thought that having been struck by me gave them the right to hit anyone else who was asleep, and there soon began a wild melee. At each slight letup sleep crept back to suck up all consciousness. I pulled each by the hair, I shook their heads wildly, I slapped them so hard on the cheeks that the imprint of my fingers remained. But even if I had struck so hard that they tasted the bones of my fist, even if I had had a fist of iron, no sooner would my violent actions stop for a moment than all would plummet towards death. Even while I went on pummeling the eleven others, watching intently their every movement, I felt suddenly buoyed up by the infinite pleasure into which my consciousness was melting. Pleasure—indeed there is nothing to compare with the gaiety and transparency of the pleasure before death. The heart begins to choke from its extremity of pleasure, as if it were licking some luscious piece of fruit. It holds no melancholy, like a forgetting of the self. What is this thing between life and death, this wave which surges up in ever shifting colors with a vapor joyous as the sky? I wonder if it is not the face of that dreadful monster no human being has ever seen—time? It gave me pleasure to think that when I died and disappeared every other man in the whole world would vanish at the same time with me. This temptation to kill every human being, this game with death enticed me, and I wavered on the point of yielding myself without further struggle to sleep. And yet, when I observed the others I would pound them with both hands, scarcely caring where I struck. To fight to keep others from death—why should such a harmful act prove beneficial? Even supposing that we managed to escape death now, it was impossible to imagine that when we were dying at some future time we could do so without the least worry, so neatly and so pleasantly as now. And yet I seemed to want them to live again. I pulled the women by the hair and beat them, kicked the men over and over. Could that be called love, I wonder? Or was it more properly to be termed habit? I was so painfully aware of the unhappy future that awaited us all that I felt like strangling each to death, and yet I was compelled by helping them to prolong their sufferings. And was this action to be called salvation? —My lips formed the words, "Go ahead and die!", but I continued to tear frantically through their sleep as though struggling with some misfortune from long years past which had never ceased in its depredations. Gradually they awakened and then, with exactly the expression of "Which one of you has destroyed my happiness?", fell to hitting those around them more savagely than ever. It seemed impossible that anyone could now sleep undisturbed. Some kept moving even while asleep, with only their hands flailing the air in motions of striking. The others, even as they were stamping, kicking, hitting, wildly pounding one another in this scene of inferno, began to fall asleep again. What at first had been round and gathered together steadily disintegrated as heads dropped between legs and trunks became interlocked. In this coagulating, amorphous mass, it was no longer possible to tell whom one struck or where the blow fell. I ranged over as large an area as I could, furiously striking everyone, for I knew that anyone who escaped would die. But lethargy is filled with a submerged terror that attacks with a ferocity only second to that of brute violence; an instant, it would seem, after arousing someone I would open my eyes to find him striking my head or thrusting his knee into my groin. Each time I awoke I would wriggle my way among the bodies around me and sink into them. Thus we moved again and again from sleep to waking.

Outside the hut changes had also been taking place. The rain had stopped, and in the moonlight streaming in through holes in the crumbling walls we could see the spider webs etched with absolute clarity. We tried to make our way outside in the hope of shaking off our drowsiness, but our legs refused to move. So we crawled out on our bellies and stared at the mountains and the sea illuminated by moonlight. Then Sasa, who was beside me, wordlessly tugged at my sleeve and pointed dementedly at a place down the cliff. I looked, my mind a blank—a thin stream of water was flowing from the rocks, making a faint splashing sound as it sparkled in the moonlight. I tried to shout "Water!" but I had no voice. Sasa went down the cliff, rubbing his knees painfully. After a few minutes he reached the spring and began to drink. His spirits were suddenly restored, and he shouted "Water! Water!" I too faintly called out at the same time.

We were saved. The others, incapable as they were of moving their legs, crawled out of the hut, each man for himself, and headed for the spring. One after another, their pale cobweb-covered faces exposed by the moonlight, they pressed their noses into the rock. The clear water filled with the smell of the rock soaked through from the throat to the stomach and down to the toes, with the sharpness of a knife. Then, as the force of life first began to operate, we all let out cries of wonder at the moon, as if we felt that this is what it meant to be really alive, and we pressed our mouths again to the rock. Suddenly I remembered the sick woman in the hut. I wondered if she might not have fallen asleep and died already. I asked the others to think of some way of getting water to her. Takagi had the idea of carrying water in a hat. We filled his soft hat with water, but after taking a few steps the water leaked out of it. Then we tried putting five hats together, one inside the other, and filled them with water. This time it did not leak noticeably, but it was obvious that by the time we got the hat to Namiko the water would be gone. "Wouldn't the quickest way," Sasa suggested, "be to pass the hat along in a relay?" The eleven of us distributed ourselves in the moonlight at intervals of about twenty feet apart. I was chosen to be the last in line, the one to give the water to Namiko. While I waited for the hat to be passed up, I kept shaking the sick woman. Although her skin still bore red marks where she had been struck, her body was crumbling into sleep under my shaking, and she showed no signs of returning to consciousness. I took her by the hair and shook her head violently. Her eyes opened, but it was no more than that, for they remained fixed in a dull stare. Just then the hat arrived, with almost all the water gone. I poured into her mouth the few remaining drops, and for the first time she seemed to open her eyes of her own volition. She placed her hand on my knee and looked around the hut. I said, "It's water. You must drink it or you'll die." I lay her over my knee and waited for the next hat. Another came and again I poured the drops into her mouth. As I repeated this over and over I seemed to see the others, shouting as they scrambled one after another back up the steep cliff from the spring, their weary bodies caught in the moonlight, and exactly as though I were pouring distilled moonlight I poured the drops of water into the sick woman's mouth.

TRANSLATED BY DONALD KEENE

EARTH AND SOLDIERS

[Tsuchi to Heitai, 1938] by Hino Ashihei (born 1907)

The most famous literary products of the "China Incidents" of the thirties were the diaries written by Hino Ashihei, an official correspondent attached to the troops. The reading public of the time found such absorbing interest in the descriptions of the fighting, with its scenes of pathos and heroism, that, in the old phrase, "the price of paper rose." Hino has been denounced for his lack of a more critical attitude toward these wars of aggression, but it is undeniable that he accomplished brilliantly the task of making reportage into a work of artistry.

•

October 28, 1937
Aboard the (Censored) *Maru.*

Dear Brother:

Again today, there is the blue sky and the blue water. And here I am writing this while lying on the upper deck of the same boat. I wish this were being written at the front, but not yet. All I can tell you is about the soldiers, lolling about the boat, the pine groves and the winding, peaceful line of the Japanese coast. What will be our fate? Nobody knows. The speculation about our point of disembarkation is still going on. Rumors that we are bound for Manchukuo are gaining strength.

Besides, there is a well-founded report that on the Shanghai front, where there has been a stalemate, our troops attacked and fought a ferocious battle. The story is that two days ago they advanced in force and rolled back the line for several miles, taking two important Chinese cities. They say that big lantern parades are swirling through the streets of Tokyo, in celebration. So the war is over! And we are to be returned, like victorious troops. That would be funny, in our case, but anyway, we are to be sent home soon!

Of course, this is nonsense, some absolutely ridiculous story. Yet we cannot avoid listening when someone talks in this vein. We cannot believe it and yet we do not wish to convince ourselves that it is not true.

This sort of life, while it is bad for the men because it is too easy, is even worse for the war horses, down in the hatch. They have been stabled below decks, in a dark and unhealthy hole. Sometimes, you can see them, clear down in the hold, standing patiently in the darkness. Some have not survived so well. They have lost weight. Their ribs are showing and they look sickly.

They have the best in food and water. Actually, they get better care than the men. Does it surprise you to know that, in war, a horse may be much more valuable than a man? For example, the horses get all the water they need. On the other hand, the supply of water for the men is limited, barely enough for washing, let alone the daily bath to which we are accustomed.

From that standpoint, the horses are much better off than we are. But the poor creatures have no opportunity for exercising, breathing fresh air, and feeling the sunlight. They are growing weaker. With my own eyes, I have seen a number of them collapse.

I never looked at a war horse, without thinking of poor Yoshida Uhei, who lives on the hillside, back of our town. In my memory, they are always together, just as they were before the war ever came. It is impossible to disassociate one from the other.

Perhaps you do not remember Uhei. He was a carter. He had a wagon, with which he did hauling jobs. His horse, Kichizo, drew it.

In all my life, I have never known such affection between man and animal. Kichizo was a big, fine chestnut, with great, wide shoulders and chest, and a coat like velvet. It used to shimmer in the sun and you could see the muscles rippling underneath the skin. Uhei cared for Kichizo like a mother with a baby.

I suppose this can be explained, at least in part, by the fact that Uhei had no children. He was already past forty, but his wife had never conceived. Undoubtedly, Uhei long ago gave up hope of having a child. So all his affection turned toward Kichizo, the horse. You have heard fathers brag about their sons? In a way, he did the same thing about Kichizo. "What strength!" he would say, "and yet how gentle he can be. He's a dear fellow, that Kichizo, even though he is so big and strong."

Then the war came. It came clear down to our little town, into the nooks and corners of the country, taking men and horses. Kichizo was commandeered by the army.

When he heard the news, Uhei was speechless with surprise for a while. I remember it very well. "The army needs your horse, Uhei," someone told him. "It is for the nation." Uhei looked at the speaker with dumb disbelief in his face. His eyes were frozen, uncomprehending. "Don't worry," they told him, "Kichizo will be all right. He isn't a cavalry horse. He won't be in any danger. They'll use him behind the lines, to pull wagons. It won't be anything different than what he does here. And the army takes good care of its horses. They're very important. Don't you worry about him."

Uhei turned away without speaking and began to run toward his home. He broke into a dead run, like a crazy man, and we saw him disappear behind the bend in the road. "He'll be all right," somebody said, "after all, it's only a horse."

That same afternoon, Uhei came back to town. He looked different then. He was smiling and his eyes were shining, and he swaggered around the streets. "Have you heard the news?" he kept saying, "Kichizo, my horse, is going to the war. They need big strong fellows for the army, so of course Kichizo was the first horse they thought about. They know what they're doing, those fellows. They know a real horse when they see one."

He went to the flagmaker and ordered a long banner, exactly like the ones people have when a soldier is called to the war.

"Congratulations to Kichizo on his entry into the army," this banner said, in large, vivid characters. Uhei posted a long pole in front of his house, high on the hillside, and attached this banner. It streamed out in the wind, where everyone could see. Uhei was bursting with pride. As soon as the banner was up, he took Kichizo out from the field and pointed up to where it floated gracefully above the house. "You see that, Kichizo," he said. "That's for you. You're a hero. You've brought honor to this village."

Meanwhile, Uhei's wife, O-shin, was carrying this human symbolism even further. She bought a huge piece of cloth and began preparing a "thousand-stitches belt" for the horse.[1]

This cloth that O-shin bought was big enough to cover four or five men. When she stood in the street, asking passers-by to sew a stitch, they all laughed, but they did it. She had a needle that she borrowed from a matmaker to do such a big piece of work. When the stitches were all in, she herself worked all through one night, finishing the belt. It was very difficult, with such a big needle, but she finished it.

They put the good-luck belt around Kichizo's middle, just as though he were a soldier. At the same time, Uhei visited a number of different shrines in the neighborhood and bought lucky articles. O-shin sewed them into the belt.

And finally, he gave a farewell party and invited all the neighbors. Uhei was not a rich man and he couldn't afford it. If he had any savings, they were all spent that night. I was among those he invited. I took, as a gift, a bottle of wine.

Most of the guests were already there, in Uhei's neat little house, by the time I arrived. They were in good humor, laughing and drinking. Uhei was excited and bustling around, seeing to everything. His eyes were glistening. "Yes, it's rare to find such a wonderful horse," he said. "You seldom find a horse with so much spirit and intelligence and at the same time so strong and vigorous. Oh, he'll show them! I'm so happy. Have a drink! Have many cups of wine for this happy occasion!"

There were tears rolling down his cheeks as he spoke and the bitter salt mingled with the wine he was drinking. Everyone was making a noise, laughing and talking and roaring jokes. O-shin kept

[1] The "thousand-stitches belt" is a talisman, with red threads sewn by well-wishers for a Japanese soldier when he leaves for the front. It is supposed to protect him from wounds.

hustling in and out of the kitchen, bringing hot food and warming the wine. She was a plain little thing, drab, I used to think. But that night, smiling and exuberant, she seemed transformed and almost beautiful.

When the party was at its height, Uhei suddenly jumped up from the table and ran outside. We heard the heavy clomp-clomp of a horse, walking through the front yard. And then, through an open window, Kichizo's long graceful neck came in. His head stretched all the way to the banquet table. He looked at us gravely; I again had the feeling that he knew all about this occasion, and knew it was for him, and what it meant.

Uhei ran into the room again and threw his arms around the horse's neck, and gave him boiled lobster and some octopus, and poured the ceremonial wine into his mouth. "To Kichizo," he cried. "Dear, brave Kichizo!" We all stood and drank and roared "Banzai!" three times. It must have seemed a little silly and sentimental. Yet, Uhei had inoculated us all with something of the love he had for that horse and it seemed natural enough to us.

In the later afternoon of the next day, I saw Uhei at Hospital Hill, returning from the army station. He had delivered Kichizo to them. I spoke to him, but he seemed not to recognize me, nor to have heard my voice, for he walked on a few paces. Then he turned and acknowledged the greeting in a distant, absent-minded sort of way. He looked haggard and sickly, as though he had lost his strength, and he left me hurriedly. All he said was "Kichizo has gone."

Later, someone told me how he brought the horse to the station. It was a terribly warm day. So Uhei took his own grass hat, cut two holes in the side for Kichizo's ears, and put it on the horse's head. Poor Kichizo, that heavy "thousand-stitches belt" must have been very warm and uncomfortable in such weather. Besides, Uhei had decorated him with national flags, so that he looked like some sacred animal on the way to dedication at a shrine. I suppose he felt just that way about him.

O-shin accompanied them, holding the reins, as they walked to the station. It was a curious and sad little trio, the man and woman with that great sleek horse in its strange attire, walking slowly down the hillside, through the village and up the other side. Everyone watched silently. No one laughed.

At the army station, a good many other horses were already gathered together in the yard. They had been examined by the army veterinarians before being accepted. Now they were merely waiting to be taken away on the train. No one knew just when it would come.

O-shin left immediately, but Uhei stayed and stayed beside Kichizo, patting its hip and running his fingers through its mane. At first, the soldiers laughed, just as the people in the village had done. But they soon saw how Uhei felt about his horse and then they told him, kindly. "Don't cry, Uncle. It's a great promotion for your horse, isn't it? He's going to serve the nation now, instead of pulling a cart around the village. That's something, isn't it? Well, then, cheer up. Besides, he'll get better care in the army than you could ever give him. Don't you worry. He's going to be all right." So they tried to console Uhei. Nevertheless, he stayed until dark.

Early the next day, he was back at the army station, fussing over Kichizo. Of course, there was nothing to be done. The army grooms had already cared for and fed and watered the horses, but the poor man wanted to see for himself. He clucked around Kichizo like a hen with its chicks. Not that day, nor for several days afterward, did the train come to take the horses away.

It was quite a distance from Uhei's house to the army station, but he came every day, faithfully. He came early and stayed until dusk.

At last the fatal day came. All the horses were loaded on the train and taken to the harbor, where they went aboard the transports. Uhei went along. He went as far as they would let him and then the grooms again told him not to worry, and promised they would take good care of Kichizo. He bowed, eyes brimming with tears. He bowed and bowed, and could only mumble, "Thanks, thanks, very much."

As the boat moved out of the harbor, he ran up to a bridge overlooking the water. It was high above the water and he stayed there until the very smoke from the steamer had vanished beneath the horizon. He waved his flag and shouted, "Kichizo," until he was hardly able to speak. And he kept his eyes riveted on the spot where the ship had disappeared.

This is all I know about the story. When I was called to the front, he was the first to come and wish me luck and help me with my preparations. On the day I left, he came again to the harbor and begged me to look out for Kichizo. "You know him," he said, eagerly. "You couldn't miss him among a thousand horses. Anyway, he has a small white spot on his left side and, on the opposite hip, the character 'Kichi' is branded. You couldn't miss him."

"If I see him, I'll be sure and write to you," I said.

"Remember, he's a beautiful reddish chestnut," Uhei continued. "Yes, tell me if you see him. And please say something to him about me. That would seem strange to you, wouldn't it, talking to a horse? All right, but just pat him on the nose, once or twice."

It seems cold and unkind of me, but only once have I asked about Kichizo since I came aboard this boat. The groom said he had not seen any such horse. Nor have I, although I have not tried to examine all the horses. But when I see one of them fall sick and die, and then go over the side to the small boat, I cannot help but recall Uhei. For his sake, I hope nothing like this has happened to Kichizo.

Speaking of the "thousand-stitches belt" reminds me of a recent episode that may give you a clear insight into our minds and hearts, these days.

As you know, there is not a man aboard ship without one of these belts. They encircle every waist and each stitch carries a prayer for safety. Mine is of white silk and has a number of charms sewn into it. I do not understand the symbolism connected with each. Some are Buddhist and others Shinto. It makes no difference, of course. All are supposed to afford protection from wounds.

Mother gave me an embroidered charm bag, which contains a talisman of the "Eight Myriads of Deities," and a "Buddha from Three Thousand Worlds." In addition to those, I have an image of the Buddha, three inches in height, of exquisite workmanship. This was a present from Watabe, who lives on the hillside. When he gave it to me, he said it had been through three wars. "No bullet ever touched the man who wore it," he said. "It is a wonderful charm." Three different soldiers had carried it in the Boxer Rebellion, the first Sino-Japanese War, and the Russo-Japanese War. According to his story, they came through without a scratch.

All the men on this ship are loaded with tokens and amulets and belts and mementoes from their family and friends. On warm days, when we take off our shirts, these articles are seen everywhere. I do not mean to scorn them, but it would be interesting to study them all, with the superstitions they embody. However, one cannot disregard the heartfelt sentiment connected with them.

There was one man who did scoff at them, and in no uncertain terms, either. He no longer does so. This man, Corporal Tachibana, is quite a character. He says he is an atheist. He likes to talk about his ideas and he deliberately provokes arguments, in which he stoutly defends the materialistic point of view. In these, he employs big, pedantic words that so puzzle the men that they cannot reply. Personally, I doubt that he himself understands the meaning of all the words he uses.

Particularly when he has had a little wine, Corporal Tachibana used to like to ridicule the men about their charms and talismans. "Absurd," he would say. "Absolutely ridiculous! If we could really protect ourselves with such things, there never would be anyone killed in war. The Chinese would use them, too, and so would every other kind of soldier. Then what kind of a war could you have, if nobody was killed? It is nonsense, and it is not befitting a member of the imperial army to do such things."

Of course, this was perfectly true and the men knew it. But still they believed in their pitiful little articles, the luck charms. To me, it seemed cruel and heartless of him. If he himself preferred not to place any stock in these ideas, very well. But why should he shake the faith of simple men who did? Strangely enough, however, he himself had a "thousand-stitches belt" around his middle.

One day recently, when it was very hot, we were all on the upper deck, lying in the shade. Suddenly, without a word, Corporal Tachibana jumped over the side and landed with a magnificent splash. He is not a good swimmer, and when the foam and spray disappeared, we saw him sink. Then he reappeared, churning the water with his arms and legs. Immediately, two of the men stripped and dived in after him. At the cry, "Man overboard," a boat was lowered.

They pulled him into the boat and finally brought him up on deck again. His dripping hair was hanging over his face and his stomach heaved. In his right hand was his "thousand-stitches belt"!

As soon as he caught his breath, he explained that when he pulled off his shirt, his belt came with it and the wind blew it into the sea. When he saw it fluttering into the water, he jumped after it.

"Not because I was afraid of being shot, if I lost it," he said, grinning. "I don't believe it can protect me in war. But my folks were so sincere about it that I couldn't just lose it in the ocean, this way. So I had to get it."

He must have thought we did not believe him, for he added, "The prayers of my people, reflecting on my brain, made me do it." Men who had been listening to him, with sly smiles on their faces, suddenly grew serious. The joking stopped. Inadvertently, it seemed to me, he had denied his own arguments and revealed a belief little different from that of the other men. Unconsciously, I put my hand on my own belt.

So much for today, I will write again soon.

TRANSLATED BY BARONESS SHIDZUÉ ISHIMOTO

THE MOLE

[*Hokuro no Tegami, 1940*] *by Kawabata Yasunari (born 1899)*

"The Mole" is a product of Kawabata's period of full maturity, and reveals the mastery of the psychology of women which is perhaps the outstanding feature of his writings.

•

Last night I dreamed about that mole.

I need only write the word for you to know what I mean. That mole—how many times have I been scolded by you because of it.

It is on my right shoulder, or perhaps I should say high on my back.

"It's already bigger than a bean. Go on playing with it and it will be sending out shoots one of these days."

You used to tease me about it. But as you said, it was large for a mole, large and wonderfully round and swollen.

As a child I used to lie in bed and play with that mole. How ashamed I was when you first noticed it.

I even wept, and I remember your surprise.

"Stop it, Sayoko. The more you touch it the bigger it will get." My mother scolded me too. I was still a child, probably not yet thirteen, and afterwards I kept the habit to myself. It persisted after I had all but forgotten about it.

When you first noticed it, I was still more child than wife. I wonder if you, a man, can imagine how ashamed I was. But it was more than shame. This is dreadful, I thought to myself. Marriage seemed at that moment a fearful thing indeed.

I felt as though all my secrets had been discovered—as though you had bared secret after secret of which I was not even conscious myself—as though I had no refuge left.

You went off happily to sleep, and sometimes I felt relieved, and a little lonely, and sometimes I pulled myself up with a start as my hand traveled to the mole again.

"I can't even touch my mole any more," I thought of writing to my mother, but even as I thought of it I felt my face go fiery red.

"But what nonsense to worry about a mole," you once said. I was happy, and I nodded, but looking back now, I wonder if it would not have been better if you had been able to love that wretched habit of mine a little more.

I did not worry so very much about the mole. Surely people do not go about looking down women's necks for moles. Sometimes the expression "unspoiled as a locked room" is used to describe a deformed girl. But a mole, no matter how large it is, can hardly be called a deformity.

Why do you suppose I fell into the habit of playing with that mole?

And why did the habit annoy you so?

"Stop it," you would say. "Stop it." I do not know how many hundred times you scolded me.

"Do you have to use your left hand?" you asked once in a fit of irritation.

"My left hand?" I was startled by the question.

It was true. I had not noticed before, but I always used my left hand.

"It's on your right shoulder. Your right hand should be better."

"Oh?" I raised my right hand. "But it's strange."

"It's not a bit strange."

"But it's more natural with my left hand."

"The right hand is nearer."

"It's backwards with my right hand."

"Backwards?"

"Yes, it's a choice between bringing my arm in front of my neck or reaching around in back like this." I was no longer agreeing meekly with everything you said. Even as I answered you, though, it came to me that when I brought my left arm around in front of me it was as though I were warding you off, as though I were embracing myself. I have been cruel to him, I thought.

I asked quietly, "But what is wrong with using my left hand?"

"Left hand or right hand, it's a bad habit."

"I know."

"Haven't I told you time and time again to go to a doctor and have the thing removed?"

"But I couldn't. I'd be ashamed to."

"It would be a very simple matter."

"Who would go to a doctor to have a mole removed?"

"A great many people seem to."

"For moles in the middle of the face, maybe. I doubt if anyone goes to have a mole removed from the neck. The doctor would laugh. He would know I was there because my husband had complained."

"You could tell him it was because you had a habit of playing with it."

"Really. . . . Something as insignificant as a mole, in a place where you can't even see it. I should think you could stand at least that much."

"I wouldn't mind the mole if you wouldn't play with it."

"I don't mean to."

"You are stubborn, though. No matter what I say, you make no attempt to change yourself."

"I do try. I even tried wearing a high-necked nightgown so that I wouldn't touch it."

"Not for long."

"But is it so wrong for me to touch it?" I suppose I must have seemed to be fighting back.

"It's not wrong, especially. I only ask you to stop because I don't like it."

"But why do you dislike it so?"

"There's no need to go into the reasons. You don't need to play with that mole, and it's a bad habit, and I wish you would stop."

"I've never said I won't stop."

"And when you touch it you always get that strange, absent-minded expression on your face. That's what I really hate."

You're probably right—something made the remark go straight to my heart, and I wanted to nod my agreement.

"Next time you see me doing it, slap my hand. Slap my face even."

"But doesn't it bother you that even though you've been trying for two or three years you haven't been able to cure a trivial little habit like that by yourself?"

I did not answer. I was thinking of your words, "That's what I really hate."

That pose, with my left arm drawn up around my neck—it must look somehow dreary, forlorn. I would hesitate to use a grand word like "solitary." Shabby, rather, and mean, the pose of a woman concerned only with protecting her own small self. And the expression on my face must be just as you described it, "strange, absent-minded."

Did it seem a sign that I had not really given myself to you, as though a space lay between us? And did my true feelings come out on my face when I touched the mole and lost myself in reverie, as I had done since I was a child?

But it must have been because you were already dissatisfied with me that you made so much of that one small habit. If you had been pleased with me you would have smiled and thought no more about it.

That was the frightening thought. I trembled when it came to me of a sudden that there might be men who would find the habit charming.

It was your love for me that first made you notice. I do not doubt that even now. But it is just this sort of small annoyance, as it grows and becomes distorted, that drives its roots down into a marriage. To a real husband and wife personal eccentricities have stopped mattering, and I suppose that on the other hand there are husbands and wives who find themselves at odds on everything. I do not say that those who accommodate themselves to each other necessarily love each other, and that those who constantly disagree hate each other. I do think, though, and I cannot get over thinking, that it would have been better if you could have brought yourself to overlook my habit of playing with the mole.

You actually came to beat me and to kick me. I wept and asked why you could not be a little less violent, why I had to suffer so because I touched my mole. That was only surface. "How can we cure it?" you said, your voice trembling, and I quite understood how you felt and did not resent what you did. If I had told anyone of this, no doubt you would have seemed a violent husband. But since we had reached a point where the most trivial matter added to the tension between us, your hitting me actually brought a sudden feeling of release.

"I will never get over it, never. Tie up my hands." I brought my hands together and thrust them at your chest, as though I were giving myself, all of myself, to you.

You looked confused, your anger seemed to have left you limp and drained of emotion. You took the cord from my sash and tied my hands with it.

I was happy when I saw the look in your eyes, watching me try to smooth my hair with my bound hands. This time the long habit might be cured, I thought.

Even then, however, it was dangerous for anyone to brush against the mole.

And was it because afterwards the habit came back that the last of your affection for me finally died? Did you mean to tell me that you had given up and that I could very well do as I pleased? When I played with the mole, you pretended you did not see, and you said nothing.

Then a strange thing happened. Presently the habit which scolding and beating had done nothing to cure—was it not gone? None of the extreme remedies worked. It simply left of its own accord.

"What do you know—I'm not playing with the mole any more." I said it as though I had only that moment noticed. You grunted, and looked as if you did not care.

If it mattered so little to you, why did you have to scold me so, I wanted to ask; and I suppose you for your part wanted to ask why, if the habit was to be cured so easily, I had not been able to cure it earlier. But you would not even talk to me.

A habit that makes no difference, that is neither medicine nor poison—go ahead and indulge yourself all day long if it pleases you. That is what the expression on your face seemed to say. I felt dejected. Just to annoy you, I thought of touching the mole again there in front of you, but, strangely, my hand refused to move.

I felt lonely. And I felt angry.

I thought too of touching it when you were not around. But somehow that seemed shameful, repulsive, and again my hand refused to move.

I looked at the floor, and I bit my lip.

"What's happened to your mole?" I was waiting for you to say, but after that the word "mole" disappeared from our conversation.

And perhaps many other things disappeared with it.

Why could I do nothing in the days when I was being scolded by you? What a worthless woman I am.

Back at home again, I took a bath with my mother.

"You're not as good-looking as you once were, Sayoko," she said. "You can't fight age, I suppose."

I looked at her, startled. She was as she had always been, plump and fresh-skinned.

"And that mole used to be rather attractive."

I have really suffered because of that mole—but I could not say that to my mother. What I did say was: "They say it's no trouble for a doctor to remove a mole."

"Oh? For a doctor . . . but there would be a scar." How calm and easygoing my mother is! "We used to laugh about it. We said that Sayoko was probably still playing with that mole even now that she was married."

"I was playing with it."

"We thought you would be."

"It was a bad habit. When did I start?"

"When do children begin to have moles, I wonder. You don't seem to see them on babies."

"My children have none."

"Oh? But they begin to come out as you grow up, and they never disappear. It's not often you see one this size, though. You must have had it when you were very small." My mother looked at my shoulder and laughed.

I remembered how, when I was very young, my mother and my sisters sometimes poked at the mole, a charming little spot then. And was that not why I had fallen into the habit of playing with it myself?

I lay in bed fingering the mole and trying to remember how it was when I was a child and a young woman.

It was a very long time since I had last played with it. How many years, I wonder.

Back in the house where I was born, away from you, I could play with it as I liked. No one would stop me.

But it was no good.

As my finger touched the mole, cold tears came to my eyes.

I meant to think of long ago, when I was young, but when I touched the mole all I thought of was you.

I have been damned as a bad wife, and perhaps I shall be divorced; but it would not have occurred to me that here in bed at home again I should have only these thoughts of you.

I turned over my damp pillow—and I even dreamed of the mole.

I could not tell after I awoke where the room might have been, but you were there, and some other woman seemed to be with us. I had been drinking. Indeed I was drunk. I kept pleading with you about something.

My bad habit came out again. I reached around with my left hand, my arm across my breast as always. But the mole—did it not come right off between my fingers? It came off painlessly, quite as though that were the most natural thing in the world. Between my fingers it felt exactly like the skin of a roast bean.

Like a spoiled child I asked you to put my mole in the pit of that mole beside your nose.

I pushed my mole at you. I cried and clamored, I clutched at your sleeve and hung on your chest.

When I awoke the pillow was still wet. I was still weeping.

I felt tired through and through. And at the same time I felt light, as though I had laid down a burden.

I lay smiling for a time, wondering if the mole had really disappeared. I had trouble bringing myself to touch it.

That is all there is to the story of my mole.

I can still feel it like a black bean between my fingers.

I have never thought much about that little mole beside your nose, and I have never spoken of it, and yet I suppose I have had it always on my mind.

What a fine fairy story it would make if your mole really were to swell up because you put mine in it.

And how happy I would be if I thought you in your turn had dreamed of my mole.

I have forgotten one thing.

"That's what I hate," you said, and so well did I understand that I even thought the remark a sign of your affection for me. I thought that all the meanest things in me came out when I fingered the mole.

I wonder, however, if a fact of which I have already spoken does not redeem me: it was perhaps because of the way my mother and sisters petted me that I first fell into the habit of fingering the mole.

"I suppose you used to scold me when I played with the mole," I said to my mother, "a long time ago."

"I did—it was not so long ago, though."

"Why did you scold me?"

"Why? It's a bad habit, that's all."

"But how did you feel when you saw me playing with the mole?"

"Well . . ." My mother cocked her head to one side. "It wasn't becoming."

"That's true. But how did it look? Were you sorry for me? Or did you think I was nasty and hateful?"

"I didn't really think about it much. It just seemed as though you could as well leave it alone, with that sleepy expression on your face."

"You found me annoying?"

"It did bother me a little."

"And you and the others used to poke at the mole to tease me?"

"I suppose we did."

If that is true, then wasn't I fingering the mole in that absent way to remember the love my mother and sisters had for me when I was young?

Wasn't I doing it to think of the people I loved?

This is what I must say to you.

Weren't you mistaken from beginning to end about my mole?

Could I have been thinking of anyone else when I was with you?

Over and over I wonder whether the gesture you so disliked might not have been a confession of a love that I could not put into words.

My habit of playing with the mole is a small thing, and I do not mean to make excuses for it; but might not all of the other things that turned me into a bad wife have begun in the same way? Might they not have been in the beginning expressions of my love for you, turned to unwifeliness only by your refusal to see what they were?

Even as I write I wonder if I do not sound like a bad wife trying to seem wronged. Still there are these things that I must say to you.

TRANSLATED BY EDWARD SEIDENSTICKER

Night Train

The pale light of daybreak—
The fingerprints are cold on the glass door,
And the barely whitening edges of the mountains
Are still as quicksilver.
As yet the passengers do not awaken;
Only the electric light pants wearily.
The sickeningly sweet odor of varnish,
Even the indistinct smoke of my cigar,
Strikes my throat harshly on the night train.
How much worse it must be for her, another man's wife.
Haven't we passed Yamashina yet?
She opens the valve of her air pillow
And watches as it gradually deflates.
Suddenly in sadness we draw to one another.
When I look out of the train window, now close to dawn,
In a mountain village at an unknown place
Whitely the columbines are blooming.

Cats

Two pitch-black cats
On a melancholy night roof,
From the tip of their taut tails
A threadlike crescent moon hovers hazily.
"Owaa. Good evening."
"Owaa. Good evening."
"Ogyaa. Ogyaa. Ogyaa."
"Owaa. The master of this house is ill."

Harmful Animals

Particularly
When something like a dog is barking
When something like a goose is born a freak
When something like a fox is luminous
When something like a tortoise crystallizes
When something like a wolf slides by
All these things are harmful to the health of man.

The Corpse of a Cat

The spongelike scenery
Is gently swollen by moisture.
No sign of man or beast in sight.
A water wheel is weeping.
From the blurred shadow of a willow
I see the gentle form of a woman waiting.
Wrapping her thin shawl around her,
Dragging her lovely vaporous garments,
She wanders calmly, like a spirit.
Ah, Ura, lonely woman!
"You're always late, aren't you?"
We have no past, no future,
And have faded away from the things of reality.
Ura!
Here in this weird landscape,
Bury the corpse of the drowned cat!

The New Road of Koide

The road that has newly been opened here
Goes, I suppose, straight to the city.
I stand at a crossway of the new road,
Uncertain of the lonely horizon.
Dark, melancholy day.

The sun is low over the roofs of the row of houses.
The unfelled trees in the woods stand sparsely.
How, how, to restore myself to what I was?
On this road I rebel against and will not travel,
The new trees have all been felled.

Hagiwara Sakutarō (1886-1942)

Composition 1063

Ours are simple fences in the Ainu style.
We plotted and replotted mulberry trees
In our inch of garden,
But even so, couldn't make a living.
In April
The water of the Nawashiro was black,
Tiny eddies of dark air
Fell like pellets from the sky
And birds
Flew by with raucous calls.
These fields full of horned stones
Where horsetails and wormwood have sprouted
Are cultivated by women
Dropping their litters
Patching together the ragged clothes of the older children,
Cooking and doing the village chores,
Shouldering the family discontents and desires,
With a handful of coarse food
And six hours sleep the year round.
And here
If you plant two bushels of buckwheat you get back four.
Are these people, I wonder,
So much unlike
The many revolutionaries tied up in prisons,
The artists starved by their luck,
Those heroes of our time?

Miyazawa Kenji (1896-1933)

Song

Don't sing
Don't sing of scarlet blossoms or the wings of dragonflies
Don't sing of murmuring breezes or the scent of a woman's
  hair.
All of the weak, delicate things
All the false, lying things
All the languid things, omit.
Reject every elegance
And sing what is wholly true,
Filling the stomach,
Flooding the breast at the moment of desperation,
Songs which rebound when beaten
Songs which scoop up courage from the pit of shame.
These songs
Sing in a powerful rhythm with swelling throats!
These songs
Hammer into the hearts of all who pass you by!

Nakano Shigeharu (born 1902)

Spring Snow

It has snowed in a place where snow rarely falls,
Steadily, piling into drifts.
The snow covers all things
And all that it covers is beautiful.
Are people, I wonder, prepared for the ugliness of the thaw?

Early Spring

Midnight
A rain mixed with snow fell,
It trickled desolately on the bamboo thicket.
The dream dealt with another's heart.
When I awoke
The pillow was cold with tears.

—What has happened to my heart?
The sun shines in mildly from tall windows,
A humming rises from the steelworks.
I got out of bed
And poked with a stick the muck in the ditch;
The turbid water slowly began to move.
A little lizard had yielded himself to the current.
In the fields
I push open black earth.
The wheat sprouts greenly grow.
—You can trust the earth.

Kitagawa Fuyuhiko (born 1900)

Morning Song

On the ceiling: the color of vermilion
  Light leaking in through a crack in the door
Evokes a rustic military band—my hands
  Have nothing whatever to do.

I cannot hear the song of little birds.
  The sky today must be a faded blue.
Weary—too tired to remonstrate
  With anyone else's ideas.

In the scent of resin the morning is painful,
  Lost, the various, various dreams.
The standing woods are singing in the wind.

Flatly spread out the sky,
  Along the bank go vanishing
The beautiful, various dreams.

The Hour of Death

The autumn sky is a dull color
A light in the eyes of a black horse

The water dries up, the lily falls
The heart is hollow.

Without gods, without help
Close to the window a woman has died.
  The white sky was sightless
  The white wind was cold.

When she washed her hair by the window
Her arm was stemlike and soft
  The morning sun trickled down
  The sound of the water dripped.

In the streets there was noise:
The voices of children tangling.
But, tell me, what will happen to this soul?
Will it thin to nothingness?

Nakahara Chūya (1907-1937)

TRANSLATED BY DONALD KEENE

MODERN HAIKU: II

Isu yosete
Kiku no kaori ni
Mono wo kaku

Drawing up a chair
In the scent of chrysanthemums
I write my verses.

Mizuhara Shūōshi (born 1892)

The Imperial Tombs at Mukden

Ryō samuku
Jitsugetsu sora ni
Terashiau

The great tombs are cold:
In the sky the sun and moon
Stare at each other.

Kareno basha
Muchi pan-pan to
Sora wo utsu

In the withered fields
A horse-carriage whip sharply
Cracks against the sky.

An Ancient Statue of a Guardian King [1]

Kaze hikari
Mukabaki no kin
Hagiotosu

Wind and the sunlight—
Here, the gilt of a cuirass
Peels off and falls.

Natsu no kawa
Akaki tessa no
Hashi hitaru

The summer river—
The end of a red iron chain
Soaks in the water.

Yamaguchi Seishi (born 1901)

[1] At the Shin Yakushi-ji, a temple in Nara of the eighth century. The contrast is drawn between the sunshine outside and the silent darkness inside the building, where the once resplendent statue stands.

Guntai no	The tramping sound
Chikazuku oto ya	Of troops approaching
Shūfūri	In autumn wind.

Banryoku no	In the midst of
Uchi ya ako no ha	All things verdant, my baby
Haesomuru	Has begun to teethe.

Sora wa taisho no	The sky is the blue
Aosa tsuma yori	Of the world's beginning—from my wife
Ringo uku	I accept an apple.

Nakamura Kusatao (born 1901)

In the middle of the night there was a heavy air raid. Carrying my sick brother on my back I wandered in the flames with my wife in search of our children.

Hi no oku ni	In the depths of the flames
Botan kuzururu	I saw how a peony
Sama wo mitsu	Crumbles to pieces.

Kogarashi ya	Cold winter storm—
Shōdo no kinko	A safe-door in a burnt-out site
Fukinarasu	Creaking in the wind.

Fuyu kamome	The winter sea gulls—
Sei no ie nashi	In life without a house,
Shi no haka nashi	In death without a grave.

Katō Shūson (born 1905)

TRANSLATED BY DONALD KEENE

THE FIREFLY HUNT

[*Sasameyuki, III, 4*] *by Tanizaki Junichirō (born 1886)*

The publication of Tanizaki's novel Sasameyuki, *begun during the war, was discontinued by government order on the grounds that it was incompatible with wartime discipline, and not until 1946-1948, when the three volumes of the completed work finally appeared, could readers judge the magnitude and beauty of Tanizaki's masterpiece. The title of the work means, roughly, snow that is falling thinly as opposed to thickly falling flakes of snow, and refers to the fragile beauty of Yukiko, one of the four sisters around whom this novel of life in the Japan of 1936-1941 is centered.*

In the episode presented here, three of the sisters, together with the daughter of Sachiko, the second sister, go to visit a family named Sugano who live in the country.

•

It was a strange house, of course, but it was probably less the house than sheer exhaustion that kept Sachiko awake. She had risen early, she had been rocked and jolted by train and automobile through the heat of the day, and in the evening she had chased over the fields with the children, two or three miles it must have been. . . . She knew, though, that the firefly hunt would be pleasant to remember. . . . She had seen firefly hunts only on the puppet stage, Miyuki and Komazawa murmuring of love as they sailed down the River Uji; and indeed one should properly put on a long-sleeved kimono, a smart summer print, and run across the evening fields with the wind at one's sleeves, lightly taking up a firefly here and there from under one's fan. Sachiko was entranced with the picture. But a firefly hunt was, in fact, a good deal different. If you are going to play in the fields you had better change your clothes, they were told, and four muslin kimonos—prepared especially for them?—were laid out, each with a different pattern, as became their several ages. Not quite the way it looked in the pictures, laughed one of the sisters. It was almost dark, however, and it hardly mattered what they had on. They could still see each other's faces when they left the house, but by the time they reached the river it was only short of pitch dark. . . . A river it was called; actually it was no more than a ditch through the paddies, a little wider perhaps than most ditches, with plumes of grass bending over it from either bank and almost closing off the surface. A bridge was still dimly visible a hundred yards or so ahead. . . .

They turned off their flashlights and approached in silence; fireflies dislike noise and light. But even at the edge of the river there were no fireflies. Perhaps they aren't out tonight, someone whispered. No, there are plenty of them—come over here. Down into the grasses on the bank, and there, in that delicate moment before the last light goes, were fireflies, gliding out over the water in low arcs like the sweep of the grasses. . . . And on down the river, and on and on, were fireflies, lines of them wavering out from this bank and the other and back again . . . sketching their uncertain lines of light down close to the surface of the water, hidden from outside by the grasses. . . . In that last moment of light, with the darkness creeping up from the water and the moving plumes of grass still faintly outlined, there, far, far, far as the river stretched, an infinite number of little lines in two long lines on either side, quiet, unearthly. Sachiko could see it all even now, here inside with her eyes closed. . . . Surely it was the impressive moment of the evening, the moment that made the firefly hunt worth while. . . . A firefly hunt has indeed none of the radiance of a cherry blossom party. Dark, dreamy, rather . . . might one say? Perhaps something of the child's world, the world of the fairy story in it. . . . Something not to be painted but to be set to music, the mood of it taken up on a piano or a koto. . . . And while she lay with her eyes closed, the fireflies, out there along the river, all through the night, were flashing on and off, silent, numberless. Sachiko felt a wild, romantic surge, as though she were joining them there, soaring and dipping along the surface of the water, cutting her own uncertain line of light. . . .

It was rather a long little river, as she thought about it, that they followed after those fireflies. Now and then they crossed a bridge over or back . . . taking care not to fall in . . . watching for snakes, for snake eyes that glowed like fireflies. Sugano's six-year-old son, Sosuke, ran ahead in the darkness, thoroughly familiar with the land, and his father, who was guiding them, called uneasily after him, "Sosuke, Sosuke." No one worried any longer about frightening the fireflies, there were so many; indeed without this calling out to one another they were in danger of becoming separated, of being drawn apart in the darkness, each after his own fireflies. Once Sachiko and Yukiko were left alone on one bank, and from the other, now brought in clear and now blotted out by the wind, came voices calling, "Mother." "Where is Mother?" "Over here." "And Yukiko?" "She is over here too." "I've caught twenty-four already." "Don't fall in the river."

Sugano pulled up some grass along the path and tied it into something like a broom; to keep fireflies in, he said. There are places famous for fireflies, like Moriyama in Omi, or the outskirts of Gifu; but the fireflies there are protected, saved for important people. No one cares how many you take here, Sugano said; and Sugano took more than anyone. The two of them, father and son, went boldly down to the very edge of the water, and Sugano's bundle of grass became a jeweled broom. Sachiko and the rest began to wonder when he might be ready to think of going back. The wind is a little cold; don't you think perhaps. . . . But we are on the way back. We are going back by a different road. On they walked. It was farther than they had thought. And then they were at Sugano's back gate, everyone with a few captured fireflies, Sachiko and Yukiko with fireflies in their sleeves. . . .

The events of the evening passed through Sachiko's mind in no particular order. She opened her eyes—she might have been dreaming, she thought. Above her, in the light of the tiny bulb, she could see a framed kakemono that she had noticed earlier in the day: the words "Pavilion of Timelessness," written in large characters and signed by one Keido. Sachiko looked at the words without knowing who Keido might be. A flicker of light moved across the next room. A firefly, repelled by the mosquito incense, was hunting a way out. They had turned their fireflies loose in the garden earlier in the evening, and considerable numbers had flown into the house. But they had been careful to chase them out before closing the doors ror the night—where might this one have been hiding? In a last burst of energy it soared five or six feet into the air; then, exhausted, it glided across the room and lighted on Sachiko's kimono, hanging on the clothes rack. Over the printed pattern and into the sleeve it moved, flickering on through the dark cloth. The incense in the badger-shaped brazier was beginning to hurt Sachiko's throat. She got up to put it out, and while she was up moved on to see to the firefly. Carefully she took it up in a piece of paper—the idea of touching it repelled her—and pushed it out through a slot in the shutter. Of the scores of fireflies that had flickered through the shrubbery and along the edge of the lake earlier in the evening, there were almost none left—had they gone back to the river?—and the garden was lacquer-black.

TRANSLATED BY EDWARD SEIDENSTICKER

THE MOTHER OF CAPTAIN SHIGEMOTO

[*Shōshō Shigemoto no Haha, Chapters IX and X, 1950*]
by Tanizaki Junichirō

The Mother of Captain Shigemoto *is a novel of ninth-century Japan, and much of its material is based on actual events, as recorded in Heian literature. It deals mainly with an old man married to an extremely beautiful young wife who is his joy and treasure. The Prime Minister, hearing of her beauty, by a ruse manages to steal her from the old man, leaving him to spend his days in fruitless attempts to forget her. Captain Shigemoto was the child of the old man and his young wife, and he appears as a small boy in the following episode.*

•

Shigemoto had one terrible memory of his father. He could never forget it. His father was at the time in the habit of sitting for days and nights on end in quiet meditation, and Shigemoto, at length overcome with curiosity about when he ate and slept, stole away from the nurse one night to the altar room and, sliding the door open a crack, saw in the faint light his father still kneeling as he had been earlier in the day. Time passed and still he knelt motionless as a statue, and presently Shigemoto slid the door shut and went back to bed; but the next night curiosity came over him again, and again he went to look and saw his father as on the preceding night. And then, the third night it must have been, he was taken with the same curiosity and tiptoed to the altar room; but this time, as he looked through the narrow crack in the door, scarcely allowing himself to breathe, he noticed that the light on the tallow wick was flickering in spite of the stillness of the air, and at that moment his father's shoulders rose and his body moved. The motion was infinitely slow and deliberate. At first Shigemoto could not see what it meant, but presently his father, one hand pressed to the matting, his breathing heavy as though he were lifting an object of extraordinarily great weight, pushed his body from the floor and stood upright. Because of his age he could have gotten up but slowly in any case, and the long hours of unrelieved kneeling had so paralyzed his legs that he could pick himself up only with this special effort. In any case he was up, and he walked, almost staggered, from the room.

Shigemoto followed him, bewildered. His father's gaze was fixed dead ahead, he looked neither to the left nor to the right. He marched down the stairs, slipped his feet into a pair of sandals, stepped to the ground. The moon was a clear, crystalline white, and Shigemoto could remember a humming of insects that suggested the autumn; but he remembered too how when he slipped into a pair of grownup's sandals himself and went out into the garden, the soles of his feet were suddenly cold, as though he had stepped into water, and the bright moonlight, laying the landscape over white as with frost, made him feel that it could indeed have been winter. His father's shadow, swaying as he walked, was sharp against the ground. Shigemoto stayed far enough behind to avoid stepping on it. He would very probably have been seen had his father turned around, but his father seemed deep in meditation still, and when presently they had gone out the gate he walked firmly ahead as though he knew clearly where he was going.

An old man of eighty and a child of seven or eight could not have gone very far. Still to Shigemoto it seemed something of a walk. He followed his father at a distance, now seeing him and now cut off from him; but there were no other travelers on the road, and his father's figure reflected the moonlight so white in the distance that there was no chance of losing him. The road was lined at first with the earthen walls of fine mansions. Presently these gave way to poor fences of woven bamboo and to low, disconsolate roofs with shingles held down by stones, and these in turn became less regular, separated more and more by pools of water and by open spaces in which autumn grasses grew high. The insects in the clumps of grass were silent as the two approached, and began humming again as they moved away, noisier and noisier, now steady as a rain shower, the farther they walked from the city. Finally there were no houses at all, only a field of autumn grass stretching wide in every direction and a narrow country road twisting through it. There was but th one road, and yet as it wound now to the left and now to the right, lined with grasses taller than a man, Shigemoto's father sometimes disappeared from sight around a bend, and Shigemoto moved up to within ten or fifteen feet of him. The boy's sleeves and his skirt became soaked with dew as he separated the grasses that hung down over the road, and cold drops seeped down inside his collar.

His father crossed a bridge over a small river, and instead of following the road on ahead, turned downstream along the sand in the narrow river bottom. A hundred yards or so below, on a slightly raised stretch of level ground, there were three or four mounds of earth, each one soft and fresh, the tombstones above them a gleaming white, even the epitaphs clear in the moonlight. Some graves had small pines or cedars in place of tombstones; others had in place of the mound a railing with a heap of stones inside and on top of it a five-stone marker; and still others, the rudest of all, had neither stone nor mound, but only a straw mat to cover the body, and an offering of flowers. Several of the tombstones had fallen over in the recent storm, and a number of mounds had washed away, leaving parts of bodies exposed.

Shigemoto's father wandered among the mounds as though he were looking for something. Shigemoto followed, almost close enough now to step on his heels. If his father knew of it he gave no sign, not even once turning around. A dog, hungry for flesh, jumped suddenly from a clump of grass and scurried off somewhere, but Shigemoto's father did not glance up. The boy could tell even from behind that he was intent on his quest, that his whole spirit seemed poured into it. The old man stopped, and Shigemoto, stopping as suddenly, saw below him a sight that made his hair stand on end and his skin go cold.

The light of the moon, like a fall of snow, covered everything over with a phosphorescent light and obscured its form, and at first Shigemoto could not make out exactly what the strange object laid out there on the ground could be; but as he stared he saw that it was the bloated, rotting corpse of a young girl. He knew it was a young girl from the flesh of the limbs and from the color of parts of the skin. The long hair, however, had peeled off like a wig, scalp and all, the face was a lump that looked as though it had swollen up and been beaten flat, the entrails had begun to pour out, the body was crawling with maggots. One can perhaps imagine the horror of the scene, there in moonlight bright as day. Shigemoto stood as if tied to it, unable to turn his head, to move, much less to cry out. He looked at his father. His father had walked quietly up to the corpse, and now, bowing reverently before it, he knelt down on a straw mat beside it. Taking the same rigid, statue-like position he had had in the altar room, he lost himself again in meditation, sometimes looking down at the corpse, sometimes half-closing his eyes.

The moon came out yet brighter, as though polished to its last perfection. The solitude embracing them seemed to grow more intense. Except for a rustling in the autumn grasses as now and then a breeze passed, there was only the shrilling of the insects, ever louder. The sight of his father, kneeling there like a lone shadow, made Shigemoto feel as though he were being pulled into a world of eerie dreams; but, whether he wanted to return or not, the smell of putrefying flesh struck his nostrils with a force that brought him back to the real world.

It is not clear exactly where Shigemoto's father looked upon the dead woman. There were probably open charnels scattered over the Kyoto of the day. During epidemics of smallpox or measles, when the dead were many, a vacant space was chosen, any space would do, where bodies could be dumped and buried hurriedly under a token covering of earth or a straw mat, partly from fear of contagion, partly for want of better means of disposal. This no doubt was such a ground.

While his father knelt in meditation over the corpse, Shigemoto crouched behind the mound, trying to quiet his breath. The moon started down in the west, and as the cluster of grave markers behind which the boy was concealed sent a lengthening shadow off across the earth, his father at last arose and started back for the city. Shigemoto followed him along the road they had come. It was just as they crossed the little bridge and started off into the moor and the autumn grasses that Shigemoto was startled by his father's voice.

"My boy . . . my boy, what do you think I was doing there?" The old man stopped in the narrow road and turned back to wait for Shigemoto. "I knew you were following me. I had something to think about, and I let you do as you wanted."

Shigemoto said nothing. His father's voice grew softer, there was a gentleness in his manner. "I have no intention of scolding you, my boy. Tell me the truth. You were watching me from the start?"

"Yes." Shigemoto nodded. "I was worried about you," he added by way of apology.

"You thought I was crazy, didn't you?" His father's mouth twisted into a smile. Shigemoto would have guessed that he laughed a short, weak laugh, though it was too faint to hear. "You are not the only one. Everyone seems to think I am crazy. . . . But I'm not. There is a reason for what I did. I can tell you what it is if it will help you. . . . Will you listen to me?"

These are the things Shigemoto's father talked of as they walked side by side back to the city. There was no way for the boy to know even vaguely what they meant, and we have in his diary not his father's words but the adult observations Shigemoto later added. The question was that of the Buddhist "sense of foulness." I am ignorant myself of Buddhist teachings, and I have the gravest doubts whether I can get over a discussion of the problem without error. I am much indebted to a Tendai scholar whom I have frequently visited and who has lent me reference works. From the start I have seen that the problem is a complex one not to be mastered without effort. There would seem to be no need to become deeply involved here, however, and I shall touch on only those points that seem necessary to my story.

Though there may be others as good, I have found the best simple work on the subject to be that *Companion in Retirement* of which the author is either the priest Jichin or the priest Keisei, it has never been decided which. The *Companion* is a collection of anecdotes about the accomplishments of illustrious priests, and tales of conversion and salvation that were missed by earlier collections. In the first volume are stories like "How a Lowly Priest Perfected the Sense of Foulness in His Spare Time," "How a Lowly Individual Saw the Light After Viewing a Corpse Laid Out on a Moor," and "The Woman's Corpse in the River Bed at Karahashi," and in the second volume, "How the Lady in Waiting Displayed Her Foul Form." One can see well enough in stories like these what the sense of foulness is.

To take one example from the collection:

Long ago a saintly priest on Mt. Hiei near Kyoto had a lesser priest in his service. A priest the latter was called, but he was in fact little more than a temple servant who performed miscellaneous services for the sage. He was a young man of the greatest devotion and reliability, serving the sage well and carrying out his orders with never a mistake, and the sage had no little confidence in him. As time passed the young priest took to disappearing, no one knew where, when night fell, and returning again early the following morning. He must be visiting a woman at the foot of the mountain, the sage began to suspect. The latter's disappointment and annoyance, though he remained silent, were extreme. The youth would reappear in the morning looking somehow morose, crestfallen. He seemed to avoid the eyes of the other priests, to be always on the verge of tears; and the others, from the sage down, concluded that very likely the lady at the foot of the mountain was being difficult—undoubtedly that was it. One night the sage sent a man out to follow him. The young priest went down the west slope of the mountain to what are now the outskirts of Kyoto, and on to the Rendai Moor. The other followed after him, at a loss to explain what this might mean. The youth wandered over the moor, now here, now there, and presently, making his way up to an indescribably putrid corpse, lost himself in prayer beside it, opening his eyes, closing them, now and again giving himself up to the most unrestrained weeping. All through the night this continued, and when the dawn bells began to ring he finally dried his tears and went back up the mountain. The man following him was deeply moved. He too was in tears when he arrived back at the temple. What had happened? the sage asked. The fellow had reason to be gloomy, the other answered, and told everything he had seen. "And that is why he disappears every evening. Our crime has been a fearful one indeed for having doubted so saintly a person."

The sage was astonished. Thereafter he revered his subordinate as no ordinary individual. One morning when the youth had brought in the porridge for breakfast, the sage, making sure that no one else was present, turned to him. "They say you've mastered the sense of foulness. I wonder if it's true."

"It is not. That is for the great ones with learning, not for the likes of me. You should be able to tell from looking at me whether I would be capable of anything like that."

"No, no—everyone knows about it. As a matter of fact I've been doing honor to you myself for some time now. You must tell me everything."

"Perhaps I can say something, then. I don't pretend to have gone very far, but I begin to think I understand a little."

"You will surely be able to give us a sign of what you have done. Suppose you try concentrating on this porridge."

The young priest took the tray, put a cover on the porridge, and for a time closed his eyes in intense meditation. When he took off the lid the porridge had changed to a mass of white worms. The sage wept unashamedly. "You shall be my teacher," he said, and brought the palms of his hands together in supplication.

—That is the story of "How a Lowly Priest Perfected the Sense of Foulness in His Spare Time." It is, the author of the *Companion in Retirement* adds, a "most edifying one"; and the founder of the Tendai sect too has written that it is possible for even the unwise to gain insight into the nature of things by going to the edge of a grave and looking at a foul corpse. Our humble priest no doubt knew of the method. It is written in the *Method of Suspension and Contemplation*[1] that "mountains and rivers are foul, food and

[1] *Maka Shikan*, a major text of the Tendai sect of Buddhism.

clothing are foul, rice is like white worms, clothing is like the skin of a stinking thing." So wonderful was the understanding of the priest that quite spontaneously his works fell into harmony with the teachings of the holy texts. An Indian monk once said that a bowl is like a skull and rice like worms, and in China the priest Tao Hsüan taught that a bowl is like a man's bones and rice like his flesh. But a thing of surpassing promise it was for an ignorant priest, who can have known nothing of these pronouncements, to be able to demonstrate their truth. Even if one cannot follow him to the ultimate point he reached, one can still find the five desires growing weaker, the workings of the spirit changing, if one but recognizes the principle taught. "Those who have not seen the truth are stirred to the deepest covetousness by that which seems of good quality, and their resentment is not small at the rag that seems the opposite; the fine and the base may change, but that from which arises the cycle of birth and rebirth is eternal. . . . How pitiful, how profitless are worldly illusions. One can but think that only the trivia of a dream cause men to look with dread on resting in the eternal."

To come back to our story. It is clear from Shigemoto's diary that his father too was trying to train himself to the sense of foulness, that the enchanting figure of the beauty who had deserted him—the "lost crane" of the Po Chü-i poem, "whose voice has gone silent behind the green clouds, whose shadow is sunk in the brightness of the moon"—was always with him; and that in the excess of his grief he had summoned up his will to beat back the vision. He first explained the sense of foulness that night, then told how he wanted somehow to forget his bitterness at the woman who had deserted him, and his love for her, to wipe away the image still shining in his heart, to put an end to his suffering. Some might consider him insane, he said; but such was the discipline he had chosen.

"Then you've been out before?" Shigemoto asked. His father nodded with the greatest emphasis. For some months now, choosing moonlit nights, he had waited for the house to be quiet and gone out in search of enlightenment, not to one specific place but to any charnel on the edge of the moor, and had stolen back again at dawn.

"And has it helped you?" Shigemoto asked.

"No." His father stood quiet in the road. He heaved a deep sigh and looked off toward the moon over the distant hills. "It hasn't helped me forget. This enlightenment isn't so easy to come by as they say." He ignored Shigemoto after that even when the boy spoke to him, and captive of his thoughts, said scarcely a word the rest of the way back to the house.

That was the only night Shigemoto went out after his father. Since his father had stolen out unnoticed so many times before, undoubtedly he wandered out afterwards too. Late the next night, for instance, Shigemoto thought he heard his father's door open softly. His father did not ask him to come along, however, and Shigemoto did not try to follow.

Sometimes in later years Shigemoto wondered what could have made his father pour forth his heart thus for a still naive and uncomprehending child; but that was the only time in his life that he and his father talked together at such length. I use the expression "talk together" although in fact his father did most of the talking. At first the words were grave, they had a gloomy heaviness that weighed down the boy's heart, but presently it was as though the old man was appealing to his son, and at the end—Shigemoto could not be sure it was not his imagination—the voice seemed to contain a sob. Shigemoto could remember a childish fear that his father, so deranged that he quite forgot it was but a small child he was talking to, could not hope for enlightenment, that his labors would come to nothing. Shigemoto was sorry for his father, tormented day and night by that beloved image until he sought relief in the way of the Buddha. He could think of his father as a wretched and piteous figure. But, to speak plainly, Shigemoto could not repress a certain hostility, very near anger, at the father who made no attempt to preserve the beautiful figure of his mother, who sought rather to turn it into the loathsome image of a corpse left by the road, into a thing putrid and revolting.

He was only a little short, indeed, of calling out to his father, "I want to ask a favor. Please don't turn my mother's memory into something dirty." Several times during the talk he was on the point of bursting out with it, and each time he was only able to restrain himself with difficulty.

Some ten months later, toward the end of the following year, his father died. Was he able finally to gain release from the world of fleshly desire? Was he able to see her for love of whom he had so burned as no more than a worthless lump of putrefying flesh; was he able to die purified, ennobled, enlightened? Or was he, as young Shigemoto had foreseen, even at the last unredeemed by the Buddha; was that eighty-year-old breast, when it drew its final breath, aflame with passion, tortured again by the image of its love? Shigemoto had no way of knowing. To judge from the fact that his father's death was not one to arouse envy for its peace and repose, however, Shigemoto thought that those forebodings of his had not been without point.

Ordinary human sentiment would suggest that a husband unable to forget his runaway wife might do well to love all the more the only son she has borne him, that he might try to ease his pain even a little by transferring some of his affection to the boy. Shigemoto's father made no such attempt. If he could not have back the wife who had deserted him, he would not be distracted, he would not be led aside, by anyone else, not even by the child in whom his blood was joined to hers—so intense was the love of Shigemoto's father for his mother. Shigemoto had some few memories of times when his father had spoken softly to him, but without exception they were occasions when the two were talking of Shigemoto's mother, and on any other subject his father was only chilly to him. Shigemoto did not resent his father's coldness. As a matter of fact it made him happy to think that his father was so filled with love for his mother that he could give no attention to the child Shigemoto himself. His father grew colder and colder after that night, until it came to seem that the boy had quite disappeared from his mind. He was as one who gazes always at the blank space before his eyes. Shigemoto learned nothing from his father of his spiritual life during that last year, but he did notice that his father returned again to the wine he had given up, that even though he was shut up in the altar room as before the image of the Bodhisattva disappeared from the wall, and that in place of the sutras he presently took again to reciting the poetry of Po Chü-i.

TRANSLATED BY EDWARD SEIDENSTICKER

VILLON'S WIFE

[*Villon no Tsuma, 1947*] *by Dazai Osamu (1909-1948)*

Dazai Osamu, a member of a rich and influential family, was widely known during his lifetime, particularly to the younger generation, for his dissipation and excesses. His writings are autobiographical at least to the extent that we find in most of them the personage of a dissolute young man of good family, but Dazai was also gifted with a fertile imagination. His celebrity as a writer came after the war, with such stories as "Villon's Wife" and the novel The Setting Sun.

•

I was awakened by the sound of the front door being flung open, but I did not get out of bed. I knew it could only be my husband returning dead drunk in the middle of the night.

He switched on the light in the next room and, breathing very heavily, began to rummage through the drawers of the table and the bookcase, searching for something. After a few minutes there was a noise that sounded as if he had flopped down on the floor. Then I could hear only his panting. Wondering what he might be up to, I called to him from where I lay. "Have you had supper yet? There's some cold rice in the cupboard."

"Thank you," he answered in an unwontedly gentle tone. "How is the boy? Does he still have a fever?"

This was also unusual. The boy is four this year, but whether because of malnutrition, or his father's alcoholism, or sickness, he is actually smaller than most two-year-olds. He is not even sure on his feet, and as for talking, it's all he can do to say "yum-yum" or "ugh." Sometimes I wonder if he is not feeble-minded. Once, when I took him to the public bath and held him in my arms after undressing him, he looked so small and pitifully scrawny that my heart sank, and I burst into tears in front of everybody. The boy is always having upset stomachs or fevers, but my husband almost never spends any time at home, and I wonder what if anything he thinks about the child. If I mention to him that the boy has a fever, he says, "You ought to take him to a doctor." Then he throws on his coat and goes off somewhere. I would like to take the boy to the doctor, but I haven't the money. There is nothing I can do but lie beside him and stroke his head.

But that night, for whatever reason, my husband was strangely gentle, and for once asked me about the boy's fever. It didn't make me happy. I felt instead a kind of premonition of something terrible, and cold chills ran up and down my spine. I couldn't think of anything to say, so I lay there in silence. For a while there was no other sound but my husband's furious panting.

Then there came from the front entrance the thin voice of a woman, "Is anyone at home?" I shuddered all over as if icy water had been poured over me.

"Are you at home, Mr. Otani?" This time there was a somewhat sharp inflection to her voice. She slid the door open and called in a definitely angry voice, "Mr. Otani. Why don't you answer?"

My husband at last went to the door. "Well, what is it?" he asked in a frightened, stupid tone.

"You know perfectly well what it is," the woman said, lowering her voice. "What makes you steal other people's money when you've got a nice home like this? Stop your cruel joking and give it back. If you don't, I'm going straight to the police."

"I don't know what you're talking about. I won't stand for your insults. You've got no business coming here. Get out! If you don't get out, I'll be the one to call the police."

There came the voice of another man. "I must say, you've got your nerve, Mr. Otani. What do you mean we have no business coming here? You amaze me. This time it is serious. It's more than a joke when you steal other people's money. Heaven only knows all my wife and I have suffered on account of you. And on top of everything else you do something as low as you did tonight. Mr. Otani, I misjudged you."

"It's blackmail," my husband angrily exclaimed in a shaking voice. "It's extortion. Get out! If you've got any complaints I'll listen to them tomorrow."

"What a revolting thing to say. You really are a scoundrel. I have no alternative but to call the police."

In his words was a hatred so terrible that I went goose flesh all over.

"Go to hell," my husband shouted, but his voice had already weakened and sounded hollow.

I got up, threw a wrap over my nightgown, and went to the front hall. I bowed to the two visitors. A round-faced man of about fifty wearing a knee-length overcoat asked, "Is this your wife?", and, without a trace of a smile, faintly inclined his head in my direction as if he were nodding.

The woman was a thin, small person of about forty, neatly dressed. She loosened her shawl and, also unsmiling, returned my bow with the words, "Excuse us for breaking in this way in the middle of the night."

My husband suddenly slipped on his sandals and made for the door. The man grabbed his arm and the two of them struggled for a moment. "Let go or I'll stab you!" my husband shouted, and a jackknife flashed in his right hand. The knife was a pet possession of his, and I remembered that he usually kept it in his desk drawer. When he got home he must have been expecting trouble, and the knife was what he had been searching for.

The man shrank back and in the interval my husband, flapping the sleeves of his coat like a huge crow, bolted outside.

"Thief!" the man shouted and started to pursue him, but I ran to the front gate in my bare feet and clung to him.

"Please don't. It won't help for either of you to get hurt. I will take the responsibility for everything."

The woman said, "Yes, she's right. You can never tell what a lunatic will do."

"Swine! It's the police this time! I can't stand any more." The man stood there staring emptily at the darkness outside and muttering, as if to himself. But the force had gone out of his body.

"Please come in and tell me what has happened. I may be able to settle whatever the matter is. The place is a mess, but please come in."

The two visitors exchanged glances and nodded slightly to one another. The man said, with a changed expression, "I'm afraid that whatever you may say, our minds are already made up. But it might be a good idea to tell you, Mrs. Otani, all that has happened."

"Please do come in and tell me about it."

"I'm afraid we won't be able to stay long." So saying the man started to remove his overcoat.

"Please keep your coat on. It's very cold here, and there's no heating in the house."

"Well then, if you will forgive me."

"Please, both of you."

The man and the woman entered my husband's room. They seemed appalled by the desolation they saw. The mats looked as though they were rotting, the paper doors were in shreds, the walls were beginning to fall in, and the paper had peeled away from the storage closet, revealing the framework. In a corner were a desk and a bookcase—an empty bookcase.

I offered the two visitors some torn cushions from which the stuffing was leaking, and said, "Please sit on the cushions—the mats are so dirty." And I bowed to them again. "I must apologize for all the trouble my husband seems to have been causing you, and for the terrible exhibition he put on tonight, for whatever reason it was. He has such a peculiar disposition." I choked in the middle of my words and burst into tears.

"Excuse me for asking, Mrs. Otani, but how old are you?" the man asked. He was sitting cross-legged on the torn cushion, with his elbows on his knees, propping his chin on his fists. As he asked the question he leaned forward toward me.

"I am twenty-six."

"Is that all you are? I suppose that's only natural, considering your husband's about thirty, but it amazes me all the same."

The woman, showing her face from behind the man's back, said, "I couldn't help wondering, when I came in and saw what a fine wife he has, why Mr. Otani behaves the way he does."

"He's sick. That's what it is. He didn't used to be that way, but he keeps getting worse." He gave a great sigh, then continued, "Mrs. Otani, my wife and I run a little restaurant near the Nakano Station. We both originally came from the country, but I got fed up dealing with penny-pinching farmers, and came to Tokyo with my wife. After the usual hardships and breaks, we managed to save up a little and, along about 1936, opened a cheap little restaurant catering to customers with at most a yen or two to spend at a time on entertainment. By not going in for luxuries and working like slaves, we managed to lay in quite a stock of whisky and gin. When liquor got short and plenty of other drinking establishments went out of business, we were able to keep going.

"The war with America and England broke out, but even after the bombings got pretty severe, we didn't want to be evacuated to the country, not having any children to tie us down. We figured that we might as well stick to our business until the place got burnt down. Your husband first started coming to our place in the spring of 1944, as I recall. We were not yet losing the war, or if we were we didn't know how things actually stood, and we thought that if we could just hold out for another two or three years we could somehow get peace on terms of equality. When Mr. Otani first appeared in our shop, he was not alone. It's a little embarrassing to tell you about it, but I might as well come out with the whole story and not keep anything from you. Your husband sneaked in by the kitchen door along with an older woman. I forgot to say that about that time the front door of our place was shut, and only a few regular customers got in by the back.

"This older woman lived in the neighborhood, and when the bar where she worked was closed and she lost her job, she often came to our place with her men friends. That's why we weren't particularly surprised when your husband crept in with this woman, whose name was Akichan. I took them to the back room and brought out some gin. Mr. Otani drank his liquor very quietly that evening.

Akichan paid the bill and the two of them left together. It's odd, but I can't forget how strangely gentle and refined he seemed that night. I wonder if when the devil makes his first appearance in somebody's house he acts in such a lonely and melancholy way.

"From that night on Mr. Otani was a steady customer. Ten days later he came alone and all of a sudden produced a hundred-yen note. At that time a hundred yen was a lot of money, more than two or three thousand yen today. He pressed the money into my hand and wouldn't take no for an answer. 'Take care of it please,' he said, smiling timidly. That night he seemed to have drunk quite a bit before he came, and at my place he downed ten glasses of gin as fast as I could set them up. All this was almost entirely without a word. My wife and I tried to start a conversation, but he only smiled rather shamefacedly and nodded vaguely. Suddenly he asked the time and got up. 'What about the change?' I called after him. 'That's all right,' he said. 'I don't know what to do with it,' I insisted. He answered with a sardonic smile, 'Please save it until the next time. I'll be coming back.' He went out. Mrs. Otani, that was the one and only time that we ever got any money from him. Since then he has always put us off with one excuse or another, and for three years he has managed without paying a penny to drink up all our liquor almost singlehanded."

Before I knew what I was doing I burst out laughing. It all seemed so funny to me, although I can't explain why. I covered my mouth in confusion, but when I looked at the lady I saw that she was also laughing unaccountably, and then her husband could not help but laugh too.

"No, it's certainly no laughing matter, but I'm so fed up that I feel like laughing, too. Really, if he used all his ability in some other direction, he could become a cabinet minister or a Ph.D. or anything else he wanted. When Akichan was still friends with Mr. Otani she used to brag about him all the time. First of all, she said, he came from a terrific family. He was the younger son of Baron Otani. It is true that he had been disinherited because of his conduct, but when his father, the present baron, died, he and his elder brother were to divide the estate. He was brilliant, a genius in fact.

In spite of his youth he was the best poet in Japan. What's more, he was a great scholar, and a perfect demon at German and French. To hear Akichan talk, he was a kind of god, and the funny thing was that she didn't make it all up. Other people also said that he was the younger son of Baron Otani and a famous poet. Even my wife, who's getting along in years, was as enthusiastic about him as Akichan. She used to tell me what a difference it makes when people have been well brought up. And the way she pined for him to come was quite unbearable. They say the day of the nobility is over, but until the war ended I can tell you that nobody had his way with the women like that disinherited son of the aristocracy. It is unbelievable how they fell for him. I suppose it was what people would nowadays call 'slave mentality.'

"For my part, I'm a man, and at that a very cool sort of man, and I don't think that some little peer—if you will pardon the expression—some member of the country gentry who is only a younger son, is all that different from myself. I never for a moment got worked up about him in so sickening a way. But all the same, that gentleman was my weak spot. No matter how firmly I resolved not to give him any liquor the next time, when he suddenly appeared at some unexpected hour, looking like a hunted man, and I saw how relieved he was at last to have reached our place, my resolution weakened, and I ended up by giving him the liquor. Even when he got drunk, he never made any special nuisance of himself, and if only he had paid the bill he would have been a good customer. He never advertised himself and didn't take any silly pride in being a genius or anything of the sort. When Akichan or somebody else would sit beside him and sound off to us about his greatness, he would either change the subject completely or say, 'I want some money so I can pay the bill,' throwing a wet blanket over everything.

"The war finally ended. We started doing business openly in black-market liquor and put new curtains in front of the place. For all its seediness the shop looked rather lively, and we hired a girl to lend a little charm. Then who should show up again but that damned gentleman. He no longer brought women with him, but always came in the company of two or three writers for newspapers and magazines. He was drinking even more than before, and used to get very wild-looking. He began to come out with really vulgar jokes, which he had never done before, and sometimes for no good reason he would hit one of the reporters he brought with him or start a fist fight. What's more, he seduced the twenty-year-old girl who was working in our place. We were shocked, but there was nothing we could do about it at that stage, and we had no choice but to let the matter drop. We advised the girl to resign herself to bearing the child, and quietly sent her back to her parents. I begged Mr. Otani not to come any more, but he answered in a threatening tone, 'People who make money on the black market have no business criticizing others. I know all about you.' The next night he showed up as if nothing had happened.

"Maybe it was by way of punishment for the black-market business we had been doing that we had to put up with such a monster. But what he did tonight can't be passed over just because he's a poet or a gentleman. It was plain robbery. He stole five thousand yen from us. Nowadays all our money goes for stock, and we are lucky if we have five hundred or one thousand yen in the place. The reason why we had as much as five thousand tonight was that I had made an end-of-the-year round of our regular customers and managed to collect that much. If I don't hand the money over to the wholesalers immediately we won't be able to stay in business. That's how much it means to us. Well, my wife was going over the accounts in the back room and had put the money in the cupboard drawer. He was drinking by himself out in front but seems to have noticed what she did. Suddenly he got up, went straight to the back room, and without a word pushed my wife aside and opened the drawer. He grabbed the bills and stuffed them in his pocket.

"We rushed into the shop, still speechless with amazement, and then out into the street. I shouted for him to stop, and the two of us ran after him. For a minute I felt like screaming 'Thief!' and getting the people in the street to join us, but after all, Mr. Otani is an old acquaintance, and I couldn't be too harsh on him. I made up my mind that I would not let him out of my sight. I would follow him wherever he went, and when I saw that he had quieted down, I would calmly ask for the money. We are only small business people, and when we finally caught up with him here, we had no choice but to suppress our feelings and politely ask him to return the money. And then what happened? He took out a knife and threatened to stab me! What a way to behave!"

Again the whole thing seemed so funny to me, for reasons I can't explain, that I burst out laughing. The lady turned red, and smiled a little. I couldn't stop laughing. Even though I knew that it would have a bad effect on the proprietor, it all seemed so strangely funny that I laughed until the tears came. I suddenly wondered if the phrase "the great laugh at the end of the world," that occurs in one of my husband's poems, didn't mean something of the sort.

And yet it was not a matter that could be settled just by laughing about it. I thought for a minute and said, "Somehow or other I will make things good, if you will only wait one more day before you report to the police. I'll call on you tomorrow without fail." I carefully inquired where the restaurant was, and begged them to consent. They agreed to let things stand for the time being, and left. Then I sat by myself in the middle of the cold room trying to think of a plan. Nothing came to me. I stood up, took off my wrap, and crept in among the covers where my boy was sleeping. As I stroked his head I thought how wonderful it would be if the night never never ended.

My father used to keep a stall in Asakusa Park. My mother died when I was young, and my father and I lived by ourselves in a tenement. We ran the stall together. My husband used to come now and then, and before long I was meeting him at other places without my father's knowing it. When I became pregnant I persuaded him to treat me as his wife, although it wasn't officially registered, of course. Now the boy is growing up fatherless, while my husband goes off for three or four nights or even for a whole month at a time. I don't know where he goes or what he does. When he comes back he is always drunk; and he sits there, deathly pale, breathing heavily and staring at my face. Sometimes he cries and the tears stream down his face, or without warning he crawls into my bed and holds me tightly. "Oh, it can't go on. I'm afraid. I'm afraid. Help me!"

Sometimes he trembles all over, and even after he falls asleep he talks deliriously and moans. The next morning he is absent-minded, like a man with the soul taken out of him. Then he disappears and doesn't return for three or four nights. A couple of my husband's publisher friends have been looking after the boy and myself for some time, and they bring money once in a while, enough to keep us from starving.

I dozed off, then before I knew it opened my eyes to see the morning light pouring in through the cracks in the shutters. I got up, dressed, strapped the boy to my back and went outside. I felt as if I couldn't stand being in the silent house another minute.

I set out aimlessly and found myself walking in the direction of the station. I bought a bun at an outdoor stand and fed it to the boy. On a sudden impulse I bought a ticket for Kichijoji and got on the streetcar. While I stood hanging from a strap I happened to notice a poster with my husband's name on it. It was an advertisement for a magazine in which he had published a story called "François Villon." While I stared at the title "François Villon" and at my husband's name, painful tears sprang from my eyes, why I can't say, and the poster clouded over so I couldn't see it.

I got off at Kichijoji and for the first time in I don't know how many years I walked in the park. The cypresses around the pond had all been cut down, and the place looked like the site of a construction. It was strangely bare and cold, not at all as it used to be.

I took the boy off my back and the two of us sat on a broken bench next to the pond. I fed the boy a sweet potato I had brought from home. "It's a pretty pond, isn't it? There used to be many carp and goldfish, but now there aren't any left. It's too bad, isn't it?"

I don't know what he thought. He just laughed oddly with his mouth full of sweet potato. Even if he is my own child, he did give me the feeling almost of an idiot.

I couldn't settle anything by sitting there on the bench, so I put the boy on my back and returned slowly to the station. I bought a ticket for Nakano. Without thought or plan, I boarded the streetcar as though I were being sucked into a horrible whirlpool. I got off at Nakano and followed the directions to the restaurant.

The front door would not open. I went around to the back and entered by the kitchen door. The owner was away, and his wife was cleaning the shop by herself. As soon as I saw her I began to pour out lies of which I did not imagine myself capable.

"It looks as if I'll be able to pay you back every bit of the money tomorrow, if not tonight. There's nothing for you to worry about."

"Oh, how wonderful. Thank you so much." She looked almost happy, but still there remained on her face a shadow of uneasiness, as if she were not yet satisfied.

"It's true. Someone will bring the money here without fail. Until he comes I'm to stay here as your hostage. Is that guarantee enough for you? Until the money comes I'll be glad to help around the shop."

I took the boy off my back and let him play by himself. He is accustomed to playing alone and doesn't get in the way at all. Perhaps because he's stupid, he's not afraid of strangers, and he smiled happily at the madam. While I was away getting the rationed goods for her, she gave him some empty American cans to play with, and when I got back he was in a corner of the room, banging the cans and rolling them on the floor.

About noon the boss returned from his marketing. As soon as I caught sight of him I burst out with the same lies I had told the madam. He looked amazed. "Is that a fact? All the same, Mrs. Otani, you can't be sure of money until you've got it in your hands." He spoke in a surprisingly calm, almost explanatory tone.

"But it's really true. Please have confidence in me and wait just this one day before you make it public. In the meantime I'll help in the restaurant."

"If the money is returned, that's all I ask," the boss said, almost to himself. "There are five or six days left to the end of the year, aren't there?"

"Yes, and so, you see, I mean—oh, some customers have come. Welcome!" I smiled at the three customers—they looked like workmen—who had entered the shop, and whispered to the madam, "Please lend me an apron."

One of the customers called out, "Say, you've hired a beauty. She's terrific."

"Don't lead her astray," the boss said, in a tone which wasn't altogether joking, "she cost a lot of money."

"A million-dollar thoroughbred?" another customer coarsely joked.

"They say that even in thoroughbreds the female costs only half-price," I answered in the same coarse way, while putting the sake on to warm.

"Don't be modest! From now on in Japan there's equality of the sexes, even for horses and dogs," the youngest customer roared. "Sweetheart, I've fallen in love. It's love at first sight. But is that your kid over there?"

"No," said the madam, carrying the boy from the back room in her arms. "We got this child from our relatives. At last we have an heir."

"What'll you leave him beside your money?" a customer teased.

The boss, with a dark expression, muttered, "A love affair and debts." Then, changing his tone, "What'll you have? How about a mixed grill?"

It was Christmas Eve. That must have been why there was such a steady stream of customers. I had scarcely eaten a thing since morning, but I was so upset that I refused even when the madam urged me to have a bite. I just went on flitting around the restaurant as lightly as a ballerina. Maybe it is only conceit, but the shop seemed exceptionally lively that night, and there were quite a few customers who wanted to know my name or tried to shake my hand.

But I didn't have the slightest idea how it would all end. I went on smiling and answering the customers' dirty jokes with even dirtier jokes in the same vein, slipping from customer to customer, pouring the drinks. Before long I got to thinking that I would just as soon my body melted and flowed away like ice cream.

It seems as if miracles sometimes do happen even in this world. A little after nine a man entered, wearing a Christmas tricornered paper hat and a black mask which covered the upper part of his face. He was followed by an attractive woman of slender build who looked thirty-four or thirty-five. The man sat on a chair in the corner with his back to me, but as soon as he came in I knew who it was. It was my thief of a husband.

He sat there without seeming to pay any attention to me. I also pretended not to recognize him, and went on joking with the other customers. The lady seated opposite my husband called me to their table. My husband stared at me from beneath his mask, as if he were surprised in spite of himself. I lightly patted his shoulder and asked, "Aren't you going to wish me a merry Christmas? What do you say? You look as if you've already put away a quart or two."

The lady ignored this. She said, "I have something to discuss with the proprietor. Would you mind calling him here for a moment?"

I went to the kitchen, where the boss was frying fish. "Otani has come back. Please go and see him, but don't tell the woman he's with anything about me. I don't want to embarrass him."

"If that's the way you want it, it's all right with me," he consented easily, and went out front. After a quick look around the restaurant, the boss walked straight to the table where my husband sat. The beautiful lady exchanged two or three words with him, and the three of them left the shop.

It was all over. Everything had been settled. Somehow I had believed all along that it would be, and I felt exhilarated. I seized the wrist of a young customer in a dark-blue suit, a boy not more than twenty, and I cried, "Drink up! Drink up! It's Christmas!"

In just thirty minutes—no, it was even sooner than that, so soon it startled me, the boss returned alone. "Mrs. Otani, I want to thank you. I've got the money back."

"I'm so glad. All of it?"

He answered with a funny smile, "All he took yesterday."

"And how much does his debt come to altogether? Roughly—the absolute minimum."

"Twenty thousand yen."

"Does that cover it?"

"It's a minimum."

"I'll make it good. Will you employ me starting tomorrow? I'll pay it back by working."

"What! You're joking!" And we laughed together.

Tonight I left the restaurant after ten and returned to the house with the boy. As I expected, my husband was not at home, but that didn't bother me. Tomorrow when I go to the restaurant I may see him again, for all I know. Why has such a good plan never occurred to me before? All the suffering I have gone through has been because of my own stupidity. I was always quite a success at entertaining the customers at my father's stall, and I'll certainly get to be pretty skillful at the restaurant. As a matter of fact, I received about five hundred yen in tips tonight.

From the following day on my life changed completely. I became lighthearted and gay. The first thing I did was to go to a beauty parlor and have a permanent. I bought cosmetics and mended my dresses. I felt as though the worries that had weighed so heavily on me had been completely wiped away.

In the morning I get up and eat breakfast with the boy. Then I put him on my back and leave for work. New Year's is the big season at the restaurant, and I've been so busy my eyes swim. My husband comes in for a drink once every few days. He lets me pay the bill and then disappears again. Quite often he looks in on the shop late at night and asks if it isn't time for me to be going home. Then we return pleasantly together.

"Why didn't I do this from the start? It's brought me such happiness."

"Women don't know anything about happiness or unhappiness."

"Perhaps not. What about men?"

"Men only have unhappiness. They are always fighting fear."

"I don't understand. I only know I wish this life could go o forever. The boss and the madam are such nice people."

"Don't be silly. They're grasping country bumpkins. They me drink because they think they'll make money out of end."

"That's their business. You can't blame them for it. But that's not the whole story is it? You had an affair with the madam, didn't you?"

"A long time ago. Does the old guy realize it?"

"I'm sure he does. I heard him say with a sigh that you had brought him a seduction and debts."

"I must seem a horrible character to you, but the fact is that I want to die so badly I can't stand it. Ever since I was born I have been thinking of nothing but dying. It would be better for everyone concerned if I were dead, that's certain. And yet I can't seem to die. There's something strange and frightening, like God, which won't let me die."

"That's because you have your work."

"My work doesn't mean a thing. I don't write either masterpieces or failures. If people say something is good, it becomes good. If they say it's bad, it becomes bad. But what frightens me is that somewhere in the world there is a God. There is, isn't there?"

"I haven't any idea."

Now that I have worked twenty days at the restaurant I realize that every last one of the customers is a criminal. I have come to think that my husband is very much on the mild side compared to them. And I see now that not only the customers but everyone you meet walking in the streets is hiding some crime. A beautifully dressed lady came to the door selling sake at three hundred yen the quart. That was cheap, considering what prices are nowadays, and the madam snapped it up. It turned out to be watered. I thought that in a world where even such an aristocratic-looking lady is forced to resort to such tricks, it is impossible for anyone alive to have a clear conscience.

God, if you exist, show yourself to me! Toward the end of the New Year season I was raped by a customer. It was raining that night, and it didn't seem likely that my husband would appear. I got ready to go, even though one customer was still left. I picked up the boy, who was sleeping in a corner of the back room, and put him on my back. "I'd like to borrow your umbrella again," I said to the madam.

"I've got an umbrella. I'll take you home," said the last customer, getting up as if he meant it. He was a short, thin man about twenty-five, who looked like a factory worker. It was the first time he had come to the restaurant since I started working there.

"It's very kind of you, but I am used to walking by myself."

"You live a long way off, I know. I come from the same neighborhood. I'll take you back. Bill, please." He had only had three glasses and didn't seem particularly drunk.

We boarded the streetcar together and got off at my stop. Then we walked in the falling rain side by side under the same umbrella through the pitch-black streets. The young man, who up to this point hadn't said a word, began to talk in a lively way. "I know all about you. You see, I'm a fan of Mr. Otani's and I write poetry myself. I was hoping to show him some of my work before long, but he intimidates me so."

We had reached my house. "Thank you very much," I said. "I'll see you again at the restaurant."

"Good-bye," the young man said, going off into the rain.

I was wakened in the middle of the night by the noise of the front gate being opened. I thought that it was my husband returning, drunk as usual, so I lay there without saying anything.

A man's voice called, "Mrs. Otani, excuse me for bothering you."

I got up, put on the light, and went to the front entrance. The young man was there, staggering so badly he could scarcely stand.

"Excuse me, Mrs. Otani. On the way back I stopped for another drink and, to tell the truth, I live at the other end of town, and when I got to the station the last streetcar had already left. Mrs. Otani, would you please let me spend the night here? I don't need any blankets or anything else. I'll be glad to sleep here in the front hall until the first streetcar leaves tomorrow morning. If it wasn't raining I'd sleep outdoors somewhere in the neighborhood, but it's hopeless with this rain. Please let me stay."

"My husband isn't at home, but if the front hall will do, please stay." I got the two torn cushions and gave them to him.

"Thanks very much. Oh, I've had too much to drink," he said with a groan. He lay down just as he was in the front hall, and by the time I got back to bed I could already hear his snores.

The next morning at dawn without ceremony he took me.

That day I went to the restaurant with my boy as usual, acting as if nothing had happened. My husband was sitting at a table reading a newspaper, a glass of liquor beside him. I thought how pretty the morning sunshine looked, sparkling on the glass.

"Isn't anybody here?" I asked. He looked up from his paper. "The boss hasn't come back yet from marketing. The madam was in the kitchen just a minute ago. Isn't she there now?"

"You didn't come last night, did you?"

"I did come. It's got so that I can't get to sleep without a look at my favorite waitress's face. I dropped in after ten but they said you had just left."

"And then?"

"I spent the night here. It was raining so hard."

"I may be sleeping here from now on."

"That's a good idea, I suppose."

"Yes, that's what I'll do. There's no sense in renting the house forever."

My husband didn't say anything but turned back to his paper. "Well, what do you know. They're writing bad things about me again. They call me a fake aristocrat with Epicurean leanings. That's not true. It would be more correct to refer to me as an Epicurean in terror of God. Look! It says here that I'm a monster. That's not true, is it? It's a little late, but I'll tell you now why I took the five thousand yen. It was so that I might give you and the boy the first happy New Year in a long time. That proves I'm not a monster, doesn't it?"

His words didn't make me especially glad. I said, "There's nothing wrong with being a monster, is there? As long as we can stay alive."

TRANSLATED BY DONALD KEENE

TOKYO

[*Shitamachi, 1948*] *by Hayashi Fumiko (1904-1951)*

Most of the characters in Hayashi Fumiko's writings belong to the Tokyo lower classes. She portrays them with realism and compassion, probably because as a young woman she experienced the hardships of their life. Her descriptions of postwar Tokyo are among the most somber and moving. Asakusa, where much of the action of "Tokyo" takes place, is an amusement district vaguely corresponding to Montmartre. It has a Buddhist temple dedicated to Kannon, the Goddess of Mercy. A description of the same scene sixty years earlier may be found in The River Sumida.

•

It was a bitter, windy afternoon. As Ryo hurried down the street with her rucksack, she kept to the side where the pale sun shone down over the roofs of the office buildings. Every now and then she looked about curiously—at a building, at a parked car—at one of those innumerable bomb sites scattered through downtown Tokyo.

Glancing over a boarding, Ryo saw a huge pile of rusty iron, and next to it a cabin with a glass door. A fire was burning within, and the warm sound of the crackling wood reached where she was standing. In front of the cabin stood a man in overalls with a red kerchief about his head. There was something pleasant about this tall fellow, and Ryo screwed up her courage to call out,

"Tea for sale! Would you like some tea, please?"

"Tea?" said the man.

"Yes," said Ryo with a nervous smile. "It's Shizuoka tea."

She stepped in through an opening in the boarding and, unfastening the straps of her rucksack, put it down by the cabin. Inside she could see a fire burning in an iron stove; from a bar above hung a brass kettle with a wisp of steam rising from the spout.

"Excuse me," said Ryo, "but would you mind if I came in and warmed myself by your stove a few minutes? It's freezing out, and I've been walking for miles."

"Of course you can come in," said the man. "Close the door and get warm."

He pointed towards the stool, which was his only article of furniture, and sat down on a packing case in the corner. Ryo hesitated a moment. Then she dragged her rucksack into the cabin and, crouching by the stove, held up her hands to the fire.

"You'll be more comfortable on that stool," said the man, glancing at her attractive face, flushed in the sudden warmth, and at her shabby attire.

"Surely this isn't what you usually do—hawk tea from door to door?"

"Oh yes, it's how I make my living," Ryo said. "I was told that this was a good neighborhood, but I've been walking around here since early morning and have only managed to sell one packet of tea. I'm about ready to go home now, but I thought I'd have my lunch somewhere on the way."

"Well, you're perfectly welcome to stay here and eat your lunch," said the man. "And don't worry about not having sold your tea," he added, smiling. "It's all a matter of luck, you know! You'll probably have a good day tomorrow."

The kettle came to a boil with a whistling sound. As he unhooked it from the bar, Ryo had a chance to look about her. She took in the boarded ceiling black with soot, the blackboard by the window, the shelf for family gods on which stood a potted sakaki tree. The man took a limp-looking packet from the table, and unwrapping it, disclosed a piece of cod. A few minutes later the smell of baking fish permeated the cabin.

"Come on," said the man. "Sit down and have your meal."

Ryo took her lunch box out of the rucksack and seated herself on the stool.

"Selling things is never much fun, is it?" remarked the man, turning the cod over on the grill. "Tell me, how much do you get for a hundred grams of that tea?"

"I should get thirty-five yen to make any sort of profit. The people who send me the stuff often mix in bad tea, so I'm lucky if I can get thirty yen."

In Ryo's lunch box were two small fish covered with some boiled barley and a few bean-paste pickles. She began eating.

"Where do you live?" the man asked her.

"In the Shitaya district. Actually I don't know one part of Tokyo from another! I've only been here a few weeks and a friend's putting me up until I find something better."

The cod was ready now. He cut it in two and gave Ryo half, adding potatoes and rice from a platter. Ryo smiled and bowed slightly in thanks, then took out a bag of tea from her rucksack and poured some into a paper handkerchief.

"Do put this into the kettle," she said, holding it out to him.

He shook his head and smiled, showing his white teeth.

"Good Lord no! It's far too expensive."

Quickly Ryo removed the lid and poured the tea in before he could stop her. Laughing, the man went to fetch a teacup and a mug from the shelf.

"What about your husband?" he asked, while ranging them on the packing case. "You're married, aren't you?"

"Oh yes, I am. My husband's still in Siberia. That's why I have to work like this."

Ryo's thoughts flew to her husband, from whom she had not heard for six years; by now he had come to seem so remote that it required an effort to remember his looks, or the once-familiar sound of his voice. She woke up each morning with a feeling of emptiness and desolation. At times it seemed to Ryo that her husband had frozen into a ghost in that subarctic Siberia—a ghost, or a thin white pillar, or just a breath of frosty air. Nowadays no one any longer mentioned the war and she was almost embarrassed to let people know that her husband was still a prisoner.

"It's funny," the man said. "The fact is, I was in Siberia myself! I spent three years chopping wood near the Amur River—I only managed to get sent home last year. Well, it's all in a matter of luck! It's tough on your husband. But it's just as tough on you."

"So you've really been repatriated from Siberia! You don't seem any the worse for it," Ryo said.

"Well, I don't know about that!" the man shrugged his shoulders. "Anyway, as you see, I'm still alive."

Ryo closed her lunch box, and as she did so, she studied him. There was a simplicity and directness about this man that made her want to talk openly in a way that she found difficult with more educated people.

"Got any kids?" he said.

"Yes, a boy of six. He should be at school, but I've had difficulty getting him registered here in Tokyo. These officials certainly know how to make life complicated for people!"

The man untied his kerchief, wiped the cup and the mug with it, and poured out the steaming tea.

"It's good stuff this!" he said, sipping noisily.

"Do you like it? It's not the best quality, you know: only two hundred and ten yen a kilo wholesale. But you're right—it's quite good."

The wind had grown stronger while they were talking; it whistled over the tin roof of the cabin. Ryo glanced out of the window, steeling herself for her long walk home.

"I'll have some of your tea—seven hundred and fifty grams," the man told her, extracting two crumbled hundred-yen notes from the pocket of his overalls.

"Don't be silly," said Ryo. "You can have it for nothing."

"Oh no, that won't do. Business is business!" He forced the money into her hand. "Well, if you're ever in this part of the world again, come in and have another chat."

"I should like to," said Ryo, glancing around the tiny cabin. "But you don't live here, do you?"

"Oh, but I do! I look after that iron out there and help load the trucks. I'm here most of the day."

He opened a door under the shelf, disclosing a sort of cubbyhole containing a bed neatly made up. Ryo noticed a colored postcard of a film actress tacked to the back of the door.

"My, you've fixed it up nicely," she said smiling. "You're really quite snug here, aren't you?"

She wondered how old he could be.

2

From that day on, Ryo came regularly to the Yotsugi district to sell tea; each time she visited the cabin on the bomb site. She learned that the man's name was Tsuruishi Yoshio. Almost invariably he had some small delicacy waiting for her to put in her lunch box—a pickled plum, a piece of beef, a sardine. Her business began to improve and she acquired a few regular customers in the neighborhood.

A week after their first meeting, she brought along her boy, Ryukichi. Tsuruishi chatted with the child for a while and then took him out for a walk. When they returned, Ryukichi was carrying a large caramel cake.

"He's got a good appetite, this youngster of yours," said Tsuruishi, patting the boy's close-cropped head.

Ryo wondered vaguely whether her new friend was married; in fact she found herself wondering about various aspects of his life. She was now twenty-nine, and she realized with a start that this was the first time she had been seriously interested in any man but her husband. Tsuruishi's easy, carefree temperament somehow appealed to her, though she took great care not to let him guess that.

A little later Tsuruishi suggested taking Ryo and Ryukichi to see Asakusa on his next free day. They met in front of the information booth in Ueno Station, Tsuruishi wearing an ancient gray suit that looked far too tight, Ryo clad in a blue dress of kimono material and a light-brown coat. In spite of her cheap clothes, she had about her something youthful and elegant as she stood there in the crowded station. Beside the tall, heavy Tsuruishi, she looked like a schoolgirl off on a holiday. In her shopping bag lay their lunch: bread, oranges, and seaweed stuffed with rice.

"Well, let's hope it doesn't rain," said Tsuruishi, putting his arm lightly round Ryo's waist as he steered her through the crowd.

They took the subway to Asakusa Station, then walked from the Matsuya Department Store to the Niten Shinto Gate, past hundreds of tiny stalls. The Asakusa district was quite different from what Ryo had imagined. She was amazed when Tsuruishi pointed to a small red-lacquered temple and told her that this was the home of the famous Asakusa Goddess of Mercy. In the distance she could hear the plaintive wail of a trumpet and a saxophone emerging from some loud-speaker; it mingled strangely with the sound of the wind whistling through the branches of the ancient sakaki trees.

They made their way through the old-clothes market, and came to a row of food-stalls squeezed tightly against each other beside the Asakusa Pond; here the air was redolent with the smell of burning oil. Tsuruishi went to one of the stalls and bought Ryukichi a stick of yellow candy-floss. The boy nibbled at it, as the three of them walked down a narrow street plastered with American-style billboards advertising restaurants, movies, revues. It was less than a month since Ryo had first noticed Tsuruishi by his cabin, yet she felt as much at ease with him as if she had known him all her life.

"Well, it's started raining after all," he said, holding out his hand. Ryo looked up, to see scattered drops of rain falling from the gray sky. So their precious excursion would be ruined, she thought.

"We'd better go in there," said Tsuruishi, pointing to one of the shops, outside which hung a garish lantern with characters announcing the "Merry Teahouse." They took seats at a table underneath a ceiling decorated with artificial cherry blossoms. The place had a strangely unhomelike atmosphere, but they were determined to make the best of it and ordered a pot of tea; Ryo distributed her stuffed seaweed, bread, and oranges. It was not long before the meal was finished and by then it had started raining in earnest.

"We'd better wait till it lets up a bit," suggested Tsuruishi. "Then I'll take you home."

Ryo wondered if he was referring to her place or his. She was staying in the cramped apartment of a friend from her home town and did not even have a room to call her own; rather than go there, she would have preferred returning to Tsuruishi's cabin, but that too was scarcely large enough to hold three people. Taking out her purse, she counted her money under the table. The seven hundred yen should be enough to get shelter for a few hours at an inn.

"D'you know what I'd really like?" she said. "I'd like us to go to a movie and then find some inn and have a dish of food before saying good-bye to each other. But I suppose that's all rather expensive!"

"Yes, I suppose it is," said Tsuruishi, laughing. "Come on! We'll do it all the same."

Taking his overcoat off the peg, he threw it over Ryukichi's head, and ran through the downpour to a movie theatre. Of course there were no seats! Standing watching the film, the little boy went sound asleep, leaning against Tsuruishi. The air in the theatre seemed to get thicker and hotter every moment; on the roof they could hear the rain beating down.

It was getting dark as they left the theatre and hurried through the rain, which pelted down with the swishing sound of banana leaves in a high wind. At last they found a small inn where the landlord led them to a carpeted room at the end of a drafty passage. Ryo took off her wet socks. The boy sat down in a corner and promptly went back to sleep.

"Here, he can use this as a pillow," said Tsuruishi, picking up an old cushion from a chair and putting it under Ryukichi's head.

From an overflowing gutter above the window the water poured in a steady stream onto the courtyard. It sounded like a waterfall in some faraway mountain village.

Tsuruishi took out a handkerchief and began wiping Ryo's wet hair. A feeling of happiness coursed through her as she looked up at him. It was as if the rain had begun to wash away all the loneliness which had been gathering within her year after year.

She went to see if they could get some food and in the corridor met a maid in Western clothes carrying a tea tray. After Ryo had ordered two bowls of spaghetti, she and Tsuruishi sat down to drink their tea, facing each other across an empty brazier. Later Tsuruishi came and sat on the floor beside Ryo. Leaning their backs against the wall, they gazed out at the darkening, rainy sky.

"How old are you, Ryo?" Tsuruishi asked her. "I should guess twenty-five."

Ryo laughed. "I'm afraid not, Tsuru, I'm already an old woman! I'm twenty-eight."

"Oh, so you're a year older than me."

"My goodness, you're young!" said Ryo. "I thought you must be at least thirty."

She looked straight at him, into his dark, gentle eyes with their bushy brows. He seemed to be blushing slightly. Then he bent forward and took off his wet socks.

The rain continued unabated. Presently the maid came with some cold spaghetti and soup. Ryo woke the boy and gave him a plate of soup; he was half asleep as he sipped it.

"Look, Ryo," Tsuruishi said, "we might as well all stay the night at this inn. You can't go home in this rain, can you?"

"No," said Ryo. "No, I suppose not."

Tsuruishi left the room and returned with a load of quilted bedrolls which he spread on the floor. At once the whole room seemed to be full of bedding. Ryo tucked up her son in one of the rolls, the boy sleeping soundly as she did so. Then she turned out the light, undressed, and lay down. She could hear Tsuruishi settling down at the other end of the room.

"I suppose the people in this inn think we're married," said Tsuruishi after a while.

"Yes, I suppose so. It's not very nice of us to fool them!"

She spoke in jest, but now that she lay undressed in her bedroll, she felt for the first time vaguely disturbed and guilty. Her husband for some reason seemed much closer than he had for years. But of course she was only here because of the rain, she reminded herself. . . . And gradually her thoughts began to wander pleasantly afield, and she dozed off.

When she awoke it was still dark. She could hear Tsuruishi whispering her name from his corner, and she sat up with a start.

"Ryo, Ryo, can I come and talk to you for a while?"

"No, Tsuru," she said, "I don't think you should."

On the roof the rain was still pattering down, but the force of the storm was over; only a trickle was dropping from the gutter into the yard. Under the sound of the rain she thought she could hear Tsuruishi sigh softly.

"Look Tsuru," she said after a pause. "I've never asked you before, but are you married?"

"No. Not now," Tsuruishi said.

"You used to be?"

"Yes. I used to be. When I got back from the army, I found that my wife was living with another man."

"Were you—angry?"

"Angry? Yes, I suppose I was. Still, there wasn't much I could do about it. She'd left me, and that was that."

They were silent again.

"What shall we talk about?" Ryo asked.

Tsuruishi laughed. "Well, there really doesn't seem to be anything special to talk about. That spaghetti wasn't very good, was it?"

"No, one certainly couldn't call it good. And they charged us a hundred yen each for it!"

"It would be nice if you and Ryukichi had your own room to live in, wouldn't it?" Tsuruishi remarked.

"Oh yes, it would be marvelous! You don't think we might find a room near you? I'd really like to live near you, Tsuru, you know."

"It's pretty hard to find rooms these days, especially downtown. But I'll keep a lookout and let you know. . . . You're such a wonderful person, Ryo!"

"Me?" said Ryo laughing. "Don't be silly!"

"Yes, yes, you're wonderful . . . really wonderful!"

Ryo lay back on the floor. Suddenly she wanted to throw her arms around Tsuruishi, to feel his body close to hers. She did not dare speak for fear that her voice might betray her; her breath came almost painfully; her whole body tingled. Outside the window an early morning truck clattered past.

"Where are your parents, Tsuru?" she asked after a while.

"In the country near Fukuoka."

"But you have a sister in Tokyo?"

"Yes. She's all alone, like you, with two kids to take care of.

She's got a sewing machine and makes Western-style clothes. Her husband was killed several years ago—in the war in China. War, always war!"

Outside the window Ryo could make out the first glimmer of dawn. So their night together was almost over, she thought unhappily. In a way she wished that Tsuruishi hadn't given up so easily, and yet she was convinced that it was best like this. If he had been a man she hardly knew, or for whom she felt nothing, she might have given herself to him with no afterthought. With Tsuruishi it would have been different—quite different.

"Ryo, I can't get to sleep." His voice reached her again. "I'm wide awake, you know. I suppose I'm not used to this sort of thing."

"What sort of thing?"

"Why—sleeping in the same room with a girl."

"Oh Tsuru, don't tell me that you don't have girl friends occasionally!"

"Only professional girl friends."

Ryo laughed. "Men have it easy! In some ways, at least. . . ."

She heard Tsuruishi moving about. Suddenly he was beside her, bending over her. Ryo did not move, not even when she felt his arms around her, his face against hers. In the dark her eyes were wide open, and before them bright lights seemed to be flashing. His hot lips were pressed to her cheek.

"Ryo . . . Ryo."

"It's wrong, you know," she murmured. "Wrong to my husband. . . ."

But almost at once she regretted the words. As Tsuruishi bent over her, she could make out the silhouette of his face against the lightening sky. Bowed forward like that, he seemed to be offering obeisance to some god. Ryo hesitated for a moment. Then she threw her warm arms about his neck.

3

Two days later Ryo set out happily with her boy to visit Tsuruishi. When she reached the bomb site, she was surprised not to see him before his cabin, his red kerchief tied about his head. Ryukichi ran ahead to find out if he were home and came back in a moment.

"There are strangers there, Mamma!"

Seized with panic, Ryo hurried over to the cabin and peered in. Two workmen were busy piling up Tsuruishi's effects in a corner.

"What is it, ma'am?" one of them said, turning his head.

"I'm looking for Tsuruishi."

"Oh, don't you know? Tsuruishi died yesterday."

"Died," she said. She wanted to say something more but no words would come.

She had noticed a small candle burning on the shelf for family gods, and now she was aware of its somber meaning.

"Yes," went on the man, "he was killed about eight o'clock last night. He went in a truck with one of the men to deliver some iron bars in Omiya, and on their way back the truck overturned on a narrow bridge. He and the driver were both killed. His sister went to Omiya today with one of the company officials to see about the cremation."

Ryo stared vacantly before her. Vacantly she watched the two men piling up Tsuruishi's belongings. Beside the candle on the shelf she caught sight of the two bags of tea he had bought from her that first day—could it be only two weeks ago? One of them was folded over halfway down; the other was still unopened.

"You were a friend of his, ma'am, I imagine? He was a fine fellow, Tsuru! Funny to think that he needn't have gone to Omiya at all. The driver wasn't feeling well and Tsuru said he'd go along to Omiya to help him unload. Crazy, isn't it—after getting through the war and Siberia and all the rest of it, to be killed like that!"

One of the men took down the postcard of the film actress and blew the dust off it. Ryo stood looking at Tsuruishi's belongings piled on the floor—the kettle, the frying pan, the rubber boots. When her eyes reached the blackboard, she noticed for the first time a message scratched awkwardly in red chalk: "Ryo—I waited for you till two o'clock. Back this evening."

Automatically she bowed to the two men and swung the rucksack on her back. She felt numb as she left the cabin, holding

Ryukichi by the hand, but as they passed the bomb site, the burning tears welled into her eyes.

"Did that man die, Mamma?"

"Yes, he died," Ryo said.

"Why did he die?"

"He fell into a river."

The tears were running down her cheeks now; they poured out uncontrollably as she hurried through the downtown streets. They came to an arched bridge over the Sumida River, crossed it, and walked along the bank in the direction of Hakuho.

"Don't worry if you get pregnant," Tsuruishi had told her that morning in Asakusa, "I'll look after you whatever happens, Ryo!" And later on, just before they parted, he had said, "I haven't got much money, but you must let me help you a bit. I can give you two thousand yen a month out of my salary." He had taken Ryukichi to a shop that specialized in foreign goods and bought him a baseball cap with his name written on it. Then the three of them had walked gaily along the streetcar lines, skirting the enormous puddles left by the rain. When they came to a milk bar, Tsuruishi had taken them in and ordered them each a big glass of milk. . . .

Now an icy wind seemed to have blown up from the dark river. A flock of waterfowl stood on the opposite bank, looking frozen and miserable. Barges moved slowly up and down the river.

"Mamma, I want a sketchbook. You said I could have a sketchbook."

"Later," answered Ryo. "I'll get you one later."

"But Mamma, we just passed a stall with hundreds of sketchbooks. I'm hungry, Mamma. Can't we have something to eat?"

"Later. A little later!"

They were passing a long row of barrack-like buildings. They must be private houses, she thought. The people who lived there probably all had rooms of their own. From one of the windows a bedroll had been hung out to air and inside a woman could be seen tidying the room.

"Tea for sale!" called out Ryo softly. "Best quality Shizuoka tea!"

There was no reply and Ryo repeated her call a little louder.

"I don't want any," said the woman. She pulled in the bedroll and shut the window with a bang.

Ryo went from house to house down the row calling her ware, but nobody wanted any tea. Ryukichi followed behind, muttering that he was hungry and tired. Ryo's rucksack dug painfully into her shoulders, and occasionally she had to stop to adjust the straps. Yet in a way she almost welcomed the physical pain.

4

The next day she went downtown by herself, leaving Ryukichi at home. When she came to the bomb site she noticed that a fire was burning inside the cabin. She ran to the door and walked in. By Tsuruishi's stove sat an old man in a short workman's overcoat, feeding the flames with firewood. The room was full of smoke and it was billowing out of the window.

"What do you want?" said the old man, looking round.

"I've come to sell some Shizuoka tea."

"Shizuoka tea? I've got plenty of good tea right here."

Ryo turned without a word and hurried off. She had thought of asking for the address of Tsuruishi's sister and of going to burn a stick of incense in his memory, but suddenly this seemed quite pointless. She walked back to the river, which reflected the late afternoon sun, and sat down by a pile of broken concrete. The body of a dead kitten was lying upside down a few yards away. As her thoughts went to Tsuruishi, she wondered vaguely whether it would have been better never to have met him. No, no, certainly not that! She could never regret knowing him, nor anything that had happened with him. Nor did she regret having come to Tokyo. When she had arrived, a month or so before, she had planned to return to the country if her business was unsuccessful, but now she knew that she would be staying on here in Tokyo—yes, probably right here in downtown Tokyo where Tsuruishi had lived.

She got up, swung the rucksack on her back, and walked away from the river. As she strolled along a side street, she noticed a hut which seemed to consist of old boards nailed haphazardly together.

Going to the door, she called out, "Tea for sale! Would anyone like some tea?" The door opened and in the entrance appeared a woman dressed far more poorly than Ryo herself.

"How much does it cost?" asked the woman. And, then, seeing the rucksack, she added, "Come in and rest a while, if you like. I'll see how much money we've got left. We may have enough for some tea."

Ryo went in and put down her rucksack. In the small room four sewing women were sitting on the floor around an oil stove, working on a mass of shirts and socks. They were women like herself, thought Ryo, as she watched their busy needles moving in and out of the material. A feeling of warmth came over her.

TRANSLATED BY IVAN MORRIS

OMI

[from Kamen no Kokuhaku, 1949] by Mishima Yukio (born 1925)

With the publication of the novel Confession of a Mask, *from which these extracts are taken, Mishima Yukio established himself as a writer of the first rank. The novel is apparently autobiographical, although Mishima has denied this. In the following sections the "I" of the novel is about fourteen years old.*

•

One morning just after a snowfall I went to school very early. The evening before, a friend had telephoned to say there was going to be a snowfight the next morning. Being by nature given to wakefulness the night before any greatly anticipated event, I had no sooner opened my eyes too early the next morning than I set out for school, heedless of the time.

The snow scarcely reached my shoetops. And later, as I looked down at the city from a window of the elevated train, the snow scene had not yet caught the rays of the rising sun and looked more gloomy than beautiful. The snow seemed like a dirty bandage hiding the open wounds of the city, hiding those irregular gashes of haphazard streets and tortuous alleys, courtyards and occasional plots of bare ground, which form the only beauty to be found in the panorama of our cities.

When the still almost empty train was nearing the station for my school, I saw the sun rise beyond the factory district. The scene suddenly became one of joy and light. Now the columns of ominously towering smokestacks and the somber rise and fall of the monotonous slate-colored roofs cowered behind the noisy laughter of the brightly shining snow mask. It is just such a snow-covered landscape which often becomes the setting for a tragic riot or revolution. And even the faces of the passers-by, suspiciously wan in the reflection of the snow, reminded me somehow of conspirators.

When I got off at the station in front of the school, the snow was already melting, and I could hear the water running off the roof of the express company building next door. I could not shake the illusion that it was the radiance which was splashing down. Bright and shining slivers of it were suicidally hurling themselves at the sham quagmire of the pavement, all smeared with the slush of passing shoes. As I walked under the eaves, one sliver hurled itself by mistake at the nape of my neck. . . .

Inside the school gates there was not yet a single footprint in the snow. The locker room was still closed fast, but the other rooms were open.

I opened a window of the second-year classroom, which was on the ground floor, and looked out at the snow in the grove behind the school. There in the path which came from the rear gate, up the slope of the grove, and led to the building I was in, I could see large footprints; they came up along the path and continued to a spot directly below the window from which I was looking. Then the footprints turned back and disappeared behind the science building, which could be seen on a diagonal to the left.

Someone had already come. It was plain that he had ascended the path from the rear gate, looked into the classroom through the window, and, seeing no one there, had walked on by himself to the rear of the science building. Only a few of the day students came to school by way of the rear gate. It was rumored that Omi, who was one of the few, came each morning from some woman's house. But he would never put in an appearance until the last moment before class formation. Nevertheless, I could not imagine who else might have made the footprints, and judging by their large size, I was convinced that they were his.

Leaning out the window and straining my eyes, I saw the color of fresh black soil in the shoe tracks, making them seem somehow determined and powerful. An indescribable force drew me toward those footprints. I felt that I wanted to throw myself headfirst out of the window to bury my face in them. But, as usual, my sluggish motor nerves protected me from my sudden whim. Instead of diving out the window, I put my satchel on a desk and then scrambled slowly up onto the window sill. The hooks and eyes on the front of my uniform jacket had scarcely pressed against the stone window sill before they were at daggers points with my frail ribs, producing a pain mixed with a sort of sorrowful sweetness. After I had jumped from the window onto the snow, the slight pain became a pleasant stimulus, filling me with a trembling emotion of adventure. I fitted my overshoes carefully into the footprints.

The prints had looked quite large, but now I found that they were almost the same size as mine. I had failed to take into account the fact that the person who had made them was probably wearing overshoes too, as was the vogue among us in those days. Now that the thought occurred to me, I decided that the footprints were not large enough to be Omi's. . . . And yet, despite my uneasy feeling that I would be disappointed in my immediate hope of finding Omi behind the science building, I was still somehow compelled to follow after the black footprints. Probably at this point I was no longer motivated solely by the hope of finding Omi, but instead, at the sight of the violated mystery, was seized with a mixed feeling of yearning and revenge toward the person who had come before me and left his footprints in the snow.

Breathing hard, I began following the tracks.

As though walking on steppingstones, I went moving my feet from footprint to footprint. The outlines of the prints revealed now glassy coal-black earth, now dead turf, now soiled packed snow, now paving stones. Suddenly I discovered that, without being aware of it, I had fallen into walking with long strides, exactly like Omi.

Following the tracks to the rear of the science building, I passed through the long shadow which the building threw over the snow, and then continued on to the high ground overlooking the wide athletic field. Because of the mantle of glittering snow which covered everything, the three-hundred-meter ellipse of the track could not be distinguished from the undulating field it enclosed. In a corner of the field two great keyaki trees stood close together, and their shadows, much elongated in the morning sun, fell across the snow, lending meaning to the scene, providing the happy imperfection with which Nature always accents grandeur. The great trees towered up with a plastic delicacy in the blue winter sky, in the reflection of the snow from below, in the lateral rays of the morning sun; and occasionally some snow slipped down like gold dust from the crotches formed against the tree trunks by the stark, leafless branches. The roof ridges of the boys' dormitories, standing in a row beyond the athletic field, and the copse beyond them, seemed to be motionless in sleep, and everything was so silent that even the soundless slipping of the snow seemed to echo loud and wide.

For a moment I could not see a thing in this expanse of glare.

The snow scene was in a way like a fresh castle-ruin—this legerdemain was being bathed in that same boundless light and splendor which exists solely in the ruins of an ancient castle. And there in one corner of the ruin, in the snow of the almost five-meter-wide track, enormous Roman letters had been drawn. Nearest to me was a large circle, an *O*. Next came an *M,* and beyond it a third letter was still in the process of being written, a tall and thick *I*.

It was Omi. The footprints I had followed led to the *O,* from the *O* to the *M,* and arrived finally to the figure of Omi himself, just then dragging his overshoes over the snow to finish his *I,* looking down from above his white muffler, both hands thrust in his overcoat pockets. His shadow stretched defiantly across the snow, running parallel with the shadows of the keyaki trees in the field.

My cheeks were on fire. I made a snowball in my gloved hands and threw it at him. It fell short.

Just then he finished writing the *I* and, probably by chance, looked in my direction.

"Hey!" I shouted.

Although I feared that Omi's only reaction would be one of displeasure, I was impelled by an indescribable passion, and no sooner had I shouted than I found myself running down the steep slope toward him. As I ran a most undreamed-of sound came reverberating toward me—a friendly shout from him, filled with his power:

"Hey! don't step on the letters!"

He certainly seemed to be a different person this morning. As a rule, even when he went home he never did his homework but left his school books in his locker and came to school in the mornings with both hands thrust in his overcoat pockets, barely in time to shed his coat dexterously and fall in at the tail end of the class formation. What a change today! Not only must he have been whiling away the time by himself since early morning, but now he welcomed me with his inimitable smile, both friendly and rough at the same time—welcomed me, whom he had always treated as a snotnosed child, beneath contempt. How I had been longing for that smile, the flash of those youthful white teeth!

But when I got close enough to see his smiling face distinctly, my heart lost its passion of the moment before, when I had shouted "Hey!" Now suddenly I became paralyzed with timidity. I was pulled up short by the flashing realization that at heart Omi was a lonely person. His smile was probably assumed in order to hide the weak spot in his armor which my understanding had chanced upon, but this fact did not hurt me so much as it hurt the image which I had been constructing of him.

The instant I had seen that enormous *OMI* drawn in the snow, I had understood, perhaps half unconsciously, all the nooks and corners of his loneliness—understood also the real motive, probably not clearly understood even by himself, which brought him to school this early in the morning. . . . If my idol had now mentally bent his knee to me, offering some such excuse as "I came early for the snow fight," I would certainly have lost from within me something even more important than the pride he would have lost. Feeling it was up to me to speak, I nervously tried to think of something to say.

"The snow fight's out for today, isn't it?" I finally said. "I thought it was going to snow more though."

"H'm." He assumed an expression of indifference. The strong outline of his jaw hardened again in his cheeks, and a sort of pitying disdain toward me revived. He was obviously making an effort to regard me as a child, and his eyes began to gleam insolently. In one part of his mind he must have been grateful to me for not making a single inquiry about his letters in the snow, and I was fascinated by the painful efforts he was making to overcome this feeling of gratitude.

"Humph! I hate wearing children's gloves," he said.

"But even grownups wear wool gloves like these."

"Poor thing, I bet you don't even know how leather gloves feel. Here—"

Abruptly he thrust his snow-drenched leather gloves against my cheeks. I dodged. A raw carnal feeling blazed up in me, branding my cheeks. I felt myself staring at him with crystal-clear eyes. . . .

On the switchboard of my memory two pairs of gloves crossed wires—those leather gloves of Omi's and a pair of white ceremonial gloves. I did not seem to be able to decide which memory might be real, which false. Perhaps the leather gloves were more in harmony with his coarse features. And yet again, precisely because of his coarse features, perhaps it was the white pair which became him more.

Coarse features—even though I use the words, actually such a description is nothing more than that of the impression created by the ordinary face of one lone young man mixed in among boys. Unrivaled though his build was, in height he was by no means the tallest among us. The pretentious uniform which our school required, resembling a naval officer's, could scarcely hang well on our still immature bodies, and Omi alone filled his with a sensation of solid weight and a sort of sexuality. Surely I was not the only one who looked with envious and loving eyes at the muscles of his shoulders and chest, that sort of muscle which can be spied out even beneath a blue serge uniform.

At my school it was the custom to wear white gloves on ceremonial days. Just to pull on a pair of white gloves, with mother-of-pearl buttons shining gloomily at the wrists and three meditative rows of stitching on the backs, was enough to evoke the symbols of all ceremonial days—the somber assembly hall where the ceremonies were held, the box of Shioze sweets received upon leaving, the cloudless skies under which such days always seem to make brilliant sounds in mid-course and then collapse.

It was on a national holiday in winter, undoubtedly Kigensetsu. That morning again Omi had come to school unusually early.

The second-year students had already driven the freshmen away from the swinging-log on the playground at the side of the school buildings, taking cruel delight in doing so, and were now in full possession. Although outwardly scornful of such childish playground equipment as the swinging-log, the second-year students still had a lingering affection for it in their hearts, and by forcibly driving the freshmen away they were able to adopt the face-saving pretense of indulging in the amusement half derisively, without any seriousness. The freshmen had formed a circle at a distance around the log and were watching the rough play of the upperclassmen, who in turn were quite conscious of having an audience. The log, suspended on chains, swung back and forth rhythmically, with a battering-ram motion, and the contest was to make each other fall off the log.

Omi was standing with both feet planted firmly at the mid-point of the log, eagerly looking around for opponents; it was a posture which made him look exactly like a murderer who has been brought to bay. No one in our class was a match for him. Already several boys had jumped up onto the log, one after another, only to be cut down by Omi's quick hands; their feet had trampled away the frost on the earth around the log, which had been glittering in the early morning sunlight. After each victory Omi would clasp his hands together over his head like a triumphant boxer, smiling profusely. And the first-year students would cheer, already forgetting he had been a ringleader in driving them away from the log.

My eyes followed his white-gloved hands. They were moving fiercely, but with marvelous precision, like the paws of some young beast, a wolf perhaps. From time to time they would cut through the winter morning's air, like the feathers of an arrow, straight to the chest of an opponent. And always the opponent would fall to the frosty ground, landing now on his feet, now on his buttocks. On rare occasions, at the moment of knocking an opponent off the log, Omi himself would be on the verge of falling; as he fought to regain the equilibrium of his careening body, he would appear to be writhing in agony there atop the log, made slippery by the faintly gleaming frost. But always the strength in his supple hips would restore him once again to that assassin-like posture.

The log was moving left and right impersonally, swinging in unperturbed arcs. . . .

As I watched, I was suddenly overcome with uneasiness, with a racking, inexplicable uneasiness. It resembled a dizziness such as might have come from watching the swaying of the log, but it was not that. Probably it was more a mental vertigo, an uneasiness in which my inner equilibrium was on the point of being destroyed by the sight of his every perilous movement. And this instability was made even more precarious by the fact that within it two contrary forces were pulling at me, contending for supremacy. One was the instinct of self-preservation. The second force—which was bent, even more profoundly, more intensely, upon the complete disintegration of my inner balance—was a compulsion toward suicide, that subtle and secret impulse to which a person often unconsciously surrenders himself.

"What's the matter with you, you bunch of cowards! Isn't there anyone else?"

Omi's body was gently swinging to the right and left, his hips bending with the motions of the log. He placed his white-gloved hands on his hips. The gilded badge on his cap glittered in the morning sun. I had never seen him so handsome as at that moment.

"I'll do it!" I cried.

My heartbeats had steadily increased in violence, and using them as a measure, I had exactly estimated the moment when I would finally say these words. It had always been thus with moments in which I yield to desire. It seemed to me that my going and standing against Omi on that log was a predestined fact, rather than merely an impulsive action. In later years, such actions misled me into thinking I was "a man of strong will."

"Watch out! Watch out! You'll get licked," everyone shouted.

Amid their cheers of derision I climbed up on one end of the log. While I was trying to get up, my feet began slipping, and again the air was full of noisy jeers.

Omi greeted me with a clowning face. He played the fool with all his might and pretended to be slipping. Again, he would tease me by fluttering his gloved fingers at me. To my eyes those fingers were the sharp points of some dangerous weapon about to run me through.

The palms of our white-gloved hands met many times in stinging slaps, and each time I reeled under the force of the blow. It was obvious that he was deliberately holding back his strength, as though wanting to make sport of me to his heart's content, postponing what would otherwise have been my quick defeat.

"Oh! I'm frightened—how strong you are! —I'm licked. I'm just about to fall—look at me!" He stuck out his tongue and pretended to fall.

It was unbearably painful for me to see his clownish face, to see him unwittingly destroy his own beauty. Even though I was now gradually being forced back along the log, I could not keep from lowering my eyes. And just at that instant I was caught by a swoop of his right hand. In a reflex action to keep from falling, I clutched at the air with my right hand and, by some chance, managed to fasten onto the fingertips of his right hand. I grasped a vivid sensation of his fingers fitting closely inside the white gloves.

For an instant he and I looked each other in the eye. It was truly only an instant. The clownish look had vanished, and instead, his face was suffused with a strangely candid expression. An immaculate, fierce something, neither hostility nor hatred, was vibrating there like a bowstring. Or perhaps this was only my imagination. Perhaps it was nothing but the stark, empty look of the instant in which, pulled by the fingertips, he felt himself losing his balance. However that may have been, I knew intuitively and certainly that Omi had seen the way I looked at him in that instant, had felt the pulsating force which flowed like lightning between our fingertips, and had guessed my secret—that I was in love with him, with no one in the world but him.

At almost the same moment the two of us fell tumbling off the log.

I was helped to my feet. It was Omi who helped me. He pulled me up roughly by the arm and, saying not a word, brushed the dirt off my uniform. His elbows and gloves were stained with a mixture of dirt and glittering frost.

He took my arm and began walking away with me. I looked up into his face as though reproving him for this show of intimacy. . . .

For all that, it was a supreme delight I felt as I walked leaning on his arm. Perhaps because of my frail constitution, I usually felt a premonition of evil mixed in with every joy; but on this occasion I felt nothing but the fierce, intense sensation of his arm—it seemed to be transmitted from his arm to mine and, once having gained entry, to spread out until it flooded my entire body. I felt that I should like to walk thus with him to the ends of the earth.

But we arrived at the place for class formation, where, too soon, he let go of my arm and took his place in line. Thereafter he did not look around in my direction. During the ceremony which followed, he sat four seats away from me. Time and time again I looked from the stains on my own white gloves to those on Omi's.

TRANSLATED BY MEREDITH WEATHERBY

SHORT BIBLIOGRAPHY

GENERAL WORKS

Aston, W. G. *A History of Japanese Literature.* London, 1889.

Bonneau, Georges. *Histoire de la littérature japonaise contemporaine.* Paris, 1940.

Keene, Donald. *Anthology of Japanese Literature.* New York, 1955.

———. *Japanese Literature.* New York, 1955.

Okazaki, Yoshie. *Japanese Literature in the Meiji Era,* tr. by V. H. Viglielmo. Tokyo, 1955.

Sansom, George. *The Western World and Japan.* New York, 1950.

PROSE

Akutagawa, Ryūnosuke. *Hell Screen,* tr. by W. H. H. Norman. Tokyo, 1948.

———. *Kappa,* tr. by S. Shiojiri. Osaka, 1947.

———. *Rashomon and Other Stories,* tr. by T. Kojima. New York, 1952.

Dazai, Osamu. *The Setting Sun,* tr. by Donald Keene. New York, 1956.

Elisséev, Serge, tr. *Neuf nouvelles japonaises.* Paris, 1924.

Futabatei, Shimei. *An Adopted Husband,* tr. by B. Mitsui and G. M. Sinclair. New York, 1919.

Hino, Ashihei. *Wheat and Soldiers,* tr. by Baroness Shidzué Ishimoto. New York, 1939.

Kobayashi, Takiji. *The Cannery Boat.* New York, 1933.

Mishima, Yukio. *The Sound of Waves,* tr. by Meredith Weatherby. New York, 1956.

Nagai, Kafū. *Le Jardin des pivoines,* tr. by Serge Elisséev. Paris, 1927.

Natsume, Sōseki. *Kokoro,* tr. by I. Kondo. Tokyo, 1941.

———. *La Porte,* tr. by R. Martinie. Paris, 1927.

Osaragi, Jirō. *Homecoming,* tr. by B. Horwitz. New York, 1954.

Ozaki, Kōyō. *The Gold Demon,* tr. by A. and M. Lloyd. Tokyo, 1905.

Tanizaki, Junichirō. *Ashikari and the Story of Shunkin,* tr. by R. Humpherson and H. Okita. Tokyo, 1936.

———. *Some Prefer Nettles,* tr. by E. G. Seidensticker. New York, 1955.

POETRY

Bonneau, Georges. *Anthologie de la poésie japonaise*. Paris, 1935.

——. *Lyrisme du temps présent.* Paris, 1935.

Hughes, Glenn and Iwasaki, Y. T. *Fifteen Poets of Modern Japan.* Seattle, 1928.

——. *Three Women Poets of Modern Japan.* Seattle, 1936.

Ishikawa, Takuboku. *A Handful of Sand,* tr. by S. Sakanishi. Boston, 1934.

Matsuo, Kuni and Steinilber-Oberlin. *Anthologie des poètes japonais contemporains.* Paris, 1939.

Yosano, Akiko. *Tangled Hair,* tr. by S. Sakanishi. Boston, 1935.

DRAMA

Bowers, Faubion. *Japanese Theatre.* New York, 1952.

Iwasaki, Y. T. and Hughes, Glenn. *New Plays from Japan.* London, 1930.

——. *Three Modern Japanese Plays.* Cincinnati, 1923.

Kikuchi, Kan. *Tōjūrō's Love and Four Other Plays,* tr. by Glenn W. Shaw. Tokyo, 1925.

Kurata, Hyakuzō. *The Priest and His Disciples,* tr. by Glenn W. Shaw. Tokyo, 1922.

Tanizaki, Junichirō. *Puisque je l'aime,* tr. by C. Jacob. Paris, 1925.

Yamamoto, Yūzō. *Three Plays,* tr. by Glenn W. Shaw. Tokyo, 1935.

NOTE: A much more extensive bibliography may be found in Borton, Hugh, *et al., A Selected List of Books and Articles on Japan in English, French and German.* Cambridge (Mass.), 1954.